A Realm of Ash and Shadow
By: Lara Buckheit

D1293092

A Realm of Ash and Shadow

Lara Buckheit

Published by Sword and Silk Books, 2023.

A REALM OF ASH AND SHADOW

First edition. April 11, 2023.

Copyright © 2023 Lara Buckheit.

ISBN: 979-8986599847

Written by Lara Buckheit.

CHAPTER 1

F alling from Mason Kennedy's trellis was not how I wanted to start my morning.

I hit the ground with a bone-rattling thud, a string of swears slipping through my kiss-bruised lips.

Mason's head popped out of the window, dark hair ruffling in the breeze. He stared down at me with a grin splitting his boyish face in two and pointed to the splintered bits of wood that dusted the grass like freshly fallen snow. He laughed, breathy and quiet, before he whisper-shouted, "Val, you broke the trellis."

"That's what you're concerned about?" I snapped, forgetting his mother was still asleep. I climbed to my feet, shifting to test my weight on each of my ankles. No injuries, save for my wounded ego. "I'm fine, by the way."

"Good, so I'll see you later for our run?"

A rumble of thunder sounded in the distance, and I turned my face toward the sky, searching for storm clouds. There weren't any yet. But there was a shock of black soaring across the paling indigo curtain hanging above us like spilled ink.

A raven. Nosy little shit.

I glanced back at Mason and forced a smile. "Yep. I'll meet you at seven."

Before he could respond, I rushed home, continuously checking to see if the bird was following me. They weren't. Fifteen sweaty minutes passed, and I sprinted through the gate and into my front yard. I stopped to catch my breath only to find the raven perched on the steep, multi-faceted roof, watching me, waiting for me.

My steps crunched against the gravel as I stalked across the driveway. To my annoyance, the raven made a deep caw as I drew closer to the porch. I answered them with a flip of my middle finger. It cawed again as if saying, *Real classy, Valeria.*

Whatever.

Goosebumps pricked my skin as I climbed the steps of the old and creaky porch, knowing what I'd find waiting for me at the top. The swing off to the left swayed softly back and forth, the groaning a welcome distraction from the single, dreadful envelope fastened to the front door.

Nope. I wanted nothing to do with *that.*

I wrenched the door open quickly, like pulling off a band-aid, and made my way inside and upstairs to my bedroom. Rummaging through the piles of clothes, books, and shoes strewn across the worn wooden floor, I searched for a somewhat clean pair of shorts. I slipped them on, along with my worn gray running shoes. My hands worked deftly as I threw my knotty blonde hair up into a messy bun using one of the elastic hair ties I snatched from around the door handle.

Once downstairs, I yelled, "I'm going for a run with Mason!"

If my keeper, Mistress Marjorie, heard me, she didn't reply.

Shutting the door behind me, I nearly jumped out of my skin.

The stupid envelope was no longer fastened to the door. Instead, the ridiculously oversized raven had torn it down and dropped it onto the porch, a few inches away from where their sharp talons clicked against the wood as if they were growing impatient with me.

My father's Celestians—shape-shifting warriors bound to protect mortals from demons and gods alike—always became moody when I didn't obey them straight away. I glared at the bird.

Often, I caught them flying around Oakwood, even though there hadn't been any supernatural activity since Mistress Marjorie and I were exiled here nearly eighteen years ago. If there were demons lurking about, my keeper would've handled them quickly and quietly.

We didn't need their help.

I waved my hands at the bird. "Shoo. Fly away. Be free."

They tilted their head to the side, exposing several silver scars jutting across their neck and down their body.

"You poor thing." I softened, taking a step closer to them. I petted their head once, twice. "What happened to you?"

They leaned into my touch for the briefest of moments before they pecked at the envelope.

"Seriously?" I dropped my hand back to my side. "I already know what it's going to say: 'Soon you will be where you were meant to be all along, my dearest Valeria.'"

The raven's feathers rustled, impatient.

"Fine," I muttered, snatching the letter up and tearing it open. "Oh, would you look at that?"

Sure enough, that fifteen-word sentence stared back at me.

Cryptic and annoying.

"There," I hissed, ripping the letter up and dropping the pieces into the empty planter hanging from the porch railing. "Go tell my father I read *his* letter, and I'm *so* eager to return home."

As if they were satisfied, the raven cawed once and then soared toward the sky.

I clenched and unclenched my fists. I had spent my entire life hidden in the Realm of the Mortals knowing I was different. *Feeling* different. The annual letters and ravens were a reminder I didn't need for a handful of reasons. The first being that they were evidence my father didn't want the hassle of protecting me in Empyrean, so he pawned me off on—

No, I wouldn't let myself go there.

With a frustrated sigh, I bolted toward my normal running route, passing Mason along the way. He called after me, but I didn't stop. Didn't look back. My feet slammed against the pavement until the sidewalk gave way to dirt, and I followed those trails I knew by heart deep into the woodland.

Despite the sweat dripping down my forehead, I couldn't help but take in the sunrise, knowing it was one of the last I'd ever see.

Here. One of the last sunrises I would ever see *here*.

My time left in the Realm of the Mortals was limited, but returning to my own realm, Empyrean, wasn't *actually* a death sentence—even if I often treated it like one.

To be fair, I hadn't become a bitter hot mess about returning to Empyrean until my father started treating me like I was nothing more than an inconvenience. Long letters filled with promises to visit me had turned into fifteen-word sentences written by another's hand.

Mistress Marjorie told me that Daddy Dearest was too busy running Empyrean to write me himself. I always countered with something snide about how maybe he'd be too busy to remember to collect me, too. His diminishing amount of contact over the last few years suggested as much.

The soft golden hue of dawn crept through the blanket of lush green leaves that hung overhead, bathing the forest with muted streaks of marigold light. Tiny drops of dew kissed my ankles, and every soundless step brought me closer to a bliss that would obliterate my annoyance. Deeper and deeper, I ran into the thick glen of trees that surrounded the pleasant, insignificant town I'd call home for only six more days.

I collapsed to my knees, my legs trembling from the run. Tears pricked my eyes as the other reasons I hated those letters became a cyclone of torment in my mind. Reasons that sent me to this realm to begin with. Reasons that, no matter how deep I buried them, always clawed their way back to the surface.

Inhaling deeply for five counts and exhaling through my nose for seven, I tried to pull myself together before Mason caught up to me. Before he started asking questions I didn't know how to answer.

But I was spiraling.

Tomorrow. I was *supposed* to be ripped from the Realm of the Mortals tomorrow, on my eighteenth birthday. But by some miracle, Mistress Marjorie was able to bargain for more time—six glorious days so I could attend graduation. Though I was thankful for the extension, those days wouldn't be enough to quell the ache that the years I'd spent in this realm would become nothing but a distant memory.

At least I'd get a piece of paper that proved I completed *something*, proved that for a brief stint in time, I was an Oakwood High School student, even if I was someone the teachers wouldn't remember and the yearbooks had me listed as *Not Pictured.*

I'd get to experience the rite of passage that the movies made seem so monumental. The promise that everything changed once you walk across that stage, that you become something *more* when you toss your cap into the air.

And for me, that would be true. I'd walk across the stage and right into a portal that led me to my too-perfect realm, to the throne, and to my father.

A searing pain pinched my sides. *Breathe.*

Despite training for most of my life, I'd pushed myself more and more these last couple of weeks. I was five when I learned how to throw a punch, seven when I first wielded a blade, and ten when I *finally* passed Mistress Marjorie's proficiency exam. Now, I ran four miles in the mornings and spent most afternoons slaughtering training dummies with a variety of weapons. Anything to keep my mind quiet.

The crack of branches snapping under the weight of encroaching footsteps roused me from my pity party as a familiar face barreled through the tree line and into the small clearing where I sat.

"Jesus, Val. I could barely keep up with you," Mason gasped, his breathing haggard.

He dropped his running backpack onto the ground as he leaned over, hands finding his knees.

"You can never keep up with me," I teased, hastily wiping a few rogue tears from my eyes. I grabbed the bottle of water from the side pocket of his bag and drank, swishing a mouthful around to rid myself of the sour taste of my past and future that lingered on my lips. "Drink."

Mason didn't catch the glass container I tossed in his direction, and it hit the ground with a thud; he was never one for anything even slightly coordinated. He brushed dirt from the lid before he downed what was left. Black hair slick with sweat, the lump in Mason's throat bobbed as he swallowed. His bare chest heaved with every breath he tried to catch. I longed to run my hands through his silky hair, the way I did last night as he laid between my legs, our bodies entwined. Mason's lips were the perfect distraction as his ink-stained hands wandered up and down my naked thighs, hungry—

"Stop looking at me like that," he said, tugging me to my feet. His emerald eyes danced in the morning light with feverish excitement.

I wiped dirt from the thin fabric of my shorts. "Looking at you like what?"

"With your bedroom eyes, Val. You said last night was a one-time thing."

"A one-time thing that's happened." I tapped my chin. "Oh, I don't know... a hundred or so times over the last two years."

Mason grinned. "Then maybe you should stop saying it every time you come sneaking in through my bedroom window."

To absolutely no one's surprise, Mason and I fooled around. A lot. Rumors spread like wildfire through a high school like ours. No one believed that we were just *friends*, but we were.

Friends who often shared a bed.

"Well, since I broke your trellis, that won't happen nearly as often," I said, clearing my throat and pushing away memories of late nights tangled in his plaid sheets. "Have you decided who you're going to prom with?"

Mason had no shortage of offers, all of which he politely declined. Whereas I had *zero* people ask me to be their date. Present company included.

I didn't *need* someone to go to the dance with, but like graduation, I wanted my night to be as cliché as it could get with the fancy gown, the corsage, a date, *and* a limo. I wanted spiked fruit punch and the warmth of Mason's body against mine as we swayed in time to the music in the middle of a sea of people. For me, prom was another mundane high school milestone that proved I did something with my time here other than read smutty paperbacks and binge-watch trash tv—that I had somewhat of a life outside of Mistress Marjorie's wards, lessons, and the safety of our hidden home.

"Mmm." Mason rubbed his lips together. "Are you asking me?"

I shook my head. "Are *you* going to ask *me*?"

Mason drew closer and tilted my chin upward so I looked at him. Gods, he was adorable. The scent of body spray with a tinge of sweat filled the almost non-existent gap between us. Purple shadows pooled beneath his delicate eyes, courtesy of our sleepless night.

"Valeria," he said, bringing his mouth a breath away from mine. If he kissed me right now, I'd pull him to the ground and feel the weight of his body on mine until we were late for school. My cheeks warmed at the thought. "Will you do me the honor of being my *date* for prom?"

I bristled. Every fiber in my being longed to correct him that this wouldn't be a date. It *couldn't* be a date. Dates made things serious. Serious meant feelings. Feelings meant he had the power to hurt me, or worse, be taken from me.

I clamped down on that train of thought, letting Mason's words swirl around me like a brief gust of wind through an open window. "I would love nothing more."

Mason pulled away, pursing his lips.

"What?" I asked, confused.

"Aren't you going to snap at me about no boyfriend-y things?"

"Not this time."

"If I didn't know better, I'd say I'm wearing down your resolve." Mason laughed, and I wished I could bottle the sound and take it back with me to Empyrean to open whenever I missed him. Which, I imagined, would be all the time.

He was the only friend I'd ever known.

My throat constricted. Everything was going to change in less than a week, and Mason had no idea. No idea that I wasn't really going to be taking a fucking trip abroad, but that I'd be leaving him. For good. Leaving him for so much more, yet somehow, so much less.

It wasn't fair that I'd have to say goodbye to tacos at two a.m. and energy drinks that Mistress Marjorie swore would rot my teeth. There would be no more midnight texts back and forth with Mason when neither of us could sleep. On Friday nights, I wouldn't be able to shove my face with popcorn in the passenger seat of Mason's beat-up car at the drive-in theater or make out with him under the bleachers at an Oakwood Thorns' football game.

No, I'd have to give it all up. Give *him* up. If someone, anyone, had asked me, I would have told them I wanted to stay here, in this bubble, and pretend that I belonged.

Mostly.

Despite everything I loved here, there was something deep down in the pit of my stomach that called to me, beckoning me to Empyrean.

Probably my unresolved daddy issues. Ugh.

"Val, you're spacing out again." Mason snapped his fingers in front of my face to draw my attention back to our conversation. "Are you still upset about your birthday falling on prom?" Right. I had totally forgotten about *that*. He added, "It's not going to be as bad as you think it is, babe."

I narrowed my eyes. "Don't push it, Kennedy."

Mason bumped his shoulder into mine. "That's my girl."

"Whatever. Let's walk back. I don't want to run anymore today."

Threading a hand through his hair, he said, "I think that's the sexiest thing you've ever said to me."

The birds chirped a mourning melody as if they were bidding us farewell from their forest. Soon the expanse of trees looming over us dwindled, and the sun barely peeked out from behind a handful of fat storm clouds, warming the air with the promise of summer rain.

I'd miss this about Mason, too. His comfortable silence, not needing to fill the void with—

"So, do you have a dress?" Mason glanced at me from the corner of his eye.

"A dress?"

"For prom? It's tomorrow. What were you going to show up in? Your *leather ensemble*?"

Kicking a loose stone on the road, I groaned. Mason caught me in my leather ensemble one time a few years ago, following an afternoon spent sparring with Mistress Marjorie in the attic, and I never heard the end of it.

Did Mistress Marjorie get me a dress? She knew how badly I wanted to go...

Mason ground to a halt. "If you're worried about money, we can go to the mall and put a dress on my mom's credit card." He tucked a wisp of hair behind my ear. See. Boyfriend-y things I tried to avoid. "You can consider it a birthday present," he added softly.

"That won't be necessary." My keeper's voice cut through the air, and Mason jumped away from me, his hand falling limp to his side. "I've already purchased Valeria a dress for prom."

Mistress Marjorie stood several feet away from us on the sidewalk, her long, white hair cascading around her in loose waves. The hooded cloak she normally donned was nowhere to be seen, and there was a faint iridescent glimmer around her face. I knew if I drew near enough, I would see through her glamour to the cloaked figure beneath. To a mortal, like Mason, they saw nothing but the friendly face of the person they believed to be my mother. Little did they know they were looking upon the only being in all four realms who was powerful enough to keep me safe and hidden for the last eighteen years. Even if she used dark magic to do so.

I smiled at Mason. "Looks like that's a no for the leather ensemble."

Ignoring me, Mason took a step toward Mistress Marjorie with his head tilted to the side. He narrowed his eyes as if in a trance, his lips parting. My keeper didn't fidget under the weight of his stare, but if Mason didn't stop acting so weird, Mistress Marjorie would spiral into suspicion.

Instinctively, I grabbed his hand and spun him toward me, placing a kiss on his lips—something to distract him from whatever he might be thinking. He softened against me, wrapping his arms around my waist to pull me closer. But before he could deepen the kiss, I tore away, telling him, "See you at school."

My keeper waved to Mason, who returned her gesture before heading to his home on Windermere Street. When he was out of sight, Mistress Marjorie snapped her fingers, and in a cloud of thick, black smoke, we appeared in front of our massive three-story house tucked away on the outskirts of town. Spindles and brackets adorned the scalloped shingles in a dull white paint. The decorative trim was similar to that on the gingerbread houses Mistress Marjorie and I would glue together and decorate every holiday season like we were mortals.

My gaze wandered to my bedroom window located in the embellished round tower on the left. Many of my silliest fantasies were dreamt in that room, like the desire to remain in this realm, blissfully unaware of the happenings of the other three realms.

A girl can dream. A princess cannot.

Yeah, yeah. The memory of Mistress Marjorie's words echoed in my mind without her having to repeat them. She harped on the concept enough that one would think I'd heed her warning to quit daydreaming about the things I couldn't change. I didn't, though. Not usually.

The porch was blessedly empty, with the raven from earlier nowhere to be found. Before I charged through the wrought-iron gate and into our yard, Mistress Marjorie said a quick spell in a language only she knew, permitting us to enter. If my keeper wasn't home, the place was always heavily warded, even though there'd been no attempts on my life since we'd immersed ourselves in the Realm of the Mortals.

"Every night you spend with that boy creates a wedge between you and your allegiance to Empyrean," Mistress Marjorie said, her glamour gone and black hood drawn.

After all this time, I'd never seen her face. Not once. She even warded her bedroom after she caught me sneaking in once while she slept, wanting a peek of what lingered beneath her hood. My next attempt to sneak in left me with watery eyes that burned like someone blew pepper straight into them. I never tried again.

I bounded up the porch stairs, purposely ignoring the shredded letter, my mind set on a hot shower and large bowl of sugary cereal. "Don't be so dramatic. I know what's expected of me."

"Let's hope Mason will let you leave without causing a fuss."

I'd barely opened the front door when I turned, peering at her, my hand gripping the handle. My heart hammered in my chest. "What do you mean? I thought..."

"You thought what, little one? That your lie about taking a year off to go adventuring would be enough to make him forget you? To make him stop looking for you when you stopped answering his calls and never came back?"

"No." I shook my head. "I thought you'd... you know." I snapped my fingers. "Use magic or something to make him... make *everyone* forget me."

"Is that what you want?" she asked. "Do you want me to make the boy forget you?"

I opened my mouth to speak, but the words were nowhere to be found. Mistress Marjorie pushed past me into the house, leaving me reeling, breathing shallowly next to the open door. The sound of cupboards opening and closing drifted down the hallway and through the screen, creating a rhythm for Mistress Marjorie to hum to.

Of course I didn't want Mason to forget me. Our friendship was something we both cherished and to take that from him would be wrong. But could I bear to vanish from his life the same way his father did? Without something as simple as a goodbye? Would years spent wondering if *he* was the reason the ones he loved kept leaving turn him into a shell of his former self? Someone too heartbroken and frightened to care? Someone like me?

Mason was my *friend*. It didn't go any deeper than that. There was no promise of forever between us, and there never would be. He'd be *fine*.

A tiny voice in the back of my mind whispered one word over and over. It insulted me; it recognized me for what I was—a liar.

CHAPTER 2

I would be late to school for the millionth time this month, and the only person to blame was Mistress Marjorie. I had showered, dressed, and downed a bowl of cereal in less time than it took her to complete the potion she was brewing.

She flitted about the kitchen, pouring precise measurements of herbs and roots into a cauldron of boiling water. It was actually a pot from a department store, but she hunched over it like a storybook witch, so it was much more fun to pretend.

When she was satisfied with the consistency, Mistress Marjorie ladled the contraceptive into a porcelain teacup and gestured for me to drink it.

Of course, I couldn't just take the Pill like every other girl my age.

Mistress Marjorie would have none of that. She had more faith in her home-brewed concoctions than anything a pharmaceutical company could create.

Even if they were disgusting most of the time.

Okay, *all* of the time.

Squeezing my eyes shut and pinching my nose, I downed the nasty substance in one swift gulp. "Ugh." My face scrunched up. Yep, tasted like sewage. "I don't think I'll ever get used to *that*."

"Stop spending your nights with that boy, and you wouldn't have to," Mistress Marjorie clucked as she left the kitchen. "Come. You should try on the dress your father sent."

My prom dress was from *my father*? Surprise swept through me as my wet hair hung in tangles past my shoulders, dripping tiny beads of water onto the granite counter. Why would he take the time to choose and send me a dress for prom, but wouldn't take the time to handwrite a letter? *Parents.*

Mistress Marjorie's tone suggested trying on the dress wasn't a request. I wiped the drops of water from the counter with my hand and dried it on my jeans before chugging the fruity leftover milk from my cereal bowl. It was much, much tastier than the contraceptive.

Catching a glimpse of the clock beside the fridge, I slipped out of the kitchen and bounded up the stairs. I didn't have much time left before the first bell.

In a rare show of respecting my privacy, Mistress Marjorie waited outside my bedroom door. I entered before her, quickly surveying the room for anything she could question me about, and snatched the paperback I'd been reading from my bedside table and shoved it in the drawer. The cover image of a half-naked man and a woman in a torn dress peered back at me before I slammed the drawer shut. If she knew what *that* book was about, she'd make me drink that stupid concoction after every chapter.

Moments later, Mistress Marjorie entered my room and perched on the edge of my bed, sitting atop the quilt I sewed by hand a few summers ago. It was a one-time hobby that left my wrist aching for weeks.

"Let me brush my hair first," I said, padding across the space to grab a brush from the vanity I found at a yard sale.

Filtered sunlight streamed through sheer curtains. Strewn about the room were various pieces of antique furniture from the shop I frequented on Cornelia Street. There was something about antique shopping I loved. Maybe it was because, at one point in time, those items meant something to someone else. Until they didn't.

As I ran the brush through my tangles, she asked, "Have you thought any more about wiping the boy's mind? It might make things easier."

"No." Wiping Mason's mind would make my leaving easier for him, not for me. All our stupid inside jokes and bickering over reality-competition shows and our first awkward kiss on a balmy summer night while fireworks colored the sky were memories that would haunt me while he would simply forget that I existed. "It feels... weird. Weird to think I'd remember what we shared, and he wouldn't."

"I see." She waved a hand, swinging the bedroom door shut.

A woven black garment bag hung from a satin hanger on the back of the door. With a flick of her wrist, the bag unzipped itself, revealing a stunning, ruby red floor-length gown; delicate gems glittered like diamonds around the midsection that led to a trailing tulle skirt.

My breath caught in my throat. "It's beautiful."

"Empyrean has the best designers," she said. "Try it on."

Whenever Mistress Marjorie spoke about Empyrean or showed me glimpses of the realm, it made it so much harder for me to dread leaving the Realm of the Mortals. While Empyrean wouldn't have fast food or Wi-Fi, I could picture the serenity of what awaited me—a castle massive enough to get lost in, a bustling market filled with delicacies and smiling faces, and fashion that rivaled the best couture. My favorite part about those delicacies and fashion? None of it cost a dime because money didn't exist in Empyrean. A perfect world.

With another wave of her hand, the outfit I was wearing vanished, leaving me in the lacy undergarments I recently bought from the mall. I sat the brush down as the dress slid from the hanger and over my head, enveloping me in a sea of soft fabric. The back of the gown laced itself up, tugging my waistline in so that it clung to my curves. My breasts spilled from the top in a manner that was far too sexy for prom, but I loved it anyway. A squeal burst from my lips. Mason was going to die when he saw me in this.

The hem tickled my ankles as I spun round and round with an invisible dance partner. Mistress Marjorie snapped her fingers, and brassy instrumental music softly echoed around us. My invisible partner twirled with me in one of Empyrean's most popular dances—a mix between the waltz and the salsa.

"I actually feel like a princess," I said with a giggle. My violet eyes twinkled every time I caught a glimpse of my reflection. "If I dress like this all the time, maybe the Empyreans will overlook the whole mortal-raised thing."

Mistress Marjorie *tsked*, folding her hands in her lap. "Every conversation about Empyrean comes back to your desire to belong."

I stopped mid-spin, letting my hands drop to my sides. "That's not true."

"You may not realize it, but there's a void inside you that bedding that boy doesn't fill, and once you leave here, you're going to try and fill it with winning over your people."

Yeah, right. I didn't have a *void* inside of me.

"I don't know what you're talking about." I folded my arms across my chest.

"Tell me, little one, what are you truly willing to risk to belong in Empyrean? Your life? Would you accept the same fate as your mother if it meant sitting on the throne and being adored by your people?"

I sucked in a sharp breath, wanting to rip the gown from my body. It was suddenly too tight. Too constricting.

We rarely spoke about my mother. Her murder led to my... well, my exile. It was a wound I didn't like to think about. No matter what words were spoken, they felt like salt. Salt in a festering sore that wouldn't heal.

Mistress Marjorie leveled her gaze on me, though I couldn't see it beneath her cloak. I felt it—hard and stony. "The transition from the Realm of the Mortals isn't going to be easy for you, and I will shoulder some of the blame for that. I... I felt guilty when your father became distant. All you wanted was to be loved by him, and with each passing day that he didn't give you the attention you craved, I saw something in you darken. But then you met the boy, and you seemed brighter, more hopeful. Now that you must leave the only happiness you've ever known, I fear..." She let her sentence trail off as the music faded and silence took its place.

"You fear what, Margie?" The nickname slipped out, and it was like I was three again, unable to pronounce her name.

She sat quietly for a beat longer before she spoke. "I fear you'll have to become someone other than yourself when you leave this realm. Someone cold and calculating. Someone you won't recognize when you look into the mirror. Because when you return to Empyrean, you'll need to embrace that you aren't a mortal. You are a princess with power and that... that could very well be something that takes what's already inside of you, everything dark and vengeful, and draws it closer to the surface."

I stared at her, trying to remember whatever dark place she was talking about. I couldn't place it. I'd always been angry. Angry at my father, angry at what happened to my mother, angry at the world I was born into. But I never felt... dark? I was a baby when my father pawned me off on Mistress Marjorie, and I was a child when I realized that he had done so not only to keep me safe, but to ease his pain. Looking at me must have been a reminder of all he had lost. Both the sight and the thought of me *must* have caused him pain. It was the only logical explanation for why he couldn't bear to visit or write.

A part of me hated him for it. Hated him for making me weather his pain. Hated him for making me hate myself.

But he sent me this dress for prom. Maybe with graduation approaching and my return to Empyrean, he was ready to welcome me home. Maybe he was willing to overlook that pain and be my father again. Maybe we'd heal our festering wounds together.

"I think your paranoia has gotten to your head. This fear of yours is overkill, even for you," I said.

"I'm serious, little one. Things will be different for you."

"Well, you have nothing to worry about. I know the transition is going to be hard, but I've got until graduation to say my goodbyes." When she didn't say anything, I softened. "You've done all you could to prepare me for this. You've taught me everything I need to know about Empyrean. I'll be fine. Everything will be fine because I have *you*."

I didn't know why I felt the urge to comfort her. Maybe it was because, after eighteen years, she finally admitted, in her way, that our relationship ran deeper than keeper and... keepee? The kept? Whatever.

Perhaps Mistress Marjorie was, in a roundabout way, trying to tell me that she *cared*.

"I won't be going with you."

If the record player tucked into the corner of my room was playing, it would have scratched to a halt. Like those moments in the movies when the music stops, and the main character freezes in place, everything pausing around them. My heart dropped into my stomach. I must have misheard her. "I'm sorry. I think I spaced. What did you say?"

"I won't be going back to Empyrean with you."

"What?" I asked again, shaking my head. "You hate the Realm of the Mortals more than anything. I've heard you rant about it for years. Of course you're coming back with me."

"I'm not going with you, Valeria. I have other things I need to take care of."

Valeria. Not *little one*. Clenching and unclenching my jaw, I looked away from her. "Oh, so you were stuck with me for eighteen years, and now you're seizing my departure as an opportunity to get away from me?"

The grandfather clock downstairs chimed eight long tolls.

She stood silently. With a wave of her hand, the dress peeled itself from my body and floated back to the hanger and into the bag hanging on the back of my bedroom door.

"You're late for school." She clapped her hands, and I vanished from the house in a cloud of thick black smoke. Flashes of glittering starlight spun around me until I stood in the tree line adjacent to Oakwood High School in a pair of jeans and a thrifted t-shirt.

Blinking the magic away, I chewed my bottom lip. I couldn't believe... I couldn't believe she was choosing to leave me. Why? Was there a seed of resentment from being stuck with me deep in her belly that had fully bloomed?

Where would she go, if not to Empyrean?

Something viler than bitterness wrapped its claw-like fingers around my heart and squeezed as I crossed the football field and snuck into the school through the unlocked glass doors on the side of the building.

I guess Mistress Marjorie needed a break from me.

She had other things to take care of like I was a *thing* she'd dealt with for too long, and she'd had enough. She was always a mom to me, but I was never a daughter to her. I rubbed a hand over my chest to alleviate the burning there, ignoring the stinging behind my eyes.

CHAPTER 3

Later that day during lunch, I found myself watching Ellody Sinclair, resident bitch and head of the prom committee, make idle chit-chat with tiny keychain versions of herself.

If there were one person in this school I wouldn't miss, it was her. She's had it out for me ever since Mason chose me over her in a competition I didn't even know we were in.

As I sat alone at a pale-blue lunch table, Mason trudged toward her, clad in a band t-shirt and black jeans. He ran his hand through his hair, leaving it more disheveled than it was before.

Ellody's eyes lit up and I couldn't look away. I needed to see the look on her face when he asked for the prom tickets and *only* the tickets.

No promposal for her.

Last year, when Mason told me she liked him, I encouraged him to date her. She was pretty with bronze skin, chocolate curls that cascaded around her heart-shaped face, and eyes in a similar shade of milky brown.

"Why would I want to go on a date with Ellody Sinclair when I have you?" His hand brushed against my bare skin in a way he'd done time and time again.

"You don't have *me."*

Sometimes I wondered if he knew then that I could love his body and his friendship, but I'd never love *him*.

But Ellody could. She could give him what I couldn't—a future. He didn't listen, though. Of course, she blamed me for the rejection since I was fucking him and ruined my reputation by spreading slut-shaming rumors.

Ellody's friends dispersed, leaving her alone with Mason. She tossed her hair over one shoulder, laughing as if Mason said something funny, and then touched his arm. This was when someone who had *actual* feelings for another person would feel some kind of jealousy, right? I surveyed my feelings for an inkling of it.

Nope, nothing.

Mason shifted from foot to foot and snuck a glance in my direction.

I unpacked my lunch, pretending I wasn't paying them any attention. It was the same meal as every other day—a plain turkey sandwich, chips, and an apple. Mistress Marjorie was hell-bent that I only eat what she packed to prevent poisoning. As if Wendy, the lunch lady, knew who I really was and wanted to take me out. I popped a chip into my mouth; Mistress Marjorie's paranoia knew no bounds.

I still couldn't believe she wasn't going back to Empyrean with me.

The reminder made my stomach churn.

As I tore the crust from my sandwich, I peeked up at Ellody and Mason. I was too far away to hear their conversation, but when her face fell, I knew he'd asked for only the prom tickets. I pressed my lips together, stifling a giggle as her eyes met mine, and she glared daggers at me. While Mason pulled cash from his wallet, she flipped me off and I blew her a kiss.

I didn't know what it said about me that I got so much enjoyment from watching Ellody seethe in place, her face green with jealousy.

The cafeteria was buzzing with excited energy. Around me, other students sat with their friends, making idle conversations about their overbearing parents who caught them sneaking out, their plans for the summer, and the *what ifs* surrounding prom.

Prom was *tomorrow*.

And so was my birthday, but who cared about that.

My attention drifted back to Mason, where Ellody still had him ensnared. Needing yet another way to keep myself busy, I rummaged through Mason's backpack. My eyes landed on his sketchbook.

"Ooh. Mason's trove of secrets," I whispered to myself as I cracked the book open.

Mason let me look through his other sketchbooks, but never this one. This one was off-limits. The cover was a leather-like material, torn at the top, and covered in stickers from bands he liked and quirky one-liners from shows. He had filled the off-white pages with all kinds of illustrations, some in charcoal, some in ink. I recognized the real-life inspiration for a few of the drawings from tiny details like the neon sign at the drive-in theater, my front porch, and even Mrs. Kennedy, his mom, doing dishes. She was smiling in that one.

It was almost as if this was his diary.

I flipped through page after page until I came across one riddled with all sorts of creatures.

Not creatures. *Demons*. What the hell?

Like... Realm of the Forsaken baddies that not even I had seen in the flesh. Over the years, Mistress Marjorie summoned apparitions of various demons to familiarize me with the creatures, but some of these drawings were even more terrifying.

I studied the faces of the various beasts. If I squinted, I could make out the face of a Night Hag, all angles and sharp teeth. There were so many sketches that they could be his imagination running wild—the consequence of watching too many horror movies. Yet my heart pounded in my ears.

Mason slid into the seat beside me, his hand finding my thigh. I jumped, dropping the sketchbook onto the table.

Clearing my throat, I tilted my head toward his hand. "Um. Boyfriend-y thing."

"I earned it." He grinned, leaving his hand where it lay. But then his smile faded as his eyes drifted from my face down to the table where his open sketchbook stared back at us. "Where did you find that?"

I pointed to his backpack. "I was bored. Have you been watching too many horror movies again?"

"No, I haven't." He snatched the book from the table and buried it in his bag.

A shiver danced along my skin. "Why are you being so weird?"

Mason brushed a lock of hair away from his forehead without answering me.

"Mace," I tried again.

His eyes darkened. "Just fucking drop it."

A couple of students from a table a few feet away glanced over at us. I offered them a small smile before turning back to Mason.

"Here." I shoved my meal toward him. Crap. Something was seriously off to make him lash out. He never talked to me like that. And... it was *Mason*. We didn't keep secrets from each other. Well, *he* didn't keep secrets from *me*. I knew him better than I knew myself. I chewed on my lip and took a deep breath. "You spent half of lunch entertaining Ellody to get our prom tickets. The least I can do is give you the rest of my lunch."

Mason picked up my sandwich and shoved it in his mouth, chewing quickly. Once he swallowed, he turned to me. The darkness was gone from his eyes as he lowered his voice. "I want to tell you about the sketches, but they might be listening."

My palms slickened with sweat, and I sat up straighter. "Who might be listening, Mace?"

I studied him. His brows knit together as his eyes darted all around the cafeteria before meeting mine. Worry lingered on his expression.

He leaned in closer, his familiar scent of cheap body spray and laundry detergent wafting around me. "Monsters, Val. They're real. I've caught them creeping around town, outside *Antiquities* and *Begin Again Books*. But it's like they're growing restless. They're lurking around the school, and I think"—his attention shifted to the table of students sitting several feet from us before sliding nervously back to me—"they're getting close to whatever they're searching for."

"Mason—"

He squeezed my hand. "I know it sounds crazy, but I need you to believe me. Okay?"

"Okay." I drew out the word. "Have you told anyone else about these... monsters?"

"My therapist told me it's my brain's messed up way of dealing with trauma from Dad's disappearance."

That would be perfectly reasonable. Mason's father vanished when we were kids, and I remember the way Mrs. Kennedy begged Mistress Marjorie to babysit Mason, so she could visit the police station. Margie obliged, and we spent the afternoon playing board games on our porch. My mouth twisted as I recalled that day and how I kept finding Mason staring at Mistress Marjorie like she was something otherworldly. I stiffened.

No, he *couldn't*... no way.

The bell rang, signaling that lunch and this conversation were over. Mason shot a hesitant glance at me before leading the way to sixth period, where we found our assigned seats.

Throughout the lecture, I couldn't take my eyes off him. If Mason's drawings weren't from his imagination... if they were of demons from the Realm of the Forsaken, I needed to tell Mistress Marjorie *now*.

I picked at the rip on my jeans. Mason might be able to see through a demon's glamour. And if that was the case, it only meant one thing—Mason had the Sight. He was a *Seer*.

But Seers weren't easy to identify. They blended in with the rest of the mortals, sometimes not knowing what they were until it was too late.

Mason's words played on a loop in my mind. *Monsters, Val. They're real. They're lurking around the school, and I think they're getting close to whatever they're searching for.*

If the Realm of the Forsaken was sniffing all over Oakwood, it'd be for one reason and one reason only—they had grounds to believe I was here. And if that was true, they'd stop at nothing to find me, take me, and use me as ransom. *Bastards.*

My lunch threatened to come up as a burning sensation crept across my flesh.

Panic. Was I panicking?

The air in the classroom felt like it was thick with invisible smoke, making it hard to breathe.

I'd be fine.

Wouldn't I?

Goosebumps raised the blonde hairs on my arms. Out of the corner of my eye, Mason's face mirrored mine. Definitely panic. Shoving my shit into my backpack, I stood, knocking over my chair.

"Sit down," Mrs. Lengyel barked.

I opened my mouth to tell her I had to leave, but all that escaped my throat was a guttural scream. One choked breath later, it felt as if my chest cracked open, like a furious bolt of lightning shattering through me. Howling in white hot agony, I fell to the scuffed floor. My hands clawed at my clothing, at the burning sensation swelling beneath my skin.

A collective of furrowed brows and tight lips soon stood over me. Some of them snickered, and I hated them for it. Mrs. Lengyel called for help, her voice frantic. I tried to tell her no one at this school could help me, but I couldn't stop screaming to form the words.

Mason knelt at my side, trying desperately to stop my hands from peeling away my skin.

I was burning alive from the inside out.

My bones, my blood, my nerves, my soul.

A tingling sensation licked at my left wrist as Mason's sketchbook whirred through my mind.

The Night Hag, the Drozols, the Hellhound.

Demons.

The Realm of the Forsaken had found me.

I reached for Mason, fearing this was the last time I'd ever be able to. My ghostly-white knuckles gripped his shirt, pulling him closer so I could memorize the various shades of green in his eyes, the specks of black that lingered on the edges of his iris, and the concern that shimmered in his gaze.

Before the world around me went dark, I swallowed my screams and a final warning slipped through my lips. "They're real."

CHAPTER 4

Black dots sprinkled the edges of my vision as I came to. The warm glow of early afternoon streamed in through the curtains, casting shadows on the walls.

"Margie?" I croaked, wincing at the incessant burning that raged in my throat.

The heaviness of several thick blankets gave way as I reached for the cup on my nightstand. Next to it, there was a note written in Mistress Marjorie's familiar scrawl: *Drink this when you wake, little one.*

Sniffing the contents, I blanched. Mistress Marjorie's home-brewed cough syrup—extra chalky, extra thick. Downing it in three large gulps, it coated my throat as I swallowed, numbing the pain within seconds.

My entire body sighed in relief.

My heavy bones filled with dread as I forced myself out of bed and toward the standing mirror, dodging heaps of clothes, books, shoes, and candy wrappers.

I tried not to flinch at my reflection. One large bandage was taped across my chest. Peeling it off, I gasped. Dozens of jagged scratches, in varying lengths, some deeper than others, marred my chest and the space between my breasts, from where I tried to rip myself apart. Margie had applied one of her sticky salves to the wounds. Its scent was earthy, smelling of grapes, olive oil, and moss. I smoothed the bandage back into place, grabbed a tank top from the floor, and slipped it on.

Taking another look at myself, I scowled. A deep purplish bruise flowered on my elbow, and the right side of my face was puffy and red.

I was going to look like complete shit at prom tomorrow.

Sunlight reflected from the mirror, illuminating a glittering mark on my left wrist—a geometric hourglass of sorts.

I scratched at the mark. Fear sprouted in the deepest recesses of my mind when it didn't come off.

I dashed from my room and down the hall to the bathroom. My palm crushed the soap dispenser and globs of peony-scented goo oozed into my other hand. Pulling a washcloth out from the closet next to the sink, I lathered it up and used it to scrub the mark, leaving the area red and raw.

It did nothing to erase the golden ink from my wrist.

A pounding headache bloomed in my temples. No amount of scrubbing would rid me of the brand; it was still there, bright as honey. Two golden overlapping triangles, each with the point facing the opposite's base, a small diamond shape formed in the middle.

It was fine. Everything was fine. No need to lose it. Pinching the bridge of my nose, I urged myself to take deep, calming breaths.

Mistress Marjorie brought me home from school. She had to have seen it. And if she wasn't concerned, maybe I shouldn't be either. I always wanted a tattoo anyway. The brand hummed as if in agreement. I stared at it, the hairs on the back of my neck standing up straight.

Did this thing *just agree with me?*

Leaving the bathroom, I headed toward Mistress Marjorie's door and knocked. No answer. I jiggled the handle. As always, it was locked up tight.

"Mistress Marjorie," I called out.

The clanging of metal trickled into the hallway from downstairs as if in answer. I scrubbed my face with my hands. That sound only meant one thing, and I didn't want anything to do with it. Why would Mistress Marjorie test me today of all days, knowing what happened earlier at school?

"Mistress Marjorie, now is *not* the time."

After scanning the remaining upstairs rooms, both filled with mismatched furniture, thread-bare rugs, and floral wallpaper that curled from the seams, I groaned.

Margie was hiding downstairs, and so was my opponent.

I crept down the staircase, avoiding the creaky spots, and dared a peek into the drawing room opposite the foyer. Nothing and no one.

Edging my way toward the kitchen, I peeked around the corner. Several floating pots and pans banged against one another, begging for my attention. But they were a distraction. If I could get to the dining room, I'd—

A figure rushed me from the side, tackling me to the ground and knocking the air from my lungs. A sense of worry pulsed through the brand, igniting something inside me that wanted to comfort it. With a knee to my back, the figure pressed me onto the cold hardwood floor. The scratches on my chest shrieked in pain.

My bruised elbow connected with the figure's face, and I hissed from the blow before hurrying into the dining room on my hands and knees. The figure grabbed my ankles and yanked me toward them, splitting my fingernails against the wooden floor.

"Not my nails!" I hollered, kicking their face, barely able to break free of their grip. I'd been growing them out specifically for prom. I took a second to survey the damage. They were bloodied and splintered. "Oh, you're going to *pay* for this."

My opponent didn't care. It wasn't programmed to feel. It was on me again, landing a punch against my face. I bit my tongue, and I yelped. Shoving the figure away from me with all my might, it flew backward, knocking into a flowery paint-by-numbers painting on the wall. The picture fell to the ground with a clatter, and the frame broke in two.

"Great," I muttered, rushing for the table and sliding beneath it to grab the short sword Mistress Marjorie secured there for emergency use. Or, you know, training. The pots and pans continued to clang against each other in time with my pounding heart.

Like a viper in the grass, I waited for their heavy footsteps to draw closer to the table. When the soles of their boots stepped onto the rug, I slid the edge of the blade against the back of their ankles, slicing the thick tendons. They fell to the ground with a grunt, and I pounced, jamming the sword into the spot where their heart would be.

If they had one.

If they were real.

"Exceptional," Mistress Marjorie crooned. My head whipped in the direction of her voice. She sat in the corner of the room in a black tufted chair, one leg across the other. "I think you beat your best time."

A tremendous sense of relief flooded through the brand, and I touched it gently. Why did it feel concerned for me? My mouth parted to ask Mistress Marjorie, but a voice that was not my own spoke first.

"Can someone explain to me what the hell is going on?" Mason stood in the doorway to the dining room. His sparkling green eyes were wide, roving over the sight before him: a knife protruding from a lifeless body, and me straddling that corpse, breath ragged.

"It's not what it looks like." I yanked the sword free, and the body faded to dust beneath me.

"What are you?" he whispered, curiosity and fear in his voice. His words were a slap to the face, and I couldn't help but flinch. When I met his eyes, I realized he wasn't looking at me.

He was staring at Mistress Marjorie.

Standing, she gestured for him to take a seat at the table before turning to me. "Come with me."

"I'll be right back," I called over my shoulder as I followed Margie, leaving Mason reeling in the dining room with his arms folded tightly across his chest and wide-eyed shock plastered on his face.

In the kitchen, Mistress Marjorie filled a tea kettle with cold water and placed it on the smallest stove burner. With a snap of her fingers, the burner ignited. She murmured a chant, and an opaque bubble sealed off the doorway to the dining room.

"It's a soundproofing spell. Something tells me Mason's the eavesdropping type."

I forced a laugh. "What gives you that impression?"

"He broke into our house." She pointed at the shattered window to the right of the front door that was now piecing itself back together. "A mortal boy walked through our gate, shattered our window, and entered our sacred grounds without even a cut. Something must be off with my wards."

I winced, leaning against the counter and fidgeting with a loose thread on my top. "It's not your wards. There's something you need to know about Mason."

"And what's that?"

"He might be a... Seer."

She folded her hands in front of her. "Then we must tell him the truth about who you are. If he doesn't take it well, then we wipe his memory and be done with it."

I recoiled from her suggestion, lips curling as a bitter tang dripped down my throat. *Be done with it.* Like she'd be done with me in six days?

The kettle whistled a high-pitched scream, steam escaping from its spout.

Mistress Marjorie busied herself with pouring the boiling water into an enchanted teapot and placing several bags of chamomile tea into it. She readied a tray with three teacups, the tea, milk, and sugar.

"And if he's a Seer?" I asked.

"Then we use him to keep you safe."

Mistress Marjorie snapped her fingers, the soundproof bubble and invisible blanket of dark magic disappearing in an instant. She motioned for me to lead the way. I did as she directed, still reeling over how calm she was.

In the dining room, Mason sat at the table, worrying his lip. Taking the seat farthest away from him, I surveyed the damage to my nails. They were splintered and bloodied and would look awful at prom tomorrow. I glared at the tiny pile of dust where the training dummy had crumbled.

Worry worked its way into my bloodstream, flowing through me.

Was this the moment where Mason left because he saw me for who I truly was? Not a normal mortal girl, but a princess with baggage?

Maybe this would help him let me go and make it easier to end things between us.

Or he'd want me more. The thought was fleeting and selfish.

It didn't matter how much he wanted me because soon he'd need to find another friend and another body to warm his bed.

He would need to move on.

The tray carrying the afternoon tea floated into the room, and Mistress Marjorie sauntered in behind it, her long black cloak brushing soundlessly against the wooden floors. Mason watched, eyes wide, as the teapot poured the perfect amount of tea into each cup, leaving enough room for a splash of milk.

"This is the quietest you two have been since you met." She handed each of us a cup on a matching saucer and took a seat at the head of the table. When neither of us responded, she added, "I don't appreciate you breaking into our home, Mason."

"I heard Val scream." His gaze was glued to the bewitched teapot before he shot his scrutinizing eyes upon Mistress Marjorie. "Take off that stupid hood."

"Mason," I warned. My eyes darted between Mistress Marjorie and him as they stared at one another. This was turning into a pissing contest.

Mason folded his arms across his chest while Mistress Marjorie ran a long white finger around the brim of her teacup. "I cannot remove my hood, child. While you may be able to see through the glamour, Valeria cannot."

Now it was my turn to look at her with raised eyebrows. "What do you mean?"

"My cloak was a gift. I didn't know it was enchanted until it was too late." The lilt in her voice was far away. "Until there's peace between the realms, I'm physically unable to remove my hood in the presence of an Empyrean for both their safety and my own."

"Empyrean?" Mason asked, taking a hesitant sip of tea. The name of my realm on his tongue was bittersweet. His hand shook when he set the teacup down. "What's that?"

"Mason..." I fumbled for what else to say. How was I supposed to tell him I hailed from a realm that was created by a fallen god? Where would I even start without diving into a history lesson? I glanced at Mistress Marjorie for help.

"Valeria is... not of this world," she offered. "She is the Princess of Empyrean, exiled to the Realm of the Mortals to be raised in hiding."

Mason let out a long breath. "You're a *princess*? What does a princess have to hide from?"

"The person... the person who murdered my mother." I picked at the skin around my ruined nails. My heart pounded. "Eighteen years ago, my realm was rocked by terror. Bastile, the god who created

Empyrean, was brutally murdered during a battle with Vemdour, God of the Forsaken. My brother, Cayden, saw this as an opening to seize the throne from my father who Bastile had named king in his will." The rest of the words poured out of me in a rush. "Cayden murdered our mother and tried to kill my father and me too, but failed."

Saying the words out loud to a story I longed to forget caused an aching in my chest. It rattled through me until the soft embrace of concern wrapped around me like a throw blanket I couldn't shrug off. My eyes darted to the brand. *So weird.*

Mason blinked. "But why?"

"Power," Mistress Marjorie answered. "He aligned with the Realm of the Forsaken—"

"Realm of the what?"

"It's what mortals call Hell," I offered, then sighed. "So, there are four realms that make up our universe. The Realm of the Mortals, which is here. Empyrean, The Realm of the Forsaken, and what mortals call Heaven is actually the Realm of the Divine."

"I wish I was taking notes." Mason laughed. It wasn't his usual laugh, the one that lit up any space he was in. This one was breathy and uncomfortable. Nervous. He was *nervous.* "What's the point of Empyrean? I mean I get the whole Heaven and Hell thing, but what does your realm *do*?"

"My people protect the Realm of the Mortals from both the Realm of the Forsaken and the Divine. Contrary to what you've been taught to believe, Empyrean is the realm that has mortals' best interests at heart." My knee bounced up and down, rattling the spoon against the saucer that held my untouched tea. "Think of Empyrean as your realm's guardian angels."

His brow furrowed. "I get needing to protect us against Hell, but why do we need to be protected from Heaven?"

"Because the Realm of the Divine is full of selfish gods who view mortals as nothing but playthings for their amusement and enslavement," I said gently.

"We won't bore you with the politics," Mistress Marjorie said. "All you need to know is that Valeria's father exiled her to this realm to keep her safe."

I drummed my fingers on the table I'd thrifted from Antiquities on Cornelia Street. "And the father of the year award goes to..."

Mason shot me a questioning look, and I shrugged. Guess I could tell him all about my daddy issues now. Mistress Marjorie ignored my sarcasm as if what she said was fact. Sure, *that* was why my father sent me here. To keep me safe. Not to pawn me off while he dealt with Cayden's aftermath. Not to ensure I didn't get in his way while he rebuilt Empyrean.

Cayden and his demonic horde slaughtered almost the entire Celestian army—Empyrean's most noble warriors and guardians of the Realm of the Mortals—leaving the realm defenseless with shattered wards that no demon had ever been able to cross before. To make matters worse, the prick had help from Vemdour to do so. I fought against a shiver that crawled its way across my skin at the thought of the god ravaging a peaceful realm like Empyrean.

Margie had warned me against Vemdour and his reach from a very young age. He was ruthless and powerful and would stop at nothing to get what he wanted, to get *me*.

"The thing Valeria stabbed today? That was one of the Realm of the Forsaken's... monsters?"

Mason's voice drew me back to the conversation. "Demons. The Realm of the Forsaken has demons, not monsters. And that"—I pointed to the pile of dust in the doorway—"is what's left of an enchanted training dummy."

"And your leather ensemble?"

"Training gear. Though, sometimes, I spar in gowns to spice things up." I winked.

"Val, you're a *princess*." He looked at me, eyes wide with wonder. "That means I'm dating—"

"Not dating," I corrected him. "Fucking."

Mason coughed, cheeks flaming red.

Mistress Marjorie sighed. "So vulgar."

His eyes darted to my keeper, and I waved his embarrassment away. "Don't worry. She already knew."

Mason blushed harder, and I grinned, relief washing over me. I didn't have to lie to him anymore. About *anything*. The truth was out, and it felt good to no longer keep him in the dark.

Now we had six glorious days to spend together without any lies getting in the way.

He shook his head, the pink fading from his face. "What about what happened today? Was that caused by demons?"

I looked to Mistress Marjorie for help, again.

"Tell me what happened before you fainted," she said.

I brought her up to speed, starting with Mason's sketchbook, which she demanded to see.

Mason excused himself from the table and rushed from the dining room only to rush back fifteen seconds later with his backpack. As he pulled the notebook free and handed it to my keeper, the sticker-covered front taunted me. Once he sat, we both watched with bated breath as Mistress Marjorie ran her long, pale fingers over the drawings. They sparked against her touch as she ripped the ink from the pages and brought apparition after apparition of demon to life. Mason stared at the tiny glowing creatures, mouth agape.

"Valeria is correct." Mistress Marjorie slammed the sketchbook shut and the drawings faded back into harmless ink. "You do have the Sight, Mason."

"The Sight?" Mason asked, running a shaky hand through his hair. "What does that even mean?"

Mistress Marjorie was quiet, likely mulling over how much to share with him. "The Sight is a gift, and a curse, that some mortals bear. It's a peculiar type of magic—almost like a third eye—drawn from a deep awareness of your surroundings and a connection to nature and its various energy frequencies. These *monsters* you've seen are demons or gods in their purest form, beyond their glamour."

Mason opened and closed his mouth as if he was trying and failing to formulate a sentence.

"Around most mortals, there is a veil," Mistress Marjorie continued. "Many years spent disbelieving in magic and denying the truth of what they've seen has caused mortals to turn a blind eye to the world around them. Which in turn makes them easy prey for both gods and demons alike.

"You see, the gods often come to the Realm of the Mortals in different forms to seduce mortals into eternal servitude. And while the gods have their fun, the demons seek their own enjoyment. They inhabit the bodies of mortals, snatching their lives from them and dragging their souls to the Realm of the Forsaken long before death is meant to claim them."

I could've sworn a shiver spread throughout the dining room.

Mistress Marjorie paused before adding, "Mortals without the sight wouldn't even know these things were happening, but Seers would see beyond the veil to the truth—to the blinding glory inhabiting mortal or animal flesh and to the demon's truest form lurking beneath the face of their neighbor."

Mason snapped his jaw shut as shock riddled his face. A moment passed as Mistress Marjorie's words set in, and then he stopped fidgeting, laying his hands flat on the table. "I... I think I've seen demons beneath the faces of some of the students at Oakwood."

The hairs on the back of my neck stood on edge as I sucked in a breath.

A demon possession was a horrifying ordeal from start to finish, if there *was* a finish.

The God of the Forsaken made it so demons could shift from their physical form to their innate essence—sometimes that was a billow of smoke or a trail of sludge—so they could slither into a mortal's body through their mouth and down their throat, latch onto their soul, and take control of them. All the while, the mortal was completely aware of how their body was being used, but there was nothing they could do to stop it.

Even exorcisms weren't an option; the gods gave up on helping mortals a long, long time ago. It was Empyrean's Celestians who learned that the only way to free a mortal from demonic possession was by challenging the demon.

Demons weakened themselves when taking control of a mortal. They had no access to their powers, no access to anything but a portal between the Realm of the Mortals and the Forsaken to drag souls under. If they were challenged enough to fear death, they'd release their mortal husk to be able to wield their full power, preventing the mortal from facing a fate worse than death. But that was a big if. Most demons would never release their mortals. The only way to kill them would be by sacrificing the mortal's life, too.

I held in the curse that threatened to spill from my lips as I glanced at Margie.

"Little one, if the demons snatched the bodies of your peers, then you are no longer safe in Oakwood. Perhaps—"

"Don't even *think* about finishing that sentence," I cut in. "Demons or not, I'm going to prom."

"Val..." Mason tried.

"We're going," I snapped. "I'm not being chased from what's left of my life here just because some demons *might* know I'm here. This could all be a terrible coincidence."

Mistress Marjorie sipped her tea. "Very well. You will go to prom, so long as you're armed."

"I'm pretty sure Oakwood High has a 'no weapons' policy," I said.

"They will be none the wiser."

"Fine, whatever."

We were all quiet for a beat longer before Mason asked with a soft, shaky voice, "How did I even get the Sight? Is it... is it because of my friendship with Val?"

Of course he'd blame me. I swallowed the snappy comeback crawling up my throat as Mistress Marjorie answered him. "No, any mortal can have the Sight so long as their mind is open to seeing the truth." She paused, as if weighing if she wanted to add more. "The Sight is easier to tap into when nurtured through bloodlines, though. Your father—"

"What about him?" Mason asked, chest heaving. "You think he had the Sight?"

"Possibly."

"No." He shook his head. "I would've known if Dad suffered from this. I would've... He didn't. Right, Val?"

"I don't know, Mason." I lifted a shoulder. "I mean... He could've? Maybe that's why he disappeared? Maybe he panicked and left Oakwood when the demons started showing up?"

Mason carved his upper teeth into his bottom lip. If he didn't stop that, he'd draw blood. "I know my dad, and he wasn't a Seer."

"Okay," I murmured, fighting the urge to reach across the table and give his hand a squeeze. "Margie, do you know of any other Seers who could help Mason figure this shit out?"

"Not in Oakwood," Mistress Marjorie said. "But that doesn't mean there aren't more. The last Seer I'd known personally was Aulus Damus—"

"Aulus Damus?" I laughed. "That is the fakest name I have ever heard in my life."

Mistress Marjorie ignored me as she added, "I met him in Empyrean shortly after he accepted his role as ambassador to the realm."

A flicker of hope danced in Mason's eyes when he looked at me, and my gut told me I had to squash it.

"I won't allow you to come to Empyrean with me, Mason." The words were harsh, but my voice was small. I pointed at Mistress Marjorie. "You know Aulus wasn't just an *ambassador* to Empyrean. Tell him the truth."

"Aulus was never forced to do anything he didn't volunteer for. Rumors say he went mad using his gift to aid the realm, fleeing to the Realm of the Mortals to live a life of total isolation. Others say he's still in Empyrean, hiding among its people." Her voice lowered. "The life of a Seer is a lonely one if they survive long enough to live it."

My stomach flopped at the thought of someone, or something, hurting Mason.

He sighed. "So what am I supposed to do now? Sit around and wait for someone else to figure out I have the Sight?"

"We will use your gift to keep Valeria safe at prom and during her remaining days in Oakwood," Mistress Marjorie said simply, as if she had this planned all along.

Before I could object, Mason's ears perked up. "Consider it done. Do you need me to swear my allegiance to Val through a blood oath or something?"

I rolled my eyes as she waved away his proclamation. "No, that won't be necessary. But it would be helpful if you sketched any demons you see, so I can gauge what creatures we're up against." She conjured two notebooks from thin air, holding one out to Mason. "Use this for your sketches." He took the offered book from her and flipped through the bright white pages. "Whatever you draw in there will appear in its twin, so it'll be easier for you to report back to me."

I wasn't too fond of the idea of bringing Mason into the genuine dangers of my world, but I trusted Mistress Marjorie and her judgment. If she thought Mason helping could be worthwhile, I'd go along with it.

Mason had stopped glaring at Mistress Marjorie and now leaned in whenever she spoke, transfixed on whatever he was hearing. There was a stillness smoothing his features as if the confirmation that there wasn't something wrong with him put him at ease.

The tension in my shoulders relaxed just a little bit. At least he'd get to keep his memories.

Explaining the events that transpired during class were more difficult to articulate. How could I describe what had happened to me? It was as wild and bizarre as a fever dream.

"Go over it again," Mistress Marjorie urged. "What did it feel like?"

"Like my chest cracked open and invisible fire filled my body, burning me from the inside out. It was suffocating and unbearable."

"That sounds like a bonding spell." Mistress Marjorie used one finger to trace along the edges of the brand. "I studied it earlier while you were asleep, but I couldn't get a read on it. Now that you're awake, I can tell that this magic is a different kind of magic. Neutral magic."

I'd only ever heard of two kinds of magic. Dark magic, the kind Mistress Marjorie, Vemdour, and some demons in the Realm of the Forsaken wielded, and holy magic, the kind that pulsed throughout Empyrean and the Realm of the Divine.

"It's a scarce type of magic. One that's a mixture of dark and holy magic." She angled my wrist under the bright chandelier light, and the brand buzzed in response.

"This is going to sound crazy," I said, and Mason snorted. I glared, and he offered me a lop-sided grin. "Since the brand appeared, I've felt some... emotions come through it."

"Emotions?" Mistress Marjorie dropped my hand suddenly, and I cradled it against my chest.

"It's the best way I can describe it. Unexpected feelings that I normally wouldn't feel under the circumstances. Like during the test with the training dummy, I felt genuine fear and urgency pulsing through me. But when I killed the dummy, I felt relieved. And... and I had the urge to comfort whoever or whatever was worried for me. But I didn't know *how*. I didn't know how to make them feel that I was all right."

Mason's eyes met mine; a flicker of jealousy shimmered there, and I bit back the urge to shake him and remind him I wasn't his girlfriend.

"I see," Mistress Marjorie finally said, running another finger around the brim of her teacup.

"So what kind of bond is it?" I asked, an unfamiliar feeling burrowing its way into my bones.

She took a sip of her now cold tea, her gaze on me from beneath the cloak. "If I were you, little one, I wouldn't concern myself with what kind of bond it is but *who* you are bound to."

CHAPTER 5

The question of who I was bound to kept me up until the pitch black of night faded into the dawn's bleeding glow of bubblegum pink and peach, bathing my room with pastel light.

I should've crawled out of bed and met Mason for a run, but I didn't.

Instead, I laid there staring at the golden tattoo.

Who are you? I asked for the thousandth time, sending the question down whatever invisible tether we shared. Much to my annoyance, there was no reply.

I could have received any number of presents for my birthday, but what did I get? A creepy magical bond to someone I didn't know, who felt what I felt and experienced what I experienced. With my luck, it was probably some toothless old dude.

"Happy birthday to me," I muttered to myself over the faint laugh track of a sitcom rerun playing on the small TV mounted to my wall.

The bond was too much, too soon. It was an invasion of privacy, and I wanted it *gone*. But there was no user manual for magic, no off switch to be found.

What do you want from me? I tried again.

Nothing.

I hated this stupid thing.

Grabbing a fleece throw blanket and wrapping it around my shoulders, I slipped out of bed and through the double doors to the terrace, taking a deep breath of chilly morning air. Chipped white paint covered the railing, and I mindlessly picked at it, the tips of my fingers numb from the salve Mistress Marjorie put on them last night.

I sighed.

Five days. I had five days left before she sent me back to Empyrean without her.

Who would I have once I left the Realm of the Mortals? Not Mason. Not Mistress Marjorie.

I'd be utterly alone. I shivered at the thought.

That wasn't totally true. I'd have my father. Though there was no guarantee he'd have time for me. It wasn't like being in the same realm would free him up for anything other than Take-Your-Kid-To-Work-Day.

I'd be able to visit my mother's grave and walk among the people she gave her life for. That brought a small smile to my lips. Mistress Marjorie told me Mom was loved by all and feared by none. I could only hope the people of Empyrean would feel the same about me.

Doubt slithered its way into the recesses of my mind.

What if they didn't like what they saw? What if they rejected me? I didn't belong here in the Realm of the Mortals. Maybe I didn't belong in Empyrean either.

The mark on my wrist sparked a flicker of gold before that all too familiar embrace of comfort wrapped itself around me, trying its damnedest to convince me that my thoughts were wrong.

But it didn't matter. The worries were still there, poking and prodding.

I glared at the brand on my wrist. *Stop comforting me.*

I thought those three words so loudly that beads of sweat swelled on my forehead.

No response.

There had to be someone who could help me understand what this bond was and how to use it or control it.

A slight breeze rustled through the leaves, and I pinched the fuzzy blanket tighter around my shoulders.

"Little one," Mistress Marjorie called from behind me. "Are you well?"

I turned to look at her, my eyelids heavy with exhaustion. "I'm fine. I was up all night wondering about the bond."

"Get back in bed. I'll make some breakfast and fetch your birthday present."

I arched my brow. "You got me a present?"

"Why are you so surprised? I've given you a gift every year for your birthday, haven't I?"

Because you're leaving me, I wanted to say so badly, but I let the words die on my tongue.

Today was my birthday, and prom, and I wouldn't let Mistress Marjorie's future abandonment cast a shadow on how happy I should be.

"No reason," I lied.

She studied me for a beat longer before tucking her hands into her pockets and wandering out of the room, leaving me to pad across the wooden floor, climb into bed, and wait.

LESS THAN FIFTEEN MINUTES later, Mistress Marjorie sauntered into my bedroom with a tray floating behind her. On it was a steaming cup of hot chocolate, filled to the brim with already melting marshmallows, and a plate with a waffle bigger than my face, coated in powdered sugar and topped with fresh cut strawberries.

My favorites.

"Thank you," I said, scooting over to give her space to sit on the bed beside me.

As she made herself comfortable, careful not to tilt my tray, I flicked through the channels on the TV, landing on a game show I was absolutely terrible at. But Mistress Marjorie enjoyed this one, and I ate in silence as she rattled off the answers to whatever questions the host asked the contestants.

Once I was fed, Mistress Marjorie turned off the TV with a wave of her hand and summoned a slender velvet box.

I'd always been jealous of the way Margie used magic freely, as if it was as simple as breathing. Whenever I'd complain about my inability to wield magic, she'd teach me spells that anyone could do with the right incantations and ingredients—a scrying spell to help me find a missing earring (I never found it), a communication spell to send a fire letter to my father so he could attend Oakwood Middle School's father-daughter dance (he didn't come), and even a truth spell (which she only used on me once after I tried to run away when I was twelve)—but none of that would ever measure up to the allure of her abilities, to the power she wielded.

My fingers traced the crushed velvet of the box and the delicate silver roses embroidered across its edges. The sheer beauty of the case told me this gift was not from the Realm of the Mortals. It was hand-crafted in Empyrean.

I cracked it open. A gasp slipped from my lips.

There wasn't a piece of jewelry waiting for me, but a dagger.

Where a polished silver blade should be was lethal clear crystal. Carefully, I took the gift from the case. I wrapped one hand around the black, leather-bound hilt, and the crystal transformed, embodying a spinning galaxy—shades of mulberry blended into starry ink and shimmering gold.

"You are to take this to prom with you," Mistress Marjorie said, folding her hands in her lap. "It's designed to be hidden, as I've enchanted it with a one-word command. All you must do is say 'conceal.'"

There was no time like the present to try it out for size.

"Conceal," I whispered.

A strange sense of otherness seeped from it as the straps of leather unwound and curled around my right wrist. What was once a stunning dagger was now a thick cuff adorned with a single incandescent jewel. In the center of the gem, flecks of glitter swirled around and around like snowflakes in a snow globe.

I stared at it, amazed. "This is incredible."

"To turn it back into a dagger, all you have to do is take it off."

I tried that too and watched as it took the shape of the dagger once more. Carefully, I placed it back in the velvet box. "I think this year's gift is by far my favorite."

"I'm glad you like it," she murmured as she stood, gathering the tray stacked with empty dishes. "You should rest, little one. You have a long night ahead of you."

AFTER A THOUSAND FINGER snaps and claps, Mistress Marjorie stood in front of me, impressed with her handiwork.

"I think I did well," she said for the second time. "I'm no trained handmaiden, but you look radiant."

"Can I look now?" I asked, bouncing on the edge of the bed.

Mistress Marjorie pointed to the arched full-length mirror, gilded in gold, leaning against the wall. "Yes."

I launched myself toward it in four-inch heels and scrutinized my reflection. My blood buzzed with excitement. "Holy shit."

Mistress Marjorie wasn't lying. She did a *damned* good job with both my hair and makeup, covering up any bruising and enhancing my delicate features. Woven into my hair was a crown of black roses, plucked straight from our garden in the backyard. The bronze and smoky onyx shades she layered around my eyes gave them a tenderness I didn't recognize; what was once a vibrant lilac storm was now a canopy of wisteria on a sunny day, soft and calm.

"Do you approve?" She approached me from behind and wrapped a ribbon around my neck, tying it in a hidden bow underneath my loose honey-colored waves. The choker matched the roses in my hair, stark compared to the ruby dress that clung to my curves.

"I wouldn't change a thing." I spun around to admire the way the gemstones shimmered.

I'd have to thank Daddy Dearest for picking a dress that hid the healing scratches on my chest.

"All that's left is your birthday present." Mistress Marjorie clapped her hands, and the long, velvet box she gave me this morning appeared. She handed me the dagger, and I said the one-word command that would turn it into a bracelet. I ran my finger over the stone absentmindedly. "Should you have to use it, remember to aim for the heart because the blade is enchanted."

"Enchanted?

A knock from downstairs drew my attention away from the bracelet to the clock next to my bed.

Mason was early.

I threw my arms around Mistress Marjorie, and she stiffened under my embrace. Swallowing the shaking in my voice, I murmured, "I wish you'd change your mind about coming back to Empyrean with me, Margie."

She softened just a little, and a kernel of hope sprouted within me. Maybe she'd change her mind. Maybe—

"You should know me well enough by now to know that I rarely change my mind. Now, go. Have fun. The Seer's waiting."

Whatever hope I had faded fast. I hid my disappointment with a reluctant nod before making my way out of the room and down the wooden staircase, habitually avoiding the spots that creaked.

Mason was a shapeless blob beyond the acid-etched window, giving me a moment to steady myself. I smoothed out my gown and ran my fingers through my hair, careful not to disrupt the black roses pinned in a crown around my head.

Once I was settled, I opened the door just as Mason raised his fist to knock again. He stood on the porch, one hand tucked into his pants pocket, the other holding a gift bag. He wore a simple black suit with a deep red rose tucked in where a pocket square would go. His slicked-back hair reminded me of the heartthrobs in black and white films; all he needed was a leather jacket and a bad boy attitude—both of which he didn't have.

Moments passed between us, his jaw slack. "Wow. Thank you."

"You're thanking me? For what?"

"Not wearing your leather ensemble."

Playfully shoving his arm, I welcomed him into the foyer.

"Happy birthday." He pulled me into a hug. As he released me, he added, "I made you something."

Mason handed me the gift, our fingers brushing during the exchange. He glanced at me with those eyes that made every thought of his transparent on his face. He was smitten. I looked away to rummage through the glittery tissue paper, finding a framed picture.

"Mason." I inhaled sharply, staring at the life-like portrait of myself. "It's beautiful."

He shifted his weight from foot to foot. "I meant to draw you for the longest time, but I could never get your eyes right."

I stared at my graphite reflection. "What do you mean?"

"They always lacked something whenever I drew them. Last night I realized what they were missing."

My gaze returned to the illustration in front of me, studying his drawing of my eyes. Delight and strength mixed with a tiny bit of chaos lingered beneath the stare.

"And what was that?"

"Fire." He gave a lopsided smile.

That's when I saw them—subtle purple flames dancing around the pupils, challenging whoever met their gaze with a flickering taunt.

"The likeness is uncanny," Mistress Marjorie said from over my shoulder. Mason jumped, unfamiliar with her shadow-like movements. "Are you leaving now?"

Mason nodded. "We should get—"

"No!" I shouted, cutting him off. "We need to take pictures—in front of the fireplace and on the staircase."

I set Mason's gift on the credenza in the hallway and slipped into the drawing room. Mason handed Mistress Marjorie his phone, and we stood in prime prom position in front of the hearth.

She snapped a few photos, which I swiped through and approved, and then we repeated the process on the stairs. When I was happy with the results, we said our goodbyes and left the house.

I stopped midway on the driveway. "Mason, what is *that*?"

"Val," he warned. "Don't talk shit on Ol' Bessie."

I folded my arms across my chest. "You promised me a limo."

Mason laughed, opening the passenger door for me. "Our town has one limo and it was already booked, so Ol' Bessie is our chariot for the night."

Together we crammed my gown inside the passenger seat of his beat-up, piece-of-shit car, and I huffed. When he took his seat behind the steering wheel, he doubled over, laughing at the sight of me drowning in an endless sea of red tulle.

"Just drive," I said, laughing along with him.

"Of course, Your Highness," he said with an unidentifiable fake accent.

I rolled my eyes and let the wind carry away his words.

CHAPTER 6

Prom was everything I imagined it would be.

As soon as we walked through the doors to the gym, we crossed under an arch of balloons and sandy driftwood with various seashells woven in and took pictures in front of a cheesy underwater backdrop.

I was overdressed compared to the other girls in their sequin mini-dresses and slim-fitting gowns, but I didn't mind.

I felt beautiful.

Mason placed a hand on my lower back and led me through a sea of couples kissing and dancing to a table lined with fish-shaped fresh-cut fruit and tiny sandwiches and several bowls of bright blue punch.

"Is it spiked?"

He poured himself a small cup and took a sip, shaking his head. "Not yet."

Pulling a silver flask from his pocket, he emptied a clear liquid into two cups. With a mischievous grin, he swished the drinks around and handed me one.

It burned as I downed it. "It's disgusting."

"It's supposed to be."

Pop song after pop song blared through the speakers while bubbles floated in the air, bursting sporadically above the ocean of people grinding against one another.

The dancing... it was everything I'd imagined it'd be from the reality shows I'd watched where people went to clubs and got wasted.

"Do you want to dance?" Mason's breath was warm on my ear.

"Not like that." I gestured to a cheerleader gyrating her ass on the front of someone who was *not* her boyfriend.

Mason laced his fingers through mine before turning around to angle his body in front of me. I looked up into his frantic jade eyes, searching for an explanation. "What's wrong? We can dance like that if you want, I just think it's weird—"

"They're here."

My stomach sank.

"How many?" The brand on my wrist pulsed in time with my racing heart.

His eyes darted from the left to a spot over my shoulder. "Too many. We need to get you out of here." With sweaty palms, he dragged me in the direction of the nearest exit sign. The four red letters were a beacon promising us we'd make it out unscathed. A few more steps, and we'd be free.

"Where do you two think you're going?" I recognized her voice before she stepped into our view. *Ellody*. I glanced at Mason, and his grip tightened on my hand before he shot me a fearful nod. She was one of them. But when had she been claimed?

I feigned ignorance. "Probably Mason's bedroom. His mom's working the night shift."

Her eyes darted to Mason, and she licked her red lips.

"Ellody, get out of our way," he said, trying to maneuver us around her.

She hissed. "I don't think I will."

Maybe if I challenged the demon, it would release Ellody's body.

"I'm going to enjoy this." It was a quick warning before my fist collided with her face. She hit the ground, smacking the linoleum floor. We ran past her toward the exit—only a few more feet to go. Mason's hands were on the door's metal bar separating us from freedom when Ellody grabbed my ankle, yanking me to the floor with her and away from the door—ripping my dress in the process.

"You bitch," I growled through gritted teeth.

She scrambled on top of me. "You've got a bounty on your pretty little head, lost princess."

"A bounty?" Fear and anger warred within me.

She donned a feral grin. "It didn't specify alive or dead."

Mason snatched a tacky, papier-mâché decoration from one of the tables and whacked her with it.

"Let her go!" He dropped the frilly shark when she turned to him and snarled.

I snapped the bracelet's strap, and the dagger materialized, the weight of the hilt a comfort. Mistress Marjorie had etched survival into my bones the way protection runes were carved into the walls of our hidden house.

I could do this. I would get us out.

Thankful for the shadowy area of the cafeteria, I let go of the breath I was holding. The blade pierced Ellody's soft skin, straight in to the hilt and into her flat stomach. She gasped with wide eyes and struck me across the face. My teeth bit my cheek. The coppery taste of blood pooled in my mouth as I yanked the dagger free and jammed it in again and again, even as she struck me, until her body went slack.

My eyes flickered around us to ensure no one saw what just transpired and when I deemed the coast clear, I shoved her off of me with trembling, bloodstained hands. Ellody was the first person I'd killed—the first *demon* I killed.

My heart pounded in my chest. I was going to be sick.

It was totally normal to feel like this. Killing wasn't supposed to be easy.

But I didn't know it would make me feel so... alive.

Mason tugged me to my feet as I slipped and slided. Warm blood made the floor slick. "We have a problem."

I groaned. "What now?"

He pointed toward a group of at least twenty students. No. All of them couldn't be... could they?

The brand on my arm burned with concern, questioning if I was all right, wondering if I needed help.

I did.

Help me, I begged. *Please.*

Like this morning, there was no reply.

Useless, stupid bond.

The air around the students shimmered as their demon veils weakened. Pitch-black eyes turned to stare in our direction and sharp teeth poked out from behind their sickening scowls.

Welp, I guess they *could* all be demons. Shit. Across the gym, teens smiled and danced without a care or fear in the world—oblivious to what happened behind the veil. If I left now, who knew what would happen. Maybe the demons would follow me or maybe they'd stay and turn prom into a massacre. I couldn't risk it. But I could stay and try to free the possessed students before they were taken and trapped in the Realm of the Forsaken forever. I could buy some time until Mistress Marjorie arrived and protected us all.

"Mason." I lowered my voice, trusting he could hear me over the blaring music. "You need to go and take the rest of the unpossessed students with you."

"I'm not leaving you." He looked between our classmates and me, desperation in his eyes. "Come with me?"

"Pull the fire alarm and get them out of here," I said, making my choice clear to him. "And then go get Mistress Marjorie."

He hesitated before saying, "You better make it out." Worry creased his forehead as he cast one more glance at the students. He pulled me toward him, pressing his lips to my hair. "I —"

"Don't." I stepped away from his embrace. "Don't say whatever it is you were going to say."

Mason nodded and dashed toward the red box on the wall, pulling the lever. A siren wailed and strobe lights blinked in time with the music. The muffled commotion of students rushing toward the exits at either side of the building drowned out Mason's warning shouts.

Mrs. Lengyel approached the horde of demons, unable to see through their glamour, demanding they exit too. I watched in horror as sludge poured from a student's mouth in a thick, black stream until their body crumpled to the ground unconscious but breathing. Spared from a life of terror in the Realm of the Forsaken. From that sludge, a huge, muscular Hellhound formed and leaped toward Mrs. Lengyel, ripping open her throat with its teeth. Crimson blood sprayed as her body hit the floor, and I cried out. I might not have liked her, but she didn't deserve that. She didn't deserve to die because of *me*.

The Hellhound wagged its long, mangled tail.

I searched the room for Mason, but he was gone. There was no one else left in the gym.

Ice-cold fear coursed throughout my body. Whether it was my own or from the bond, I couldn't be sure. But it was there, restraining me, freezing me in place. The demons circled me like prey.

I was outnumbered twenty to one.

I took a deep breath, and ethereal calm and focus pulsed through me. My whole life, I'd been training for this.

Instinct took over. With one careful movement, I snatched the dagger from Ellody's body, and the demons began shedding their husks as easily as they snatched them, with smoke and sludge snaking from their mouths. As each unconscious body smacked the floor, I felt a rush of relief. I inched further away from the students, luring the demons toward the opposite side of the gym.

As I continued backward, a demon shed the skin of a girl from my math class, smoke pouring from her mouth, triggering the sprinkler system. Her body fell limp to the floor, and a Night Hag hovered over the ground in her place. The sprinklers drew the horde's attention to the ceiling as they watched water rain down on them.

Morons.

I lunged for the Night Hag and sliced. She howled in anger. In a series of slashes, my dagger met her decaying flesh until she collapsed in a heap, writhing in pain, her paper-thin hands torn to shreds.

A Drozol demon with long black claws and dinosaur-like feet charged toward me but slipped on the blood-soaked floor. Darting around it, I slid on my knees in the direction of an Ympe perched on the refreshment table. With one quick flick of my wrist, the blade flew toward the bark-covered creature and impaled it through the heart. In a matter of seconds, it burst into dust.

My eyes went wide. Mistress Marjorie said the blade was enchanted, but she didn't say it would do *that*.

Rushing to the pile of dust, I grabbed the dagger.

A demon with four eyes and a round belly covered in barnacles yelled, "She'll kill us all if we go at her one-on-one."

"We have our orders," another demon replied through the body of Oakwood High's star quarterback. It looked like it refused to release its mortal vessel. "The bounty may not have specified whether to claim her alive or dead, but we know *he* wants her alive."

He. Cayden or Vemdour?

"Oh, fuck all of you." The words were a trembling growl from my throat. With a snap of my wrist, the dagger soared and lodged in the jock's neck. "And fuck *him*."

If either of those pricks were coming, I needed to end this. Now.

The brand on my arm seethed in worry.

Snatching the dagger from the Oakwood MVP of the Year's throat, I charged toward the horde. Red and black blood splattered along the walls and the floor with every strike. A chorus of laughter rose above the music when one of their own fell, shoving me into another fight. For every final blow I landed, they inflicted minor flesh wounds on me. Fiery slices of shredded skin peppered my body. They weren't beyond hurting me, but they wouldn't kill me.

My adrenaline waned as several demons lay dead at my feet. I couldn't keep going like this. The dagger slipped from my grip, my movements sluggish from exhaustion and pain, hitting the floor with a clatter.

A Hellhound wasted no time making quick work of my blunder. It pounced, knocking me to the floor and pinning me in place. Massive jaws full of rows of yellow teeth chomped at my face, bathing me in thick, sticky saliva. I gagged at the putrescent stench coming from its open mouth while struggling beneath its weight.

Fine. Eff it. "Just take me to him already."

I was tired. Too tired to go on.

No. The smooth, deep sound of a male's voice echoed throughout my mind. His words were short as he demanded, *Keep fighting.*

It was a failed attempt at empowerment. It'd be so much easier to give in.

Craning my neck to the side, I caught a glimpse of an incandescent portal sparking to life behind the Hellhound. My breathing came in short gasps as I braced myself for Cayden or Vemdour to step through and drag me out of the gym to the Realm of the Forsaken.

I—

Suddenly, a guy leapt out of the portal and onto the beast's back. The Hellhound bucked wildly, and I scrambled out from underneath it, just in time to watch the strobe lights reflect off the shiny blade of a long-sword as the guy swung and connected with the neck of the Hellhound—beheading it and showering the floor in ink-dark blood.

He rolled off the dead body and sprung to his feet, bounding toward me.

"Give me your hand," he said with the same voice that was in my head just moments ago.

Grasping his forearm, he hauled me to my aching feet. The brand sparked as we touched, golden bits of light spilling out around us. When he pulled away, a mirror image of my brand shone brightly on his wrist.

I gasped. "It's *you*."

He patted his hands over my body as if he was making sure I was still in one piece. His touch electrified my skin, igniting something deep within me. A dash of strength wormed its way into me, easing my sore muscles and boosting my adrenaline. Cupping his cheek with a bloodied hand, I confirmed that he was real. I didn't imagine this. The person I was bound to was *here*.

And... he was hot? Sun-kissed skin, blue eyes, golden hair that whispered against his nape.

I shook my head. Now was *not* the time for that.

Satisfied with his inspection, he offered me a curt nod before turning his attention to the swarm circling us. "Now this"—he pointed his sword at the Drozol, a devilish grin upon his lips—"is a fair fight."

The guy set upon the demons in a way unlike anything I had ever seen before. His movements were unyielding and refined, a sign of impeccable training. Sheesh. I needed to be taught by whoever trained him. I snatched my dagger from the floor and cut through the opposite side of the horde with a feline grace I didn't have moments ago until his back met mine in the center of the circle. It was warm and sturdy, a comfort amidst the chaos.

Together, we fought as one, as if fate predestined our bodies to move in sync—like planets circling the sun.

If I dodged, he struck. If he ducked, I sliced.

At one point, he spun me around and dipped me to the floor, running his sword through the pus-filled belly of an Uretheros. Its stomach exploded from the impact, mixing with the blood, sweat, dust, and water coating the flooring.

Demons continued to charge at us to no avail. We danced around them, landing blow after blow until they laid in pieces at our feet.

When the boy ran his sword through the last demon, disemboweling it, I vomited and collapsed to the ground, shivering in my blood-soaked and torn dress. The strength he loaned me seeped back into him, leaving me weak and ravaged. The steady thumping of music pounded in my head at a muted low.

The devastation left in our wake was shocking.

We tore all the demons to bits.

I glanced at him, and he wiped his sword on his thigh before sheathing it onto his back.

His hands weren't shaking at all.

CHAPTER 7

The guy wasted no time scooping me into his arms and carrying me out of the cafeteria, kicking the emergency exit open without breaking his stride.

The further away from the building we got, the better I felt, and the heat from his body calmed the trembling in my own. He placed me on a patch of grass and laid down next to me.

"I can't believe you're here," I whispered, staring at him.

His face was immaculate, albeit a little bruised. Sweet sassy molassy, he was gorgeous—obviously not from Oakwood—with sun-kissed skin and lean muscle for days.

"I'm sorry I couldn't get here sooner, Princess Valeria."

His velvety voice drew my eyes to his square jaw, then to his full lips, and I wanted him to say my name again and again.

Wait.

I stared in shock. "You know who I am?"

He looked at me from the side, and I sucked in a breath. His eyes were the deepest shade of blue, rivaling the depths of the oceans. I had to look away before they pulled me under.

"Of course. You're the lost princess."

I snorted. "Lost princess?"

That was what the demons called me, too. I could count on one hand the terms to describe what kind of princess I was to Empyrean—cast aside, forgotten, unwanted—but *lost*? Nope.

Lost was definitely not one I'd heard before.

His gaze swept over me, and I swear to the gods it left me naked. He shrugged, his broad shoulders brushing against the grass. "It's what our people call you since you were exiled."

Empyrean. He was from Empyrean. No freakin' way—a real-life person from Empyrean. My mouth felt dry.

"Who *are* you?" I asked, dying to know his name.

"Gideon."

"Gideon," I repeated, and the corners of his lips twitched upward.

Burning charcoal and fresh-cut grass—early summer staples—filled the air. The scents were a welcome reprieve to the horrors inside the cafeteria. Somewhere in the distance, the cries of shaken teenagers were muffled by sirens drawing closer to Oakwood High School. This quiet town had never seen such horrors. Above us, the sky was still. No hint of my father's ravens.

I frowned as I searched the parking lot for Mason's car, but it was gone. I was positive that meant he made it to Mistress Marjorie, if Ol' Bessie didn't break down on the way there, and alerted her of what was happening.

She'd come for me.

All I had to do was wait.

Kicking off my heels, I massaged the soles of my aching feet as the next question I had for Gideon sprung to mind. "How did you find me?"

He held up his wrist, his brand gleaming in the moonlight. Fresh blood seeped through his once-white cotton shirt.

My muscles stiffened. "Are you hurt?"

"No." He groaned as he inspected his side. "We've got to get moving. More will come."

"We'll never make it anywhere in your condition." My heartbeat picked up in sudden worry. For this perfect stranger. Weird. Sure, he had helped me. Sure, he looked like a model, but why was I so concerned for his well-being?

He shot me a wary look and sat up, wincing in pain. "I'll be fine."

"Take off your shirt."

He raised an eyebrow. "But we just met."

I scoffed, my cheeks burning underneath the blood drying on my face.

So he was hot, *and* he was a flirt. Double trouble.

Gideon lifted his arms above his head like a child ready to put on his pajamas. *Well, allow me, I guess.* My fingers grazed his taut torso as I lifted his shirt up and over his head and placed it on my lap. The light scent of citrus and spice lingered against his sweat-soaked skin.

He tried his best to pretend he wasn't in pain, but the grimace when my hand brushed the reddened area along his ribs said enough. Purple pooled along the spot, the beginning of a nasty bruise likely caused by one or two cracked ribs. There was a deep and angry gash below the bruising, the edges stained black with spider-like veins protruding from it.

It looked terrible, but I didn't tell him that.

Mistress Marjorie would have a salve to fix it up in a matter of hours.

He took his shirt from me and tore it into one long strip of fabric wide enough to wrap around his body.

A moment later, Gideon rose to his knees, attempting to tie the shirt in place. I placed my hands on his, stopping him, trying my best to ignore the way his roughened hands felt in mine. I untied the satin ribbon from my neck and secured the fabric in place with it. He winced as I tightened the knot.

"This should do until we get back." He slung his sword over his shoulder and stood before he extended a calloused hand to me.

"Get back? To where?" I asked, unmoving.

"Empyrean. I'm taking you home."

I shook my head and scrambled to my feet, putting distance between us. "No, I'm not going back yet. My keeper bargained for time so I could stay until graduation. I have five more days."

A flicker of surprise danced across his features. "Valeria, you're no longer safe here."

"No," I said again through clenched teeth. "I just need to get back to my keeper. She'll keep me safe until it's time for me to leave. I'm *not* missing graduation."

He closed the distance between us with three steps, grasping my hands as he towered over me. I had to tilt my head back to look at him. His blue gaze glowed in the starlight. "You would put more lives in danger for something so... *mortal?*"

I swallowed under the weight of his stare. When he said it like that, it sounded *bad*. But all I said was, "It's important to me."

"Selfish. So incredibly selfish."

Well, now I wanted to slap his face. Hot or not. "Don't talk to me like that. You don't even know me. Now release me. I'm staying."

"I'm not going to let innocents die because you're too wrapped up in playing mortal to comprehend the consequences."

"How *dare* you!" I tried to pull my hands from his to deliver the slap I needed to give him, but he didn't let go. Instead, he snaked an arm around my waist and pinned me to him. I pushed against him with whatever remaining strength I could muster, but it was as useless as fighting against stone.

He pulled a tiny vial full of silver liquid from his pocket.

"No. Don't you dare use that." Mistress Marjorie had shown me a vial just like that one, with the same silver-flecked liquid swirling inside. It was meant to open a portal. How could something so pretty feel like a death sentence?

With bloodstained hands, I struggled to pry free from his grip.

"Stop wiggling! You're going to make me drop it." His arm around me was like a vice.

"That's the point, fuckwit." I slammed my heel onto the top of his foot.

He gave a satisfying wince. "Princess, I'm trying to help. Can you just stand still for half a second?"

I tried to headbutt him, but he dodged it before he sighed and tossed me over his shoulder like I weighed nothing.

He didn't react to the pounding of my fists and the wriggling of my body. Time for different tactics. Putting the most sugar I could muster into my voice, I begged, "Gideon, please. I still have time here. This is my *life*."

Truth was, it *was* my life and dammit, stupid or not, graduation mattered to me.

When my begging didn't work, I threatened him. "Put me down, or I swear I'll make your life miserable."

He laughed. He actually *laughed* at my threat.

And then a burst of cool air whipped around us, ruffling my tattered skirt. Incandescent light washed over us, casting our shadows against the lawn.

He must have shattered the vial.

As if I was being carried toward my execution, I screamed bloody murder, biting and clawing at him. "Stop, Gideon! I don't want to go!"

My mind spun as wet hot tears burned my eyes. "Please." I repeated the word over and over until it turned to screams. This was really happening. He was kidnapping me.

Mason's frantic shouts from behind us echoed my name.

Desperately, I raked my nails across Gideon's back, splitting the skin, as I cursed him. He ignored me as if I was nothing more than a minor annoyance, stepping into the inky blackness without breaking his stride. This was it. So long, Realm of the Mortals. Goodbye, freedom. As quickly as the portal opened, it closed. Sealing me off from the only home I'd ever known.

The world around me spun as blood rushed to my head. A guttural scream clawed its way up my throat, demanding he put me on my feet.

Gideon marched along an obsidian bridge that glistened with silver starlight. "Promise not to do anything rash, and I'll let you go."

Ha. The bastard. "Is punching you in the face considered rash?"

"That's all you want to do?" He put me down. "Then do it."

Without giving him any sign it was coming, I let my fist fly right into his perfect nose, hard enough to split my knuckles.

"Not bad." He chuckled, eyes sparkling with amusement. I hit him again, this time busting his lip. He stopped laughing then. "Okay, that's enough."

"I'll tell you when it's enough." I cocked my fist to throw another punch.

He grabbed my hand mid-swing. "Punching me won't change the fact that I can't take you back to the Realm of the Mortals. The only way out of the Void is through."

A chill crawled up my spine, pricking the tiny hairs on the back of my neck. Darkness flecked with bits of twinkling lights surrounded us as we walked side-by-side among the stars. Regret crept into the corners of my mind, caressing the raw parts of me that longed to run from here, run from *him*.

His regret.

"Get the hell out of my head," I snapped.

"Sorry." He raised his hands in surrender. "I'm still getting used to the bond and how it works."

The bond.

This nightmare of an evening was all the bond's fault.

It allowed him to track me down and kidnap me. It let him slip words and feelings into my mind to try and manipulate me into forgiving him for taking *everything* from me.

Maybe he was the one who bound me to him in the first place.

And if he did, then maybe my father would punish him and free me of this curse.

"Does my father know about our bond?" I asked as I studied the strange bridge. It reminded me of an overstretched piece of taffy without the stickiness.

"No. No one does."

I tilted my head to the side, knotted blonde hair spilling over my shoulder. The fresh flowers that once crowned my head were crushed and ruined, tangled into the knots. "So how are you going to explain bringing me to Empyrean five days before I was due to arrive?"

"That's what took me so long to get to you," Gideon said. "I had to alert the King's Council of demonic activity in Oakwood and hope they would allow me to intervene instead of a Celestian."

I pursed my lips. "You're not a Celestian?"

"I am not." He frowned, a blush creeping over his cheeks like he was embarrassed.

Bastile, the Father of All and the creator of Empyrean, created Celestians to be the most prestigious and notorious warriors to ever exist. As a child, all I ever wanted was to become a Celestian. I asked Mistress Marjorie every day to train me like one, and every day she would refuse. *Celestians serve, while you were born to be served,* she would say. Maybe if she trained me like a Celestian, I would have been able to save myself tonight.

"I'm not surprised you haven't been chosen to become a Celestian," I said finally, hoping to rub salt in the wound. "Clearly, you're unworthy."

He let the conversation drop.

We continued to cross the Void drawing closer to a metal dome-like structure in the distance—the Gateway, the central hub for all four realms.

From where we were, I could spy three different bridges attached to the Gateway. The bridge to the Realm of the Mortals, the one we were on, was stationed to the south and glistened like the night sky. To the west, a bridge made of molten lava, with a smoke and shadow railing, led to the Realm of the Forsaken. My eyes unwillingly lingered on that bridge for far too long until they snapped to the opposite side. To the east arched a bridge made of fluffy, golden clouds. It floated along into buttery light, leading to the Realm of the Divine.

"Where's the bridge to Empyrean?" I wondered aloud.

Excitement poured through the bond as Gideon gave me a sideways glance. "You'll see."

"I don't like surprises." Sweat pricked the back of my neck.

"Trust me. It's worth the wait."

"Trust you? I don't even know you."

His lips were a thin line, and the brand on my wrist turned the blood in my veins to ice. Numbness spread up my arm as we continued toward the Gateway.

At least I was still alive to feel something.

By now, Oakwood High had to have been stormed by the police and paramedics. What would they make of the corpses they'd find? What would they say caused their deaths?

Whatever happened, I hoped those who died found peace in the Half-Light. Except Ellody. She deserved to rot in the Realm of the Forsaken for the hell she put me through for years.

It used to be that all mortal's souls were forfeited to the Realm of the Forsaken when they died. But centuries after Bastile made Empyrean, he also created the Half-Light—a place for those the god deemed worthy to spend their afterlife beside him, living in peace. How he got the God of the Forsaken to agree to releasing *any* souls from his realm was beyond me, but he did and then he died by Vemdour's hand and ascended into the Half-Light himself.

Gideon stopped in his tracks, blood seeping through the makeshift tourniquet around his torso. "Your thoughts are slipping into my head."

I bristled. "I don't know how to turn the bond off."

"Well, do you hear my thoughts or feel my feelings?"

I thought about it for a moment. "Not really."

He nodded. Beads of sweat clung to his paling skin, and the bond hummed unevenly.

Placing the back of my hand against his forehead, I cursed. He was hot to the touch and shivering. Feverish. "You need to see a doctor."

He swatted my hand away. "I'm fine."

"So you're a kidnapper *and* a liar. No wonder you're not a Celestian."

His eyes were a deadly storm of pain. Whether he wanted to admit it or not, he was hurting. My mind flashed to the inky tendrils around his wound—likely some kind of poison.

If we didn't move fast, he was going to pass out or die.

And I didn't know what that meant for me.

I bolted toward the Gateway, my bare feet pounding against the bridge with every step. He kept up with me, his breathing more labored with each passing minute. It was like jogging with Mason.

I'm not going to die. The words flickered in my mind.

I shot him a look.

There had to be a way to prevent my thoughts from slipping into his mind.

"How do you keep your thoughts to yourself?" I asked.

He shrugged. Judging by his grimace, it took more effort than necessary. "I picture a wall in my mind and ensure it's up whenever I don't want you to hear what I'm thinking. And when I do want to say something to you, I lower that wall just a bit."

"Sounds like a lot of work," I mumbled under my breath.

The corners of his lips twitched upward. "So you're selfish *and* lazy. No wonder *you're* the lost princess."

"Oh, fuck off."

The archway was a few feet ahead—a swirling galaxy of stars glittering and spinning round and round, waiting for us to pass through. Gideon slowed to a stop, his hands resting on his knees. When he caught his breath, he grabbed my hand and pulled me through the door.

We stood in the middle of a lavish room with all sorts of symbols and shapes depicting the four realms etched on the walls of the dome. Intricate doors guarded each bridge. Skulls and bones lined the Realm of the Forsaken entrance, while the Realm of the Divine shined like unfiltered sunlight. My eyes landed on the door to Empyrean. It was arched like a pair of wings and glittering in shades of black and silver. The handle was the head of a raven. Its eyes glowed as I approached and tried to open it. It was locked.

"Why won't it open?" I asked, spinning toward Gideon.

"Where would you like to go?" An unearthly voice boomed through the dome.

"Empyrean," Gideon answered, clutching his side. "Quickly, Kai. Lake Fortunate's entrance."

I gasped, thinking of the apparition Mistress Marjorie once showed me of Kai.

He was a beast made of pieces from each realm, anchored in the Gateway as a neutral party to ensure the realms never ventured further than they were given permission.

Kai soared into the room from above. He had the body of a man, but the rest of his features were horrifyingly inhuman. Large, flesh-like wings protruded from his back, and razor-sharp teeth prevented his mouth from closing. Reptilian scales covered his arms, and his legs ended in hooves.

He stalked toward us with soundless steps. Nothing that massive should be that silent. I froze in place, looking between him and Gideon. He cocked his head to the left while his eyes studied me. They were a sunflower without the center, pupil-less.

"Valeria Breault, Princess of Empyrean," Kai said at last. "The throne awaits you."

"How—"

I was interrupted by the screeching of metal; a long chain dangled from the ceiling, and Kai grasped the teardrop-shaped handle.

Gideon wrapped his arms around me in a way that would make one think he had done it a thousand times. His breath was warm against my cheek when he murmured, "Surprise."

The floor dropped from under us, and we were free-falling into the Void.

CHAPTER 8

No air whizzed by as we fell through the darkness.

My nails dug into Gideon, and his arms tightened around me. We turned and turned, falling through the emptiness until we soared headfirst into a muted, sunny day, clouded by an opaque sheen of smoke, before crashing through a pool of shimmering, placid water.

"You prick!" I croaked when we breached the surface of the lake of liquid silver.

He chuckled, running a hand through his wet hair. Every trace of blood and dirt, along with the tourniquet from earlier, disappeared from his body. He stood shirtless in black leather pants that clung to him, molded to his muscular thighs. I stared at the contours of his chest and abs, chiseled as if sculpted by Bastile himself.

My breath hitched at the sight of him, perfection incarnate.

He kidnapped you, you idiot.

I was pretty sure I wasn't supposed to find the bastard who abducted me attractive. But, gods, his body made it incredibly difficult. Briefly, I wondered what he was like in bed. Would he pepper my skin with tender kisses or would he wind my hair around his fist as he took me from behind? My eyes traveled over his torso, landing on the spot where his wound had been bound by a makeshift tourniquet moments ago. It was completely healed, save for a faint silver scar.

My mouth hung open. "What *is* this place?"

"Lake Fortunate," Gideon said, wading in the vast body of water. "It's a healing lake. Legends say Bastile decides who is worthy enough to heal and what is worth mending." He held up his torn shirt, and I watched as it cleaned and mended itself. He slipped it on, grinning.

I shivered against the cool water as it tickled my body, swishing around me like a gentle washcloth, tending to my wounds. The bruises that kissed my knuckles, the cuts that marred my skin from my cheeks to my ankles, and the ruined gown that hung in shreds were mending, changing, morphing under the power of magic.

It was extraordinary.

Gideon watched in amusement, eyes glittering and lips tugging upward, as I swam and splashed around in the warm lake. Every fiber in my being willed the dress to shift into something easier to walk in, but equally stunning. A dress that would impress, a dress that would seduce.

As if the water had listened to me, the ruby dress morphed into something else entirely—a tight-fitting black gown with a plunging neckline, exposing the curves of my breasts, and a slit that met the middle of my left thigh. One black cuff materialized around my wrist, hiding the brand, leaving my dagger bracelet where it was. Soft, satin flats slid onto my once-bare feet.

Gideon's eyes raked over me, his jaw clenching the longer he took me in. But he didn't speak. He didn't have to. Various words floated through the bond, caressing my mind like a lover's whisper.

Beautiful. Radiant. Enchanting.

I plastered the sweetest smile I could muster onto my face and said, "Kidnapper. Liar. Prick."

Again, he laughed at me.

He closed the space between us, placing a hand on the small of my back, leading me out of the lake.

Empyrean was magic. Pure, undiluted magic.

"Imagine if the Realm of the Mortals had access to a place like Lake Fortunate," I said. "They wouldn't be so fragile."

"Careful," he warned. "You're starting to sound like Bastile."

"And that's a bad thing?"

Bastile was damned to live among the mortals as punishment for his infatuation with them and his desire to protect them from the Realms of the Forsaken and the Divine. While both realms enjoyed the opportunity to use mortals as they saw fit—for servitude, entertainment, torture—Bastile saw how fragile the mortals were and helped them by thwarting the gods through lies, deception, and dark magic. When the gods learned of Bastile's undermining and trickery, they wanted nothing to do with the god who dared to challenge them. So they clipped his thread to the Realm of the Divine and never imagined he'd use his banishment to create a realm sworn to protect the mortals—one that challenged the gloriousness of their own.

Gideon gave a half shrug. "Your father might not like it too much."

Jealousy sparked within me that Gideon may know more about my father than I did. "Well, I don't care what he likes."

It was both the truth and a lie. I didn't care what my father liked unless it was *me*. I wanted him to like me, to like the daughter he gave up and the woman she became without him.

We trekked down a winding dirt path through a forest of pine trees, reddish-brown dried needles crunching under our steps. The familiarity sent a jolt of homesickness through me. I had forgotten that Empyrean was carefully crafted to mirror the Realm of the Mortals. All the landscapes, architecture, spices, and fabrics, even the mannerisms and languages the Empyrean people used, were all inspired and taken from the Realm of the Mortals.

Gideon led the way like he knew these woods the same way I knew the forest in Oakwood. I searched the tree trunks for any indication of how he knew where he was going. There was nothing. No broken bark, no snapped twigs or other markings.

He drew to a stop. The devilish grin was back on his full lips, and my heart did that fluttering thing that I didn't like. He was just so beautiful in a way that promised heartbreak. In a way that swore he'd ruin me with a kiss and shatter me with a touch. His bright blue eyes, framed by thick lashes, rivaled the cloudless sky above. Standing this close, his scent caressed every part of me—citrus, spice, and something that reminded me of a fire in the dead of winter, warm and lingering.

"Close your eyes," he whispered, reaching for my hand.

And that was all it took to snap me out of whatever spell his beauty had cast on me. I snatched away from him and folded my arms across my chest, defiant. "Absolutely not. No more surprises."

He frowned. "Princess, trust me."

My laugh was breathy. "Need I remind you that you kidnapped me? I'm not going to trust you. Not now, not *ever*."

The tiny sliver of me that *wanted* to trust him, even after his betrayal, was the part of me that I needed to ignore. That sliver was thinking with pleasure in mind, not survival.

Stupid, useless hormones.

I may be bound to him, but I wasn't required to trust him. And I wouldn't let him manipulate me with his excruciating good looks or his pretty words. The brand on my wrist pulsed as if it was annoyed with me. I glared at it before gesturing for him to continue ahead.

After a short hike and one turn, the sun burned my shoulders, no longer hidden behind the trees.

Gideon climbed onto a ledge made of rock and bent to pull me up to stand beside him. I opened my mouth to scold him about not needing his help, but the words wouldn't come out.

I was too awestruck by the view.

In the distance, a ruined village lay at the feet of a massive marble statue of a god with broad glorious wings, while he held a towering city above the clouds. It was as if Bastile rose from the ashes of destruction and ripped the land from the ground itself.

No amount of squinting brought Seraphicity, the city above the clouds, into view. We were too far away, and it was too high up. My gaze drifted to the rolling fields between us and the floating city. Storybook cottages with thatched roofs woven with flowers and farms with crops and pens of animals were connected by time-worn dirt paths that led all the way to the looming statue of Bastile.

There was so much to take in at once, and I didn't know where to look first.

All I knew was that from where we stood, everything was at peace.

Home. Gideon whispered the word into my mind.

Home to me was my hidden house in Oakwood, but... I could get used to this. The dread that lingered in my belly quietly dissipated, replaced by an unfamiliar feeling.

"Hope." He bumped his shoulder into mine. Something flickered in his eyes, but I couldn't place it. "That's what you're feeling right now, isn't it?"

I cast one more glance at the view and smiled.

THE JOURNEY TO THE outskirts of the city took longer than I thought it would. No matter where we were after climbing down from the overlook, the statue of Bastile could be seen towering over the trees.

The sun had set and risen again beyond the effigy illuminating the realm and bathing us in glorious, vibrant color. Everything about Empyrean, from the skies to the sunsets, reminded me of the Realm of the Mortals, and I knew that was intentional. Bastile loved the

Realm of the Mortals so much, he wanted his realm to be a superior version of it.

We spent the night in the middle of a field of flowers without a fire to keep us warm. During the night, I woke to find Gideon's shirt draped over me while he slept several feet away. I'd be lying if I said I didn't watch him until the sun rose and stirred him awake.

Now, every step we took toward the city was a rush of adrenaline pushing me forward. I was sore, tired, and on the brink of becoming hangry.

"Is this the fastest way to Seraphicity?" I asked after hours of silence.

Gideon nodded. "Coming from Lake Fortunate, yes."

I arched my brow. "Are there other ways in from the Gateway?"

He rubbed the light blond stubble on his chin. "Technically two. The first is a bridge to the north of the Gateway. The second is through Lake Fortunate, which leads to a hidden entrance through the Bygone."

I wracked my brain for any history on the Bygone but came up blank. "The Bygone?"

He gestured to the destroyed village that lay at the statue's feet.

I squinted, hoping it'd give me a better view. It didn't. "What happened there?"

"Your brother." He looked away from me as if he was trying to mask his pain, but I felt it. A profound sadness burned through me. Either his mental wall wasn't up, or his grief was too vast to keep in check.

"Celestians lived in that village as Seraphicity's first line of defense. Cayden knew if he struck there first on his quest for power, he'd leave Empyrean weak." His voice hitched. "It's taken years to regain our strength, and our ranks aren't even close to where they were before the attack."

I stopped walking and turned to him. "You lost someone that night, didn't you?"

"Yes." He stared ahead, the muscle in his jaw feathering. "A lot of innocent people died that night."

"Innocent people die all the time, Gideon."

"That doesn't make it right."

"No." I swallowed. "It doesn't."

I SMELLED THE BYGONE before I saw it—a stench of rot and mold mixed with ash and despair. Scorched ground and broken buildings blocked the path to the base of Bastile's statue. Whatever happened here had been a massacre. I stepped over and around shattered pieces of weapons and skeletal remains. There were so many bones, both beast and human. I thought the destruction we left in Oakwood High School was terrible, but it was nothing compared to this wasteland.

Countless bodies were left to decay where the demons slew them, their clothing destroyed and now one with their skeletons. They deserved a proper burial so their souls could pass into the Half-Light. But was it too late now?

Empyrean souls that weren't buried or burned risked turning into a specter—a vengeful ghost that haunted the land until it was put to rest and filtered into the Half-Light or Realm of the Forsaken.

Raspy caws escaped the beaks of an unkindness of ravens that flew around the village, and I jumped, half-expecting it to be a warning that specters were nearby. Faint traces of writing marked the buildings though none of it was legible, washed away by weather and time. I shuddered. What did the Realm of the Forsaken have to say about Empyrean?

Gideon's warmth seeped into me as he tugged me close, steering me toward the base of the marble statue, and for once, I didn't pull away.

My heart gave a painful squeeze as shock and disbelief bled into one. "Why didn't my father do something about this?"

I thought there would be a few dilapidated buildings, maybe a handful of slain demon carcasses, but not *this*. Not Empyreans left to rot, their souls forever imprisoned in a disgusting and forgotten village while the rest of the realm carried on as if they hadn't sacrificed their lives so they could live. It was sacrilegious and despicable, no matter the reason Gideon gave. I rubbed my slick palms on my dress.

"Your father didn't want to risk another attack, so they fortified Seraphicity instead." He looked around us, frowning. "No one comes down here anymore. It's better that way."

Better for who? I left the question on the tip of my tongue.

A lump swelled in my throat. Those left here couldn't find peace in the Half-Light without being buried or burned, and that cut deep.

Bastile wouldn't like that my father forgot his warriors. Why would he risk a god's wrath?

Maybe I could talk some sense into him. Maybe I could do *something*. Like bury our dead and then burn the rest of the village down—start anew and imbue this land with new life. They died for my family. Putting them to rest was the least I could do.

Gideon led me to the area between the Father of All's gigantic feet where the imprint of two doors was visible on the insides of his ankles. Those must be what the Realm of the Forsaken used to storm Seraphicity. He pulled his dagger free from the sheath on his thigh. With a quick slice to his palm, he squeezed his fist. Blood dripped through the creases of his fingers onto the soil, and the rocky earth shook below us.

A pillar of blinding light shot up from the ground. It hummed in sync with my brand, beckoning for me to come closer. Was it made of neutral magic, too?

Without a word, Gideon scooped me into his arms and leapt into the light.

The world whirled around us in a kaleidoscope of colors. I threw my head back like a kid spinning too fast on a merry-go-round. It was beautiful. Magic was so godsdamned beautiful, but I couldn't help but worry that whatever awaited me in Seraphicity wasn't.

CHAPTER 9

We ascended through an opening in the ground, and I stared in awe as the soil stitched itself back together, erasing the entrance from view.

Like it was never there at all.

Gideon stiffened beside me, and I followed his gaze to find seven Celestians pointing their swords at us. The sun glistened against their chainmail armor, and their birdlike metal helmets were a frightening sight to behold. I couldn't help but want to reach out and touch one of the beaks. Bastile's crest, a pair of wings in the deepest shade of onyx adorned with specks of silver, was emblazoned across each of their chests.

A symbol of his everlasting presence.

I snuck a glance at Gideon. Did he lie about having permission to take me from Oakwood early? Oh, I was going to *kill* him, if they didn't first.

"Gideon." A deep voice drew my attention to a man whose armor resembled stardust, a combination of pitch black and shining stars. Unlike the others whose jaws were exposed, his entire face was hidden behind an iron mask where silver tears seeped from his eyes and down his cheeks as if frozen by time. It was a permanent display of weeping—a symbol of power and mercy, worn only by the highest in command.

The captain of the Celestians.

Maybe the only captain left after what happened below.

A heavy dose of dread poured through our bond, and I relished in Gideon's unease as he addressed the man with the mask. "Malachi."

"We've been awaiting your arrival at the North Gate."

He cleared his throat. "We had to enter through Lake Fortunate."

"That was not the plan." Malachi's tone was sharp, and Gideon flinched, his cheeks flushing from the reprimand. Heat radiated from his body, and I wanted to wear it like a coat. Seraphicity, the floating island Bastile's statue held above the clouds, was colder than I expected. I rubbed my arms against the chill.

Gideon's mouth opened and closed like a fish out of water. Gone was the man who was so sure of himself when he was the one in charge.

It filled me with glee. *That's what you get, biiiiitch.* Smiling, I folded my hands in front of me—a picture-perfect image of grace.

Malachi removed his helmet and rested it on his hip. To my surprise, he wasn't much older than me. His eyes were as endless as the Void in such a deep shade of brown they could almost pass for black. A long white scar marred his warm, golden skin, trailing from the outer corner of his right eye to the middle of his cheek. He had a sharp jawline and a head of ebony hair held back in a bun. Something stirred in the back of my mind at the sight of his scars.

Like Gideon, he looked like bad news.

"I apologize for your delayed arrival, Your Grace." Malachi bowed quickly then stood, and his men sheathed their swords, each placing one hand over their chest. "We sent a novice to secure your safe return."

I smirked at Gideon. "It seems you did."

The corners of Malachi's lips twitched, but he bit back his smile as he brushed sweat from his forehead with the back of his hand; more scars lingered there. Were they from the battle below? Because of my brother? My stomach sank at the thought. If the rest of these warriors were to remove their helmets, would they also be scarred?

"We should get going." He gestured to a simple black carriage hitched to two white horses parked a few feet behind the guards. On the door was another pair of silver wings.

My chest tightened.

How was it only a day ago that I climbed into Mason's passenger seat, swimming in a sea of red tulle? What was he doing right now? Was he pacing the worn carpet in his bedroom worrying about me? Or maybe he was with Mistress Marjorie? If so, she was probably preventing him from doing something stupid.

Malachi opened the door to the carriage, and Gideon helped me inside, one hand on my back, the other on the train of my dress. I slid onto the fine leather seat and Malachi sat across from me, resting his helmet on the empty space next to him.

"Get in," Malachi ordered Gideon.

I frowned. "Can't he walk?"

Malachi forced back another smile. "No, he cannot."

Gideon grinned, and I swallowed the urge to punch him again.

"Whatever," I muttered under my breath.

Once Gideon settled in next to me, two cracks of a whip answered Malachi's knock on the ceiling. The horses lurched forward, careening us toward the castle.

Riding in a carriage was so unlike riding in a car that I couldn't help but scowl. The faster the horses moved, the more it felt like driving on a road filled with potholes of varying sizes and purposely hitting every single one. We followed a dirt path until the ground shifted into weathered gray cobblestone, and we entered the heart of Seraphicity.

The carriage slowed to a crawl through the market, and I stared slack-jawed out the window. It was like we took a step back in time.

Sparks flew as weaponsmiths sharpened swords, and smoke billowed toward the bright, cloudless sky from several pigs roasting on spits. Chickens fluttered in cages and goats slept on short leashes tied to tables. Woven awnings, of the prettiest silver, arched over the market stalls, casting the merchants in cool pockets of welcomed shade.

Trash and waste, crumpled pink and red flower blossoms, and bits of torn fabric littered the ground. So did people. Men with long, dirty beards and women with matted hair sat cross-legged with empty glass jars perched in front of them. Some of them sang while others begged. The stench of body odor and something rotten mixed with the sweet perfume of flowers and pastries. It was a disgusting combination—one that made you choose to breathe through your mouth.

This wasn't how Empyrean was supposed to be.

"Malachi, let's stop for a quick bite," Gideon said.

Malachi drew his lips into a thin line. All business. "We mustn't. The king is—"

"Waiting? Let him wait," I cut in. I waited eighteen years for him to visit me, now it was his turn to wait.

Malachi knocked once on the carriage ceiling. "As you wish."

We came to a stop, and for a fleeting moment, I felt like I had true power in this realm.

Gideon hopped out and took my hand, igniting another spark that set my skin on fire. I ripped mine from his and wiped it on my dress. It didn't help. His touch lingered.

There were curious glances as I turned in place, taking in Seraphicity, my eyes wide with wonder. Looming in the distance, the palace was a magnificent building, beautifully sculpted from white marble with silver veins that glittered in the twilight. Bestrewn across the castle's sides were hundreds of windows and terraces. Beyond it were mossy mountains lounging like sleeping giants.

"Empyreans have taken to calling that area the Pry." Gideon pointed to the homes west of the castle. They were massive works of art, failing in comparison to my new home, but beautiful nonetheless. Each house in the Pry had pillars and porches and privacy, which was a stark difference from the houses in the east. "I'm sure you can guess why... prying bastards."

Malachi's attention cut to Gideon before returning to survey the crowd.

"And there?" I gazed at the unsightly rundown houses.

"The Commons. That's where those of non-noble rank and class reside."

The Commons was a stretch of land that was nowhere near as decadent as the Pry with derelict homes stacked against one another like cargo bins.

The Commons must be the slums of Seraphicity.

But Empyrean shouldn't have slums. Empyrean shouldn't have differing classes at all.

Shaking my head, I turned to Gideon. "And which are you? A prying bastard or a commoner?"

"A bit of both." He grinned, kindling something warm in my chest. The brand purred in response. Ugh. I hated it *and* him.

"All right. The market is secure," Malachi said. "Gideon, keep an eye on the princess while I grab her something to eat."

"Um, hello?" I waved a hand in front of myself. "Don't talk about me like I'm not here. Why can't I order for myself?"

"Well, to start, you don't have any *corones*."

My brow furrowed. "*Corones?*"

He rummaged around in his pocket, tossed a silver coin to me, and disappeared among the crowd. The coin was heavy, about the size of a quarter, and stamped on both sides with a symbol resembling a raven with a red-colored eye.

This was all wrong. Empyrean was a utopia. There was no money, only trading and bartering in perfect harmony. Gideon rested a hand on my lower back that I wanted to step away from, but his warmth fended off the goosebumps prickling across my arms.

I looked around us.

It wasn't hard to tell who lived in the Pry and who lived in the Commons. Tattered wool tunics, muted homespun dresses, and filthy, unkempt appearances mixed with embroidered form-fitting tops, vibrant gowns, and shimmering jewels.

A medley of status, all together in one place.

In the Realm of the Mortals, money could be the deciding factor between life and death. But here, all of these people existed outside of that constraint. Or, at least, they were supposed to. They were meant to bring balance to all three realms. Not this. Whatever *this* was.

Empyreans were made equal in every way. How could the entire realm have changed course? Bastile had only been dead for eighteen years. Surely, that wasn't enough time to overwrite thousands of years. Could it? And what would my father gain from diverting from Bastile's path? Was this what he was busy with? Pumping *corones* into the realm and starving his people?

I rubbed my forehead.

A scraggly child—no more than seven or eight—with a sandy beige complexion streaked with layers of dirt and grime, bare feet, and ripped clothes that hung way too loose on her thin body, approached a bearded man holding a large bag of goods.

She tugged on the back of his burgundy tunic. "Sir? Can you spare a *corone*?"

The man turned, glaring down at her. He flashed a set of shiny white teeth and shoved her away from him with one of his meaty hands; several rings glimmered on his fat fingers. "Get out of here, filthy rat."

"Hey!" I shouted, drawing several confused looks from the people around me, including Gideon.

The child hit the cobblestones, scraping her knee. Tears streamed down her cheeks as she continued to beg. "Please, I'm so hungry. *Please.*"

My heart sank into my empty stomach. No one was doing anything. People watched as the child begged for food, for a single coin, for help. And they did *nothing.*

My blood boiled, a silent rage brewing inside of me.

She was a *child.*

The man laughed at her. And when he finished laughing, he spat on her.

I charged at him, shoving him hard enough that he dropped his goods. They fell to the ground, spilling around us.

Anger flashed in his dark eyes. "Mind your business, shrew."

I raised my hand to slap him just as the tip of a blade met his throat.

"Mind your tongue when you talk to Her Highness, or I'll remove it from your skull," Malachi hissed from behind him.

The man grunted and begged apologies as Malachi shoved him away from us.

"Where are your parents?" Gideon asked as he knelt beside the little girl.

She pointed to the back of the market.

I smiled at her. "I'm Valeria. What's your name?"

The little girl squinted at me, pulling the skin tight over her cheeks. "Brini."

"Come." I offered her my hand. "Take me to your parents."

Brini hesitated before placing her tiny hand in mine, and then she led us to a patch of trees beyond the market. She stopped in front of several makeshift tents made of dry-rotted fabric, twine, and slender branches, all woven together to create some semblance of a home. I shuddered. Empyreans weren't supposed to live like this.

"They're in there," she said. A wretched stench wafted out from within the tent her parents were in. "Mama, Papa, there are people here to see you. It's time to wake up now."

When there was no movement inside the tent, Gideon and Malachi exchanged a knowing glance.

Gideon nodded once and popped his head into the tent before muttering, "By Bastile."

"What is it?" I pushed Brini behind me.

A second later, Gideon slipped out and inhaled a lungful of fresh air. His eyes met mine, and I knew. Her parents were dead.

Malachi balled his hands into fists, squashing the doughnut he purchased for me. I snatched it from him before it was beyond saving.

"Here, little one." I offered Brini the treat. "Eat this while I talk to the guys, okay?"

She smiled and took the doughnut, tearing into it ravenously as she sat on the ground a few feet away.

"How long have they been dead?" I whispered.

"Hard to tell. A week, maybe more."

Malachi cursed, clenching and unclenching his fists.

"We can't just leave them like that," I said. "You two need to bury them while I take Brini back to the castle with me."

Gideon and Malachi exchanged another look, and I raised my eyebrows.

"Your father would never allow Brini to come with you," Gideon said softly.

"She's all alone." My voice hitched. "She needs food, shelter, and someone to take care of her."

Malachi clutched my shoulders. "You will go back to the castle and pretend like we didn't take this detour. Gideon and I will ensure the bodies are buried and the child is taken somewhere safe."

I frowned. "But why would I have to pretend?"

Gideon lowered his voice. "Because the king would have our heads if he knew we exposed you to this."

This. The reality of Empyrean. I chewed my lip. None of this was making sense. My dad was an inconsiderate asshole, sure. But was he capable of this? Capable of turning Empyrean into something so far from what Bastile created it to be? Not a place to be revered, but a place to live in fear and hunger? A city where Empyreans died on the streets instead of in defense of the mortals?

The guys stared at me expectantly.

"Fine," I said at last. Too tired and confused to fight them. "But I want to meet whoever's going to look after Brini."

I left them to talk things over, taking a seat next to the child. "How are you feeling?"

She drew shapes in the dirt with a finger. "Still hungry, miss."

"Please, call me Valeria," I told her, watching as Gideon ran back into the market, disappearing among the people.

"We had a princess named Valeria," she murmured. "But she's lost to us now."

I poked her arm, a teasing smile on my lips. "Maybe she isn't so lost anymore."

She inspected me, taking in the dress adorning my body, eyes trailing me from head to toe. "Are *you* the lost princess?"

I nodded, and she squealed, tossing her little arms around my neck in a hug. Malachi startled, reaching for his sword, and I waved him off.

"Shh," I murmured, glancing around us. I caught the eye of a beautiful woman with ghost-like skin and vibrant red hair as she walked beside Gideon. Brini released me, brown eyes glimmering. I patted her head. "It's our little secret, okay?"

As I stood and approached the woman, excitement spread over her freckled, delicate features. Gideon took a step away from her, angling his body slightly in front of me. She didn't pay him any mind as she pushed past him and threw her arms around my neck, much like Brini had, and squeezed. "I'm relieved to see you alive, princess."

It was odd, experiencing anything but venom from another woman. Skeptically, I hugged her back.

Malachi tapped a booted toe on the dirt impatiently and the woman released me, curtsying before casting her full attention on the captain.

"Princess, this is Sabel," Malachi said quietly. "She will take care of Brini until we find a permanent home for her."

"Are you sure you can take care of her?" I wound a strand of gleaming hair around my finger. "It's not too much to ask of you?"

A warm, welcoming look filled her eyes, brightening them from pale green to jade. "Of course! I'm having a room made up for her as we speak."

I opened my mouth to ask more questions, but one look from Malachi silenced me. They had handled the situation, and they needed to get me back to the castle before my father learned of our *detour*. Before we lost our *heads*.

Sabel approached Brini with an extended hand. Brini glanced at me, and I offered her an encouraging nod. Within moments, they both slipped quietly into the market, hand-in-hand.

We made our way back to the carriage. My mind raced, but I didn't know where to start with my questions.

Once settled inside the cabin, I let out a long breath. "So who's Sabel?"

Malachi looked to Gideon, amusement shining in the onyx flecks of his eyes.

"She's a friend," Gideon answered.

My gaze met his and he glanced away. If she was a friend, why did it feel like she was something more? Why did Gideon's thundering heart roar through the bond? Why did he look like he wished we never stopped the carriage?

We continued down a paved road lined with willow trees that bent and arched around us, dancing in a light breeze. Excitement and dread warred in my stomach like this was the first day of school after a long summer break. My hair clung to my neck from sweat, and my knees bounced nervously.

Breathe, I told myself. In for five counts, out for seven.

An intricate wrought-iron gate, also adorned with Bastile's sigil, swung open—the only thing welcoming us.

I let one last question slip from my lips, hoping one of them would answer honestly. "Is he a kind man?"

Gideon's hard eyes met Malachi's before they drifted to mine. And I knew his answer.

My father was not a kind man.

CHAPTER 10

No guards or wards prevented us from approaching the two windowless wing-shaped doors, arching at least fourteen feet high.

Mistress Marjorie wouldn't approve.

Malachi gave the door one sharp knock, and a breath later, the doors groaned open, revealing a well-dressed man and two guards, twins by the look of them. Their tawny skin and sharp, hazel eyes focused on me as they moved in sync, resting their roughened hands on the hilts of their sheathed swords.

The twins said nothing as the man they guarded glared at Malachi and Gideon before leveling the weight of his scrutiny on me. "That's not the dress we sent for your arrival. Where's the red one? The king specifically asked for the red one."

"Um." I bit my bottom lip. "It's kind of a long story."

"You know what?" His smooth brown skin crinkled on his forehead as he pinched the bridge of his nose. "It'll do." He spun on his heel, clearly expecting us to follow him.

Aion, your father's footman, Gideon whispered into the tether between us. *Also a prick.*

I snickered, and the footman scowled over his shoulder.

We hurried down a hall past countless purposely broken and chipped statues. Only Bastile was allowed to create perfection. Each bust glorified various stages throughout the god's life, from infant to man, from beloved to fallen.

I shivered as the eyes of his statues followed us.

The hall's marble floor was an intricate pattern of constellations as if we were walking among the stars. There was only one other person I knew who would appreciate their beauty—Mason. Gods, I missed him.

We passed through another set of heavy wooden doors, and my eyes were instantly drawn to a glorious throne perched on a dais. It was carved from pure obsidian with a silver, bejeweled raven etched into the back. I drew nearer to it, and my blood sang as my finger traced the stone. The throne beckoned and begged for me to sit and to claim it as mine.

Don't let the king see you do that, Gideon warned. It was a gentle warning, followed by a tug to come back to his side.

I relented, not wanting to stir up trouble on my first day back.

Behind the throne, light spilled through a stained-glass window depicting a beautiful man falling from the heavens—the Realm of the Divine—with fiery wings spread wide behind him. It stained the floor in such a vibrant shade of purple that it was hard to believe it didn't match my eyes. I itched to take a closer—

The sharp bang of a staff colliding against marble rattled off the walls and startled me from my thoughts. Guards and servants, even Malachi and Gideon, lowered their eyes to their shoes.

Not me.

I couldn't care less about protocol. He was my father first, king second.

A black mantle, lined with charcoal and white fur, trailed along the floor as he entered the room. He slowed to a stop in front of me, roughly grasping my chin in his fingers to turn my face in several directions. Agitation whipped through the bond, and the back of Gideon's hand brushed against the back of mine, grounding me.

"Valeria." My father's unrecognizable voice was barely above a whisper. I studied him, unable to glean a trace of resemblance between us. His muddy brown eyes simmered with silent rage. He had a long nose, thin lips, and a round face. On top of his bald head rested a crown that matched the throne—pure silver chiseled with seven ebony feathers that jutted toward the domed ceiling.

"Father." His nails dug into my chin for a moment longer before he released me, waving his hand. I rubbed his touch away, my skin throbbing from phantom pressure. The room emptied, except for the guys, my father, and me.

"Where is the dress I sent? The crone did give it to you, did she not?"

He did not just call Mistress Marjorie a *crone*.

"Demons attacked me at prom," I told him, picturing my keeper crushing his hand with one snap of her fingers. "They ruined it."

"And you survived the attack without a scratch?" He glanced between Gideon and me, a look of annoyance hardening his features. He tossed a leather pouch to Gideon, and it jingled when he caught it. "Your reward."

Gideon bowed his head, blond hair falling into his face, as he slipped the pouch into his pocket.

"Reward?" The word was sour on my lips.

"You may go," my father said with another wave of his hand.

Gideon met my gaze for a beat longer, silently pleading for me to keep my cool. I glared at him and willed my mind to carry a promise through the tether. *I will free myself of this bond to you if it's the last fucking thing I do.* And then I pictured building a fortress in my mind, brick by brick.

He flinched and followed Malachi out of the room without a backward glance.

I *knew* I couldn't trust him. He didn't save me because he felt my panic through the bond. He saved me and kidnapped me for a pocket full of *corones*.

My father's face was a mask of indifference as I seethed in place.

"Is it her?" a woman asked as she glided into the room, her heels clacking against the starry floor. She was as lovely as a picture with long dark hair and pale skin. She wore a violet floor-length gown adorned with pops of silver jewelry. The dress did nothing to hide the belly she cradled in her hands. "Ward, is it her?"

My father nodded once, never taking his eyes off me.

"How can you be sure?" Her distrust flung at me like the dagger I used in Oakwood High School.

"Her eyes," my father murmured, staring at me again. "I could never forget those eyes."

The woman shifted from foot to foot, releasing a long breath from her red-stained lips. "My dearest Valeria. Welcome home."

I blanched. *My dearest Valeria?* Three words I'd recognize anywhere.

Soon you will be where you were meant to be all along, my dearest Valeria.

It was her. She wrote me those letters.

"Who are you?" I asked.

"I'm Lirabeth." She smiled as if that was enough explanation, extending a hand to me. Her nails were painted the same shade of ruby as her lips. My father's gaze flickered between the woman's waiting hand and me, the muscle in his neck twitching. I shifted under his stare, taking her hand so that I could get away from his scrutiny. "Come. I'm sure you're exhausted after the journey all the way here."

We left the room without another word and walked down a hallway toward a magnificent set of stairs. A gentle knock came from somewhere around us, and I searched for its origin before realizing it was in my head. Gideon was *knocking* on my mental fortress. I removed an imaginary brick, and his words came trickling through.

Valeria, I can explain—

Nope. None of that. I put the brick back.

Lirabeth watched me intently from the corner of her eye.

The hairs on the back of my neck stood on edge as Gideon tried to barrel through my little fortress. I smirked, knowing my mind was far too stubborn to betray me that easily.

We followed the marble staircase up as far as it would go. There was a small alcove at the top of the stairs leading to a plain, white door with an iron handle. Lirabeth pulled a tiny key from her pocket and shoved it in the lock before pushing the door open.

She smiled. "These are your chambers, princess."

I stepped through the threshold, my breath catching in my throat. My *chambers* were several rooms combined into one that dazzled in at least a dozen shades of silver shining on every surface. From the oversized chaise to the humongous four-poster bed tucked away in the back of the room, nothing was beyond its glimmer.

Pale pink gossamer curtains hung in front of arched floor-to-ceiling windows that lined the entire wall to the right of the bed, with two glass doors perched in the middle that opened to a terrace alive with pink and coral peonies, some twined around the gilded railing while others were part of stunning bouquets tucked into crystalline vases. The view overlooked the market.

I didn't know how to feel about that.

A bookshelf worthy of a library took up at least half of the left wall, also from floor-to-ceiling, with a sliding ladder propped against it. The book spines were leather-bound and embossed with silver.

Somehow, I knew none of them contained smut. Such a shame.

Lirabeth made herself comfortable in the carnation-tufted chair in front of a marble fireplace, a grin plastered on her face. She pointed to the ceiling, and I gasped. Painted above us was the bluest of skies with fluffy white clouds scattered across it. If I closed my eyes, I could pretend that I was in the Realm of the Mortals with soft grass tickling my neck as I laid outside under the sun, trying not to fall asleep while Margie told me stories of near and far.

"It's beautiful," I breathed.

"It is." The woman shifted in the seat, kicking off her satin slippers to rest her swollen feet on the matching velvet stool. "In pictures, it looked like the prettiest thing in the Realm of the Mortals."

"It was beyond difficult to find *anything* pretty about that realm. I will never understand Bastile's obsession with it." My father strode into the room without his crown or mantle. He ran the back of his hand across Lirabeth's cheek in such a loving manner that something in me fractured. "Thankfully, I had Lirabeth to help."

"We should throw a ball." She idly spun a diamond ring around her finger. "There's no better way to celebrate Valeria's safe return than a ball."

I glanced between her and my father, the words I wanted, needed, to swallow clawing their way out of me. "You remarried?"

"Of course I did."

"But what about my mother?" *And what about me?* I wanted to add.

"It's not like she was coming back, Valeria." His icy words were brutal and sharp, cutting straight to the quick. My heart burned viciously with betrayal. My father didn't exile me to keep me safe. It was never about what was best for *me*. It was about what was best for *him*. He left me in the Realm of the Mortals because it was easier to play the part of a widow, or a bachelor, if he didn't have a child to take care of. He wanted a new life, a new wife, and a child that wouldn't know what it felt like to grow up without a father's love or a mother's touch. "You have no idea how lonely I was," he added.

"I have no idea?" I sucked in a breath. "I was left alone in the Realm of the Mortals with only my keeper for eighteen years while you remarried and conceived another child. I was cast aside for years while you... while you *replaced* me."

I squeezed my hands into fists, trying and failing to rein in my temper.

"It's time I make something clear." He cocked his head to the side, a lethal look in his eyes. "You're here because I have use of you."

"You have *use* of me?" I folded my arms over my chest. "And what use is that?"

"Stop asking questions. I am your king, and you will do whatever I say for the crown."

A laugh bubbled out of me, unbidden. My father clenched his jaw and closed the distance between us, placing a hand on my shoulder before bringing the other across my face. The slap was louder than a whip. It stung. I staggered back, clutching my cheek, feeling the raised welt left by his ring.

The fortress crumbled. My emotions, thoughts, and pain were too vast to contain.

Gideon's worry came trickling down the bond. *Valeria, what's wrong?*

My eyes watered as I avoided my father's stare, afraid he'd strike me again for simply looking at him wrong.

"Next time you disrespect me in *my* realm, you will be punished." He came toward me again and grabbed my chin, forcing me to look at him. "Do you understand me?"

The unburied Celestians down below, Brini, the Commons, the warnings about my father's temper... it all rushed back to me, zapping away any sense of self-preservation and filling me with rage.

He was the reason Empyrean was no longer a utopia.

"You're a monster."

My father laughed, tightening his grip. The brand burned. If I removed the cuff to reveal it, I bet it'd glow in honeyed anger.

"Oh, Ward. That's enough," Lirabeth said sharply, rising to her feet. "You made your point."

He released me, and I stumbled backward, holding my breath until they left the room, locking the door behind them.

I exhaled, shoulders trembling.

I was a prisoner here until my father had *use* of me.

My knees buckled, and I fell onto a soft fur rug. The snapping and crackling of the fire were the only background noise for Gideon's frantic concern. *Valeria, what happened? Are you okay?*

I couldn't answer him. I didn't know how.

And he wouldn't care, anyway.

He was as useless as this bond unless *corones* were involved, and no amount of coin would convince a wannabe Celestian to go against the crown.

Tears drenched my cheeks, stinging the welt. I knew all along that my father didn't love me. Because how could you abandon a child you loved? But it was something else entirely to have that feeling confirmed. It was life-shattering.

Rising from the floor, I crossed the room to sit in front of a trifold vanity, embossed with silver filigree. All three mirrors revealed how badly bruised my face would be tomorrow. Did they even have makeup here to cover it up?

I sighed, blinking away fresh tears and knowing what I needed to do now.

It was what I'd trained to do my entire life.

Survive.

CHAPTER 11

Muted white light streamed into the room as a faint voice whispered my name. I didn't know how long I slept, but the tiredness lurking in my bones told me it wasn't long enough.

I groaned. "Go away."

Someone shook my shoulder. "You must wake up, Your Grace."

I bolted upright, drawing the covers to my chest to find a light-skinned woman, with a scattering of freckles across her nose and cheeks, staring at me. "Who are you? Why are you in my room?"

"My name is Mae." She tucked a stray lock of reddish-brown hair behind one ear. She had friendly, deep-set eyes that resembled the caramel candies old people in the Realm of the Mortals liked. "I'm one of your handmaidens."

I totally forgot about *that* part of being royal. I smiled, wincing at the pain in my cheek. Bringing my fingers to the tender spot on my face, I touched the imprint of my father's ring.

"A bit of makeup will hide it." She frowned as she added, "His Royal Highness is requesting your presence this morning."

Great. I had a dreamless sleep last night and awoke to a living nightmare.

Reluctantly, I slipped from the too-soft bed, taking a moment to help her make it.

"Your Grace, I am fully capable of making your bed."

"I know." I sighed. "It's... I'm not used to people doing things for me."

She chewed her lip before blurting, "May I be frank?" I nodded, curiosity getting the best of me. "You're royalty, princess. People are going to do things for you. The best thing you can do is let them."

The corners of my mouth twitched. "Noted."

"I've drawn you a bath." She pointed to the open door across the room. "Go wash. Then I'll cover up that nasty bruise."

My body refused to move from where I stood, feet rooted in place, not because I didn't want to bathe—I did, desperately—but because the sooner I was presentable, the sooner I had to face *him*.

My father.

With a gentle push from Mae, I inched my way into the bathroom to find a space as ample as my bedroom in the Realm of the Mortals. The same pinkish hues carried into this room and glittered against the silver fixtures like a jewelry store. Etched into the marble floors were tiny flowers that continued up the wallpapered walls.

"Your Grace, is something the matter?" Mae's voice startled me, causing a tiny nudge of worry to trickle through the bond.

I glared at my wrist and imagined putting up another mental fortress, one with slabs of concrete rather than bricks. I meant what I said about finding a way to sever this bond with Gideon, and no amount of false worry would change my mind.

"Everything's fine." I waved away her concern as I approached the clawfoot tub in the center of the room. Steam rose toward the ceiling and pale pink rose petals floated on top of the water alongside bubbles. "I can handle it from here."

She curtsied, leaving and shutting the door behind her.

Stripping down, I climbed into the water and hissed at its heat. It burned in the best possible way. My neck rested on a tiny, cushioned pillow as the scent of jasmine and vanilla wafted around me.

Stars twinkled on the ceiling, out of place among the pastels and florals. I hoped they glowed, like the silly green ones Mason scattered all over his ceiling when we were ten. Back when he wanted to be an astronomer. We spent hours pinning them in place. I was much shorter, so my job was to put the putty on the backs and pass the assembled stars to him. It was beautiful until he tore them all down last summer and painted the ceiling black.

Somewhere in my room, Mae hummed a tune as she busied herself.

I wondered what Mason was doing as I grabbed a sponge and lathered it with a deliciously scented soap— a mixture of eucalyptus, rosemary, and honey—before dragging it across my body. Probably losing his fucking mind. After I was scrubbed clean, I went to work on my hair. By the time I finished, the bathwater was as frigid as my heart. A stack of fluffy towels rested on top of a nearby round table. Standing, I wrapped one around me and padded out of the bathroom to the vanity.

Mae offered me a tight smile as she ushered me into the high-backed chair. With one look in the mirror, I cringed. Deep shades of grayish blue and the reddened imprint of a raven from my father's ring stood out against my creamy skin. But the mark left by his fury wasn't what drew my attention to my face. It was the sheer unhappiness that masked my features—the frown on my lips, the crestfallen sadness in my eyes, the worry in my brow. Things makeup couldn't hide.

"Please do your best to cover it up," I whispered.

Mae nodded, resting a hand on my shoulder. An unspoken exchange passed between us that told me she knew what I wanted her to remedy.

Empyrean was nothing like Mistress Marjorie said it would be. And my father was not even *close* to what I imagined. People were starving while he remarried, while he conceived another child, while he pumped *corones* into the realm and destroyed Bastile's utopia.

I may blame Gideon for kidnapping me, but it was done by the will of my father's hand and coin. He *knew* what graduation meant to me, and he took me before then anyway. Somehow, I'd make him pay for that.

Mae spent what felt like a lifetime hiding the proof on my face of my father's rage and my displeasure with these circumstances while I fumed, imagining a world where I was on the throne instead of him. The thoughts were a fantasy at best, treasonous at worst, and I swallowed, checking my mental fortress to ensure nothing slipped into Gideon's mind.

I pictured it so vividly—me on the throne making decisions with Empyreans and mortals and what was best for both of them in mind. Ensuring no one felt the vicious bite of hunger again. Giving Brini these chambers and making sure she grew up loved and cared for while I took the King's Chambers and turned them into the Queen's Quarters.

If I was in charge, I would restore Empyrean to its former glory.

I would help instead of hurt.

I would prove that I belonged.

"We'll angle your hair over the bruise to mask it further," Mae said, startling me from my treacherous thoughts.

"I'm not picky. Do whatever you want."

She grinned as she pulled and pinned, studying me in the mirror with a single eyebrow raised and hair pins between her lips.

Once she was satisfied with my appearance, she dashed into the walk-in closet and came out holding one of the ugliest gowns I had ever seen in my life. It was high-necked and long-sleeved, with thick, heavy skirts the color of crushed pomegranate.

"I'm not wearing that," I said flatly.

"Your Grace?"

I clutched the itchy fabric in my fist. "This is the kind of dress a grandmother would wear!"

Mae frowned. "I'm sorry, princess. But this is one of your father's approved dresses, and you must wear it."

I scowled and padded past her into the closet to find it filled with an entire assortment of the same kind of dresses—prim and unsensible with layers and layers of skirts.

"But this doesn't make any sense..." I let my words trail off as my brow furrowed. Why would my father send me such a beautiful gown for prom and then force me to dress like a spinster here?

A sharp knock ricocheted through the room.

Mae mumbled a swear and held up the dress that she originally picked out. "Please, Your Grace. You don't want to be late to a meeting with His Royal Highness."

"This is a nightmare," I muttered as she helped me into the gown, quickly buttoning up the back.

Once the dress was on, she sighed and crossed the space to heave the door open.

A plain-faced man with wiry gray hair stood in the hallway, the same emblem on the guards' armor embroidered on his black sweater. "I'm here to escort the princess to His Royal Highness."

MY FATHER SAT BEHIND a large desk littered with various scrolls and leather-bound books. He wore a navy tunic with silver feathers embroidered around the collar. It was hideous, so it suited him. A bowl of porridge sat untouched in front of him along with a crystal glass half full of amber liquid. The air was thick with the scent of cinnamon and wood. I wasn't surprised my father drank whiskey with his breakfast.

"Sit," he commanded without looking up from the papers in front of him. Like a dog, I sat on command in one of the uncomfortable chairs opposite his desk. My layers of skirts pooled around me. "I'm sure you're wondering why I summoned you after our *incident* last night."

"I'm quite the curious person," I offered, studying the dimly lit room. My eyes landed on a crusty whip next to a long, dust-covered bookshelf. Would he use it to punish me if I disrespected him again? Or did he have something worse in mind?

He leaned back in his chair, taking a sip from his glass. "I wonder who you get that from."

"I wouldn't know."

"Of course you wouldn't. You know nothing of this realm."

He had no idea what I knew of this realm and how he destroyed it. I mirrored his stance and half shrugged. "And yet you still have use of me."

His grip around the tumbler tightened. I shouldn't have said that. I braced myself for what would come next.

Face red with anger, he spat, "Learn how to mind your sharp tongue before it gets you into trouble."

"Sorry," I said sheepishly.

A moment passed, then two. His grip loosened, white knuckles slowly regaining color. He reached for the crystal decanter on the shelf behind his desk and topped off his glass. "I summoned you because we're throwing a ball in your honor tonight."

A few days ago, I would've been giddy at the thought of a ball, but now... now, it seemed excessive and unnecessary. But I couldn't tell him that.

I forced a smile. "That's... nice."

"You will be on your best behavior." He pushed his chair away from the desk, the wood scraping against the stone floor, and came to stand behind me. I stiffened when his brutal hands clasped my shoulders and squeezed, his breath hot on my ear. "You will dance when asked to dance, and you will laugh when everyone else laughs. You will smile until your cheeks hurt, and then you will smile some

more, and I better not catch that pathetic frown on your face."
Another squeeze. "I brought you back to Empyrean to show strength
and unity, and you will play the part I tell you to play, or I will
remove you from the game."

Balling my shaking hands into fists, I willed myself not to react.
"Yes, Your Highness."

"Good girl," he purred, releasing me. "Now get out."

I bolted from his study and down the hallway like a madwoman,
taking turns left and right, clutching the skirts of my dress until I lost
my way in a marble labyrinth and entered a quiet garden.

Sinking to the ground, I leaned against the trunk of a flowering
dogwood tree and focused on my breath.

The feeling of my father's grip lingered on my shoulders,
pressuring me to conform, forcing me to change myself from a
sharp-tongued mortal-raised girl into a quiet and obedient servant
to the crown.

Mistress Marjorie's words came rushing back to me. *I fear you'll
have to become someone other than yourself when you leave this realm.*

In the same breath, she had told me I was a princess with power,
but if that were true, then why did I feel so powerless?

And gods, I *hated* feeling powerless.

Biting my lip, my mental fortress threatened to shatter as Gideon
pried his way into my mind, questioning me again if something was
wrong. I couldn't tell him *everything* was wrong without risking his
betrayal. He could report me to my father and reap the reward.

No, I couldn't trust anyone in Empyrean.

Not even my own father.

I didn't get it. Why did he have so much hatred for me? I was his
flesh and blood. Yet disgust riddled his eyes when he looked at me as
if the sight of me made him sick.

The crack of his hand against my face rattled in my ears.

If Bastile saw my father now, saw what he had done to Empyrean, would he regret making him king? Regret putting a monster in charge of a monster-less land?

Bastile loved Empyrean more than anything. And yet, his dying wish was to see my asshole of a father on the throne in his place?

It didn't make sense. There were too many loose threads on this tapestry of lies, and I'd have to keep tugging at them until I uncovered the truth.

Rising to my feet, I brushed dirt from the back of my gown. I might as well enjoy whatever freedom I had before the guards found me and dragged me back to my chambers.

The garden was a beautiful and lush sanctuary. Clusters of thorny black roses, pearly narcissus, and silver calla lilies grew wildly on both sides of the brick path while lavender wisteria hung overhead, creating a fragrant canopy.

The brand hummed as I drifted deeper into the garden until buttery light spilled into an entrance leading to a courtyard where I heard two familiar voices arguing.

"We should have warned her," Gideon growled.

"You did," Malachi said flatly. "You cannot blame yourself for what happens now."

I peeked around the corner to find the guys in the center of a patch of grass surrounded by trim, green hedges. Malachi stood with his feet shoulder-width apart, one hand on the hilt of the sword strapped to his hips while Gideon ran a hand through his hair, sunlight bathing him in gold.

Of course, this stupid bond led me to *him*. I held back a sigh, craning my neck to listen closer.

"It wasn't enough," Gideon said. "I should have been clearer about what she was walking into."

Something akin to a sigh slipped from Malachi's lips. "It's not your place."

"I know. But can't you..." He pointed toward the cloudless sky. "Go and check on her?"

Malachi chuckled. "You know I can't."

Celestians could morph into ravens, but only twice a day. It was a power granted to them by Bastile to roam the Realm of the Mortals freely to be his eyes and ears. Or, you know, deliver dreadful letters. I shuddered, despite the sun on my back. Now that power was in my father's careless hands.

Gideon frowned. "No one in the castle has seen her since her arrival. I hate—"

"You hate *what*, Gideon?" Malachi threw his hands up.

There was a long pause before Gideon finally spoke. "She blames me for bringing her here."

"You did what you had to. She'll come around."

I turned away from them, pressing into the wall. They were talking about me. Obviously. But why? Gideon got his payment, so why still pretend to care? *Maybe he wasn't pretending?*

The soft shuffling of footsteps drew near, and I held my breath, knowing I was about to be caught.

Shit.

Gideon turned the corner just as I stepped into his path. We collided into each other. My hands gripped his shirt, while his found my waist. My skin sparked at his touch, and I took in a lungful of his familiar scent—citrus, spice, and a dash of winter fire.

"Princess Valeria." His warm eyes sparkled. "Were you *spying* on me?"

"Don't flatter yourself." I stepped away from him, noticing Malachi had slipped quietly from the garden without so much as a goodbye. "Actually, I was hoping you could tell me how you bound yourself to me, so I can hurry up and undo it."

"I'm charmed you think a brute like me has that kind of power." He rubbed his full lips together before letting them slip into an easy smile. For a moment, I wondered what they'd feel like on my neck. Gods, I was pathetic. "Unfortunately, I don't."

"I don't believe you."

He shrugged. "Believe what you want, princess. Either way, I'm glad you tracked me down. I was... worried about you."

A fire lit deep in my belly, and my mouth went dry. Why did he have this effect on me?

You hate him, remember?

"You have no right to be worried about me. You're the reason I'm here."

He pulled me closer, his fingertips grazing my face. "What happened?"

Shame burned my cheeks, and I averted my gaze. "You know what happened."

"Your father did this?"

"Yes." Pressure built behind my eyes from the admission, but I blinked it away. I was a fool to confide in him. I folded my arms across my chest and added, "I guess, by association, you did this to me, too."

Gideon gritted his teeth. "Enough with the kidnapping shit." He stepped closer to me. I had to tilt my head back to meet his eyes. "I saved you from those demons, and I saved you from yourself. If I left you there, you might've died."

"Death would be a welcome respite from you and the horrors of this realm," I shouted before clamping a hand over my mouth.

He closed his eyes and tilted his face toward the sun. It highlighted the perfect curve of his jaw and the bridge of his nose. He let out a long breath. "Well, at least you're honest."

"I... I didn't mean that."

"It'll take a lot more than that to wound me, princess." He shoved his hands into his pockets as he rocked back and forth on the balls of his feet. "You're angry with me, and I'd like to understand why. Tell me what I took from you. Tell me what you miss."

I gave a half-hearted laugh. "You want to know what I miss about the Realm of the Mortals?"

"I do."

Fine. I'd humor him. "Tacos." I sighed wistfully. "And energy drinks and showers and reality TV and romance books with smut. I had a few chapters left in this paperback about a femme fatale who was hunting vampires, and it was *so* good..."

He watched me with an amused smile curved on his full lips. "Those sound like tiny things to miss."

"Little things add up."

"And the big things?"

A knot formed in my chest. "Mistress Marjorie—she was my keeper. And Mason. He was my only friend, and..."

"And graduation?" he finished for me.

Frowning, I remembered why I hated him. "Yeah, graduation. You took that from me, too."

Gideon's eyes held mine as he quietly asked, "Why is graduation so important to you?"

"Because..." I picked at the skin around my nails, weighing whether or not I should tell him the truth. "Because graduation would've given me proof... proof that for a blip in time, I belonged somewhere. That I was part of something."

"You belong *here,* in Empyrean."

My mouth hitched up at one side. "If only I didn't think you were a liar."

From behind, a hand tugged at my elbow, and I whirled around, cocking my fist. Mae blinked, a bemused smile on her lips. "Come, Your Grace. We have lots to do to prepare you for the ball."

Gideon bowed in farewell and Mae led me from the courtyard. Something within me slightly shifted. Gideon wasn't my friend, but he wasn't my enemy either. And as much as I hated him for all he took from me, I appreciated his attempt to smooth things over and his desire to understand why I was so angry with him.

Even if he was a charming prick.

I didn't know what compelled me, but I chiseled my mental fortress down just enough to send a sentence through the tether. *Come to the ball tonight.*

A faint caress through the bond told me he would.

CHAPTER 12

That night, Lirabeth waited for me at the bottom of the staircase, a vision in sapphire. Her eyes narrowed and she pursed her scarlet lips. "That gown is certainly... something."

Bex, the second handmaiden assigned to me, dressed me in another hideous contraption, though this one was far less plain and far more uncomfortable. The gown had long, lacy sleeves that flared out at the wrists and a full floral-quilted skirt fitting enough to blanket a crappy motel bed. The corset-style bodice was excruciatingly tight and snatched my waist into something that looked dreadfully unnatural.

I bit back a scowl as I pulled at the high neck. "Do you not approve? Should I change?"

She looped her thin arm through mine. "No, that's not necessary."

We meandered down the main hall as she rattled on about what I could expect from the night's events, but it was hard to focus on anything she said when the castle had transformed into something from a fairytale. Woven around the columns leading to the ballroom were silver and black roses. Strung between them were countless miniature lanterns shining like fireflies. The scent of savory meat and spices wafted down the hall, rumbling my stomach. I hadn't eaten all day, and I was starving. I'd give anything for a slice of pizza.

Stopping in front of two wooden doors, where the twin guards I met yesterday waited patiently for us, Lirabeth brought her mouth to my ear. "Try to have fun, dearest."

Her words sent a shiver down my spine. If I didn't play my part tonight, I didn't know what would happen. Nervous energy fluttered in my stomach like butterflies reluctant to fly.

She waved the hand that wasn't cradling her belly. The guards pushed open the wooden doors to the ballroom and the music drew to a halt, all eyes on Lirabeth. Like the king, her presence demanded attention. Her luxurious gown, woven from thin layers of shimmering silk and breathable mesh, billowed around her as she glided toward the dais. Hundreds of unfamiliar faces watched her. My eyes locked on my father where he sat on the throne. He inclined his head.

Right. I needed to play my part.

I smiled at the crowd, searching every face for one with magnetic blue eyes and the ability to drive me wild with one grin. My stomach sank when I didn't see Gideon, and I didn't like that one bit.

I didn't like *him.*

The brand hummed as if it disagreed. *Shut up.*

The room was massive, with vaulted ceilings covered in rich paintings that chronicled Bastile's life in all its glory, from a cherubic baby in the hands of his mother to a handsome black-haired man sitting on an obsidian throne with people kneeling at his feet. Every milestone in his life was a story to be studied.

Seven white pillars lined each side of the room. They held up the dome-shaped roof, the same flowers as in the hallway haphazardly adorning them.

My father rose from his jagged throne, extending his hand to Lirabeth as she drew closer to the dais. He brought her to stand on his left, one step behind him where my mother would've stood if she wasn't dead.

I swallowed a frown. The king didn't offer me a hand as I slid in place to his right, obediently taking a step back and positioning myself behind him.

Whispers spread among the guests, their eyes on me and the dark, diamond-encrusted tiara resting on my head.

"The lost princess, my daughter, Valeria of Empyrean, has returned to us at last." There was a slight pause before the room erupted in cheers. My cheeks burned from the attention. He added, "If anyone should want to greet the princess, please do so tonight."

The band tucked away in one corner of the room strummed an upbeat song, their fingers racing over their string quartet.

Sweat dripped down my back as I stood ramrod straight. A long line of guests approached to kiss my hands and grant me wishes of health and happiness. My jaw hurt from grinding my teeth together in a forced smile. I would've appreciated their sentiments more if those greeting me weren't the most fortunate of the realm. The wealthy, those that lived in the Pry. They didn't need to attend this ball and devour the free food and drinks. Yet, here they were, vying for my favor.

After the first hour, I thought my feet were going to bleed from standing so long in these wretched heels. Boredom tugged at my eyelids, and I nearly toppled off the dais when a hand reached out to steady me.

My eyes met Malachi's and he winked before dipping into a low bow. "Your Majesty."

The king beamed. "So great of you to join us, Malachi."

"The pleasure's all mine. May I introduce the princess to the King's Council?"

My father took a sip of wine from his silver goblet and waved. "Do what you want with her."

With one hand splayed across my back, Malachi wove us through the crowd, putting distance between us and the dais. When we were far enough away, he turned to me. "You look like you're going to faint. Have you eaten?"

I shook my head.

"Come with me." He guided me toward an overflowing table covered with countless breads, fruits, meats, and goblets filled to the brim with wine. It was a feast fit to feed a hundred families. Piling a plate full of food, he ushered me toward a corner of the room, hidden behind silver partitions and out of sight from everyone else. "Your father would throw a fit if he saw me coddling you."

"Is there anything that doesn't rile him up?" I sat my plate on my lap, lifted the hem of my dress and wiggled my feet at him. "Do you mind freeing me from these?"

He laughed. It was such a gentle sound. "Not at all." He slipped each shoe off and tossed them onto the floor. "Better?"

"Much." I sighed in relief and shoved a piece of buttered bread into my mouth.

Without his armor, silver scars similar to the ones on his face were visible, trailing down his neck. Not for the first time, I had the feeling that I knew him from somewhere... Was he the raven who brought my annual letter this year?

Malachi tucked a lock of ebony hair behind his ear. "It's not polite to stare."

"Sorry." I took a large gulp of wine, the taste bitter on my lips.

"How'd you get that bruise, princess?"

My eyes met his in a playful challenge. "How'd you get those scars, captain?"

Another chuckle revealed something childlike underneath his rough exterior. "That's not a story for tonight."

AFTER I ATE, MALACHI led me around the room and introduced me to the members of the King's Council. Most of them were well-dressed, gray-haired, and forgettable.

By far the most exhausting was Ekon Zadzora, the preceptor for the Assignment—a set of trials for Empyreans to complete in order to become a Celestian. He reeked of arrogance and assumptions, treating me like I knew nothing of our customs. Of course, I pretended to eat up whatever he had to say, all while ignoring the urge to roll my eyes.

After we said our farewells to Ekon, I turned to Malachi. "Why are there no women on the King's Council?"

He leaned in close. "Your father doesn't think women can lead. He says they don't have the stomach for it."

I schooled my face into an expression of indifference. Gods, I hated that prick. Not only was he a careless ruler, but he was a sexist pig.

Mistress Marjorie's words echoed in my mind. *You are a princess with power.*

Somehow, I'd figure out what that power was and use it to help Empyrean.

Malachi came to a stop in front of a man with eyes of amber. "This is Aurick Lythewood. He is the last of the king's trusted advisors. And you've met his son, Gideon, and his betrothed."

My breath hitched when Gideon stepped around Aurick, the rest of the room fading away. He looked nothing like his father, as he stood tall in a tailored black tunic that clung to his muscular frame. A thick metal ring adorned his index finger. He was so heartbreakingly beautiful with his high cheekbones, full lips, and slicked-back golden hair. I wondered what it would feel like to run my fingers through it, what he would do if I grabbed a fistful while he was deep inside me.

I shook my head, scolding myself. *Enough with the thirsting already.*

His eyes washed over me from the tip of my tiara to the hem of my dress, making my cheeks flush as he sent three words into the bond. *Beautiful. Radiant. Enchanting.* The exact words he said to me as I waded in Lake Fortunate. Only now, he was lying because I looked absolutely *ridiculous* in this dress.

I opened my mouth to say something, *anything*, as Malachi's words clicked into place. The heat in my cheeks cooled. The fire in my belly raged.

He was *betrothed.*

I grimaced. "Betrothed?"

The girl from the market slid into place beside him. Sabel.

Oh no.

You said she was a friend. I flung the sentence down the bond, hoping he'd hear me.

His lips twitched, and I wanted to punch him.

Sabel's mossy-green gown matched her wide eyes and accentuated her lithe frame. She wrapped a dainty hand around Gideon's forearm. I willed my emotions to settle, but something akin to jealousy flared inside me. Envy? Was I *envious* of her? Or was I pissed that he lied to me...again?

Maybe it was a mixture of both.

Malachi and Aurick struck up a conversation as they excused themselves and ventured in the direction of the dais, leaving the three of us near the edge of the dance floor.

"Are you having a good night?" Sabel asked, breaking the dragging silence.

I smiled, unable to be angry with her. She'd done nothing wrong. She was kind and beautiful and Gideon's *betrothed.*

"I spent most of it socializing with self-centered old men. You?"

"It's been great. Except this one"—she tugged on Gideon's arm—"has yet to ask me to dance."

There were a lot of things I could picture Gideon doing right now, most of which were vulgar and violent, but dancing wasn't one of them.

Me on the other hand? I could dance.

"To hell with him then," I said, extending an arm to her. "I'll dance with you."

Her eyes lit up as she slipped her arm from Gideon's and wound it around mine and together, we took to the dance floor, leaving Gideon and his lingering gaze in the sea of people behind us.

Sabel and I spun and twirled around for all of two songs, laughing carelessly even when I stepped on her toes. I liked that she was polite enough not to comment on my rusty skills. By the time the third song began, a tap on my shoulder had us halting in place to find Gideon standing behind me.

My smile vanished as I stared up into those deep blue eyes as endless as the ocean.

"May I have this dance?" he asked, extending his hand toward Sabel.

She giggled, placing a quick kiss on my cheek. "Save me another dance later, princess?"

A stinging sensation prickled through the bond as she took his hand, as if revolting from her touch. The brand burned. Unable to look away from her betrothed, unable to hear anything but the roar of desire in my veins rushing my ears, I stared at him. Did he feel the burning, too? Why did I feel this way? So hot and bothered and ready to scream. It was frustrating. I barely knew Gideon. And the parts of him I did know, I hated. He was a liar that I couldn't trust, and yet, all I could think about was him satisfying the heat between my thighs.

A blush crept across Gideon's sun-kissed cheeks. *I didn't lie to you. Sabel's a friend. Nothing more, nothing less.*

I bristled at his words and how they mirrored my own when it came to my *friendship* with Mason. Maybe that was why we were bound, because we were both selfish enough to fuck our friends and ignore the possible consequences.

Except I never intended to *marry* Mason. I never intended to marry anyone.

The happy couple maneuvered around me. The back of Gideon's free hand brushed against my arm, sending a shiver of heat through me. That two-timing bastard. If Mason were here, he'd be the perfect distraction to whatever spell Gideon had over me. He'd know what to do to make me lose my train of thought, to make time pause, to make me feel lost in pleasure.

I flashed a quick glare at the brand. Was *it* the culprit for this sexual tension boiling inside of me? Or was it something deeper? My body craved Gideon's closeness, begged for his touch, and every moment I denied myself of him, the tether grew more irritated with *me*.

Gods, I had *issues*.

Malachi pushed through the crowd, his face a mask of concern. "What's wrong? You're scowling."

"That's just my face."

"Your face is far too beautiful to be riddled with such a look. Would you like to dance?"

My eyes met his, and I grinned. He would be a fine distraction. "Yes."

He took my hand in his and spun me around the floor in time to the music. When it faded, and the band switched to an upbeat song, I danced like the girls had at prom. His hands found my hips as I ground against him, breath hot on my neck.

The weight of Gideon's gaze was something I recognized without having to confirm he was staring. His mental wall was down and his emotions whipped through the bond. This wasn't one-sided. He felt the same way seeing me in Malachi's arms that I felt seeing Sabel in his.

This was why I didn't fucking do feelings. And I definitely wouldn't let myself develop feelings for *him*.

Something deep within me taunted me, telling me it was too late—that Gideon had already wormed his way into my soul, and if given the chance, my heart and body, until I was consumed by him. I swallowed. Not going to happen. I wouldn't give him that power over me.

When I turned to Malachi, I brought my lips just an inch away from his and whispered, "Come with me."

I wandered out of the ballroom and down a hallway lit by several sconces. Malachi trailed behind me. All I could hear was the pounding of my heart telling me that hooking up with him wouldn't change how Gideon made me feel, that no one but him would make me feel satiated, make me feel whole.

Gideon's voice whispered throughout my mind. *Don't do something you'll regret, princess.*

The brand burned, and it would continue to burn until I gave in.

We turned a corner into a shadowy alcove, and Malachi wasted no time, pushing me flush against the stone wall. His lips met mine in a fury, all tongue and teeth. He bit my lower lip as he hiked up my skirts and lifted me, wrapping my legs around his lean waist. My fingers wound through his thick hair while I pulled him closer. The thumping of his heart drowned out whatever words Gideon sent through the bond until they were nothing but gibberish.

One of Malachi's scarred hands roamed my body, cupping my breast, and then squeezed my ass until a small moan escaped my lips, giving us both a moment to breathe. When his mouth found mine again, his hand slipped under my dress.

He pulled away, cursing. "By Bastile, you're not wearing anything under here?"

Panting, I shook my head, and a carnal sound escaped his throat as he kissed me again.

Gideon's eyes flashed in my mind, and I imagined it was him kissing me. That it was his hand exploring my skin. I breathed in the imaginary scent of citrus and spice, pretending it was his winter fire igniting my blood in a sensual song.

One that bound us as lovers.

As Malachi's hand dipped between my legs, I moaned his name.

He stopped, rearing back to look at me with wide, wild eyes. "Well, that's a first."

I blinked, mortified. I hadn't moaned his name—I'd moaned Gideon's.

"I didn't—"

"Princess, you can use me as a weapon in whatever way you see fit." He cupped my cheek, gently stroking it with his thumb. "But never against Gideon."

And then he put me down, straightened his clothes, and disappeared down the hallway as the ghost of Gideon's laughter trickled down the bond.

CHAPTER 13

Standing alone in the shadows of flickering fire, I waited until my heartbeat slowed, the flush in my cheeks faded, and my lips were no longer swollen before I moved from where Malachi left me.

I groaned, embarrassment and mortification shuffling together inside my stomach. How could I be so stupid? I lost control and let the bond prove it was right. Partially. I *was* attracted to Gideon. Even after he ruined everything. Even after he lied.

I wandered the castle, following the clanging of pots and pans. It reminded me of Mistress Marjorie and her tests. The noise grew louder the closer I got to the kitchen, and when I entered the room, several cooks and servants stopped to gawk at me. Crowding the far wall were three ovens and two large fireplaces with mouths big enough for me to stand in. The counters were vast, providing plenty of room to prep meals. Several mortar and pestles sat next to small glass jars of finely crushed spices and bulbs of garlic.

I maneuvered around sacks of flour, potatoes, and barrels of wine, swiping a half-filled bottle of what looked like a variant of rosé and tucked it under my arm as I wound my way to the back of the kitchen to an icebox. Opening it, I frowned. It was empty save for some wrapped meats and mason jars filled with gods knew what.

"I gotta bring this castle into the modern century," I muttered, taking a swig from the wine bottle. There was no way I was going to live out the rest of my life without snacks.

The staff went back to work cleaning up and chucking leftover food into the garbage. So much was going to waste when it could be going to those in the Commons.

I ventured into the pantry to scan the shelves. There wasn't much there to work with. After pushing some pickled vegetables out of the way, my eyes landed on a single jar of peanut butter.

It would do.

Silverware was haphazardly thrown into a crate on a lower shelf, and I grabbed a spoon before sitting on the filthy ground. Cross-legged, I wrenched the top of the jar free and dug in. It was thick and creamy, doing its job to fill the spots where holes poked into my resolve. A pounding in my temples bloomed as the servants cleaned, chatting and laughing with one another. They spoke to each other like friends.

That could never be me, even if I wanted it to be.

And gods, did I *want*.

Every fiber in my being burned for Gideon, even now, and I couldn't make it stop. I'd never felt so out of control around anyone—so desperate and consumed. And I *hated* it so fucking much. Not because it was Gideon, but because... it scared me. It scared me to want.

I didn't deserve to.

Not after what my brother did. Not after doing so brought chaos to Oakwood. And not after the destruction my father brought upon Empyrean.

Goosebumps spread across my skin, and I glanced up to find Gideon leaning against the doorframe, watching me. I didn't have to question how he found me; the glowing golden ink on his wrist gave it away. His hair was messy and the top of his shirt was unlaced, his tanned skin peeking out.

The air around us thickened with heat as he entered the pantry, crouching in front of me. When I didn't say anything, he grabbed a spoon from the crate and sat down. I handed him the jar, still working on my own spoonful.

We sat in silence, taking turns scooping peanut butter and sipping wine from the bottle.

After a while, he asked, "What's a fuckwit?"

I choked mid-swallow. Coughing, I managed, "Huh?"

"The day I took you from the Realm of the Mortals. You called me a fuckwit. What is it?"

"Oh, right." I laughed. "It's just a random mortal insult."

Genuine amusement flooded through the bond. My gaze dropped to his mouth, where a tiny bit of peanut butter lingered on the corner of his lips. Without thinking, I brushed it off with my thumb.

His shoulders relaxed before his expression turned serious. "Valeria, were you *trying* to make me jealous?"

"No," I lied.

"Really? Because you screamed, 'I'm going to fuck Malachi to make Gideon jealous!' so loud down the bond that it gave me a headache."

I sighed. That *did* sound like something I'd say. What was the point in lying if he'd see right through it?

"Fine, yes. Maybe? I don't know. I just felt so… overwhelmed, out of control, and pissed that you hid the truth about Sabel. I needed an escape, and I thought Malachi was it."

He was quiet for a moment. "I feel it, too—the pull to you. I've felt it since the day this brand appeared on my wrist. It only deepened the moment I laid eyes on you, drenched in demon blood with a scowl on your face. But you haven't made it easy considering you take pleasure in reminding me that you despise me."

My heart did a flippy thing in my chest. "I don't despise you."

"Well, you certainly don't like me."

I let out a long breath. "I don't *trust* you, or this bond, or myself."

There, I said it.

He twirled the ring on his index finger. "That's why I'm wearing this ring. It's enchanted so my mind cannot be manipulated by magic. Not even our bond can penetrate its shield."

My eyes went wide. I had heard of charms like his, but I'd never seen one in person. He slipped it off his finger and handed it to me. There was filigree on the sides and an anemone flower insignia in the center, symbolizing protection against evil and ill omens. Charms like this were incredibly rare, taking both dark and holy magic to enchant them.

"Lucky you," I muttered, handing it back to him.

He grinned, pulling a slim, velvet box from his jacket pocket. "Lucky *us*."

Skeptically, I took the box from him and opened it to find a long silver chain with a miniature dagger dangling from it. A black sapphire shimmered on the hilt, and a teardrop ruby hung from the tip, dripping like blood.

"Gideon," I breathed. "This is beautiful."

"Consider it a belated birthday present." He took the necklace from the box to put it around my neck, brushing my wavy hair out of his way. His fingertips grazed my skin as he latched the clasp. "It's enchanted like my ring. All thoughts you have from this point on are your own."

I shifted to look at him. "It must have cost a thousand *corones*."

"It's a family heirloom. My mother used to wear it before she..." His words trailed off and the lump in his throat bobbed as he tried to finish his sentence. His gorgeous features took on a sheen of aching sadness from the furrow in his brow to the downturned corners of his lips. His eyes became glossy, filled with pain from a festering wound.

I knew what he couldn't say.

I placed a hand on his knee. "Before she died?"

"The night of Cayden's attack. A demon found her and snapped her neck."

Tears pricked my eyes. He understood loss, understood the heartache of growing up motherless, the guilt of surviving when she didn't. But he had his father, Malachi, and this realm. He lost his mom and didn't fear friendships, didn't fear relationships.

Didn't fear the wanting.

He was *engaged*, after all.

"I can't accept this." I reached to take the necklace off. "It's a lovely gift, but you're with Sabel, and contrary to what happened tonight with Malachi, I'm not interested in breaking the two of you up."

"Believe me." He grabbed my hand. "Sabel and I are *friends*. We're betrothed in the eyes of the king, but not in our own. Trust me when I tell you, we don't want to be together." When I didn't respond, he added softly, "You can ask her. She'll tell you our engagement is nothing but a ruse."

Why would they want to trick the king? Unless... it was about rising in station. Gideon said he was both a prying bastard and a commoner. Could his engagement to Sabel help him rise in rank?

"It doesn't matter," I said, more to myself than him. "There's nothing between us but this bond, and once it's broken, I'll stop feeling like this. I'll stop..." *I'll stop wanting*, I didn't say. I took a deep breath. "I should go."

He stood, tugging me to my feet. "Would you like me to escort you?"

"No... but I want to visit my mother's grave." I screwed the lid back onto the jar of peanut butter and grabbed a couple of clean spoons to take back to my room with me. "Would you... would you take me there sometime?"

His eyes searched mine, and he nodded, understanding why I asked him to come with me.

Our heartache was the same.

And for a moment, I wondered if maybe, just maybe, Gideon wasn't a curse but an infuriating, super sexy last-ditch effort from the universe to give me some shred of friendship in a realm ravaged by despair.

GIDEON SUMMONED ME a few days later to escort me to my mother's tomb. I wanted to go sooner, but he said he had things to take care of, and I didn't ask what, mainly because the thought of being pushed to the side for mysterious *things* reminded me so much of Mistress Marjorie and her abandonment that I couldn't breathe.

Of course, my father was not happy with my show at the ball, so I spent those days waiting locked in my room with only my handmaidens to keep me company. Bex, a pretty woman with cool tawny skin, a blunt black bob, and a perpetual smirk, asked for stories of my time in the Realm of the Mortals to keep us entertained.

It was nice.

But trashy reality TV and bowls filled with snacks would've been loads better.

"Watch your step," Gideon said, bringing my attention back to the dreadful courtyard we were standing in.

For the last fifteen minutes, he'd tried to clear a path for us to walk through. But he was getting nowhere. It was around noon and the sun glared down on us. Sweat clung to the back of my neck.

The courtyard would have been beautiful if it weren't for the wildly overgrown, bloomless rose bushes, thick with thorns, and scattered naked trees—skeletal even though it was peak growing season. Weeds grew through the cracks between black, basket-woven bricks, destroying what would've been charming. Vines wound around various statues, all bearing Bastile's likeness. Some of them were knocked over and smashed into the ground as if they were purposely destroyed.

While Gideon cut through a tangled web of thorns, I trekked through the overgrown grass and pushed aside the ivy crawling up and around the arched windows to peek inside the northern wing of the castle. It housed a library filled with countless rows of packed bookshelves, several tables, and two staircases that led up and up and up. It was straight out of a fairytale.

Gideon swore and wiped sweat from his forehead as I ventured back to the path.

Opposite the library there was calf-high grass and thick clusters of greenish blossoms attached to thin stems. Beyond the neglect was a dry fountain carved from shimmering black limestone and several matching benches set around it.

"I don't care about ripping this ridiculous dress. Give me a *corone*."

He sighed, rummaging around in his pockets until he found one and tossed it to me. I caught it and trudged through the weeds over to the fountain.

Many years ago, I bet it had been stunning with silver water pouring from the statue's eyes and spraying from its sword, like blood during a battle. With a full basin, it'd create a makeshift pool similar to Lake Fortunate. If the water ran today, maybe it would heal the yellowing bruise on my cheek.

Closing my eyes, I flicked the coin into the fountain. The tiny dink of silver hitting stone was a symphony as I cast my wish.

Gideon looked at me, his brow furrowed. "What was that for?"

I grinned like a child in a candy store. "I made a wish."

"A wish?"

"It's something the mortals do whenever they see a fountain."

I wasn't foolish enough to believe wishes were real when magic existed. But it was such a small thing that made me feel closer to home. A reminder that I was mortal-raised through and through. No one and nothing in Empyrean could take that from me. Not even my father.

Gideon hung behind as I made my way back to the path, my cranberry skirt snagging on a protruding thorn from one of the bushes. When I pulled free, I turned to him. "Are you coming?"

"You go ahead"—he pointed to an iron gate overcome by greenery—"the mausoleum is through that gate."

With another glance at him, I shrugged and headed toward it. Tearing away vines woven through the lock, I found the gate was rusted shut. Even throwing my entire body weight against it didn't make it budge.

"It's stuck!" I yelled. Gideon jogged toward me and pushed on the gate. I glared at him. "What, do you think you have the magic man-touch?"

"I *am* stronger than you, princess." He flexed and muscles rippled beneath his shirt. "But you're right, it's not going to budge. C'mon, I'll boost you over."

I glanced between the oversized dress I was wearing and the gate. "You can't be serious."

He crouched and laced his fingers together to give me a sturdy foothold. Apparently, he was *very* serious.

After I placed one hand on his shoulder and my foot in his clasped-together hands, he thrust me over the gate. The bottom of my dress caught on a finial shaped like a chess piece and tore as I fell face-first onto the ground.

"Ow," I grunted. "That would've been so much easier in jeans."

Gideon hopped over the gate and helped me to my feet, brushing dirt and pieces of dried grass from my hair. My heart pounded a little bit harder standing this close to him, the smell of sweet citrus and winter spice beckoning me to lean in.

The dagger dangling around my neck was ice-cold against my skin. These thoughts were *all* mine. Of course, I had studied the necklace the night he gave it to me. Looking for the tiny black and gold star that signified it was actually what he said it was—a protective charm. He hadn't lied, and that made my opinion of him even more conflicted than before.

I took the smallest of steps away from him.

Similar to the courtyard, this area was a desolate wasteland of forgotten greenery. No one had cared for it in years. But that didn't diminish how grand the mausoleum was, even beneath the moss-covered stairs and ivy-laden marble.

It was fit for a god.

Like most of Bastile's architecture choices, seven columns surrounded the eternal resting place with two raven-like gargoyles perched by the door, warding off trespassers. Under the moss, the stairs were black as ash leading up to ornate double doors made of pure silver. A repeating crisscross pattern decorated them, and filigree lined the frames.

Two stained glass windows on the front of the building added to the gloriousness of it all. Like the castle's windows, they depicted images of Bastile, that much I was sure of, with his flowing black hair and dark eyes, his fiery wings spread out behind him. The only difference was there was a familiar woman with him, and they looked... happy.

As happy as blurred pieces of melted glass could look, anyway.

Were my mother and Bastile closer than I thought?

Etched into the white marble were the words *By His Grace Alone We Enter the Half-Light.*

A pang spread throughout my chest. This building was far too beautiful to house such heartbreak.

Navigating the distance between the gate and the mausoleum, I bounded up the stairs, Gideon following close behind. The door swung open without struggle.

He grabbed a torch from the entryway and lit it with a strike of a match. The flames cleared our path of cobwebs and scared off any creepy critters that may have snuck their way inside. We descended further into the tomb, where dry, stale air filled my lungs with the type of itchiness a cough couldn't soothe.

My heart stopped as we approached two marble sarcophagi lying side-by-side. One was sleek and white, with a melted and embossed tiara infused at the top where the body's head would be under its lid. Embellished sides with black feathers bled into the sarcophagus next to it. The other was grand, made of obsidian and embossed with silver speckles and snowy feathers. Another crown adorned the head of this one, a mirror image to the one my father wore.

The sarcophagi balanced each other, light and dark, feminine and masculine, young and old, all blending to create harmony amidst despair.

"Is this her?" I ran my hand over the white marble slab.

"It is. And if you believe the rumors..." Gideon tapped the jagged crown. "This is Bastile."

I stilled in place. "What rumors?"

"That Bastile was in love with your mother and demanded that her final resting place be beside his when the time came."

Why didn't Mistress Marjorie ever tell me that? She said my mother and Bastile were close, but not *that* close.

My voice hitched. "Did they have an affair or something?"

"I don't know. No one speaks of your mother anymore because of what happened and no one speaks of Bastile because it angers your father."

I chewed my lip. That was weird. Empyrean was Bastile's realm. My father had no right to get angry over people worshipping the god who loved and cared for them for thousands of years. Then again, my father had no right to do a lot of the things he had done.

Bouquets of dried and brittle irises and narcissus hung from the walls. Open trunks full of glittering jewels and tiaras along with thick, dust-covered leather-bound books crowded the room. I didn't want to think about what would be left in this mausoleum if the castle grounds weren't so heavily guarded. There were enough riches in here to feed a thousand families. Heaps of rotted clothes and shoes towered in the corner as if they were carelessly thrown there. I ran my fingers over various odds and ends, picturing my mother reading in the sun or pacing the castle halls in one of the dresses piled in the corner. Even in their ruined state, none of those gowns were as hideous as what my father forced me to wear. My mother's entire life was in this mausoleum, boxed up and forgotten, hidden away and neglected.

The stones were cold beneath me as I sank to the ground, my forehead pressing against the marble of the sarcophagus. The reality that she was gone clawed at the back of my eyes, pricking them with soft tears that soon turned to harsh cries.

She was *gone*.

After all this time, the tiniest part of me thought that maybe Mistress Marjorie got it wrong, that maybe my mother wasn't dead, that it was all a misunderstanding.

I never let that part of me fully grieve. I locked it up and waited until now. Sobs wracked through me, rattling against my ribcage. She was murdered by her son, and her memory was murdered by her monster of a husband. Everyone had forgotten her.

"I'll make them pay," I cried, anger flaring within me. Cayden would die for what he did, and my father would die because of the monster he had become. "I'll make them both suffer."

My words were too loud. I shouldn't have said such treasonous things, but I couldn't stop.

I hated my father.

Maybe I'd always hated him.

Gideon shrugged off his jacket and wrapped it around my shivering shoulders before pulling me from the floor and burying my face into his chest. I breathed in a lungful of summer air and winter spice.

"When I lost my mother, I didn't know how I was going to go on living without her. But one night my father pulled me into his arms just like this and told me that even in death, my mother wasn't gone. Not really," he whispered, smoothing a hand over my hair. "The ones we lose are kept safe in our hearts until we meet them again in the Half-Light."

His lips brushed against the top of my head so gently my trembling stilled. For a brief moment, there was peace. A peace I had never known before.

Pulling away, I glanced up at him. I was frozen in place, unsure if I wanted to push him away or pull him closer. A breath passed and my mouth crashed into his as one of his hands fisted my hair. He hungrily devoured me. The taste of citrus spilled onto my tongue, and I lapped it up, kissing him like I was starved. Exhilaration rippled through the tether as a rhapsody exploded, a crescendo rising in time with my need to get lost in him. Books and jewels toppled to the ground as he lifted me against him, deepening the kiss.

One hand slipped under my skirts and he squeezed my bare thigh, while his mouth traced my jaw, panting heavily like sticky summer air. Winding my hands through his hair, I yanked his face back up to mine and crushed myself against him, needing to feel his heart beating in time with mine. One hand worked its way up his shirt, his taut back warm beneath my touch. I dug my nails into his tanned skin, and a moan escaped from his throat. I wanted to hear that sound every day for the rest of my life.

The length of him rose in his pants as I ground against him, feeling every delicious inch. A growing desire swept through me for him to strip away my anger until I was raw and vulnerable—his for the taking.

A husky throat-clearing tore us apart, leaving my lips swollen and screaming for more. Malachi didn't even try to hide his amusement as his mouth curved into a smirk. "Sorry to interrupt. The king is looking for the princess."

Gideon put me down. "I'll escort Valeria to the castle."

"I think we both should," Malachi countered as Gideon tucked his shirt into his pants and grabbed his jacket from the floor. "There are too many corners to get lost in on the way back. Right, princess?"

My cheeks burned. "Very funny."

Malachi winked and strolled out of the mausoleum.

Leaning against the wall, I closed my eyes, trying to slow my breathing. I had kissed Gideon. And he *ravaged* me. It left me dazed.

Looking around, I bent to pick up the stack of books we knocked over in our frenzy. One of the diaries had fallen open, landing on a page written in a language I couldn't read—the old tongue. And next to those unknown words was an image of the brand that glittered on my wrist.

Gideon's eyes went wide. He snatched the journal from the floor and dog-eared the page before handing it to me. "Maybe it'll have some answers."

Breathlessly, I tucked it into the waistband of my underskirts and followed him from the mausoleum, unable to think of anything but the bond and how the only person I knew who could read those pages was the same person who skirted the question when I asked her about it.

But why? What would Mistress Marjorie gain from keeping me in the dark?

CHAPTER 14

C hatter from the servants filled the halls as several of them scrubbed stone floors with buckets of soapy water, their hands red and raw. The fragrant scent of lemon tickled my nose as we passed by.

No light flickered from my father's study, and my shoulders sagged in relief. At least I wasn't being led to a whipping.

As we wound through the corridors, Malachi stopped briefly to kiss a servant on the cheek.

My eyebrows raised in surprise, considering how he kissed me days ago.

"Is she a lover of yours?" I asked, poking Malachi's side when we turned the corner into another hallway.

He shot me a sideways glance. "One of many."

At that, Gideon laughed, and it wrapped around me like an old cardigan, fending off the cold air drifting through the halls. The brand hummed as if it was content that we crossed the invisible line drawn between us. Our kiss was still fresh in my mind—the taste of citrus clinging to my lips and winter spice lingering in my hair. He was all around me, my body marked by him both inside and out.

Fear crept up my spine. I couldn't chase after the peace his embrace gave me ever again.

Giving in to the wanting was asking for heartache—which was precisely why I needed someone who could speak the old tongue and decipher the journal we found. Deep down in my bones, I knew those pages held the key to what kind of bond we shared and how to sever it.

In front of two arched doors, Aion, my father's footman, paced. As we drew closer, he huffed. "You're *late*."

"And you're a dick," I snapped.

Both Malachi and Gideon coughed to hide their laughter as voices rumbled from behind the double doors.

Malachi sighed, pushing the iron doors inward. They groaned as they opened, the chatter dropping to a dull murmur.

Both of the guys flanked my sides as we strode into a partially renovated cave with stalagmites clawing their way up from the ground. The only light in the room came from the sun glaring down through a hole in the ceiling. Shiny black gleamed all around us except from the round stone table where six members of the King's Council sat alongside my father.

"Gentlemen." Malachi bowed to the council. "Your Highness, I've brought the princess as requested."

"Sit," the king commanded, gesturing to the empty seat next to him. Gideon pulled the chair out for me before finding his own next to his father. He busied himself with several pieces of paper, and I tapped my lips.

Malachi hadn't said Gideon was on the King's Council.

But that couldn't be right because he would make the total eight, and Bastile only dealt in variables of seven. It took seven years to create Empyrean from scratch, there were seven King's Council members, seven stories in the castle, seven pillars on either side in the main hall... Everywhere I looked, that number could be found.

Seven, not eight, and certainly never nine. That was the God of the Forsaken's preferred number of choice.

I glanced around the table, taking in the familiar faces. Too bad I didn't remember all of their names.

My father's heavy gaze lingered on my torn skirt and mussed hair. Malachi approached him, drawing his attention from me. He whispered in his ear, his eyes flickering in my direction. The king returned his scrutiny to the men sitting around him, and Malachi slid in place to his left.

Unlike at the ball, I hung on every word spoken between the advisors. My father watched them earnestly, though his hollow eyes gave the impression he didn't care what they had to say.

I tried to act surprised to hear the realm was struggling, but I knew firsthand from the detour in the market. The poorest of Empyrean's people were starving, while the richest became gluttonous.

"We need to do something," Aurick, Gideon's father, pleaded, wringing his weathered hands in front of him. "Too many children are taking to the streets begging. They're *starving*."

"If we provided food to every starving family, why would anyone work and rebuild?" Ekon countered. "We can't provide handouts."

A handsome man with graying hair drew his lips into a thin line. He wore a chartreuse tunic that was bright against his deep black skin. I remembered him from last night. His name was Royston, and he'd been on the council since Bastile appointed him. Besides Gideon's father, he was one of the only men on the King's Council who greeted me like a person, not a royal he was trying to impress.

Royston rubbed the back of his head, choosing his words wisely. "Bastile wouldn't want his people to suffer like this."

The quick wham of my father's hands slapping the arms of his chair made me wince. Gideon's eyes flashed to mine before shifting to the king. "Bastile left us with a broken system that's vulnerable to attack." He hurled the words at the council. "We all felt the devastation of the Deathbringer's hand. If Empyrean is to rebuild and lead a counter-attack, we need to organize an army of the strongest in this realm."

The Deathbringer? My eyebrows drew together as I tried to place the name.

Another name for your brother, Gideon said through the tether.

Another thing Mistress Marjorie kindly left out of our history lessons.

What did the Deathbringer even mean? And why would we *want* to lead a counter-attack? There were far more demons than Empyreans. We'd be leading our people to slaughter.

"Your Highness, if I may," Aurick said, his voice soft like his amber eyes. The king nodded. "The people in the Commons deserve a fair opportunity to ascend should they be selected for the Assignment. They'll never pass the Trials if they're starving."

My father took a long sip from a jewel-encrusted goblet. "Then they weren't worthy to begin with."

I scoffed.

"Do you have something to add, Your Grace?" Ekon set his empty, lifeless eyes on me.

Malachi cleared his throat, and Gideon tensed, our bond flooding with worry.

"Yes." I kept my voice level. "Only a fool would question Bastile's decision in who is worthy enough to ascend into the role of a Celestian." I should've stopped there, but I couldn't shut up. The words flew out of my mouth like word vomit. "And by letting our people starve, by encouraging station disparities, we are diverting from Bastile's vision and purpose entirely."

Aurick and Gideon exchanged a surprised glance while Royston gave me a slight nod of encouragement. Even Malachi sat stunned in place.

On the other hand, my father slumped in his chair, rubbing the stubble on his chin.

"And how would you solve this..." Ekon waved a hand around, words escaping him. "Diversion?"

"Well, to start, I'd feed our people. There's plenty of food in this castle for that."

"What happens when the food runs out?"

I narrowed my eyes. "Empyrean is pure, undiluted magic. We can harness that magic and ensure that our food supply doesn't run out, like ever, so that no one starves again."

The king clenched his jaw and turned his glazed eyes back to the council. "Let's put it to a vote. All in favor of feeding the commoners?"

Aurick, Malachi, and Royston raised their hands.

My eyes darted to Gideon, and I hoped he could hear my question. *Why aren't you voting?*

I'm only apprenticing. I don't have any voting power.

I chewed my lip. Another thing we had in common—a lack of power.

My father smiled, his dark eyes crinkling at the corners. It was three against four.

He won.

"Looks like they'll have to fend for themselves." The king took another sip of wine. "Perhaps you will have the chance to do things differently should you inherit the throne, Valeria."

"*Should* she inherit the throne?" Aurick's voice was an octave higher now.

Ekon stood. "An excellent transition to the next issue at hand, Your Highness." He shuffled some papers. "Let us discuss your request to shift the line of succession."

I blinked. Surely, I didn't hear him correctly. "Your request to *what*?"

A murmur spread throughout the room. Rage pulsed through the brand, and I wasn't sure if it was mine or Gideon's. Did he want me to abdicate the throne to my half-sibling? Changing the line of succession was nearly impossible. The only ways were if I abdicated or the King's Council voted to remove me for instability. Or if I died, but *that* was a bit dark, even for a monster like my father. Was that why he sent me away? Because he didn't want to see me rule Empyrean? He didn't think I was capable?

Malachi's words from the ball came back to me: *Your father doesn't think women can lead.*

If he somehow managed to convince the King's Council to change the line of succession, I'd have nothing.

I'd *be* nothing.

The king grinned as if he was the one who could hear my thoughts. "The next rightful heir should be of male lineage. It's what Bastile would have wanted."

"Blasphemy," Gideon muttered.

Malachi sucked in a breath.

"What did you—"

The doors to the hall flew open, metal colliding with stone.

My father's warning to remain seated didn't stop me as soon as I saw who stood in the doorway with her hands on her hips. Rushing across the room and tripping over the torn hem of my dress, I threw my arms around Mistress Marjorie, breathing in her scent of smoke and vanilla until it settled deep in my lungs.

"Margie," I cried into her cloak. "You came for me."

"Of course I did, little one."

The aching inside of me cracked open, and her voice bathed me in an endless supply of comfort. After a few moments, she pulled away and tilted my face to the left and then the right, clicking her tongue when she noticed the fading bruise on my cheek.

I couldn't believe she was here—in Empyrean. She came for me. Foolishly, I glanced over her shoulder to see if she brought Mason.

She hadn't.

The doors to the chamber swung shut with a wave of her hand—the twin guards and Aion unconscious behind her.

"You could at least look pleased to see me." She moved toward the King's Council, pacing several feet away from the table like she was a shark in open water, and they were her prey.

"Always a pleasure." My father's tone was clipped. "To what do we owe the honor of your sudden arrival?"

"Do I need a reason to return home?"

Mistress Marjorie feasted on the men before her, her hidden gaze lingering on Gideon before looking at me. She ran a finger along the inside of her left wrist as if she could feel our tether.

The journal. She could decipher the journal and get to the bottom of the bond once and for all.

My heart pounded in my chest at this turn of events.

My father took a long gulp from his chalice and tossed it to the floor with a clatter. He ran a tongue over his wet lips. "Seraphicity is *not* your home, Witch of the Gray."

Malachi's eyes met mine, and he shook his head. It was a warning to let them hash out their differences. It was a warning I didn't heed.

"This *Witch of the Gray* raised me while you fucked around and drove Empyrean into a pit of despair," I growled. "You'll treat her with the respect she—"

My father exploded out of his chair, closing the space between us with a speed I didn't know he had, his hand ready to strike. Gideon jolted to his feet, knocking papers to the ground while Malachi's hand hovered on the hilt of the dagger sheathed on his belt.

Mistress Marjorie manifested between us, grabbing the king's wrist mid-swing. Her pale white hand was tiny in comparison, but what she lacked in strength, she made up for in magic. "Touch her *again,* and I'll burn this castle to the ground before you realize your flesh is melting."

"Treason," Ekon shouted from the table. "The witch threatened King Ward!"

Without releasing my father's wrist, she clenched her left hand
into a fist. The crunch of bone followed by Ekon's screams shuddered
throughout the room. He crumpled to the floor, clutching his
shattered leg, bone peeking through his leather breeches.

"Do I have your attention now?" Silence answered her. "Good.
It's time for a story. A week ago, someone snatched Valeria from the
Realm of the Mortals. Imagine my surprise when I came looking
for her to find Empyrean... in dire conditions. Of course, my first
thought was, that's Ward for you. Always making a mess of things.
But then, when I tried to enter the castle, I discovered there were
wards in place. Wards designed to keep *me* out." She tightened her
grip on the king's wrist. "As you can see, I shattered them quite easily.
My question is *why*? What are you hiding?"

"How dare you question me!" The king seethed, a vein in his
forehead protruding. "You are no longer welcome in Empyrean. I
will give you until sundown to leave, or I will watch your body swing
in the market."

"Father!"

"You." He turned his fury on me. "You will be unrecognizable
when I'm through with you."

I won't let him touch you. Venom coated Gideon's conviction and
fire kindled throughout me at how protective he was.

Malachi looked skyward, focusing on the soft golden hue leaking
through the skylight, his foot tapping in place.

"I've heard enough." Aurick slammed his gentle hands on the
table. Blood pooled on the ground where Ekon lay, his breathing
shallow. "Finish your story, Marjorie. Why have you come?"

"Very well." Her shoulders relaxed. "The story concludes with
me finding a way around your pathetic wards with some grave news
for Valeria."

My stomach flipped. Grave news. For me?

She released my father's wrist. He flexed his hand, nostrils flaring. When he was seated, she snapped her fingers, and a black envelope materialized with a gold cracked wax seal stuck to the back.

"Shall I read it aloud?"

The king's command was a bark from a wounded dog. "Read it, witch."

She removed an ink-stained piece of parchment from the envelope and unfolded it.

I held my breath.

"Dearest Witch of the Gray," she read. "I have something my sister wants. Or should I say, *someone*? Tell her I'll be waiting for her arrival, and if she doesn't come, I'll gift her his limbs one by one."

The room spun as a high-pitched whistle shrieked in my ears.

"Who do they have?" my father questioned, his voice sharp.

Mason.

I wasn't sure if I said his name aloud. They had him. *Mason.* I had to go rescue him. My heart thundered in my chest, threatening to rip free from its cage the way Ekon's bones tore through his skin. I had... I had to help him.

My father flicked invisible lint from his tunic. "And I should care why?"

"Because the boy they took has the Sight," Mistress Marjorie said.

The King's Council broke into a hushed panic. If the Realm of the Forsaken had had a Seer, then Mason wasn't just a bargaining chip. He was a weapon. With him, they had power over Empyrean. They could use his Sight to pin-point Celestians when they went to the Realm of the Mortals to patrol for demonic activity and wipe out our warriors one by one.

Malachi and Gideon exchanged nervous glances, speaking in a language only they understood.

This is bad, Gideon whispered to me and only me.

Bad didn't begin to explain it. This was one of the worst things that could ever happen, and it was *his* fault.

I glared at him, fury burning through me. Gideon was the reason the Realm of the Forsaken took Mason instead of *me*. He may have saved me from a fate worse than death, but he condemned my best friend to it in my place.

And now, I was going to make him pay.

Seeing nothing but red, I leaped toward him and knocked him out of his chair to the stony ground. He didn't scramble away as I climbed on top of him seething in anger.

Anger at him for taking. Anger at myself for wanting.

His regret stormed through the bond as my hands wrapped around his throat and squeezed.

CHAPTER 15

"**I**t should've been me," I screamed at Gideon. "They should've taken me!"

Malachi's strong arms ripped me from Gideon and dragged me away as I kicked and screamed. The captain tossed me over his shoulder, and I watched, upside down, as Gideon sat up, coughing, his face flushed.

"I'm sorry," he gasped, shaking his head. Golden hair spilled into his eyes. "I didn't... I didn't know."

Something primal clawed its way up my throat as Malachi carried me out of the room. Servants watched, wide-eyed and horror-stricken, as I swore and pleaded and begged for him to put me down.

He lugged me all the way upstairs to my room, and threw me onto the bed, his gaze molten. "Pull yourself together, princess. This is not Gideon's fault."

I leaped from the bed, attempting to shove him away. He didn't budge. Stupid corded muscles and impeccable training.

"You carry a torch for someone who doesn't deserve it," I hissed.

He bent over me until I fell backward onto the down comforter, staring up at him. Under any other circumstances, this would've been a major turn-on.

Mae and Bex peeked out from the bathroom.

"Is there a problem, Your Grace?" Bex asked through swollen lips, one hand on her chest as she steadied her breathing.

I squinted at them. Were they— Not important right now. "No, you both may go."

They exchanged a look before hurrying from the room.

"You don't know Gideon." Malachi glared at me. "You view him like he's nothing but an arrogant pawn for the crown, but he's more than that. *We* are more than that." I opened my mouth to interrupt, but he kept speaking. "You don't know what he's been through. He gives and gives for our people, for this realm, for *you*."

"He hasn't *done* anything for me. He's *taken* everything from me."

Something in his gaze darkened. "I thought you were different. But you're just like your father." His jaw clenched, then he added, "Maybe worse."

I flinched. "I—"

"Malachi, that's enough." Gideon strolled into the room. His reddened neck was already flowering with the shadow of a future bruise. "She's nothing like her father, and you know it."

"I don't need you to defend me," I snapped, fists clenched at my side.

"Can we please not do this again?" He held his hands up in surrender. "I'm sorry the Realm of the Forsaken took your friend."

"You think an apology will make things better?" I took a step toward him, ready to strike.

"No, but I think helping you rescue him will."

My eyes went wide. He would do that? For me?

Malachi grabbed him by the collar. "Gideon. Hallway. Now."

Gideon didn't protest as Malachi dragged him from the room, slamming the door shut behind them. I waited a millisecond before padding over to eavesdrop.

Pressing my ear to the door, I closed my eyes and listened.

"Have you lost your damn mind?" Malachi hissed. "She tried to *kill* you."

"No, she didn't," Gideon said, his voice raw. "She was just angry. If she wanted me dead, I'd be dead."

He was right. I didn't want to kill him... not really. I wanted him to hurt the way I hurt, but maybe I hadn't gone about it the right way.

Malachi let out a long breath. "We're not taking the princess to the Realm of the Forsaken. We just got her back. We need her *here* for the—"

"I thought you grew out of eavesdropping," a voice said from behind me, and I jumped, throwing my weight against the door.

"Margie," I breathed, one hand on my chest.

I was so wrapped up in their conversation I didn't register the soft crackling of dark magic purring throughout the room. It was warm and smelled of vanilla and smoke. It reminded me of home. My heart hitched.

"That was some outburst downstairs, little one."

"I lost my temper."

She crossed the room, reached for my hand and led me over to the edge of the bed, where we both sat. "It happens. But why on the boy you're bound to?"

"I—" I swallowed, trying to find the right words. "I blamed Gideon for what happened to Mason."

"It wasn't his fault. And it wasn't yours either."

I stared at her, my eyes brimming with tears. "Then who should I blame? Where should I direct all this... anger?"

It raged under my skin, begging for a release.

She was quiet for a moment. "Mason went behind my back to strike a deal with a demon for information on who took you. That's how the Realm of the Forsaken found him."

My screaming. My pleading. The way I acted as Gideon carried me through the portal. My actions were why Mason thought the Realm of the Forsaken took me, not someone from Empyrean.

If I had gone quietly...

If I hadn't resisted...

"I know that look," she murmured. "I tell you the boy made a reckless decision of his own accord, and yet you still find a way to blame yourself. Not everything is your fault."

"Sure as hell feels like it."

I should've left Mason blissfully unaware of who we both were—content with being a friend who I occasionally shared a bed with. Actually, I shouldn't have been anything to him at all. It had put us both in danger.

She placed a hand under my chin and turned my face toward her. "How are you adjusting to Empyrean?"

The question opened a floodgate. "I hate it here. It's nothing like you said it would be. And definitely not like you showed me. People are starving—they're *dying*. And I can't help them. I can't *do* anything because my father is a monster. He remarried, has another child on the way, and now he wants to change the line of succession." I didn't know when I started crying, but tears streamed down my cheeks. "Everything is so fucked."

"Shh. I'm here now."

"For how long? You wanted to get away from me, remember?" I bounded to my feet, pacing back and forth. "Why are you here? Did you think of more things to hide from me?"

"What have I hidden from you?"

My hand slipped under my dress, and I retrieved the journal, thumbing to the dog-eared page. "You're the only one I know who can read the old tongue. You've been around as long as a bond like this has. So tell me, what kind of bond is it?"

"Little one—"

"Tell me!" I screamed. Gideon and Malachi barged into the room. I held up a finger, stopping them in their tracks. "Stop hiding things from me, and just read the page. Tell me what kind of bond it is. *Please.*"

She took the journal from me and ran her finger over the pages.

"It's a dyad," she said at last. "Caused by an archaic ritual that splits a soul between two bodies, magically tying two people to each other at their very core."

"Simpler terms, Margie."

"We're soulmates, princess," Gideon said softly.

"No." The word was a sob. "That can't be what she means."

"Gideon is correct."

Soulmates. We were fucking soulmates.

I doubled over in disbelief, clutching my sides until I fell to my knees on the soft, white fur rug. If we were soulmates, that meant...

I sucked in a breath. "If we're soulmates, can the bond be broken?"

Gideon flinched.

Margie folded her hands in front of her. "I believe it can, but I don't know what the ramifications are. The last dyad I saw was a millennium ago, and even then, I wasn't privy to what happened when Bastile shattered it."

Shattered. Broken. Obliterated.

Breaking the dyad didn't sound pleasant.

Malachi looked between the three of us. "Does anyone want to fill me in on whatever it is you're talking about?"

"I'll tell you later," Gideon told him, tone frosty. "Go deal with the aftermath from the King's Council meeting."

He nodded, eyes flashing to me in silent warning.

When the door shut behind him, I whispered, "Mistress Marjorie, did you do this to me?"

"Of course not." She tugged me to my feet. "Only a god can create and destroy a dyad."

"A god? Bastile... did this?"

Gideon laughed, taking his jacket off and tossing it onto the chaise. "So Bastile thought I was worthy enough to be bound to Valeria but not worthy enough to be a Celestian? Someone make it make sense."

"Shut up, Gideon." I rubbed my temples.

He was right, though. None of this made sense.

Mistress Marjorie walked around the room, touching things, opening windows, and running her fingers over the furniture.

She knew exactly what this bond was and what it meant, but she didn't tell me.

Stilling in place, she turned to me. "Go on. Ask your question, little one."

"Why did you hide this from me? You could've warned me."

She softened. "Because I knew how you would react. You would panic. You wouldn't want to explore what such a gift could mean for you, what *he* could mean to you."

My cheeks flamed. Everything I felt for him, the heat, the tension, the hunger to be close to him, the jealousy, the burning...

The *wanting*.

It was because we were soulmates.

Was any of it real? Would we feel so hungry for each other if we hadn't been bound?

My skin tingled as my muscles grew tense. "Why would Bastile do this to me?"

"Do *what* to you?" Gideon hissed.

"Punish me."

The dyad had to be a punishment for what my father had done to Empyrean. But didn't Bastile see that I wanted to divert from my father's ways, that I wanted to restore Empyrean to the god's vision?

He raked a hand through his hair. "Is being bound to me so awful you would regard it as a *punishment*?"

"Yes," I shrieked, voice cracking. "Because now I'm tied to you in a way I never wanted to be tied to anyone."

Now I would *never* be free of the wanting.

He gaped at me with such bitterness that his ocean blue eyes shifted into a murky gray. Even when disappointed, he was beautiful. "You think so little of me that you believe I would force you to be mine? That I would cage you?"

I bit my lip, unsure what to say. I read books and watched movies. I witnessed the cages that feelings brought—the self-imposed prisons. Feelings changed people. They allowed betrayal and heartache and made things messy.

When I didn't respond, he clenched his jaw and left the room. I sank into the chaise next to where he left his worn leather jacket and its scent of citrus and spice. My chest tightened.

Silence swelled between Mistress Marjorie and me. She had something to say—some warning for me to heed or a lesson to learn.

"Having a soulmate isn't a punishment," she said at last. "You may not see it now, but Gideon was a gift to you from Bastile."

"A gift? A new pair of shoes is a gift—not another *human being*."

"He isn't required to love you, nor are you required to be anything to him that you don't want to be. Bastile simply gifted you the chance to have happiness, to fall in love and let go of your reservations so you can live freely alongside someone who will always have your best interests at heart."

I couldn't bear to hear any more about my *happiness* or my *best interests*.

Not when the Realm of the Forsaken was holding Mason prisoner.

"We need to rescue Mason," I blurted out.

She didn't seem surprised by my abrupt change in subject. "Your first reaction anytime someone is taken cannot be to rush to their aid. If you keep reacting like that, you'll be dead before you have a chance to inherit the throne."

I worried my lip. There wouldn't be a throne for me to inherit if my father got his way... Who knew how long I'd have until he extradited the succession change after my outburst during today's meeting? It definitely didn't err in my favor or prove that I was less bloodthirsty than the king. The only three people who would've been on my side before I assaulted Gideon were all very firmly on Team Gideon—Aurick, Malachi, and Royston.

I needed to swallow my pride and apologize for lashing out. Especially to Gideon. The things I said and did were awful. But how could I explain that *he* wasn't a punishment... the feelings were? How could I let him in and expect the Realm of the Forsaken not to come for him, too?

Something inside me stirred, recoiling from the image of him hurting.

The dagger necklace was cool against my skin, reminding me that even if my thoughts were a tangled mess, they were mine and mine alone.

I rubbed the back of my neck. "Then what do you suggest I do? Leave Mason there?"

She pulled a book from the middle of a shelf and cracked it open. The pages stuck together as she flipped through them. "You wait until Cayden tries to make contact again."

"They'll kill Mason if we don't leave immediately."

"Don't be foolish." She snapped the book shut and slipped it back onto the shelf. "Mason's their bargaining chip."

"How can you be so sure they won't kill him?" I shuddered. "In case you've forgotten, Cayden threatened to send me Mason's body parts."

"So many questions!" She threw her hands up in exasperation; the candles illuminating the room flickered in response. "I know you well enough to know you're going to do whatever you want to. You always have. I'm here to warn you against it. As I always have."

I stomped toward the bed. Feathers in the duvet crinkled when I flung myself onto it, burying my face into a throw pillow to scream. If we reversed the roles, Mason would come for me. He *tried*. His stupid attempt to solicit a demon for information was what got us into this mess.

He had always been there for me. When the bullies in middle school mocked me for my eye color and when boys wouldn't quit snapping my bra straps, he defended me, even if his hands shook and his voice quivered, even if it ended with him outcast alongside me or sent home with an ice pack on his eye.

"Little one, I know you're frustrated." She pulled the pink flower-shaped pillow away from my face. "We'll go for him when we're in control of the demands."

"You're going to help me?" I sat up and folded my knees under me. "You don't have other *things* to take care of?"

"I'm sorry I hurt your feelings with what I said." She cupped my bruised cheek with a frigid hand. "You must know I never considered you a burden. You were never a *thing* I had to care for."

As those words spilled from her lips, more tears sprung from my eyes. Margie and Mason were all I had, and now, the Realm of the Forsaken was punishing him for being my friend.

Whether she admitted it or not, this *was* my fault. Caring for Mason had put him in danger. Just like caring for Gideon would put him in danger. My heart seized. I... I couldn't risk him, too.

I couldn't risk Malachi's wrath or Sabel's tears. I couldn't be the reason Gideon's father outlived his son. Tethering Gideon to my soul put a target on his back. And if I let him in... if I let him consume me the way I wanted to consume him, I would never recover from that loss.

Losing him would break me, leaving me with half a soul.

And somehow, that was scarier than being alone.

If Mason were here, he'd call me on my bullshit. He'd tell me I was being overdramatic, that I could draw on the strength of others, and I didn't have to go at everything alone. That life... life wasn't a burden to shoulder without friends or family.

But he wasn't here.

The Realm of the Forsaken took him because they knew it would hurt me. And there was nothing I could do about it but *wait*. I was just a powerless, mortal-raised girl with a heart that was becoming heavier by the minute.

CHAPTER 16

Days passed without another message from Cayden. Or Gideon. Or Margie, who was off doing gods knew what to try and figure out why my father had the castle warded against her. The only person aside from my handmaidens that I had spent any time with was my stepmother.

Growing bored of listening to Lirabeth drone on about the ball she was throwing as her last hurrah before the baby came and staring at the same four walls for hours on end, I convinced my handmaidens to send word to Sabel that I'd like to stop by for a visit.

My father gave me clearance to visit Sabel's home in the Pry under one condition—Malachi was to come as my guard. I wasn't opposed to the thought, hoping it'd give me a chance to apologize to him, but every time I tried, he ignored me. He was mad, incredibly mad. Rightfully so. But still... it sucked.

Sabel folded her hands onto her lap. "Brini will be down shortly."

We sat across from each other on two high-backed velvet couches in the prettiest shade of sapphire. Her parents' mansion was bigger than any house I'd ever seen in Oakwood, and it glistened in shades of silver and vibrant jewel tones, all complementing the pure white quartz floors. Four floor-to-ceiling windows on the southern wall cast sunlight through the sheer, white curtains that overlooked an orchard of apple trees. They reminded me of Mason and the afternoons we'd spent picking apples for his mother in the fall.

My stomach sank. I hoped he was all right. I had tried using a spell Mistress Marjorie taught me to send a fire message to the Realm of the Forsaken, but the letter shriveled up into nothing but cinders. Likely because I was missing two key ingredients—parchment washed in rainwater, left out to dry under a waxing moon, and crushed elderberries for the ink. Ugh.

Attempting to distract myself, I gestured to a grand piano in the corner of the sitting room. "Do you play?"

Sabel took a sip of her warm tea. She frowned as she said, "Forgive me, Your Grace, but I'm not keen to make small talk with you."

Out of the corner of my eye, Malachi's jaw twitched.

I deserved this treatment after what I had done to Gideon—hurting him and telling him *he* was a punishment. I didn't have to wonder how much he told Sabel about what happened—the tension in her shoulders, the way her bright green eyes turned icy when they met mine, her innate desire to ignore me told me she knew. She knew everything.

"That's fair," I whispered. I hated that I may have sabotaged our friendship before it even blossomed. "How is he?"

I hadn't seen or heard from Gideon since the day we found out we were soulmates. His mental wall was up, and the bond had been cold, distant, and angry with me. As if Bastile himself was pissed off at me, too.

She pursed her lips as if she was considering how much she should tell me. "He—"

Brini bounded into the room and rushed toward me, throwing her arms around my neck. Her pretty brown eyes were shining, and her skin was glowing. She had her dark hair tied back in a braided crown around her head, and she was wearing a cute, frilly dress in the softest shade of pink. The skin was less taut across her face, and she felt heavier than she did before—no longer bony and sharp.

"Well, hello there," I said with a giggle.

Brini beamed. "Thank you for coming to visit me, princess."

"I'm sorry I couldn't come sooner." I patted the seat next to me. She sat and folded her legs underneath her.

"Brini, we've talked about sitting like a lady," Sabel chided, her pale cheeks turning the color of peonies in springtime as her eyes darted between the two of us.

Mirroring Brini's position, I tucked my legs under my dress. "Oh, ease up, Sabel. There shouldn't be constraints on how women sit."

Brini smoothed out her dress. "I can't believe I'm sitting like a not-lady with the *princess*."

I winked. "It'll be our little secret."

"You shouldn't encourage this behavior, Your Grace."

"Why?" I glanced around us. "It's just us... and Malachi. Aren't you tired of being so proper?"

Sabel sighed, her brows drawing together. "It's all I know."

"Then I declare today we'll have the most improper afternoon."

Brini shouted, "This is going to be the best day ever!"

Her sheer excitement brought a smile to Sabel's coral lips as she kicked off her shoes and folded her legs under her. She fidgeted for a moment before she admitted, "Sitting like this *is* loads more comfortable."

"What else is considered improper?"

A mischievous grin split Brini's face in two. "Swearing."

Sabel's eyes went wide. "Brini, no."

"Brini, *yes*." I laughed, knowing it was ridiculous to encourage a child to cuss. But if it brought a smile to her little face, if it eased her grief, then it was worth it. "What's one swear word you've always wanted to say, but you were too afraid?"

Brini looked between us, her eyes flashing to Malachi, before she whispered, "Shit."

I gasped in mock shock before laughing right along with everyone else.

We spent the next half an hour cursing back and forth before we set off to do a handful of other improper things: speaking with our mouths full of candies and cakes, stripping from our dresses into our underclothes (to which Malachi gave a somewhat disapproving grunt as he fixed his gaze on the painting hanging above the mantel), and dancing like madwomen to whatever upbeat tunes Sabel could muster on the piano. She was *terrible* at playing, but it got the job done. If we had a fire in the center of the sitting room, I would have imagined we were witches celebrating a full moon.

At the end of our dance party, Brini and I collapsed to the floor, breathing heavily with flushed cheeks. She hid her face behind her hands, shoulders trembling. Sabel darted toward her and kneeled, trying to peel her hands away from her face. She didn't want us to see her crying.

I understood that better than anyone. "Leave her be."

Sabel frowned, grabbing her silky violet dress from the piano bench and slipping it on. She cast one more look at Brini before leaving the room.

I pulled the child into my lap and rubbed her hair until she took a deep, stuttered breath.

Her hands fell from her face as fresh tears poured down her cheeks. "I'm sorry, princess," she cried. "I was having so much fun, and I couldn't help but think about Mama and Papa and how they would've laughed at us being so silly."

"Shh," I murmured, thinking of the words Gideon whispered to me in the mausoleum. The only words that made any sense of my pain. "A friend of mine once told me that even in death, no one is really gone. The ones we lose are kept safe in our hearts until we can meet them again in the Half-Light. Your parents... They'd want you to live your life and to be happy, Brini."

"Do you still miss your mama?"

"I was a baby when she... died. So, I didn't know her, but I used to make up stories about her and the things she liked when I was little. It helped me feel close to her. It didn't make the hurting any less painful, but thinking of her helps me keep her alive in here"—I tapped my heart—"and that's where she'll stay until I meet her in the Half-Light."

She wiped at her face with both of her hands. "Do you think Mama and Papa made it to the Half-Light?"

"I have no doubt they're feasting alongside Bastile and telling him all about how much of a troublemaker their little *shit* is."

"Hey!" She giggled. "I'm *not* a little shit."

I rolled my eyes, poking her. "Sure, you aren't."

"Thank you for coming to visit me. Lady Sabel said you're very busy doing princess things."

I snorted, and Malachi cut me a look as Sabel came back into the room, calling for Brini. "It's time for supper."

She maneuvered out of my lap and into her dress before hugging me again. "I think my parents would've liked you, princess."

They're the only ones, I thought to myself.

She released me and tore out of the room, leaving me sitting on the floor. A moment passed before I stood. Grabbing my dress from the sofa, I slipped it on, thankful that it was a simple, mauve gown with capped sleeves, an empire waist and layered tulle. During the days I spent with Lirabeth, I complained (a lot) about the monstrosities my father forced me to wear. This morning, I awoke to this gown and a note from my stepmother that read, "I'm grateful for your company this past week, my dearest Valeria."

Lirabeth may be as vapid as they came, but at least she was *trying* to be nice.

Sabel smiled at Malachi. "Will you wait outside? I'll help the princess lace up her dress."

He looked between the two of us but focused on her. "Don't do anything stupid."

She crossed her heart, and he headed for the door, shutting it quietly.

"Gideon told me everything." She tugged the back of my dress together. "He told me about the jealousy, the kiss, the fact that you're soulmates. All of it."

Guilt gnawed at my insides. "I don't have any intention of breaking you two up."

"You didn't believe him when he told you our engagement was a sham?" Her hands stilled momentarily before starting back up. Another forceful tug. I could barely breathe. "He wasn't lying to you, Your Grace."

"You can call me Valeria, Sabel." I paused, taking as deep of a breath as I could before adding, "Because friends use each other's names, not titles."

She gave the dress a final tug. "Gideon wasn't lying to you, *Valeria*. We're nothing more than friends."

"But why?" I turned around to face her.

"Because King Ward has made it a mandatory requirement to have a certain wealth ranking to serve on the King's Council." She ground her teeth together. "Aurick was appointed to the council by Bastile, so the king couldn't forcibly remove him. But for Gideon to replace Aurick, he needs to meet the newly instated conditions. The Lythewoods rejected the idea of *corones,* while my parents leaped at the chance to seize wealth and power. So while the Lythewoods became commoners, the Keoghs became rich. Marrying me would raise Gideon's station enough to qualify for the position."

I pressed my hand against my mouth, remembering the day in the market when I asked Gideon whether he was a prying bastard or a commoner and he said he was a bit of both.

My father was buying spots on the council and filling them with members he could control and manipulate. Members who would vote the way he told them to vote. Members who would help him get rid of my claim to the throne.

My chest squeezed. "Sabel, I had no idea."

"Gideon is a good friend of mine. And if you asked me two weeks ago if I would follow him blindly to the edge of the realm, I would've said yes without hesitation. But now..."

"Now what?"

"I'm not sure." She sighed. "I've never seen him like this before. He's not thinking with his head anymore. He's thinking with his heart. He's thinking with *you* in mind, not the realm."

"You're ridiculous. Gideon and I aren't even on speaking terms right now."

She leveled her gaze on me. "No, *you're* ridiculous. Maybe it's because I've known Gideon since we were children, but he was always focused on what was best for Empyrean. And now... now, he talks about the realm like he'd burn it to the ground and start it anew for *you*."

"What are you talking about?" I asked, my mind spinning.

Someone could misconstrue her words as treason... she spoke as if he was planning something that would undo everything my father had done, but what could he be plotting?

Something fluttered deep in my belly. The idea that he could be contemplating treason *excited* me. Gods, I was such a fucking mess.

"I can't tell you anything more." She folded her arms across her chest. "Just know that your unnecessary anger and resentment blind you to who he is and what he stands for. Gideon is... good." She let the words sink in before softly adding, "Maybe too good for you."

MALACHI SHADOWED ME as I walked through the castle. The way back was quick and quiet; like earlier, we didn't speak. But I didn't mind it as much since I was too wrapped up thinking about my conversation with Sabel.

She spoke about Gideon the same way Malachi regarded him—with love and admiration. The other day Malachi said they needed me for something, but *what*... what were the three of them planning that they would need help from a princess with no power?

Not wanting to return to my room, my feet carried me through the halls and into a garden where a familiar face sat alone.

The only sound Malachi made was a slight curse when I stopped in front of Gideon. He was sitting on a patch of lush grass surrounded by burgundy poppies, so dark they could pass for black, and silver hyacinths, with his long, muscular legs stretched out in front of him and a book propped in his lap. A half-eaten orange was forgotten on a cloth napkin beside him.

I found myself watching him—at the way his muscles tensed as I approached, the full curve of his lips as he frowned, and the shadow of fading bruises on his throat left by my hands. His golden hair was messy, like he couldn't stop running his hands through it the way I had in the mausoleum. I thought about that kiss often, mostly late at night with my hand between my legs. He was unimaginably handsome, and somehow, Bastile plucked him from the crowd and wove our souls into one.

I could've had it worse.

"Gideon," I said softly, standing in front of him. I felt bare and exposed, vulnerable with the knowledge of what I needed to do and what I needed to say. He looked up at me, blue eyes flashing as if he was replaying the last time we spoke—the day I called him a punishment. I hated to admit a small part of me missed having him around. Even if he was irritating most of the time. I pointed to the spot next to him. "May... may I sit?"

"You may." His gaze drifted to his friend. "Leave us, Malachi. I'll see the princess back to her rooms."

Malachi huffed and stomped out of the garden.

Slipping free of my heels, the soft grass pricked my bare feet. I sat, drawing my knees to my chest and wrapping my arms around them. "I'm... I'm sorry about hurting you."

"Which time?"

"Every time." I released a breath. "I freaked out about Mason and the soulmates thing. It... was a lot to process, and I didn't handle it in the best way."

He snapped the book shut. "You act like it's only your life impacted by the dyad."

"I know." I stretched my legs out, fiddling with a piece of tulle on my gown. "I'm selfish and violent and just like my father."

His thumb and index finger found my chin and turned my face toward him. "Don't ever compare yourself to him."

The touch sparked against my skin. His familiar scent—citrus, spice, and winter fire—blended so perfectly with the fragrances in the garden.

My eyes searched his. "Will you forgive me?"

Against my better judgment, I craved his forgiveness. I needed to know I didn't fuck everything up, that we still had a chance to be... friends... or something. It still scared me to even think of becoming anything more, but Bastile chose Gideon for me for a reason. And if I couldn't trust the only god I had faith in, who *could* I trust?

He cupped my cheek and leaned in, his lips gently brushing mine. I closed my eyes, expecting more, expecting to be devoured by the intensity he laid upon me before, but it didn't come. My lashes fluttered open to find him studying me, yet to give me a concrete answer.

Holding his gaze, I teased, "If the only way to earn your forgiveness for all that I've said and done is through kissing, I think we'll be here all night."

"Would you like that?" He twirled a strand of my hair around his finger. "To spend all night with me?"

"Depends on what you have planned."

A grin crept across his face. "Kissing, of course." He ran a finger down my cheek, neck, and over the rise and fall of my breasts. "Touching." He fisted his hand in my hair, tilting my head back. "Pulling." He brought his mouth to my shoulder and bit down, lightly. "Biting." He crushed his lips against mine, tongue demanding entrance, and I gave it freely. He broke the kiss, panting. "Tasting." He pushed me backward until my back was flush with the ground. Hovering over me, one hand slid up my dress and gripped my thigh. I arched into his touch, my body tingling. "Teasing." A heat burned low in my belly. My legs wrapped around his waist as he ground his hips against my core. "Pounding."

The length of him strained against his training leathers. His eyes met mine in a challenge, and it took everything in me not to reach up and trace the curve of his lips and the line of his jaw. I resisted the urge to lean forward and kiss the bruises I left on his skin.

He brought his mouth to my ear, his breath hot on my neck. "You said being bound to me was a punishment." He ground into me again and the friction against my center was enough to set my skin on fire. "It could be, but only in ways that brought you pleasure."

We stared at each other for a long moment before he rolled off of me and propped himself up on one elbow. "So tell me, princess. Do you want to spend all night with me?"

Sitting up, my heart pounded in my chest as he watched me, waiting for an answer. Did I want to spend all night with him? Gods, yes. He essentially told me he'd give me the fuck of my life if I did. But that was part of the problem. Obviously, there was a burning between us that had led to an insatiable wanting, and that scared me. To want him so badly that nothing else mattered.

Maybe... maybe I should be honest with him.

"Yes," I breathed. "Yes, I want to spend all night with you. I want *you* and that... scares me."

He sat up. "You're afraid of me?" I nodded, and he frowned. "Whatever for?"

"Because you make me feel things I haven't felt for anyone else, and I hate it." I pulled a handful of grass from the ground and let the blades slip through my fingers. "I hate *feelings*. They always render someone powerless in the dynamic, and I'm powerless enough as it is. I can't risk you having that kind of power over me. And I definitely can't risk someone else knowing what you are to me and then use that against me, like the Realm of the Forsaken is doing with Mason."

"And *what* am I to you?"

"My soulmate." My eyes met his, vulnerably and honestly. "An annoying, incredibly handsome *gift* that I'm stupidly attracted to."

He laughed and wrapped an arm around me, pulling me close. I rested my head on his shoulder. "You can ask anyone who knows me, and they'll tell you that you hold all the power when it comes to what we are. You are the one who decides if we are friends or lovers or something else entirely. Wherever you lead, I'll follow."

My heart lurched as a grin spread across my lips. "We'll see about that."

CHAPTER 17

M oths fluttered around the flames illuminating the alley behind the castle while stars glittered in the night sky like a fistful of diamonds tossed into the Void. The first time I ever snuck out was to warm Mason's bed and satisfy my own needs with desperate touches and bruising kisses.

Sometimes I wondered if Margie had lowered her wards to grant me that tiny moment of typical teenage rebellion because it was far easier sneaking out of our hidden house than it was to slip out of the castle without anyone realizing I was gone.

But somehow the plan I came up with worked.

Bex *forgot* to lock my door when she left my chambers for the evening, and Gideon met me upstairs with a pair of riding leathers, an oversized cotton shirt, and a thick, black cloak to hide my identity. I didn't want to know where he found pants in my size on such short notice, but something told me he had connections in Empyrean beyond my wildest imagination.

The clip-clop of hooves on cobblestone signaled Malachi's arrival in the alley with a similar carriage to the one that brought me to the castle a couple of weeks ago. This time, the driver tipped his hat to me. I waved in return.

Tonight we were going to feed the hungry.

As quietly as possible, we piled food and several barrels of water and wine onto the large wooden trailer hitched to the back. My arms screamed in agony by the time I carried the last basket of fruit to the stash. We didn't take all of the food from the castle's kitchen, considering it might make Lirabeth's perfect head explode, but we took enough that tomorrow's ball would be underserved.

In the dark of the carriage, the three of us were silent, holding our breath until we passed through the castle gates and onto the winding road that led to the Commons.

Gideon's hand found my bouncing knee, the heat from his palm seeping through my leathers. I stiffened, expecting the dread to hit me the way it would when Mason did the same thing. Instead, my skin felt like a live wire dancing on an empty street after a horrible storm—free and exposed.

"So, you two made up," Malachi said quietly. "Big surprise."

"Want an even bigger surprise?" The words rushed out before he could stop me. "Malachi, I'm sorry for what I said and did at the King's Council meeting and after. I was freaking out about Mason, and I directed my anger at the wrong person." My mouth twisted to the side before I added softly, "That doesn't excuse my behavior, though. I really am sorry."

He was quiet for a moment. "You are undoubtedly the worst person I've ever seen at managing their feelings—"

"That's probably because I'm so good at literally everything else," I cut in with a shit-eating grin.

Gideon laughed. "She has a point there."

Malachi shifted forward, his knees bumping mine. "I forgive you, but it will take some time for me to trust you."

"I understand," I whispered. "Take all the time you need. I'm not going anywhere."

The carriage carried us further and further away from the castle and closer to the Commons. The journey wasn't as long as I thought it would be, and after a few more minutes, we came to a stop.

Gideon plucked me from the carriage like a doll from a toybox.

Following the guys, my breath caught in my throat as a cloud of stench hit me, snaking up my nose. Garbage littered the ground. Gagging, I pulled my shirt over my face and breathed in the scent of citrus and winter spice. It must be one of Gideon's. I snuggled into it.

We stood before the slums of Seraphicity, where hundreds of filthy and overcrowded homes were stacked on top of each other in a manner that made my stomach churn. It was a fucking housing crisis.

The homes were unstable, weak structures that could blow away with a heavy wind, gaping holes punched into the roofing like paper, and there was a lack of toiletry, judging by the puddles of urine and piles of feces.

Malachi groaned. "How are we going to disperse all of this?"

"I didn't think that far ahead," I said.

He glanced between the food and the Commons. "Going door to door will take hours."

Gideon stretched. "I've got the time."

The guys bickered in hushed tones, trying to find an efficient solution that didn't waste time. Every minute I wasn't locked in my room was a minute we didn't have to spare.

"Malachi, you take the houses to the left." I pointed to the row of homes that curved up a mountainside. "Gideon and I will take the ones to the right. We'll rally the people to grab their share and ask them to tell others. It shouldn't take as long with their help."

Malachi tied his hair back. "What if no one answers?"

"Knock harder?"

Gideon lifted my hood, concealing my face. "Keep your identity hidden. We can't risk your father finding out you were involved with this."

"What about you and Malachi?"

He grinned. "Don't worry about us. We do this kind of stuff all the time."

My eyebrows lifted. They helped feed the people in the Commons *all the time*? The brand buzzed as if it was saying, *See. He's not all bad.*

Gideon unwound one of the leather pouches fastened to his waist and tossed it to Malachi who caught it with ease.

"What's that?" I asked.

"Salt," Malachi said. "Just in case we run into trouble."

I sucked in a breath. "You guys think... there are specters *here*?"

Gideon frowned. "We can never be too careful."

We ventured off on our separate paths, going from door to door, rousing people from their homes.

Anger nestled inside me as we approached house after house with broken windows and ramshackle roofs. Each face that greeted us was sunken in and tired, hungry and broken. And yet, they thanked us repeatedly while slipping on torn and ragged clothes that did nothing to protect them against the chill in the air. Feeding these people was just the beginning. I'd have to find a way to completely dismantle the Commons and renovate it into something safer, warmer, and healthier.

Bitter indignation wrapped its hands around my heart and squeezed.

"Don't worry." Gideon touched my arm, tugging me from my thoughts. "Things will be better when you reign."

My concern must have slipped through the bond. I hadn't put up a mental fortress in days since he had been ignoring me.

"If I reign," I corrected him, lowering my voice. "My father wants to change the line of succession, remember?"

He glanced around and pulled me into a vacant alleyway that stunk worse than anything I'd ever smelled before. We side-stepped several piles of something slick and slimy. "There's something I need to tell you."

"And it has to be in this disgusting alley because...?" He shoved his hands into his pockets. I pushed the hood from my head and stared up into his stormy blue eyes. "What's wrong?"

"I don't think there will ever be a good time to tell you what I'm about to, and I'll understand if you want to turn and run the other way, but there's something... something you need to know."

Goosebumps spread along my arms. "What is it?"

"There's a rebellion on the horizon, Valeria."

I sucked in a breath, and my knees went weak.

A rebellion. Against the king.

Against my father.

The tether between us went quiet, waiting for me to process what he had revealed.

A tiny sliver of me wondered if this was a test to see how deep my hatred for my father ran.

I grabbed him by the shoulders and shook him. "Have you lost your damn mind? My father will have you *killed* for saying, for even thinking, such things."

"I would be one of many willing to die to put you on the throne."

"Gideon—"

"No. Listen to me." He stepped out of my grip. "You've seen it firsthand, princess. Our people are dying. Empyrean is not what it was when Bastile reigned. I've seen the way you react to these injustices. I've *heard* some of the thoughts you've had about ruling. You want to do *something*."

I did want to do something, but not something that would get me or anyone else [J6] killed.

Mistress Marjorie's words came echoing back to me. *What are you truly willing to risk to belong in Empyrean? Your life? Would you face the same fate as your mother if it meant sitting on the throne and being adored by your people?*

"No, this is treason." My back straightened. "Gideon, stop talking like this."

"You said it yourself at the King's Council meeting. Your father drove Empyrean into a pit of despair, and he's diverted from Bastile's path. We believe you're our saving grace."

"Saving grace?" I snorted. "I'm not a hero, Gideon. I have no power. I have *nothing*. I *am* nothing."

"That's not what we think."

"You keep saying 'we.' Are you part of the rebellion?"

"Part of it?" He chuckled. "Princess, I *am* the rebellion. I'm the one who sparked the fire. A commoner turned prying bastard, an insider of both worlds. Our numbers have grown because of me, and they'll keep growing once people see that you're different from your father."

Blinking, I replayed every conversation of Gideon's I had overheard. Malachi said they needed me for *something*, but I didn't hear what, and Sabel said Gideon spoke as if he wanted to burn the realm down for *me*.

Gideon had started a rebellion against the king.

A deep, shaky breath rattled my ribs. "This is madness."

"What will you do now that you know? Will you condemn me to my death by ratting me out?"

Shoving him away from me, I snapped, "Is this your way of gauging how loyal I am to you? What's next? Blackmail? Either I help you with this rebellion, or *you* turn *me* over to the king?"

He closed the distance between us until my back was flush with the wall. Heat shot straight to my toes as his scent swirled around me. "I swear on my mother's grave that I'm telling you about the rebellion because you deserve to know. You deserve to have a choice in the part you play."

My heart thundered in my chest. This wasn't happening. No wonder he was so quick to help with my plan tonight. He must have seen it as my way to rebel against the crown... and it was. But delivering food wasn't the same as seizing a throne.

He cupped my face with both of his hands. "Our people can't keep going like this. They're starving and living worse than animals. Malachi fears disease might ravage Seraphicity if we don't do something."

So, Malachi was part of the rebellion, too. My father's greatest warrior was a traitor to the crown, ready to replace him with me. He was probably so upset by my outburst toward Gideon because he thought I was as violent as the king he loathed. My throat was dry and itchy. I'd felt my father's violence firsthand and witnessed his destruction. More children like Brini would starve in the streets, orphaned, if someone didn't *do* something. But what he was asking, what he wanted me to become, was... nefarious.

He was asking me to break divine law.

My father was a monster who didn't care about me, my mother, or the Empyrean people. Would it be all that bad if we freed Empyrean from his rule? Would Bastile regret bonding me to Gideon, or did he somehow know about the rebellion? Was our dyad further proof that I should join them? Mistress Marjorie said the dyad meant Gideon would always have my best interests at heart, but did an uprising fall into the Best Interests category?

I chewed my bottom lip. "I—"

Something moved in the corner of my eye and Gideon tensed as he saw it, too. We both turned to see who it was that may have overheard us.

Not a who.

A *what*.

Ripped at the edges, a fragmented soul, half here, half gone, hovered a couple feet above the ground not more than a stone's throw away from us as if she was eavesdropping. Or waiting for the perfect opportunity to strike.

The hairs on the back of my neck lifted in fear, in sorrow, for this person who was no longer a person.

A specter.

Gideon pushed away from me, completely blocking me from view. I peered around him as his hand reached for the pouch dangling from his waist just as the specter's empty eyes locked onto both of our movements.

She opened her mouth in a blood-chilling scream and lunged.

Boney hands clutched his broad shoulders, fingers digging through the fabric of his shirt. Gideon cried out and dropped the pouch as he tried to push the specter away.

But his hands slipped right through.

Half here, half gone.

She could touch him, *harm* him, but only salt and fire could harm her.

"Gideon!" I screamed his name, drawing another vicious howl from her before she lifted him and threw him into the wall, the back of his head hitting stone with a sickening *crack*. He slumped forward, chin to his chest. "Gideon!"

Every piece of me wanted to rush to his side, but I remained rooted in place, feeling through the tether for his heartbeat, for confirmation that he was alive.

His steady pulse coursed through the brand. My knees almost buckled in relief.

The specter focused her eerie gaze on me.

"Stay where you are," I hissed, searching for a way to stop her, to free her.

She approached me slowly, methodically. All bones and anger and rot.

I inched backward, nearly tripping over debris and gods knew what else. Holding my hands in front of me, I whispered, "I don't want to hurt you. Let me help you."

She halted.

My eyes darted toward the pouch of salt that Gideon had dropped, only two steps away. I could make it to it if I kept her distracted, kept her placated.

"My name is Valeria. I'm the lost princess." I waited for any sign of recognition she was listening. She gave none. "If you let me, I will free you from this pain."

The promise was soft, truthful.

The specter remained where she was, hovering in place, as if she was thinking, calculating, deciding.

I took another step toward the pouch.

Gideon stirred, his hand reaching for the back of his head, as a hiss slipped through his lips. His eyes flicked wildly between the spirit and me, a small *v* between his brows. *Valeria, whatever you're thinking, don't. They can't be reasoned with. They—*

"Show me where your body is," I said gently. "And I will release you."

She cocked her head to the side, stretching the sinew that held her together.

Who was she before she became this gruesome half-version of herself? A mother? A sister? A friend?

A final step. I bent and picked up the pouch. "Do you know what this is?"

Her head remained angled, but I saw a brief, almost imperceptible shake. She understood me. Even in death, the specters were aware. My chest squeezed painfully, rage and sorrow warring for control.

"It's salt. It's very painful for... people like you," I murmured. "I don't want to hurt you. I really don't. So, will you let me help you? Will you show me where your body is?"

A moment passed. She lifted one boney hand and pointed behind me.

I glanced over my shoulder. "You died here?"

A tight nod, a strangled sound, and then she zoomed past me in a rush of death and despair, stopping abruptly several feet down the alley.

Do you have anything to burn her body? I asked Gideon through the bond.

He tapped his pants pocket. *Always.*

A pang ricocheted through my chest. How many specters had he come face to face with? How many fractured souls had he had to release from these filthy streets?

Valeria, let me do it, he said with a gentle caress down the tether. *You shouldn't have—*

No. I glanced at the waiting spirit, finger outstretched toward her corpse. *It must be me.*

He didn't argue or try to convince me otherwise. He simply nodded and removed a flask from his pocket along with a pack of matches. I took them from him quickly and moved toward where the specter waited.

Light from the moon illuminated her corpse like a spotlight on a stage. Propped up against a rough stone wall and surrounded by filth was where she took her last breath, where she lay forgotten. A disturbing mess of bone and sinew and the muted weather-worn wardrobe of who she once was—a starving commoner.

After a deep, shaky breath, I unscrewed the lid to the flask and dumped the liquid on her corpse before dropping the flask altogether. Its smell faintly reminded me of vodka. Tears burned my eyes as I struck the match and dropped it. Both the corpse and the specter ignited in a rush of vibrant flames that cast dancing shadows along the stone wall, and it took everything in me not to focus on them instead of her.

"I wish I knew your name," I whispered as I watched her body burn.

The specter turned to me, something like a soft smile curving across her horrific face as the ripped ghastly edges of her form faded into the balmy night air. A breeze brushed past me, ruffling wisps of honey hair and carrying her name like the rustle of leaves on a crisp, autumn afternoon.

Rosalyn.

A sob lodged in my throat. "May Bastile grant you peace in the Half-Light, Rosalyn."

Gideon came up beside me, wrapping one arm around my waist and tugging me close. My head found his shoulder, and we stood there unspeaking until the flames burned out, Rosalyn's bones were charred black, and her spirit was free.

"How many?" I asked, finally breaking the silence. "How many specters have you faced and freed?"

He unsheathed his dagger and picked the flask up from where I had dropped it. Carefully, he carved a short, thin line diagonally across four others. There were row after row of similar markings.

"Dozens," he sighed, defeated. "Listen, about earlier... I didn't mean to spring the rebellion on you. And I don't want you to feel pressured into leading it, but this"—he ran his thumb over the markings on the flask, jaw clenching—"is only a fraction of how many we've lost since your father became king."

"I need time to think about this, about what you're asking me to do."

He slipped the flask into his pocket and pulled the hood back over my face. "Take all the time you need."

We left the alley without another word, the smell of smoke and char and the acidic stench of ammonia followed us, clung to us, as we continued going door to door. The tether between us pulled tight, cold and nervous, as if my decision could make or break whatever fragile understanding we had.

My temples thumped to the beat of my racing heart. How did I end up in this position? Needing to make a decision that could change my life... or end it.

What was I supposed to do? Just follow my gut?

I was guilty of fantasizing about ruling Empyrean and restoring it to Bastile's vision. Since the first day I stepped foot in Empyrean, I'd dreamt of treason, but hearing the words aloud, spoken from lips laced with temptation, was different.

It made it real. And it made the consequences unspeakable.

AN HOUR AND A HALF later, we knocked on the last door and walked back to the carriage.

My mind was still spiraling. If I joined Gideon, if I contributed to the rebellion, I would be putting my full trust in him, and I didn't know if I was ready for that. I didn't know if I was ready to be a queen, either.

A crowd of people swarmed the trailer, laughing with arms filled to the brim with fruits and cured meats. Some sipped water out of their hands with tears streaming down their sharp, dirt-ridden cheeks. I rubbed a hand over the ache in my chest. These people had nothing and were treated like nothing because of my father.

And more of them would meet a fate just like Rosalyn if things didn't change.

Malachi slid into place behind us, clapping a hand on Gideon's shoulder. Gideon winced. We watched as the people of the Commons took their helpings, nothing more than they could carry, and rejoiced for something as simple as a bite of bread.

"You should say something before they grow suspicious," Malachi said to Gideon.

Gideon flashed me a grin that didn't quite meet his eyes, fixing my hood once more before climbing on top of the carriage. The wood creaked under his weight as he stood up, towering over all of us.

A tiny voice in the back of my head whispered *you should be up there.* Maybe this was the moment where I could choose to be something greater than myself, something more to these people. But, of course, I froze.

"Enjoy your food, my friends." Gideon's voice rang out, and the people watched him with grateful smiles. "Change is coming, and it's up to us to decide when and how that change manifests."

"You lie," a raspy voice croaked. I followed the sound to find an older woman glaring at him. She was a living skeleton with skin pulled tight over her frame. "You are a messenger sent by King Ward to spread false gospel, to keep us content with scraps."

"There's no gospel, Cas. You know me. I'm one of you."

Her words riled the crowd as they pushed against one another, screaming obscenities about the king. Gideon locked eyes with Malachi, a silent message passing between them just as Malachi looped a hand around my waist and dragged me toward the carriage.

The people of the Commons began to threaten Gideon. Anger flared within me. He did nothing wrong, and they turned on him.

The same way I did days ago.

Without thinking, I wrenched myself free of Malachi's grip and climbed onto the carriage, ripping my hood off.

"Many of you know me only as the lost princess." My voice carried on the breeze, while a hush grew over the crowd as they took me in. "But I'm not lost anymore. I'm here, in the flesh, and I'm devastated to see what has become of Empyrean. You *know* that Gideon is not to blame for this. Direct your anger at the one person in this realm who warrants it."

"And who would that be?" Cas shouted.

This was it. The moment where I needed to choose—remain a powerless princess or become something more. I could tell myself I didn't want the responsibility and I didn't want the throne, but I did. I wanted *power*—to save Mason, to fix Empyrean, to free Gideon from his engagement, to provide for Brini, to get my revenge on Cayden.

I wanted it all.

A smile spread across my lips. "The king."

CHAPTER 18

Lirabeth's screams rattled through the castle the next day when she learned over half the food prepared for tonight's masquerade ball had gone missing. She laid into the kitchen staff, which I felt guilty about, but they couldn't give her any explanation as to where the food went.

It was there when the kitchen shut down for the night, and then, it wasn't.

As Mae styled my hair and did my makeup, she fed me all the juicy gossip on who the servants thought took the food, not once mentioning the guys or me. But every time my eyes met Bex's in the mirror, she gave me a knowing look and a flash of a smirk. Gideon had asked her to leave my door unlocked. She had to know it was us. But she didn't snitch, which made me wonder... was she part of the rebellion, too? And how deep did the rebellion run?

I thought I'd regret my decision to join them when morning came, but I didn't. Condemning Daddy Dearest sent the people in the Commons to their knees as they chanted my name—as if they were praying to me like I was a god.

It was weird, but I liked it.

Out of the corner of my eye, Mae brushed a piece of dark hair away from Bex's face, her fingertips trailing the length of her brown cheek.

I turned to study my handmaidens, glancing between them. "You don't have to answer this, but were you guys hooking up in my bathroom the day I was arguing with Malachi?"

Bex tilted her head quizzically. "Hooking up?"

"You know..." I smashed my index fingers together and made kissing noises.

Mae's face flamed as pink as the begonias dotting the wallpapered walls.

Guilty. They were *so* guilty.

The smell of smoke and vanilla whirled around the room, and I blinked as Mistress Marjorie manifested behind Mae and Bex. The girls jumped, muffling screams with their hands.

"Fear not, ladies." Mistress Marjorie clapped, a garment bag and a hatbox appearing in her hands. "I brought Valeria a gift."

Bex unzipped the bag, revealing a gorgeous gown that glittered like the night sky. It tied on the shoulders with onyx satin bows, and a light layer of chiffon trailed to the floor into an ombre of shining silver. From the box, Mae pulled free a matching mask with two satin horns.

Squealing, I rushed toward Margie. "This outfit is loads better than what you know who picked out."

She snapped her fingers, stripping me of my robe. *Right.* Didn't miss that. In sync, Mae and Bex quickly turned around to give me an ounce of privacy.

The dress slid over my head, clinging to my curves. The deep v down the front and back of the gown made it impossible to wear a bra, but the top fit so snug against my chest that I didn't need one. The dagger necklace dangled icily between my breasts, chilled by my protected thoughts.

When my handmaidens turned back around, they fussed over my hair and makeup until they were both satisfied with themselves. My hair fell around me in soft, loose waves, complemented by my dramatic makeup—smoky blacks and sharp winged liner. My lips were painted pitch-black to match. I smiled at my reflection, finally feeling like myself in this realm.

The entire ensemble was devilish in the best possible way.

Pleased with their work, Mae and Bex slipped out of the room, hand-in-hand, leaving me alone with Mistress Marjorie.

"Will you be attending the ball?" I asked.

"No. There's something else I must do."

I nodded, giving her a hug. She squeezed me once and vanished.

As I walked barefoot down the stairs, strappy heels in hand, my blood raced, knowing my father was going to be *pissed* when he saw me. I smiled to myself. That's exactly what I needed if I was going to expose what kind of monster he truly was.

THE BALLROOM WAS VIBRANT with joy as people danced and laughed, praising Lirabeth and her fine eye for extravagance. I scowled, making my way toward the dais, my third glass of wine in hand, where my father sat on the obsidian throne. It sang out to me, and I wished I could run my hands over it and whisper, "Soon."

Soon, that throne would be *mine*.

As I approached, my father's eyes turned black, seething with anger. The vein in his forehead protruded. "That is not the gown I sent for you."

Well, obviously. The dress he sent for me was the color of the wine lingering on my tongue, and it hid almost every inch of my skin. The mask was even worse—a thick veil that I could barely see through. The entire set was hideous and better suited for someone at a convent, not an eighteen-year-old princess hoping to get laid. A shiver skirted up my spine as I glanced around the room for Gideon.

"This one's more my style, don't you think?" I spun in place and touched my horns. The bond buzzed as if it knew what I was doing—provoking the king. "It was a gift from Mistress Marjorie."

Lirabeth narrowed her eyes. "While it's a lovely gown, princess, you look like one of Madame Alyona's whores."

I shrugged, carefully aware of how the dress pulled tight against my chest, exposing the sides of my breasts even more. "Better a whore with a heart than a monster without a conscience."

The king bounded to his feet, fists at his side, and the music stopped, all eyes falling on him.

I smiled.

He wouldn't strike me, not with everyone watching. But I needed him to. I needed to bait his anger and expose what he was behind closed doors to the wealthiest in our realm.

I held my breath.

He watched me for a moment longer before plastering a fake smile across his monstrous face. "The princess has arrived; let us celebrate tonight as a happy family."

The music picked back up. I sighed and weaved my way into the crowd without another word.

I stood in front of the tables that should've been overflowing with food and drink. Swapping my empty chalice for a fuller one, I sipped some wine, doing my best not to smudge my lipstick.

Wrapped and unwrapped gifts spilled across several tables, from baby clothes to toys to fruits and sacks of vegetables; there were more presents for that unborn child than I ever received during the years I spent in the Realm of the Mortals.

"That is quite a dress," Gideon murmured, sliding into place next to me. He was as handsome as ever in his sharp, tailored tunic and gunmetal mask, the beak of a raven jutting from it. His jaw and full lips were exposed, a grin tugging at the corners as he took in the sight of me.

I cocked my head to the left. "You look... nice."

He chuckled and reached for my hand, brushing his lips against my knuckles.

"Don't do that!" I snatched my hand away from him.

"Do what?"

I lowered my voice. "Be intimate with me in front of people that might rat us out to the Realm of the Forsaken."

"Are you saying you would like me to be intimate with you behind closed doors, then?" He pursed his lips. "Or do you simply prefer darkened hallways and mausoleums?"

"There might not be much to this dress, but I'm still armed," I teased, willing him to think the heat in my cheeks was due to the obscene amount of wine I'd consumed.

He hummed as his midnight-blue eyes slowly raked over every exposed inch of me, his deft fingers popping a strawberry into his mouth.

Tucked away in the corner of the ballroom, a band played countless melodies that inspired guests to sway around the marble floor. Malachi dipped a woman in a violet gown, his lips curved into a dangerous grin. His wolf mask partially hid his scars, and I longed to ask him about them, to ask him if he was the raven I'd met in the Realm of the Mortals. But tonight, he was a hunter with his eyes on a lamb, and I'd let him have his fun. With a small smile, I searched the dance floor for vibrant copper curls and bright green eyes before remembering Brini had come down with a fever and Sabel chose to stay home with her.

Gideon extended a hand to me, the thick ring on his index finger glinting under the flickering flames illuminating the ballroom. "Will you come with me to the gardens?"

"The gardens?"

"Yes, I have a surprise for you."

I folded my arms across my chest. "You know how I feel about surprises."

"I swear you'll like this one."

This surprise couldn't be worse than free-falling through the Void or learning Mason was kidnapped by the Realm of the Forsaken or being told about the rebellion.

My blood buzzed as I reluctantly took his hand. Slipping out of the ballroom, we entered a corridor that led to the gardens with the beautiful wisteria canopy. The area lit up with fireflies illuminating the soft shadows of calla lilies. Our steps were quiet, almost soundless. The moonlight shining down accentuated the near-perfect angles of Gideon's face, and I yearned for an ounce of Mason's artistic talent with a pen or charcoal.

Right before the turn to the courtyard, he drew to a stop, unwinding a piece of silver fabric from his wrist. There was a shine in his eyes that glittered like the moon against the sea. My breath caught in my chest. Would I ever stop being blown away by how beautiful he was?

"Take off your mask." His tone made my stomach flip in nervous excitement, heat coiling between my legs, toes curling in my heels. I did as he asked, slipping the mask free from my face. He took it from my hands, tossing it to the ground, and stepped closer to me, brushing his lips against mine. When he pulled away, he whispered, "Is it okay if I blindfold you?"

My heart hammered as I nodded.

A breathy laugh escaped his lips. His fingers trailed up my arms as he circled me. He wrapped the fabric around my head, securing it with a simple knot.

He slipped away for the briefest of moments and warmth radiated from his body as he came back to my side, placing something on my head. The sound of a zipper filled the quiet, and I drew my eyebrows together. He took my hand and slipped it through something silky, doing the same with my other arm until he zipped whatever it was up around me.

"Gideon, what is this all about?"

"Patience, princess." His voice was far away. A moment later, his calloused hand found mine again, and I jumped, startled by the touch. He tugged me forward a few steps. "Now, wait here."

Chewing the inside of my cheek, I fidgeted with the billowy sleeves of the garment he put on me.

"Okay." His voice was somewhere in front of me. "You can look now."

Reaching up, I untied the blindfold and let it slip free from my face. He stood a few feet away on a makeshift platform. Tiny jars with tea-light candles hung between the trees, illuminating the courtyard. A path of onyx and silver rose petals lined the pathway to a stage, and in front of it was a cloaked figure sitting in the lone chair. "Margie?"

She waved without turning around.

Slipped over my dress was a murky green graduation gown and on top of my head was a cap, a tassel dangling from the right in the same shade of green mixed with strands of bark brown and pure white.

Oakwood High's school colors.

Tears welled in my eyes. "What is this?"

"Valeria Edelyn Breault," he said, placing a hand over his heart. He had shrugged off his tunic and stood in his plain white shirt with his sleeves rolled up. His golden hair was slicked back and out of his face. "It's my honor to bestow upon you an achievement so grand others may fail in comparison." A soft laugh. "When your keeper and I look at you, we see not only a mortal-raised princess, but a high school graduate *and* the future queen of Empyrean."

He held a hand out toward me, and my keeper stood.

I bounded toward him, pinching myself. "Is this actually happening?"

Gideon helped me onto the rickety stage. It wobbled under our weight. "Move your tassel from right to left."

Taking a deep breath, I moved the tassel. Something in me shifted with it... changing my opinion of him. He was so thoughtful that my heart could burst.

"You've officially earned your diploma," he said, handing me a leather-bound folder embossed with "Diploma of Graduation" in thick, gold lettering. Opening it, I swallowed, my throat dry. Bolded at the top was *Oakwood High School* and right below it in fancy script was my name. Beneath that, four illegible signatures were signed around a stamped seal.

My eyes met his. This was real. It was my official diploma from Oakwood... but how?

The tears I held back poured from my eyes, and I threw my arms around him, crying into his shoulder. "You have no idea how much this means to me."

It was everything. It was the proof I needed that I did something with my time in Oakwood, that I was part of something. Not something as big as the rebellion, but something that was all mine. He hugged me tight, the tether between us rejoicing in a fiery song.

I pulled away from him and looked at Mistress Marjorie. "Did you know about this? Did you help him?"

She shook her head. "Gideon invited me after the King's Council meeting."

"You've had this planned for *that* long?"

"I've had it planned since the day I asked you what you missed most about the Realm of the Mortals." He straightened the cap on my head. "Those *things* I had to take care of after your welcome ball? It was this. I went to the Realm of the Mortals and retrieved everything."

"This is the nicest thing anyone has ever done for me."

He picked up a box from the other side of the stage. "I've been told it's custom to give a gift when someone graduates."

Ripping the present open, I laughed. Inside were at least a dozen paperback romance novels with shirtless men and women in torn dresses on the covers. "Gideon, you didn't."

"And they're filled with smut."

I arched my brow, impressed, considering he probably didn't know what smut was. "How did you manage that?"

"I charmed the Cornelia Street bookshop owner."

My heart seized. I frequented *Begin Again Books & Coffee* almost weekly. The bitter scent of coffee beans roasting among the dry and musty stacks of used books was vividly ingrained in my memory. I could imagine myself there, sitting cross-legged on the floor trying to decide which paperback I was going to buy.

Mistress Marjorie snapped her fingers, bringing me back to the present, and a cart filled with my favorite foods and desserts appeared in front of me. Pizza and tacos and a few cans of... "Phantom Energy? Margie, you *never* let me drink energy drinks."

"There's a time and place."

"Wish you would've said that at least once in the Realm of the Mortals," I muttered. "I wouldn't have had to sneak sips from Mason's behind your back."

We left the stage and sat in the grass with plates piled high with mortal delicacies.

"You weren't kidding," Gideon said between bites of a taco. "These are incredible."

It was so strange to see my worlds colliding in a way that didn't result in bloodshed. I never knew a stack of books, a slice of pizza, and a hideous graduation gown would make me so happy. I cracked a can of Phantom Energy and grinned. This was the best day of my life.

Tearing the tab from the can, I fiddled with it, thinking of Mason and how he used to collect these cans. A few summers ago, we even tried to stack a tower of empty ones as high as his bedroom ceiling, but we were never able to reach it.

My grin slowly faded into a frown. How could I think today was the best day of my life? How could I be so selfish? Here I was, relishing in all my favorite things while Mason was suffering in the Realm of the Forsaken.

"What's wrong, little one?"

I took a sip of the fruity drink. "It feels wrong to be so happy while Mason's a prisoner."

She placed a hand on my shoulder. "Being happy doesn't negate your worry or concern."

"I just wish I could do something."

Gideon took a sip of his energy drink and wrinkled his nose. "We will when the timing is right."

I squeezed his hand and slid my mental fortress into place. It was nice to know he would do what he could to help me save Mason, but even I knew his help had limits. He would never risk my life, or the rebellion, for my friend.

And he could never know I would risk everything for Mason.

Myself, the rebellion, Empyrean, I'd risk it all in a heartbeat if it meant my best friend was safe from the horrors of the Realm of the Forsaken. I got him into this mess, and I would get him out of it. Somehow, someway.

CHAPTER 19

Floating up the stairs to my bedroom, I was drunk on the taste of Gideon's lips.

After we ate, Mistress Marjorie vanished from the gardens, leaving us with ample time to give in to each other. His mouth was a welcome distraction. And his hands. Oh, gods. We made out under the glow of flickering tea lights until my body ached to know the weight of his.

The lust seeping through the bond told me he ached for me, too. Of course, he had more restraint than I did. He tore away from me, breath heavy, and tugged me to my feet. My skin tingled in places I didn't think had nerves, craving his touch. But he didn't satiate me or my need. He simply bid me farewell and ventured into the castle.

I banged the door with one foot. Bex wrenched it open, and Mae sidled up from behind her, quickly grabbing the items from my hands.

"The plates are for you guys." I nodded toward them. "They're packed with some of my favorite mortal foods."

They both thanked me profusely, and I waved their gratitude away, kicking my heels off and watching them fly across the room. They landed with a soft thud on the carpet.

My handmaidens exchanged a glance, their eyes sparkling in curiosity.

I sighed wistfully. "Tonight was a dream."

Mae handed me a long, black satin box. "A gift came for you, Your Grace."

I arched my brow and took it from her. Another gift? Is that why Gideon didn't walk me to my room? I ran my hand over the strange symbol fastened to the front. Or was this another gift from Mistress Marjorie?

"Thanks. Take the food and go. I'll be fine for the rest of the night."

They nodded and followed my orders, shutting and locking the door behind them. Slowly, I unwrapped the gift, preserving the delicate paper. A golden envelope slipped free, landing on the carpeted floor. I picked it up and used both hands to break the black wax seal. The letter crinkled, threatening to tear at the seams. In a thick, jagged script, a message that made my blood run cold stared back at me.

You, for the mortal.

A shiver crawled up my spine. It had to be from Cayden, but how did he manage to smuggle a gift into this realm? And into the castle no less?

My heart hammered in my chest as alarms sounded in my ears.

Concern flooded through the brand on my wrist.

Are you okay? Gideon asked.

I don't know.

Barely a breath passed before his next words came through. *I'll be there in a few minutes.*

Below the message was a single instruction: To respond, use any form of blood and write your reply.

Gross. Had the Realm of the Forsaken never heard of texting? Cayden could've sent me a fucking enchanted phone or something less disgusting than a blood letter. I chewed my lip. Mistress Marjorie said Cayden wouldn't kill Mason if I didn't give in to his terms. That he was too valuable. I trusted Margie and her judgment with all my heart, so now was as good a time as any to see if she was right.

I groaned, realizing the only blade I had was the one hidden on my wrist. But it was poisonous, so using it was off the table. A hairpin would do. I snatched one from the tiny jar in the top drawer of my vanity. Using enough pressure to break the skin, I dragged it across my left palm. At my writing desk, I dipped a clean quill into the gash.

Once it was coated with what looked like enough blood, my uninjured hand glided across the paper as I wrote my response. *Fuck you.*

The message faded into the paper, leaving a pale imprint of my reply.

Cayden's reply appeared word by word as if he was writing while I watched. *You'd fit in so well here with a mouth like that. It's a shame I'll have to keep you at arm's length.*

A faint tapping came from inside the gift box, and fear surged through me. Swallowing, I slid the ribbon off and opened the lid, peeking inside.

An arm sprung free just as a scream clawed its way up my throat. It clasped my mouth shut, muffling any other sounds. I stumbled backward in panic and toppled over a stool, landing hard on my back.

The arm acted like it had a mind of its own. It jumped from my mouth and wrapped its fingers around my neck, choking me. Skin gathered under my nails from scratching at the arm to no avail. It wouldn't release me no matter what I did.

Fear thundered through the bond.

My mind was too cloudy, too confused to make sense of whatever Gideon said.

The remaining air trapped in my lungs was thick and hot, threatening to burst like a balloon filled with too much helium.

A heavy pounding sounded from my left, but I couldn't make out what it was until the door flew open, chunks of cracked wood scattering along the carpet.

Bex rushed to the mantle and then to me, where she jammed a fire iron into the arm and tore it from my throat, tossing it into the crackling flames while I gasped in a breath, turned on my side, and coughed. My lungs slammed against my ribcage.

Gideon barreled inside, knocking Bex out of the way. He fell to his knees, cupping my face in his hands. "A-are you hurt?" His eyes were a shipwrecked sea as they scanned up and down my body. "What the hell did this to you?"

Shaking the fuzziness from my head, I scrambled to my feet and grabbed the paper from the desk.

Another message from Cayden waited for me: *Enjoy the mortal's arm.*

"No, no, no, no." I clutched the letter to my chest, my gaze landing on the fire blazing in the hearth. "That arm. It—It was Mason's."

The room spun, blurring around me. Bex wrapped a thick blanket around my shoulders and ushered me to sit on the tufted chair in front of the writing desk.

Gideon snatched the paper from my hands and read the messages. Anger seethed through the bond, though his face didn't show it. "Valeria, the king could have you *burned* if he found this. This is exactly the kind of proof he needs to change the line of succession."

"Give it back." I reached for it, but he held it too high up. "I have to accept Cayden's offer before he does something worse to Mason."

I pictured Mason terrified and hurt, like a rabbit in a trap. Screw Mistress Marjorie's plan of trying to negotiate. I didn't want to find out what else they were willing to take from him just to get to me.

"No, we need to show this to your keeper."

"He's my best friend." Gideon looked at me, our worries seeping into each other for different reasons. "You'd do it for Malachi."

He sighed before handing me the paper. "This is a bad idea."

"I'm full of those," I grumbled. The cut on my hand wasn't deep enough for the message I wanted to write. "I need more blood."

He pulled the dagger from the sheath on his thigh and sliced his palm, extending his hand to me. I hesitated briefly, taking in this guy who held his bleeding palm to me like an offering he would've made again and again. For me. Fear squeezed my heart. What if he was willing to spill even more blood for me? How deep did his feelings truly run? I placed a quick kiss on his cheek, an unspoken thank you, and dipped the quill into his blood.

My hand shook with every word that faded into the paper. *I want proof that he's alive. Tell him to tell me something only we know.*

The three of us stared as the ink faded. Gideon cleaned and bandaged our hands, saving a bit of blood in a dish.

"I'm sorry about breaking your door, Your Grace," Bex whispered from the doorway. "Mae has the key, and when I heard you scream, I told her to run and fetch Malachi. Kicking it was the best way to get it open."

I crossed the space of the room and pulled her into a tight hug. "You saved my life. I owe you."

When I let her go, she glanced between Gideon and me. "Your secrets are safe with me from King Ward."

Once she left to send word for Mistress Marjorie, we sat in silence. Gideon's fears prodded at the tether, testing my resolve. He didn't want me to trade my life for Mason's. I couldn't blame him. It was stupid and reckless, but somehow, I thought I could make it worthwhile. Maybe I could find a way to help the rebellion while I was there.

Cayden had to know *something* incriminating about our father.

I stared at the arm's charred remnants in the fireplace. Tears pricked my eyes, thinking that Mason would never draw again. My brother took that from him.

All he did was take and take and take.

And I would make him pay for it. I'd make him beg for mercy before I ended his pathetic life with my bare fucking hands.

Gideon's sense of rationality tried its best to seep through the bond, but I pushed it away and built my mental fortress back up brick by brick. There was no point in trying to think straight. Not when I knew the flames burning my best friend's arm matched the ones dancing in my eyes.

I wanted blood. Cayden's blood.

The doors to the terrace swung open. A slight breeze followed Mistress Marjorie into the room, billowing her long, ebony cloak. She took one glance at the broken bedroom door and waved her hand. Shards of wood and pieces of the lock molded themselves back together, repairing the door in a matter of seconds. She approached me and surveyed the tender marks on my neck, her hand stilling over the dagger necklace. "What happened?"

I pointed to the letter from Cayden. She clucked her tongue as she read the faded exchange and placed the letter back on the table. Her steps were soundless as she prowled toward the fireplace, reaching into the flames to touch the arm. Mason's arm.

Mistress Marjorie rubbed two fingers together. "Your brother wrote the letter, but this magic isn't his. It's Vemdour's."

Vemdour, the freaking *God of the Forsaken*, was one of the most lethal assholes to ever exist. My heart plummeted to the floor along with any hope of retrieving Mason safely. The words I wanted to say died in my throat as a single sharp knock drew my attention away from her.

Gideon bounded toward the door, letting Malachi into the room and shutting it behind him. "Did anyone see you come up here?"

"Of course not," Malachi said. His hair was messy, and his belt hung undone at his waist. He winked when he caught me staring.

My gaze darted back to my keeper. She clasped her hands in front of her. "I'm not surprised to find the presence of his magic here. After all, Vemdour was there the night your brother killed your mother. He was the one who freed Cayden before the guards could drag him away."

"Filthy traitor," Malachi spat.

My eyes met Gideon's and I lowered my fortress by one brick. *Is he going to be able to handle this?*

He'll be fine.

Mistress Marjorie made her way back to the letter. "There's a response, little one."

With trembling hands, I took the paper from her. In the same jagged script as before, Cayden wrote: *The mortal says you once spent an entire summer trying to convince him to have a threesome with you and some douchebag you met at a house party.*

"He's alive," I breathed, the pressure in my chest loosening. Only Mason knew a threesome was on my bucket—

Gideon reached for the letter. "What's it say?"

Instinctively, I hid it behind my back. Something told me he wouldn't like knowing Mason and I were friends... who occasionally had sex. "He's alive. That's all you need to know."

Malachi snatched the paper from my hand.

"Malachi," I snapped. "Don't."

He raised his eyebrows and read the letter aloud. My cheeks flamed as jealousy rammed its way through the bond. I slid the brick back in place to lessen the blow.

Gideon let out a low growl as he shoved Malachi, his nostrils flaring.

"That's enough." Mistress Marjorie's voice cut through the room. "If the boy lives, it won't be for long. Vemdour is impatient, and he's waited a long time for Valeria."

"Not that long for a god," Gideon muttered.

I swallowed. "But you said we had time to bargain."

"It seems that time is up."

The room grew silent as we all weighed our options. They had to know I'd trade myself for Mason in a heartbeat, but I doubted they'd let me. They'd be sending the future Queen of Empyrean into the hands of the enemy... but if my father successfully changed the line of succession, I would be no one. I wouldn't matter to the Realm of the Forsaken.

Gideon raked a hand through his golden hair. "Let's pretend we'll make the trade. Then fight our way out if we must. We can all hold our own."

Malachi scoffed. "You think the four of us can take on Vemdour *and* the entire Realm of the Forsaken? We could've gone head-to-head with Cayden, but not the *entire* realm."

"If we don't—"

"I think there's something we should consider," I said, interrupting Gideon. "If I trade places with Mason, I may be able to glean some kind of information that will help the rebellion, so we can overthrow my father and be done with all of this shit."

"Did you say *rebellion?*" Mistress Marjorie murmured from where she sat perched in the corner of the room, her legs crossed at the ankles. "You've been quite busy, little one."

"You've seen how awful Empyrean is now. Somehow, these idiots"—I pointed at the guys—"think it'll be better with me on the throne."

"This is madness, but it *could* work," Malachi said, golden light from the fireplace reflecting off his black hair. "Something's rubbed me the wrong way about the night of Cayden's raid. Why did

Vemdour help him? How long had Cayden been working with the Realm of the Forsaken before the attack?"

I nodded. "I can try to find answers."

Gideon huffed, looking between us. "This is going to be risky."

"The only problem I can think of is knowing when to extract her." Malachi snatched a hair ribbon from my vanity and tied his hair back in a low ponytail.

Right. There was *that*. How could I be sure they'd come back for me? Anxiety bubbled in my stomach as sweat clung to the back of my neck.

What if they just left me there?

Gideon held up his wrist. "Maybe we'd be able to use the dyad?"

Malachi pursed his lips. "How strong is it?"

"Strong enough." I pulled at the chiffon on the skirt of my dress. "But I still don't know how to use it properly."

Mistress Marjorie stood, placing her hands on her hips. "I'd be wary of relying on the dyad for something so crucial. The Realm of the Forsaken is warded. I doubt you'd be able to communicate through it at all."

"I say we try it." Malachi turned to me. "We'll give you a week in the Realm of the Forsaken, then slip in and steal you without anyone knowing until it's too late."

I chewed on my bottom lip, glancing between them. "You will come for me, right? You won't leave me there?"

The Realm of the Forsaken was a brutal, bloody place full of demons and rage. A place of torture and endless pain. And I was talking about going... willingly.

Gideon softened, reaching a hand toward me, but I took a step back. This plan sounded good in my head, but now... now, I was afraid I was making a mistake.

Bastile bound me to Gideon for a reason, and I believed I *could* trust him, mainly because of that, and because if I did, I'd be able to save Mason. But there was another part of me that trusted Gideon because of how I felt about him. Or at least... how I thought I could feel about him if I wasn't so afraid.

"We must reply before they grow impatient," Mistress Marjorie said.

Malachi handed me the letter. "Time's up, princess. Are you going or not?"

My heart stuttered as I locked eyes with Gideon, the taste of his lips still lingering on my own. I trusted him with my body and my soul, so maybe that meant I could trust him with my life.

A week in the Realm of the Forsaken. I could do it. For Mason, for Brini, for Empyrean.

And for power.

I dipped the quill into the tiny dish of Gideon's cold blood and made my decision. *My keeper will escort me to the Realm of the Forsaken at first light. Have breakfast waiting for me, you won't like me when I'm hangry.*

The ink faded into the parchment. Moments passed as I held my breath.

When Cayden's reply came, worry quivered through the bond. *See you soon.*

"May Bastile watch over you now." Malachi kissed his fist and brought it to his left shoulder. He flashed one knowing look at Gideon and slipped out of the room, quickly and quietly, the way I imagined he did with his lovers.

Mistress Marjorie mumbled something about how she had to prepare for tomorrow, vanishing without a goodbye.

Leaving Gideon to shift awkwardly where he stood. "I guess I'll see you in the morning before you head out."

Pieces of Mason's arm taunted me from the fireplace. What if it stitched itself back together and crawled out of the fire and finished me off while I slept?

"I don't want to be alone tonight," I blurted out. My cheeks burned at the thought of what he promised a night with him would be like. "Will you stay with me?"

His eyes met mine, and I let the fortress crumble. His thoughts and feelings were a welcome distraction from the fear that sloshed through my veins.

He grinned that stupid grin that made my knees wobbly. "I thought you'd never ask."

CHAPTER 20

G ideon was quiet when I padded into the bathroom.

I needed a bath—needed to scrub away the phantom touch left by Mason's arm. I could still feel the weight of it on my neck and the skin bunched under my nails. It left me shaken and dirty. Sinking deeper into the tub, I let the water warm my frozen bones, thawing the fear that riddled me.

In less than twelve hours, I'd trade myself for Mason. I had no idea what kind of trap I'd be walking into, but I'd do it knowing I made the most of my last night in Empyrean.

By the time I finished bathing, a thick cloud of steam followed me from the bathroom as I crept pass the bed where Gideon slept with one of my romance novels cracked open on his chest. Inside the walk-in closet, I rifled through the silver embossed dresser looking for something a little sexy. There was nothing. Just ankle-length white nightgowns with cuffed sleeves and high necks. My eyes snagged on the leather jacket hanging behind a row of gowns. It was Gideon's from the day he forgot it on my chaise. A smile curved across my lips as I slipped it on with nothing else underneath, and tip-toed to the bed.

The steady rise and fall of his breathing was such a stark difference from Mason's constant tossing and turning. Gideon was a ship sailing on a smooth sea, while Mason was a home caught in a tornado. Thinking of Mason while settling in bed next to Gideon was weird, but I couldn't help it.

Mason and I had history.

There were so many times we watched movies and laughed at the absurdity of soulmates and happily ever afters. He laughed because he thought it wasn't realistic. I laughed because I didn't believe there was such a thing as happily ever after for me. I still didn't.

Yet, here I was—watching my *literal* soulmate sleep in my bed.

Okay, *enough* with the reminiscing. Gideon promised me pleasure, and that release was what I wanted most right now.

"Gideon." I tapped his cheek. "Wake up."

"I'm awake." He opened one sleepy eye and rolled onto his side to look at me. The book fell between us with a near-silent thud onto the duvet.

"Are you?"

"I am now." His eyes swept over the length of my body. "My jacket looks a thousand times better on you, princess."

I tossed the book to the floor and climbed on top of him. "Remember what you promised me a night with you would be like?"

Gideon gazed up at me, a grin on those lips I was dying to kiss. He wrapped his muscular arms around me, bringing me closer to his face. His mouth crushed against mine, unyielding and desperate. We kissed for a few minutes before I reached for the hem of his shirt.

He pushed me onto my back and pulled away. "Before we go any further, I have to know something."

"What's that?"

"Are you in love with him?" He didn't have to say Mason's name. The uneasiness in his eyes was enough confirmation. Guilt threatened to smother me. Mason was my friend, and we fucked. But what we had was lust and fun and distraction. It wasn't *love* love. It was a different kind of love, a non-romantic kind of love. A love between best friends.

"Of course I love him," I said quietly. "He's my best friend."

"So you love him how I love Malachi? He wasn't the reason you wanted to stay in the Realm of the Mortals? You're not... together?"

It wasn't jealousy that coursed through the bond, not this time. This time it was something different, something more personal—the fear that he wasn't enough for me. How absurd.

"No, I was never able to love him in that way."

A little *v* furrowed between his brow, and I itched to rub it away with my thumb. "And me?"

"What about you?"

He peered down at me. "Do you think you'll be able to love me?"

Love... I didn't know if I'd recognize the feeling if it hit me in the face.

I think a part of me longed to feel love my entire life. But love was a scary, delicate thing that could be shattered in an instant. There was no guarantee that if I allowed myself to fall for him, he'd catch me before my bones crushed against the pavement. Not even the dyad could promise that he'd never leave or be taken from me. And that terrified me. *Love terrified me.*

Love was why I *couldn't* do feelings. I craved his body and his touch. I did want him, strings and all, but I was so fucking *scared*. Scared that those strings would snap the moment he realized I wasn't worth the trouble or the risk. That *I* wasn't enough for *him*.

The brand tingled with impatience as he waited for my response. Searching his wild blue eyes, something stirred within my chest. When the word passed my lips, it wasn't a lie. "Someday."

His lips were on mine in a flash of lightning, striking me with a bolt of yearning that left me gasping for air. Desperation to know every inch of my body coursed through the bond. He separated my knees, and the world around me faded to nothing when his hand parted the hot flesh waiting for him. All thoughts of love fluttered away, leaving only carnal desire.

Leaving only him and me.

"You're perfect." He dragged his mouth against whatever skin he could find. One finger, then two, dipped into me. He groaned. His breath was warm against my collarbone.

My head fell back as I delighted in the pleasure of his touch.

"Take it off." I clawed at his jacket, needing to feel his skin against mine. With hungry hands, he slipped the leather from my body and flung it from the bed. He pulled his shirt over his head, moaning when my nails dragged across his taut back. "I want you. I want all of you."

"I'm yours." He grazed the fresh bruises on my neck with his lips, his tongue, his teeth. "I will always be yours."

His words were strings that tugged at my heart, and I relished in them—in the unspoken promise of forever knowing we may only have tonight.

He dipped lower, tongue flicking over my nipple until he took it into his mouth and sucked. The movement was so smooth, I wondered if he'd thought about this moment a thousand times. The heat low in my stomach flared, hoping he had. Trailing lower, he pressed kisses to the inside of my knees and up my thighs until his mouth met the space between, his tongue playful. He licked, sucked, teased. I bucked against him, and he pushed my knees down, spreading me wider as I writhed in pleasure, as I shattered.

Threading my hands through his hair, I dragged his mouth back to mine and tasted myself on his lips. Our teeth grazed and tongues explored, encouraging the invisible string of fate to bind our bodies like it did our souls.

"Do you have protection?" I whispered against his lips.

He offered a shy smile. "I take a monthly elixir."

And that was all I needed to hear. My hands fumbled with his belt, helping him free himself from his pants as we trembled with need. Pushing into me, he didn't hold back as he made me his own, and I made him mine. I clung to him, savoring every delicious inch as I got lost in a haze of want.

He said nothing as he braced one hand against the headboard, pounding with rough and wild thrusts. My heels dug into his thighs, nails breaking the skin on his back. The whole bed shook as our ragged breathing and soft moans drowned out the crackling of the fire and my every worry.

One soul in two bodies.

An infinite moment unlike any I had experienced before.

Together, we rode wave after wave of ecstasy until we collapsed in a heap of sweat-soaked skin, tangled sheets, and exhausted breathing.

Outside, the stars glittered against the fading darkness, threatening to be swallowed whole by the rising sun.

THE MORNING GLOW SHINING through the sheer pink gossamer curtains stirred me from what little sleep I managed to steal and bathed Gideon in a halo of gold. His warmth kissed my bare skin, and a smile lingered on his swollen lips from the hundreds of kisses we sneaked throughout the night.

He laid on his back with messy hair, white sheets covering the lower half of his body, leaving the lean, chiseled edges of his stomach, and the faint silver scar from prom night, exposed. I longed to reach out and trace his perfect brows, nose, and jaw, but I didn't want to wake him. Instead, I watched him sleep, knowing another chance to experience this kind of stillness may not come.

With the sun glinting through the window, I wondered if this was what love was—a quiet moment of peace with the person who had a claim over your body and soul.

My breath hitched. Soon, we'd make the trade, and I hated that I might never feel this way again because of it. My plan was foolish.

Mistress Marjorie's words came floating back to me, asking me what I'd risk to belong. I should've told her *everything*. Because that was what I was doing—risking it all for Mason, for Brini, for Empyrean.

I slipped out of bed to brush my hair and teeth.

When I re-entered the bedroom, Gideon propped himself up onto his elbow and flashed that devilish grin that set my skin on fire. The sheet fell slightly, exposing the tanned muscles pointing in an arrow straight to his hips. I mentally calculated whether we had the time for round three.

He wiped sleep from his eyes. "Come back to bed."

Didn't have to ask me twice. Climbing in next to him, I pulled the blanket up to my chest, covering myself. My fears came back in full force, and I knew I couldn't stay in bed with him all morning. Mistress Marjorie would be here soon to take me to the Realm of the Forsaken, but it was so nice to pretend everything would be okay. That my plan would work, and he'd come for me in seven days. Those beliefs were all I had to rely on, all I had to look forward to.

I sighed.

"I swear on my mother's grave that I will come for you." He grabbed my hand and kissed my knuckles before turning it over and pressing his lips against our twin brand. It sent a shiver down my spine. "Sometimes I wonder if I couldn't feel anything with anyone else because of my connection to you."

My heart skipped. For the longest time, I thought the expiration date on my time in the Realm of the Mortals was the reason I couldn't fall in love with Mason. Or it was because of my aversion to feelings and the risks they posed. Perhaps that wasn't the case at all. Maybe it was because every part of me was tethered to *him*.

The smell of smoke and vanilla wafted around us, and I wrinkled my nose. Seconds later, Mistress Marjorie appeared in a cloud of charcoal smoke. Gideon leaped out of bed, hiding his crotch with a floral throw pillow. He gathered his clothes and dashed into the bathroom, his fine ass exposed for us to see.

"I figured as much would happen." She tossed me a canister of liquid. "Drink this." With a groan, I plugged my nose and downed the concoction. It was the same nasty brew she'd make after my nights spent with Mason. "You two have gotten quite close."

My mouth hitched in a half-smile. "Don't read too much into it. It's the same deal I had with Mason. Bodies only, no feelings."

"Someday, you'll let your heart love."

The brand hummed, agreeing with her. Her words mirrored my thoughts from last night about loving Gideon. Someday, sure. But not now.

"Let's get you dressed," she said. I slipped from the bed, clutching the sheet to my chest as she snapped her fingers, clothing my once naked body in a black t-shirt and worn ripped jeans. Comfort clothes for a less than comforting journey.

Gideon strolled into the room, hands in his pockets. He took one look at me and whistled. "That's how you dressed in the Realm of the Mortals?"

"Every day."

He spun his finger around, and I twirled to give him a better look. I could've sworn he murmured, "Lucky bastards," just as Mistress Marjorie said, "It's time to go."

My stomach flipped. There was something I had to do first. Darting toward the writing desk, I scribbled a short note on a piece of paper. The symbol of a raven watched me from the letterhead as my hand flew across the page.

Mae and Bex,

I can't tell you where I'm going but thank you for being so kind to me.

x

V

The note felt insufficient and impersonal, so I added one more line that plastered a smile on my face.

P.S. Please feel free to use my bed while I'm gone ;)

CHAPTER 21

We met Malachi outside of the castle grounds and used a potion similar to the one Gideon shattered back in the Realm of the Mortals to open up a shimmering silver portal to the Void.

The walk to the Gateway flew by and an hour later we stood in front of that beautiful, glittering door that wouldn't open for me the first time I saw it. Malachi turned the handle and it swung open, revealing the same lavish room Gideon and I ventured into a couple of weeks ago. It was less spacious with the four of us crowding it, and I didn't want to find out how small it felt when Kai showed up. My eyes darted toward the skulls and bones lining the door to the Realm of the Forsaken, and I beelined for it, wanting to get this shit over with.

"Valeria Breault, Princess of Empyrean," Kai's voice boomed around us, though his giant body remained hidden. "Your presence is requested in two realms. Which would you like access to?"

"The Realm of the Forsaken."

In a flash, he emerged from a hole in the ceiling, hooves clicking against the floor. The flesh-like wings protruding from his back drooped low enough to drag behind him. He cocked his head to the side. "Are you sure you wish to go there?"

A stone of dread dropped into my belly. "I'm sure."

With a wave of his hand, the door swung open, and I shivered. Smoke and screams drifted down the bridge along with the scent of burnt meat.

I glanced between Gideon and Malachi. "You'll come for me, won't you?"

Gideon's expression softened and he closed the space between us. With a gentle touch of his roughened hands, he cradled my face. "Of course I will. What's—"

I kissed him—hard and passionately, a final taste of something sweet. We kissed like it'd be the last time we'd have the chance. My throat constricted, and my heart seized as Mistress Marjorie pulled me away from him, nearly dragging me through the doorway. As I cast one more look at the guys, a realization dawned on me. *I didn't want to leave.* That was precisely why I had to go. Forcing one foot in front of the other, I moved forward. Forward to Mason. Forward to answers.

Shadows smothered the molten bridge to the Realm of the Forsaken, but I barely noticed. I was too busy focusing on the stupid fucking plan I came up with.

A trade. A life for a life. Me for Mason.

Perhaps I shared more in common with Bastile than I thought—caring for mortals, risking everything for them. The thought was a small comfort, but not enough to get me through whatever these assholes had in store for me.

I tried to ease my panic. It'd only be a week. Seven days. No time at all, really. Then the guys would come for me, and we'd take over Empyrean whether I got the intel we needed or not. I let loose a long breath that carried my worries into the Void as we approached the door at the end of the bridge.

Lodged into the wood was a dagger with a wicked sharp blade. Next to a... skull fastened to the door?

"Your blood will let us pass," Mistress Marjorie said.

I grimaced. "Why does everything they do have to include blood?"

My hands trembled as I pricked the tip of my finger and wiped the bright crimson that pooled to the surface on the skull's brow. Smoke seeped from the empty eye sockets. Several locks clicked out of place, and the door swung open.

Before we stepped into the Realm of the Forsaken, a faint tug of longing pulled on the invisible tether. Sparing a single glance back at the Gateway, I sent Gideon the emotion I first felt with him by my side.

Hope.

If he replied after the door groaned shut, I didn't feel it. The constant screams reverberating around the realm muted any chance of communication. My hand clutched the dagger hanging from my neck as I zipped it up and down the chain.

I could do this.

Couldn't I?

The path we followed reminded me of a red brick road, except it was stained in blood, not paint. Mistress Marjorie led the way, her cloak dragging against the ground. All around us, bellowing cries escaped the throats of those trapped here. Vermillion smoke billowed in the sky as winged demons flew around, dropping bodies from unfathomable heights, just to scoop them up and drop them again.

"The Harrowing of Harlots," Margie shouted. "Souls of the damned, destined to be dropped over and over."

As if confirming her words, a woman splattered to the ground, her shrieks drowned out by the deafening crack of her body.

I jumped, heart hammering in my chest. "Holy shit."

We continued along the road of blood until we entered a charred field with gray mist rising from the ground. Countless bodies hung like scarecrows, strapped to broken and jagged pieces of wood. Their gray-tinged skin rotted with open lesions while they were pecked apart by ravenous, flesh-hungry birds.

"The Pillars of Pain," she told me. I opened my mouth to ask a question, but the grotesque tang of sour meat snaked its way down my throat, causing me to gag. She kept moving forward. "Come on. Not long now."

The mist disappeared, revealing a bloody dirt path, and even more horrors flowed the deeper we went into the realm. We followed the trail along the edge of a vast red ocean, so dark it was almost black. The waves crashed onto the shore, meeting volcanic sand. Boarded-up baskets were tethered to sunken masts jutting out of the water. As the tide rose, the wooden cages filled with bodies were submerged.

I took a step off of the path. "They're drowning."

Mistress Marjorie whirled on me, her hands grasping my shoulders. "These are wicked people, little one. Any soul trapped in this realm *deserves* to be here."

"Mason doesn't."

"He's here because of his stupidity." Her bluntness knocked me over with the strength of a wave I didn't see coming. She tightened her grip before she let me go, turning around to continue down the path.

I stood there a moment longer, staring at her back as she walked away from me—the cries of the drowning victims calling out to me for salvation. But I wasn't here to be their savior. I was here for Mason and Brini and Empyrean. Jogging to catch up with Margie, I let the conversation drop along with my stomach.

Once the heavy silence between us dragged on for far too long, I broke it. "Why are you called the Witch of the Gray?"

She kept moving, her voice as steady as her stride. "Because I hail from the Gray, and I'm the only being who does."

"Where's the Gray?"

"Nowhere and everywhere."

Well, that was cryptic. I huffed, knowing better than to press her for more information.

The bloodied trail we followed led straight to the heart of the realm. After another thirty minutes of walking, a jagged, gothic-looking fortress loomed ahead of us. Bones and entrails littered both sides of the path like weeds and forgotten trash. It was a sickening sight that would likely pale in comparison to the horrors that lurked behind the castle doors.

Several Drozol perched in front of a gate, their long black claws and dinosaur-like feet tapping restlessly.

"I come with Valeria Breault in good faith of our trade for the mortal boy, Mason Kennedy," Mistress Marjorie announced. One of the Drozol bent over to sniff her, while another did the same to me. Its warm breath left a sticky film on my face. Gross. The gates slowly opened, and my heart raced. We were so close. So close to freeing Mason from this nightmare and damning me in return.

Four more Drozol flanked us as the first two led us deeper into the castle to another set of black metal doors adorned with bones dipped in gold. Minutes passed by as screams and growls and laughter rattled against the walls.

The brand on my wrist hummed as the doors to the room opened. It was strange not feeling Gideon as clearly as I did when we were in the same realm, and I didn't know why that bothered me so much. I shook my head, clearing it of thoughts of him as my eyes darted from place to place.

One of the Drozol shoved me forward and into the room. Arched stained glass windows were inlaid into the furthest wall, each displaying a different scene of mortals being tortured. From dragons setting cities on fire to sirens stabbing sailors with tridents, they took stories mortals told for generations and turned them into a deadly reality. With different inhuman faces, nine enormous statues encircled the space, their bodies eviscerated, leaking blood and tar. Crystals shone from where their organs would be.

For a room so riddled with death, I was disgusted by how alive it was.

Demons of every kind loitered around, their eyes smoldering like coals in a dying fire. Refusing to waver under their gawking, I clenched my fists tightly at my sides.

Countless orbs hung from chains attached to the ceiling at varying lengths, illuminating the space with the fluorescent glow fire could never replicate. I pursed my lips, annoyed. So this shithole had electricity, but Empyrean didn't?

In the middle of the room sat a throne on top of a staggering dais. Various bones and skulls made up the front of the seat, liquid lava coursing through and around them. But if I had thought the throne was disturbing, it didn't hold a candle to the *thing* sitting on it.

Two soulless eyes resembling pits in the center of a gaunt face stared at me. Deep in my bones, I knew I was in the presence of Vemdour, God of the Forsaken. I had never imagined a god could look so... menacing. Thousands of thin golden scars marred his upper body, carved brutally into his leather-like flesh. Nine horns twisted together to form a natural crown to adorn his head.

His eyes raked over me, and the blood drained from my face as the area around him rippled, transforming him from monster to... man? I blinked, taken aback. Somewhere beneath the surface of the sinister creature was one of the most beautiful men I'd ever seen in my godsdamned life.

With hooded eyes, a strong brow, long nose, and a wide mouth paired with full lips, he was the kind of handsome that drove women into fits of jealousy. Raven hair spilled around him, a shade or two darker than his deep brown eyes. Like before, a crown rested on his head, not made of bone but of thin, spiked gold. He had broad shoulders, long muscular legs, and smooth olive skin. Even sitting he exuded power—infernal and apocalyptic power.

I scrubbed a hand over my face. It had to be some kind of glamour because as soon as I took in his human features, the monster returned.

Horrifying and ugly. Sheeeeesh. Someone did him dirty.

Mistress Marjorie spoke first. "Vemdour."

A sickening smile of razor-sharp teeth widened across his face. "The Witch of the Gray returns."

Returns? My eyes whipped to her. Who *was* she?

"I'm here for the boy, and that is all."

Vemdour clapped his hands twice. A cloaked figure appeared with one fist wound into Mason's shaggy hair. They flung him to the ground, and he scrambled to his knees in front of the throne of bones.

"Mason!" I ran toward him. He didn't glance up at the sound of my voice or my touch. His skin was sickly and cold. Welted red gashes peeked through a torn and bloodied shirt, his once scarless skin destroyed. My eyes passed over the space where his right arm used to be.

"This is another trick," Mason whimpered. He spat at Vemdour's polished shoes. "I won't tell you shit."

A woman bounced from Vemdour's side and struck Mason across the face with the back of her hand. "Silence."

I grabbed her wrist and dug my nails into her ashen skin. "Touch him again, and it'll be the last thing you do." Turning my attention to Vemdour, I added, "You will return his arm."

Amusement danced in his coal-lit eyes as he leered at me, licking his lips. The area around him rippled once more, exposing a set of straight, white teeth where his pin-prick grin once was. Fucking weird. "That was not part of the deal, pet."

"It is now. Mason goes free with all of his limbs."

He cocked his head to the side, hair spilling over one shoulder. "Very well. But it won't be pretty."

Vemdour waved a hand at Mason. The woman sneered at me, and I let her go. She dragged Mason toward the god, his knees violently scraping against the ground.

I made a move for her just as two Drozol clutched my arms and yanked me toward my keeper.

"If you so much as leave a bruise on her, I will rip you to pieces with my bare hands," Vemdour growled. The threat sent a chill down my spine. "Now, release her."

The Drozol did as they were told, letting me slide into place next to Mistress Marjorie without a scratch.

The god chanted, the words thick and slurred.

The cloaked figure, who dragged Mason into the room, removed their hood, revealing a guy not much older than me. There was something eerily familiar about him—the curve of his jaw, the set of his eyes, his slick black hair. He looked like a younger, softer version of my father, the likeness uncanny.

Cayden. My heart hammered in my chest. He should be well older than me, but it was as if he was still that young man who murdered our mother.

From the corner of my eye, Vemdour ran his vile tongue over the raw part of Mason's arm, and bile rose in my throat. I held my breath as Mason screamed in agony, writhing in the god's clutches. Thick smoke surrounded them, a veil from prying eyes. Excited chatter and various bets of what the arm would look like buzzed around me, churning my stomach.

I fixed my gaze on Cayden.

My brother.

My enemy.

Bloodlust sizzled through me while he held my stare for a moment longer before tearing it away to focus on the throne. Gone was the smoke that surrounded it; Mason now lay in a heap on the stone floor.

"There." Vemdour leaned back, threading his fingers behind his head. "A new arm."

Crossing the distance, my heart plummeted. The tips of Mason's fingers to the middle of his arm were jet black, with thick onyx veins streaking up to his shoulder. With this arm, he could never return to the Realm of the Mortals. Maybe in some sick and twisted way, this was how it was supposed to go. Swallowing my guilt, I met the eyes of a warlock with a missing arm. He glared at me, a silent threat.

"I'm so sorry, Mason." Without realizing it, I'd started crying. Tears fell from my cheeks, gently landing on him. I mourned for the boy he used to be and the person he'd have to become. Wept for all that he was going to have to leave behind because of *me*.

"Val? Is it really you?" His words were raspy. "Is this another trick?"

Pulling him into my arms, I offered him a moment of comfort before the realms separated us again. "It's me. I'm here."

"No!" He untangled himself from me. His once emerald eyes were muddied with gray. "No, you shouldn't have come here. It's a trap."

"I know." I forced myself to chuckle. "I couldn't leave you here with these pricks. You're my best friend."

A tiny piece of me hoped the truth of my words was blatant enough that they'd never suspect I had ulterior motives. I needed them to believe I was a stupid girl making a stupid trade, so they'd be loose-lipped around me.

Mason shook his head, his mouth opening and closing. I wanted to tell him that it was all going to be okay. But I lied to him for years, and I couldn't do it again. So I said nothing at all, letting the tears streaming down my face tell him everything he needed to know.

"Enough of the theatrics." Vemdour rubbed his jaw. I leveled my eyes on him, which made his sinister grin broaden. He clapped his hands, and both Margie and Mason vanished from the realm, leaving me utterly alone in the Realm of the Forsaken. Hundreds of hungry, evil eyes swept over me, making my blood run cold. But it was the god's words that turned my insides to ice. "Oh, pet. I've waited a long time for you."

CHAPTER 22

With a wave of Vemdour's hand, the throne room emptied as if it was a gaping maw, ready to swallow me whole. Or maybe the god surveying me would do the honors. His gaze swept over me from the tips of my pierced ears to my toes twitching nervously in my sneakers, and then, slowly, dragged its way back up to meet my eyes.

I held his stare.

Neither of us spoke.

Swallowing thickly, I glanced away to study the room. The intricate designs on the walls of the chamber—wild and curving vines intertwined with intricate stars etched into the night-flecked stone—were far too pretty for whatever nightmares lurked in this fortress.

Whatever nightmares Vemdour had planned for me.

"Are you just going to stand around and stare at me for the foreseeable future?" I asked, feigning boredom, hoping it masked the scent of fear slithering through me.

"With someone as divine as you, that's quite tempting." His lips curved into something more feral than a smile. "But no, I'll show you to your chambers and let you settle in."

"My chambers?" I blinked. "You mean my cell?"

He quirked a monstrous brow. "Do you think of yourself as a prisoner here?"

"Aren't I?"

"You're here as my guest, Valeria."

"I'm pretty sure *guests* have a choice in whether or not they stay." He pointed toward the double doors at the back of the throne room. "If you'd like to go, then *go*."

There was no way he was being serious. He hadn't held Mason prisoner and traded for me just to let me go.

I hesitated. "What kind of game are you playing?"

"I don't play games with my equals."

"Your equals?"

He cocked his head to the left. The area around him shimmered, and a lock of dark hair spilled into his equally dark eyes. He brushed it away. "Your naivety is charming, pet."

"Stop calling me that," I snapped.

"Would you prefer another term of endearment?" He circled me, a playful grin on his lips. "Darling? Sweetheart? Beloved?"

My breath caught in my throat. "I am none of those things to you."

"Choose to stay, and maybe you will be."

"Hard pass." I turned abruptly, feet bounding toward the doors. My palms were slick with sweat, and I rubbed them on my jeans. "I've got a man waiting for me in Empyrean," I tossed over my shoulder.

"A man?" Vemdour laughed. "You deserve a god."

I whirled on him. "Well, I've yet to meet a god that deserves me."

He pursed his lips and stood up straighter. "Is this about the mortal's arm?"

The way he said it so casually made me shudder.

"Torturing Mason sure as hell doesn't help your meager attempt at convincing me to stay," I bit out.

"Valeria, I had to amputate his arm because he was scratched by a Succubus." He tucked his hands deep into the pockets on his slacks.

"If I didn't remove it, the poison would have spread to his heart and killed him."

I sucked in a breath. Succubi were gorgeous, murderous creatures with a poisonous touch. He *could* be telling the truth.

"So you saved Mason's life," I said, narrowing my eyes at the god. "And then you thought it'd be a great idea to enchant his amputated arm and send it to me as a fucking *present*?"

He shrugged his broad shoulders, a wicked grin on his lips. "It got you here, didn't it?"

I scoffed, spinning on my heel and beelining for the exit.

My hand had just wrapped around the crystalline handle when he blurted out, "If you stay, we can trade secrets. I'm sure there are things about Empyrean you'd like to know."

I paused, mouth parting. I steadied my gaze on the door. "And what do you get if I stay? Besides the satisfaction of ruining my godsdamned life?"

"Your presence as a guest of my court allows me to claim Empyrean and the Realm of the Forsaken are on good terms again." His words had me turning to face him, turning to find the amusement glittering in those smoldering eyes. "And that is something I can use to piss off the Realm of the Divine."

"So you're using me," I said flatly, the words tasting like ash on my tongue.

Just like my father. I was only wanted whenever there was a use for me.

"Think of it as a mutual arrangement." With a snap of his fingers, his once bare skin was covered in a pure white button-up. After rolling up the sleeves to the crooks of his arms, he motioned for us to leave the throne room, adding, "An arrangement to piss off the gods and kings who have wronged us."

I already planned to stay for a week to investigate, but he didn't have to know that. So I followed him, letting him think he convinced me as I focused on memorizing the castle's layout.

Above us, light shined dimly from the ceiling illuminating the macabre maze of halls.

The stone walls were cold to the touch and slowly became warmer the longer I skimmed my fingers against them, as if it was draining my life from me. I glanced sideways at the god, who slowed his pace to walk beside me. *He* certainly looked like someone who could take a life in an instant. I shuddered. I didn't want to know which gods and kings he spoke of, which ones dared to risk the wrath of the God of the Forsaken.

Screams and cries of the damned echoed down each corridor, and I stopped questioning the source of the stickiness underneath my sneakers when a Hellhound dragged a flayed body down the hall, leaving a thick trail of blood and entrails in its wake.

My lips curled. "This place is disgusting."

"It's all part of the image, pet."

The hall led to a single elevator with thick metal doors. They slid open, and he pressed the button that took us to the eighth floor, second from the top. We shot upward until the doors opened to a luxurious room, decked out in sheens of gold, onyx, and deep purple. It was lush and modern, a stark difference from any bedroom I'd ever had.

A decent-sized four-post bed with a sheer canopy rested against the far wall with a handful of pillows scattered about and several thick blankets. A large armoire, a writing table, and a vanity, all painted black, embossed in gold, and carved with roses and thorns, were placed against the opposite wall from the bed. Stacks of recognizable books and magazines sat in piles strewn about the room. But, no bookshelves. I frowned. Chandeliers hung from the ceiling, not lit by candles but illuminated by *actual* light bulbs.

"How is there electricity here?" I asked.

"I'm the God of the Forsaken. My realm can be whatever I want it to be." He sat on a leather couch and extended his long, muscular legs. The buttons of his shirt strained against his chest as he folded his arms behind his head. I had to admit, he looked better dressed than when the brutality of his scars were exposed. Even as a monster, he seemed... approachable. Wordlessly, he ignited the fire in the hearth. "Tell me, are you happy with the room?"

I glanced around at the windowless space and shrugged. "It'd be better with a view and some bookshelves."

He waved a hand, and the far wall shifted from gothic-looking wallpaper, deep purple with an intricate design, to floor-to-ceiling windows that stretched from one corner to the next. The windows looked over rolling fields of torture, a sickly forest full of naked trees, and steep, rocky volcanoes bubbling with lava. The vermillion sky lit up with streaks of onyx lightning as a storm broke over the horizon.

It wasn't pretty, but it would do.

Then built-in shelves manifested from thin air along the opposite wall and the books that were strewn across the floor danced their way to them, sliding into place, spines outward. I stared in absolute wonder.

"Is there anything else you'd like?" he asked simply, matter-of-factly.

Answers. Power. A one-way ticket onto the Empyrean throne.

"Not now, but I'll let you know."

"I'll leave you to get settled." He pointed to a set of ornate double doors. "There's a bathroom through there. Cayden will fetch you later for lunch."

"No, thanks."

He furrowed his brow. "No, thanks?"

"I'm not hungry."

Another grin. "Every soul that ventures into my realm is hungry for something, pet." He stood, reaching for me. I remained rooted in place as he gently tilted my head up, so I was looking into his night-dark eyes. The color was endless. "I cannot wait to learn what it is you crave, what it is you're truly hungry for."

"Fuc—"

Smoke billowed around us, and he vanished before I had the chance to finish my swear.

I bristled and sat on the soft carpet in front of the fire. Drawing my knees to my chest, I wrapped my arms around them to keep the chill in my bones from spreading to my blood.

My heart pounded as if it was in slow motion.

One week. That was all I had to stay for. One week, and I'd leave. Whether Gideon came for me or not. Vemdour said I wasn't a prisoner here, and a part of me believed him. It was that idiotic part of me that I couldn't trust. Because that sliver was in awe of his power and everything he was capable of—restoring limbs, generating electricity, changing a room based on a whim. And it was that sliver that felt the pull of familiarity beneath his glamour. Something sang out to me in a way that I recognized, but whenever the glamour faded to reveal the monster lurking within, the recognition was gone.

All that was left was something sinful and forbidden.

And, still, it called to me.

THE CRACKLING OF THE fire was pleasant compared to the screams and begging for mercy that rattled down the halls on the main floor. I couldn't get any of the horrors I'd seen or heard or smelled out of my head. The Realm of the Forsaken was brutal and unforgiving.

I didn't like it.

Sitting up, I glanced around the room. The sky had darkened over the realm, something like stars glittering amidst the inky black. My night with Gideon must have caught up to me because one minute I was brooding and the next I had passed out on the floor.

What time was it?

I rolled my shoulders and stretched before standing, cracking my neck.

In the corner of the room, something caught my eye. Not something, *someone*. Cayden sat in a chair, cloaked by the shadows. His eyes were closed with his hands folded in his lap.

I froze, weighing my options.

It couldn't be that easy to kill him. Right? Running a finger over the dagger hidden on my wrist, I imagined the weight of the hilt and the glide of the blade slicing through the soft spot on his neck. There would be a grin on my lips when his eyes flew open, half in shock, half in disbelief that his darling little sister ended his pathetic life. No, that would be too convenient. It was another trick, another test by Vemdour. I could play this game, too. I could bide my time.

I slipped into the bathroom to bathe. It was as modern as the bedroom, covered in slate. The only pop of color came from the golden fixtures on the sink, shower, and tub. The latter was massive and more like a jacuzzi, but what blew my mind was the shower. It had one of those fancy heads that made the water pour like rainfall. Gods, I loved the rain. I turned it on, stripped down, and got in, buzzing with giddiness. The water was hot and glorious, immediately relaxing my achy muscles. Stacked on a shelf were several bottles of floral-scented soaps, lavender and vanilla, rose petals and sage, and hair care products with a similar vibe. I used them greedily, singing an off-key tune at the top of my lungs, not caring if I woke the sleeping monster in my room.

By the time I finished, I was sure I'd drained Vemdour's tanks of all the hot water he had. I wiped the steam from the mirror with my hand and ran a brush through my tangled hair. A plush, black robe with golden stitching hung from the hook on the wall and I slipped it on. On bare feet, I padded out of the bathroom and over to the armoire, dreading what I'd find inside.

I took a deep breath and wrenched the engraved doors open. There were countless dresses and corsets and skirts and cloaks and silk nightgowns in the color palette of my dreams. All dark tones, from charcoals and blacks to the deepest shades of burgundy and purple, and gold. Lots and lots of gold.

I had only ever seen clothing this beautiful in magazines.

"Holy shit," I squealed.

It was a closet filled to the brim with couture.

My hands reached out, greedily, as I plucked gown after gown from the hook. With pure delight, I inspected the detailed embroidery. Roses and thorns and glittering stars and crescent moons embellished the bodices and skirts alongside pearls, ribbons, sequins and lace. So much lace. The fabrics—satin, tulle, silk, and velvet—fluttered beneath my touch as I ran my fingers over the skirts and trains.

I traced the intricate floral detailing on one of the dresses before carefully setting it back on the rack. Shelves stacked with slippers and boots and heels with varying heights, lined the space to the right of the gowns. I picked up a pair of black, velvet pumps adorned with the delicate, gold stitching of a snake, and checked the bottom. It was blood red.

With the shoe clutched to my chest, I let out another squeal of excitement. This. This was what was supposed to be waiting for me in Empyrean. Not *here*. The thought sobered me, and I placed the heel back on the shelf and slammed the armoire doors shut.

Cayden startled from his sleep and jumped to his feet. His brown eyes assessed me like they would an imminent threat. As they should.

"Did I wake you?" I asked. "Oh, wait. I don't care." I pointed at the armoire. "What is the reason for all of this?"

His brow furrowed. "As a lady of Vemdour's realm—"

"I'm not *a lady of his realm*."

"You chose to stay, did you not?"

Did choosing to stay earlier mean I didn't have a choice to leave again? Did he trick me into willingly becoming a lady of his realm? I seethed in place, stomach churning. I'd deal with that later. "Turn around so I can get dressed."

Cayden raised his brows—either because he was skeptical or amused, I couldn't tell. "Turn my back on the woman who looks like she wants to kill me?"

"If I was going to kill you, wouldn't I have tried while you slept?"

He thought about that for a moment, clasping his hands behind his back. "Why the change of heart?"

"No change of heart," I sang. "I'll kill you when the timing is right."

Cayden frowned. The man who murdered our mother and vowed to kill me actually *frowned* before reluctantly turning around.

I opened the armoire, grabbed a set of dainty, lacy undergarments, and then thought better of it. Most of these gowns were designed to be worn without anything underneath. I pulled a gown from one of the suede hangers and shimmied it up my hips, letting out a sigh of relief at the sight of a hidden zipper along my ribcage.

The gown was incredibly revealing with a see-through mesh top and tastefully placed flowers that clung to the curves of my breasts. It had a delicate train of inky silk that whispered against the floor like stolen kisses. And there was a slit up the left thigh that stopped just below my hip.

A tiny voice in the back of my head warned me against wearing something so sexy, warned me not to draw unwanted attention to myself, but I silenced that voice with the sound of the zipper gliding into place.

I grabbed the pair of velvet pumps I had admired earlier and slipped my feet into them.

Everything was a perfect fit. As if the God of the Forsaken had both the dress and the heels designed specifically for me.

I made my way over to the vanity and rifled through the drawers until I found some loose golden powder that I swiped over my eyes and a tube of matte, black lipstick that I carefully applied. A pang of sadness washed over me as I thought of Mae and Bex, but I shook the feeling off and straightened my shoulders. There was no time to miss anyone, not when I had such little time here to obtain the information we needed to overthrow my father.

On top of the vanity was a rectangular box, and I cracked it open to find an obscene amount of glittering jewels. With careful fingers, I selected several earrings and embellished my ears in gold inlaid with rubies.

Casting a final glance at myself in the mirror, I wished I could shatter it. Not because I hated how I looked, but because I actually *liked* who stared back at me. I was sexy and free and dressed a little scandalously. Slowly, a grin spread across my lips. If Vemdour wanted me to dress like I was a Lady of the Forsaken, perhaps, I should act like one, too.

Cayden studied me, one eyebrow quirked, as I crossed the room toward him. He called for the elevator. "Whatever you're planning, I suggest you think twice."

I snorted. "I'm not going to take advice from a murderer."

The elevator bell dinged, and we stepped inside, descending to the main floor in silence. I snuck a look at him, surprised to find his eyes were glassy and his jaw was clenched.

CHAPTER 23

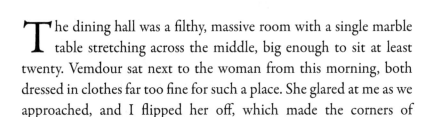

The dining hall was a filthy, massive room with a single marble table stretching across the middle, big enough to sit at least twenty. Vemdour sat next to the woman from this morning, both dressed in clothes far too fine for such a place. She glared at me as we approached, and I flipped her off, which made the corners of Vemdour's mouth twitch.

A horrible feast of mortal body parts was on display alongside candied fingernails, teeth drizzled in blood, and gurgling intestine soup. Demons were sprawled around the table, focused on their overflowing plates. Gods, there were so many breeds in this court that I'd need an encyclopedia to keep track of them all.

Cayden slid into place across from Vemdour, which left a single empty seat to my brother's left between him and a demon who reeked of decaying flesh and... mint? I glanced at him curiously, and he shrugged, causing his gluttonous body to spill over the handles of his chair into mine. Doing my best to shrink, I was careful of the dangers lurking on both sides.

My eyes lingered on a demon who took a bite out of a human arm. There was no way this was actually happening, right? Even Vemdour ate the human parts, and I wondered what the man under the monster thought about that.

Cayden leaned closer to me. "It takes a little longer to prepare our food."

Instinctively, I recoiled away from him, my elbow shoving into the beast next to me. He let out a squeal before cramming an entire handful of teeth into his mouth. They crunched like hard candy, and my hand flew to my mouth to stifle a gag.

Vemdour placed his palms flat on the table. His eyes bore into me. "Are you uncomfortable, pet?"

Should I lie? I searched his face and opted to tell the truth. "Any sane person would be uncomfortable. This is fucking disgusting."

Several of the demons stopped chewing as Cayden grabbed two goblets from an acolyte carrying a thick golden tray. He handed one to me before taking a gulp from his.

"You'll get used to it," Vemdour said with a slight shrug.

Another set of servants carried in two more plates of food and a basket of fresh bread. One placed a plate of parmesan and herb-crusted chicken, baked macaroni and cheese, and green beans in front of me. Another handed me a set of silverware, and my eyes widened.

Cayden popped a bite of chicken into his mouth and waved his fork at me. "Aren't you going to eat?"

Glancing between the plate and him, the fear that it might be poisoned overwhelmed me.

"Trade plates with me," I whispered, not wanting to make a scene.

"No."

I pushed the plate away from me, stomach screaming in frustration.

"Eat, Valeria." His tone implied it wasn't a request, and the vulgar gesture I gave him told him I didn't give a flying fuck.

"Trade her plates," the woman purred, one hand roaming Vemdour's chest, the other examining her sharp charcoal nails.

Cayden leaned forward. "Fuck off, Pyrtra. I don't answer to you."

Vemdour sighed. It reminded me of an exhausted father of two children, fed up with their constant bickering. He cut into a chunk of flesh from the calf splayed out in front of him. "I can't very well train her if she starves to death, Cayden. Swap plates."

Train me? I didn't like the sound of that.

Reluctantly, my brother did as instructed. His anger was a living thing, smothering the air around us like the smog above the skyline in a city that never slept. Whether he was angry at me or Vemdour for siding with me, I couldn't be sure. But I also didn't care. I smirked as I took an enormous bite of ridiculously flavorful and juicy chicken, humming with happiness at being fed a hearty meal.

As the night dragged on, I drank and drank and drank. If I was going to have to deal with the horrors of this realm, I might as well be drunk for it.

Servants hovered at the edges of the room ready to refill drinks, clear plates, and help where necessary. I drained my goblet and a servant dashed over and filled it to the brim with more sweet wine, without me having to do or say anything at all. I held in a giggle as I thought of rating Vemdour's catering service five-stars.

The god whispered into one of his servant's pointy ears, his eyes flicking to me.

"What's going on?" I asked no one in particular, my head fuzzy from the wine.

The demon to my left didn't answer me. But the monster to my right did. "You couldn't keep your mouth shut?"

Did I say the five-star thing out loud?

The dry taste of whatever demon wine they provided lingered on my tongue. "You need to drink more."

"You need to drink less," Cayden mumbled, pressing his lips together.

Several servants entered the room carrying trays with domed covers. The demon beside me clapped excitedly in time with the food churning in my belly. The servants sat a tray in front of each of us, their soulless eyes alight with mischief.

"It's time for dessert," Vemdour bellowed. "This one is a favorite called Worthless Witness."

The laugh that escaped those feral lips sent a shiver down my spine. Cayden balled his fists in his lap, knuckles whitening. So this wouldn't be a dessert meant for us, I guessed. I stared at the golden dome in front of me, the garnet handle begging me to lift it to reveal what was hidden under it.

Vemdour counted down from nine.

Simultaneously, we all lifted our covers.

Sitting on the tray was a man's decapitated head, his milky, opaque eyes wide and staring, his mouth holding the shape of a scream frozen in place. With a gasp, the lid slipped from my hand and clattered onto the table, knocking over the bowl of intestines. Thick liquid cascaded toward my lap, and I scrambled out of my seat.

"Sit," Vemdour commanded. Two Drozol demons flanked me, clutching my arms and pushing me back into my seat. Slick, lukewarm blood dripped from the table and seeped through my skirt. The god licked his lips. "Worthless Witness is an interactive dessert. All you have to do is dig into the sockets and rip out the eyes. They're surprisingly nutritious."

Oh, gods. I wouldn't defile someone's body like this.

Vemdour and the others dug with their fingers and claws, ripping the eyes out and popping them into their mouths, slurping the arteries like overcooked noodles. Cayden handed his set to the god before wiping his hands on a napkin.

Looking into the dead man's muddied eyes, I wondered what he'd done to deserve this.

Any soul trapped in this realm deserves to be here. Mistress Marjorie's words echoed throughout my mind.

My eyes landed on the brand on my wrist. Its faint hum tethered me to who I was. Would Gideon think less of me if I did something so foul to survive? Would Mason still want to be my friend if he knew I acted like one of the fiends who tortured him?

Vemdour tore an ear from his witness's head and tossed it in my direction. "I'm waiting."

Swallowing the bile rising in my throat, I jammed my thumbs into the sockets. It was wet and squishy as I tore the eyes free with little force. And eerily similar to those gag-worthy bowls in haunted houses that were filled with water and skinless grapes.

Not knowing what to do with them, I held the eyes out in front of me.

The table shook as Vemdour climbed onto it, crushing food and dishes. He kicked the head from in front of me, and it soared across the room. I sucked in a deep breath.

He crouched in front of me, as still as a gargoyle perched on a building.

His cruel eyes burned with elation. "Feed me."

"No," I said, still holding the eyeballs in my open palms. He glanced at them, his gaze lingering on the brand on my wrist before bringing his mouth to my hand. His teeth grazed my skin as he dragged his tongue from the tip of my middle finger to his dessert. He did it again until both of my palms were licked clean. When he finished chewing, he taunted me, blood lingering on the upturned corners of his mouth. I slapped him across the face. "I said no."

Pyrtra leaped from her seat with a blinding quickness and wound a handful of my hair between her fingers as she tore me from my chair. One hand clamped over my mouth, trapping the scream climbing up my throat. Vemdour held up a hand, and she stilled, her breath acidic on my neck. Both of my bloody hands clawed at her ashen wrist, trying to break free.

My heart thundered in my chest. I slapped the God of the Forsaken. In front of his court. During his *favorite* dessert. I tried to swallow, but my mouth was dry.

Nothing good could come of this.

Tremors spread throughout my body as images of what he'd do to me played in my mind like a low-quality film on a torn screen at the drive-in in Oakwood. Would he send me to the Pillars of Pain? Or maybe he'd prefer if he was the one who picked my bones clean with those too-sharp teeth?

Pyrtra's hand tightened in my hair, and all I saw was black as I bit her hand. She yelped but didn't let go. I stomped on the top of her foot and jabbed my elbow into her ribs.

She howled and released me, just as Vemdour yelled, "Leave! All of you."

The boom in his voice sent the room into hysteria. Demons scurried from their seats, snatching leftovers from the table and leaving crumbs and trails of blood in their wake.

Pyrtra shook strands of honey blonde hair from her hand, more debris that the servants wouldn't sweep up.

"My lord?" The lilt in her voice was unsettling as she looked to the god, waiting for her orders. He waved his hand, dismissing her. She frowned and tossed another abhorrent glance at me, exposing her teeth in an unspoken threat.

Cayden sat still, his pink-stained hands resting on the table. His gaze settled on me.

Vemdour turned to him and smiled. "You may go, too."

Sinking to the floor, I pulled my knees to my chest and pressed harder into the wall behind me.

Cayden took a sip from the goblet. "I think I'll stay and finish my wine."

The god leveled the full weight of his stare on him. "It wasn't a request, Cayden. Leave."

Cayden's chair scraped against the ground as he stood, knocking it over with a loud *thud*. He gulped down the rest of his wine and flung the empty goblet across the room. It bounced against the stone floor and clinked several times before rolling to a stop in a cluttered corner filled with bones, jewels, and coins.

Before the door to the dining hall even shut, Vemdour jerked me from the floor with a single look, pinning me against the frigid wall.

"What are you going to do to me?" My voice trembled as the force of his magic held me in place.

Stalking toward me until we were toe to toe, his black eyes simmered with bloodlust. Fear took hold only for an instant before my survival instincts kicked in. I wrenched the bracelet from my wrist, and the familiar weight of the leather-bound hilt sent a rush of relief and adrenaline through me. With a grace that mirrored Gideon's, I drove the dagger into his side. The smooth blade slid in between two of his ribs, his weathered skin breaking without much effort.

"Fuck!" Vemdour clutched the wound, dropping me in the process.

The dagger flew from my grip, and I landed on the ground. Not wasting any time, I crawled toward the weapon. He kicked it out of reach and flipped me onto my back. Holding me down with his forearm, a sickening grin coiled across his menacing lips. The power emanating from him was alluring and daunting, and I wished I could wield something so malignant. But I couldn't. Because I wasn't a god, and I was powerless.

Different tactics. "You said we were equals," I whimpered.

His grip loosened just enough for me to bring my knee to his crotch. *Moron.* He roared, releasing me long enough to scramble away and snatch the dagger. With a quick whisper of "Conceal," it wrapped around my wrist and snapped into place, like a friendship bracelet I should never have taken off.

I was going to pay for this. He was going to kill me.

Vemdour grabbed me again and climbed on top of me. I squeezed my eyes shut, my whole body tensing.

Waiting a breath longer for a blow that never came, I cracked one eye open to find him peering down at me. His chest heaved underneath his blood-stained button-up, hair hanging around him in dark curtains.

"I would tear someone to ribbons for drawing my blood," he whispered, running a feather-like caress over my cheek. One hand pressed against his wound to staunch the bleeding. "I'm the God of the Forsaken. Don't you fear me?" I blinked. Then blinked again. Was this a rhetorical question? "Answer me."

Furrowing my brows, I stammered, "I... I don't know. Do you *want* me to fear you?"

"No." He ran his thumb over my bottom lip, and I turned my face away from his touch. "I want you to feel many things for me, pet. But never fear."

I squirmed under his weight. "Then get the fuck off of me."

Vemdour sat back on his haunches. "I can't let you go without punishment."

A chill swept over me, dreading whatever it was the God of the Forsaken had in store. "You will remain in your chambers until I'm not angry with you anymore."

My mouth parted. "Are you *grounding me*?"

"Call it what you want, but that is your punishment."

My body rattled with laughter. I hadn't been grounded since I was twelve when I tried to run away from our hidden house. Margie didn't think that was as funny as I did at the time. To this day, I have no idea how she found me. Dark magic, probably. Or maybe she implanted some kind of tracking chip in my brain.

He gawked at me. "Are you *laughing* at your punishment?"

His question only made me laugh harder.

"Go ahead, do your worst." I wiggled my fingers at him. "Ground me."

Amusement glittered in his coal-lit eyes as he clapped twice, teleporting me out of the dining hall and dropping me into my room without so much as a goodbye. Bastard.

CHAPTER 24

It was a mistake to agree to—okay, laugh at—Vemdour's punishment, thinking his anger would dissipate by the time morning broke over the horizon.

It didn't.

I stood by the window, staring at the glittering stars shining in the blood-dark sky, and fought the nagging fear that Vemdour may hold onto his anger for a very long time. I wasn't sure what I would do if he planned to keep me locked up for much longer. I only had a handful of days left in this realm before Gideon came for me, and I sure as hell wouldn't spend them as some god's prisoner.

"Vemdour, I'm sorry I got drunk at dinner and slapped you," I said to the empty room. I left out the part where he deserved it. "And I'm sorry I stabbed you and laughed at your punishment. That wasn't very nice of me."

No response.

"I know you can hear me." I tested that theory this morning when I complained about being hungry and five-minutes later Cayden appeared with a breakfast—fresh fruits, pancakes, and peppermint tea for the raging migraine I woke up with. "Will you at least bring me some dinner? I'm famished."

Still no response.

With an exasperated sigh, I grabbed a couple of books from the bookshelf and padded over to the couch. As soon as I settled in and cracked open a very promising romance novel, the elevator dinged.

Cayden stepped through carrying a tray of food.

"I knew you could hear me," I muttered, shutting the book and setting it beside me.

I sank deeper into the sofa, prepared to have the same exchange with Cayden that we already had twice today. "I'd like to speak to Vemdour."

"About what?" He sat the tray on the coffee table.

I toyed with the short hem of one of the dresses the God of the Forsaken stocked my wardrobe with. The off-the-shoulder dress was fine black satin with see-through sleeves dotted with pearls. It was pretty and simple, but I longed for the days when I could lounge in raggedy sweats and thrifted tees. "I'm ready to leave."

"You have nowhere to go."

"Don't play dumb, Cayden. I'm returning to Empyrean."

Cayden pulled a piece of parchment from his pocket and handed it to me. "King Ward doesn't want you to come back. He sent a letter to Vemdour this morning."

With shaking hands, I scanned the page. A pair of thick black wings taunted me from the letterhead along with Lirabeth's familiar scrawl. The hunger in my stomach dissipated, replaced with dread.

God of the Forsaken,

I've learned Valeria has become a lady of your court. I'm sure you expect this letter to ask you for your demands on what it would take to free her, but that is not the case.

I care not for Valeria nor retrieving her.

I do ask that you pass along one message to my would-be usurper. Tell her that I've learned of her little revolt, and I'm going to put an end to it, along with any hope she may have of reigning. She is no longer welcome in Empyrean, and should she step foot in my realm... my guards will kill her on sight.

Until we meet again,

Ward

My body trembled as I read the letter over and over, committing his words to memory.

I care not for Valeria nor retrieving her.

I clutched the paper, tears burning my eyes. I didn't know why I was so caught up on that one line. I already knew he didn't care about me, didn't want me.

So why did it hurt so much to read it?

Cayden reached out a hand toward me. "I'm... I'm sorry, Valeria. Ward is—"

"Don't." My voice cracked. "I don't want your fucking pity. I don't want anything from *you*. Get out."

He didn't move.

I picked up the tray and hurled it across the room toward the elevator. It hit the doors, plates shattering with food and drink flying everywhere. "I said get the fuck out!"

He sighed and stood, stepping over the broken dishes without another word.

I hated him. Hated this realm.

My father may not want me, but Empyrean did. They had to. Because if they didn't, I didn't know what that meant for me. All I knew was I couldn't stay here a moment longer. Empyrean needed me. If the king knew about the rebellion, I had to figure out a way to seize the throne before the rebels lost *everything*—me included.

The elevator doors dinged, and I picked up a book to chuck at Cayden. "I told you to get—"

Vemdour sauntered in, glass crunching under his polished shoes. My eyes trailed up his towering, powerful frame. He was nothing but muscle. Taking one look at me, he frowned. "You're angry."

Angry? Oh, he had no idea the things I dreamt of doing to him once I saw his beautiful, monstrous face again. Without a second thought, I chucked the book at him and pegged him square in the jaw.

He blinked. "Is that all you got?" I reached for another book. "Come on, pet. You can do so much more than *that*. Throwing books? It's child's play."

With a force to be reckoned with, I flung the book and smacked him between the eyes. They didn't even water. All he did was bend over, pick up the books, and place them on the table.

I scowled. "I'm leaving."

"Cayden showed you the letter, did he not?" The glamour around him rippled. Two red welts marred his olive skin. With a wave of his hand, the mess I made in front of the elevator vanished. "Your father is aware of whatever rebellion you'd started before coming here and has forbidden you from returning."

"And? That doesn't change the fact that I want to leave." I threw my hands into the air. "I hate you. I hate this realm. You grounded me because I wounded your ego. You proved your point. Now, let." I poked his rock-hard chest. "Me." Another poke. "Go." A final poke.

He tilted his head, amused. "I punished you because I thought it would unlock your power."

"Listen, asshole." I clenched my fists at my sides. "I don't have any power."

"Believe me." His eyes met mine, and I noticed tiny flecks of gold swirling around in their endless depths. "You have power, pet."

My breath hitched in my chest. I wanted to believe him, believe this sugar-coated lie he was telling me. Because if I had power, I could go head-to-head with my father without risking anyone else's life. If I had power, I would never feel helpless again.

"You have more power than you know." He stepped closer. "It calls to me—a wicked darkness, unstable but strong. Let me help you shape it until you can wield it."

My feelings were all tangled up. I was angry with Vemdour. I wanted to leave, wanted to be free of this realm and him. But I was also intrigued. Mistress Marjorie told me long ago that there was a void inside me. What if what she saw wasn't a void? What if it was *power*? And what if I used that power against Vemdour and against my father to help Empyrean?

"Fine." My heart crashed against my ribcage. "Teach me."

THE DUNGEON STUNK WORSE than the Bygone. Beneath the filth was the scent of death, despair, and decrepit rot. It was a palpable thing snaking its way down my throat. No amount of wheezing would get the horrid taste out of my mouth.

Kneeling naked in front of us were three paper-thin bodies, black sacks covering their faces. A vine of thorns tied their hands behind their backs as they wriggled and writhed in place, trying to break free. Crimson dripped to the floor in sticky droplets with every attempt.

Vemdour pointed at them. "Pick one to practice on."

"To practice on?"

"Using your anger will help you draw out your power and give you a starting point for learning to control it. Now, pick one of these pathetic souls to torture."

I groaned, reminding myself of what Mistress Marjorie said before she left me here to rot. *Any soul trapped in this realm deserved to be here.* "Um, I don't know." I looked them over. Two males and a female. Both males on the left and right trembled in place, but the female in the center... she remained perfectly still as if she was ready for whatever came next. For both of our sakes, I hoped she was. "The one in the middle."

His steps were loud against the wet stone as he snatched the prisoner up with one hand. She yelped, kicking as he carried her into an empty chamber with me following close on his heels. He nodded toward an iron table against the back of the cell. "Grab a weapon."

I shrunk away from him. How was this the same being who told me he didn't want me to fear him? Who called me his equal? Rubbing my temples, I inched toward the table, remembering just who I was dealing with—the God of the Forsaken.

An assortment of tools sprawled across the top of a slimy table. From saws to pliers and blades so sharp they'd glide through skin like butter. It was like I stepped into a horror movie, and I was the antagonist.

Vemdour strung the woman up. Leather straps wrapped snug against her ankles and wrists and tight enough around her throat that if she thrashed, she wouldn't be able to move her head.

Grabbing a knife, I crossed the chamber.

He reached for the sack covering her face. "I find it funny that you chose this soul to torture."

"And why's that?"

Another sinister grin spread across his haunted face. "Because she tortured you for years."

My stomach sank as he yanked the sack away. The room around me spun. Strung up like a pig in a meat freezer was Ellody. Once beautiful, still stupid, Ellody.

She gaped at me, her eyes blinking rapidly to adjust to the lighting. Her gaze met mine, and she choked out a sob. "Valeria? Valeria, please help me. Please—" Her pleading stopped when she saw the weapon in my hand, the expensive dress adorning my body.

Vemdour laughed, and it cut me deep.

"Ellody." Her name crawled up my throat, and the knife slipped from my white-knuckled grip, landing on the ground with a clatter—loud and sharp, like her cries. I turned to Vemdour. "How did you know we had history?"

"Because I found her at your school when I went to clean up the mess she made."

My chest tightened. "Didn't you send the demons there with a bounty on my head?"

"Of course not." He scoffed as if the accusation was absolutely preposterous and flicked a piece of invisible lint from his shoulder. "I'm a *god*. I don't operate in bounties, and I don't send fledgling demons to do my bidding."

I glanced between the god and the demon. "Then who did?"

Ellody laughed. It sent a chill down my spine. "Blond hair. Violet eyes. Red dress. Prom night. The bounty didn't specify dead or alive, but we thought it'd be a two for one special if we got rid of the King of Empyrean's little problem and gifted it to the God of the Forsaken."

I drew closer to her, vicious-hot anger rippling under my skin. "You're saying *my father* put a bounty on my head?"

Another chilling laugh bubbled out of her, rattling her thin frame. "So pretty, but so naive."

Her words made something sinister lap underneath my skin as it wove its way through me, expanding and filling me until I felt like I would burst.

"Silence," Vemdour commanded. He kicked the blade away, eyes glinting with wicked intent. "Your wrath is a living thing, pet. It vibrates through you. It's ravenous. Feed it."

"Believe me, I want to," I whispered. "But I don't know how."

"Let me help you," he murmured as he wrapped his arms around me from behind, breath stirring my hair.

The back of my head brushed against his button-up. I was like a doll in his embrace, tiny in comparison to his broad frame. And strangely enough... I felt safe? Like he truly wanted to coax whatever powers he saw within me to the surface. Like he truly wanted to help me.

Darkness pulsed around us as he lowered his voice. "Magic is as simple as wanting and wishing. Tell me, what do you want to do to her?"

His large hand splayed across my stomach. Warmth nipped at my skin from his touch, from the heat that seeped through my dress as if the slow circles he traced were directly on my skin.

I considered this for a moment. What *did* I want to do to her? Memories of Ellody's torment over the years flashed throughout my mind—how she bullied me relentlessly for not having a father, for having curves, for liking to read, for *existing*, and how she turned my classmates against me with slut-shaming rumors and blatant lies. She was willing to sell me out for a bounty, and if the roles were reversed, she would have easily let me die.

"Is Ellody still in there?" I whispered to the god.

"She is."

"Good. I want her to feel how I feel." I swallowed the knot forming in my throat and pushed any regrets deep within me as I added, "I want to rip her fucking heart out."

Without breaking his tantalizing touch, he took my hand in his. He placed my palm flat against Ellody's chest. "Now, wish it. All you must do is imagine it."

"I really don't think I have that kind of power." My voice cracked. "I think you might be wrong about me."

His breath was hot on my ear, and my toes curled. "I'm rarely ever wrong, pet. Humor me."

My vision darkened until there was nothing but my hand pressing against the body in front of me. *My father put the bounty on my head.* The thought made my chest ache. I imagined reaching into Ellody and ripping her heart free from its bony cage, just so I could crush it the way my father did mine. A roaring fluttered in my ears as heat coursed through me, flickering and sparking under my skin. Something sizzled on my fingertips, pooling under the surface. The thought took root, and she screamed in agony as my hand dipped into her, as if her skin was melting away, parting for me and my touch. It was warm and wet, a rapid pounding that called to me, and I pushed in deeper until there was only the thumping of her heart beating in my palm. Ripping it free, I held the vessel as lavender flames danced along my skin. Any guilt that threatened to surface from what I had done was quickly stifled and replaced by pure, unbridled excitement.

My eyes went wide in astonishment. "How... how is this possible?"

"Power, Valeria. You have more of it than you know."

There was no way.

Margie... she knew. *You are a princess with power and that... that could very well be something that takes what's already inside of you, everything dark and vengeful, and draws it closer to the surface.*

"She was right." The words came breathlessly as I whirled around to face him, shaking my head. Maybe *he* was the key to unlocking my power completely. "And so were you. What else can I do?"

"Truthfully? I'm not sure. Your magic... it's different from mine." He brushed the sleeve of my dress up to expose my left wrist. Running a thumb over the brand, he added, "It's limited, confined to your wrath. This dyad of yours... I believe it's holding you back from tapping into your full potential."

My full potential.

Did my father know I had powers, and that was why he tried to have me killed? Or did Bastile know there was a darkness inside of me, and he bound me to Gideon to stifle it? To stifle what I could be?

Someone other than myself?

Maybe he feared what I'd become.

A shiver crawled down my spine and not from being afraid.

With this power, I could take back Empyrean. I could use it to make the realm a better place for everyone. I could create change. Screw gaining incriminating evidence against the king. Instead, I'd sucker Vemdour into teaching me everything I needed to know about my power. And once I leveled up, once I could wield this magic beyond my wrath, then I'd leave the Realm of the Forsaken and take the Empyrean throne by force.

"Thank you," I whispered to Vemdour, peering up through my eyelashes. I squeezed Ellody's heart until it was mush in my hand, and then I extended it toward him. "Hungry?"

CHAPTER 25

The last few days went by in a blur, a lot like those cheesy training sequences in movies that show the passing of time. That was exactly how it felt since the day I ripped Ellody's heart from her chest. Sometimes guilt gnawed away at my insides for what I'd done to her, but I couldn't allow myself to dwell on my actions or else it'd eat me alive. If I didn't think too much about it, I could straddle the fine line between regret and triumph and wake up each morning with a burst of energy, excited to meet with Vemdour and coax whatever power I had to the surface.

Breakfasts together in my bedroom turned into training sessions where he'd challenge me to small tasks—changing the color of a pen with a blink, pulling a book from the bookshelf with a wave of my hand, tying and untying shoelaces with a single thought.

I wasn't particularly good at any of it.

I had foolishly hoped I'd be able to master tapping into my power before Gideon came for me, but tomorrow marked a week since I'd left Empyrean, and I was swiftly running out of time.

"Again," Vemdour commanded. He sat beside me on the couch in my room, his muscular thigh pressed firmly against mine.

I stared at the fireplace and imagined it roaring with the same heat that rolled off the god in waves. Beads of sweat dotted my forehead as I concentrated, willing it to light.

It didn't.

I groaned. "I can't do this."

"Yes, you can," he said gently, resting his hand on my knee. "You just need to focus and call on your anger."

The warmth from his hand was a distraction from all thoughts of Gideon and my time in the Realm of the Forsaken slipping away as easily as sand in an hourglass.

I closed my eyes and cleared my mind of everything else.

My fingertips buzzed with energy. I reached for the familiar purring deep within me and tugged on the ribbons that wound around my buried powers until I felt the magic drift closer to the surface.

It was time.

Wrath simmered beneath my skin, but to wield my power, I needed it to boil. I pictured the starving Empyreans in the Pry, the crack of my father's hand against my face, Rosalyn's sad smile as she faded away into nothing, and Brini sleeping in a makeshift tent next to her dead parents.

My breath hitched.

I held my hand out, palm upward, and called the power of the sun to me, longing for a tiny burning ball of fire that I could use to light the hearth. Sweat dripped down my back, as I concentrated. *Come to me*, I thought over and over again until the sweet scent of magic in the air brought a small smile to my lips, and the single squeeze on my knee made me grin.

My eyelids fluttered open and found my palm engulfed in the same lavender flames I had conjured when I tore Ellody's heart from her chest. With a wave toward the hearth, the fire flew from my hand and ignited the room in soft purple light.

"Well done, pet," Vemdour said. "At this rate, you may be able to wield your powers freely by the time you're fifty."

I beamed at his praise, not letting the rest of his words sour my good mood.

He snapped his fingers and the fire instantly extinguished.

"Hey!" I frowned. "I worked hard on that."

"And you'll do it again and again until lighting a hearth is as easy as breathing." I opened my mouth to object, but he gave me a *look* and added, "But, not today. Today, we're going to do something fun."

"I can only image what the God of the Forsaken thinks of as fun."

A mischievous grin spread across his feral lips as he tucked a lock of dark hair behind his ear. "I did provide you with a swimsuit, didn't I?"

"STOP THAT," VEMDOUR growled, from where he sat on a pier, bare feet dangling in the lake.

After rifling through my wardrobe and finding one, delicately embroidered bikini, Vemdour had spirited us away to Crescent Lake. Aptly named for its shape, the lake was hauntingly pretty with knotted and twisted oak trees dotting the perimeter and grainy sand, black as night, carving up the shoreline.

"Oh, is the big, scary demon god afraid of a little water?" I teased, splashing him again.

Beads of liquid trailed down the taut muscle of his broad chest, and those thin, golden scars marring his olive skin glowed as if they were alive.

His night-flecked eyes met mine in challenge. "What did you call me, pet?"

A small smile tugged at the corners of my lips as I asked sweetly, "To your face or behind your back?"

He shook his head as I lifted my hands. "I'm warning you, don't—"

I conjured up the image of a wave crashing over the god and called my magic to me. It listened almost immediately and shot toward him, drenching him from head to toe. I burst out laughing as he glared at me.

Vemdour stood and reached for the top button of his sleek, black slacks and slowly kicked them off, leaving him standing before me in nothing but his swimming trunks (also in the god's favorite color—black).

My eyes swept over him, from his thick, dark hair, bound back by a leather strap, his powerful frame, all the way down to his muscular thighs, toned calves, and back up again. Gods, he was absolutely delicious. My cheeks flushed as I remembered just who I was gawking at.

The God of the Forsaken.

The number of scars lining his body were far too vast for me to count, and I longed to reach out and trace them, to feel the purring of whatever magic they were imbued with.

He dove from the pier, like an agile swimmer from a diving board, arcing into the water with more grace than I ever could. I spun in circles, kicking aimlessly as I waited for him to surface and splash me back.

He didn't.

Twenty seconds passed. Thirty. After a minute, I began to panic.

"Vemdour?" I swam toward the center of the lake and reached around blindly for him. My hands swiped at nothing but lukewarm water. "You can come up now."

I inhaled a deep breath and dove under the crystal-clear water, searching for the god. He was nowhere to be found. Surfacing, I called out for him again. "Vemdour? This isn't funny."

A slight breeze weaved through the notched branches of the trees on the shoreline. The lake was still, not even a ripple, save for where I waded in place. Goosebumps pricked my skin. Where did he go?

"Vemdour, please. You're—"

Something latched around my legs, eliciting a scream from me, and yanked me under the surface with barely enough time to suck in a breath. I kicked and clawed to no avail as I was dragged deeper and deeper into the dark depths.

My lungs burned, and I thrashed in panic, clamping my lips shut and willing them not to open, not to let in an involuntary gulp of water. I pinched my nose and placed a hand over my mouth, hoping it would stop me from gasping for air, but the tether between Gideon and I pulled taut, screaming one simple truth.

I was going to drown.

CHAPTER 26

Black spots dotted my vision as Vemdour's blurry face came into view, with a smirk that told me precisely what he would say if he could speak underwater—*who's the big, scary demon god now?*

My body felt weightless as I floated in front of him, unable to breathe, unable to do anything but stare into his infinite eyes as he watched my life slip away.

He drew closer to me and pressed his full lips against mine, parting my mouth. I waited for the taste of his tongue, for the clashing of his teeth, for his kiss of death.

None of those things came.

The god breathed air deep into my lungs, slowing my heartbeat and edging away my panic. Finally, I understood. He wanted to scare me, not drown me. The bastard. My fingers twitched as I inhaled and held as much air as I could.

When he pulled his mouth away from mine, he smiled.

I punched him.

Vemdour only grinned as he grabbed my hand, laced his fingers through mine, and dragged me further into Crescent Lake's depths. I tugged him back, frantically shaking my head and pointing toward the surface. The thought of going deeper underwater frightened me.

He squeezed my hand once as if saying, *you're fine,* and then tightened his grip on me as he led us carefully into a rocky cove, stopping only once more to breathe air into my lungs. After what felt like a lifetime, but was only a minute or two, we kicked our way to the surface, and I gasped in lungful after lungful of air and spit the taste of salt and death from my mouth.

My lips tingled as if I'd burnt them from drinking something hot. I scowled. "I can't believe you kissed me."

"That wasn't a kiss." Vemdour's face was alight with amusement as he removed the leather strap from his hair and twined it around his wrist, securing it with a simple knot. "It was a breath of life."

"Same thing."

"A kiss from a god is *very* different, pet."

"Oh?" I folded my arms across my chest. This was bound to be interesting. "How so?"

"Because when I kiss you, your body will beg for more. Your knees will quake, your heart will pound, and desire will consume you until you're left with an aching that only I can satisfy." He looked me dead in the eyes. "No kiss from another will *ever* compare to mine."

I laughed. Hard. The sound ricocheted off the cave walls, making it seem like an entire audience laughed with me. I wiped away tears of amusement as I pulled myself together and said, "Man, you're a bit full of yourself for a big, scary demon god."

All he did was hold his hand out to me. "Come, there's something I want you to see."

With a roll of my eyes, I let him guide me out of the swimming hole and down three rough-hewn stairs to a worn, smooth path, as if it had seen a million steps just like ours.

Once my feet were steady on the slick stone, I slipped my hand from his. My traitorous heart skipped when the god flexed his fingers, as if he missed my touch, just before he raked it through his hair.

As we walked along, Vemdour pointed to the ceiling. Hanging above us was a delicate sheet of glowing flowers that illuminated the ceiling of the cave like a curtain of turquoise and marigold stars.

"It's beautiful," I said, quietly. In truth, it was a little unsettling to see how much beauty could be found in a realm full of horrors.

"Yes," he agreed, and I felt the weight of his gaze shift to me. "Beautiful indeed."

His arm lightly brushed against mine. Heat radiated from him, and I found myself pressing closer to the god to take advantage of his warmth.

We continued down the stone path, guided by the stars above us, until we took a sharp left turn and stepped into a small cavern with a pocket of luminescent water. Steam rose from it in welcome.

"The Realm of the Forsaken has hot springs?" I asked in disbelief.

"Yes," he said simply. "They're warmed by the volcanoes just north of here. You can see them from the pool at the castle."

"Wait, we have a pool?" I asked, as I toed the deliciously warm water.

"Yes, *we* have a pool."

"I didn't mean—"

He waved away my words and ushered me into the hot spring. The water felt amazing against my skin, like cashmere on a winter day.

Vemdour climbed in behind me. We were close, too close, in this small spring of warmth, but I didn't feel the urge to back away. I glanced up at the god and gently ran my finger over one of his glowing scars.

He shivered beneath my touch.

"What are these?" I whispered. The restless purring beneath them told me they were imbued with dark magic. But who's?

"Proof that I am more monster than man."

My finger stilled in place as realization dawned on me. "They're tallies, aren't they?"

His sad eyes searched mine before he nodded. "Every soul I've ever claimed before they were truly meant to die is carved into my flesh as a constant reminder of who I am—a prisoner in his own skin."

So he *was* cursed, but why? Who was powerful enough to curse the God of the Forsaken?

Another god?

"Who did this to you?" I asked softly, laying my hands flat against his broad chest. "Was it Bastile? Is that why you... murdered him?"

He tensed, then took a step away from me. My hands fell limp to my sides. "I did not *murder* Bastile." He gestured to his markings. "I do not bear the weight of his death on me."

"Don't try to lie, Vemdour." I sank deeper into the warmth of the water, leaving only my head bobbing above the surface. "I know you killed Bastile hours prior to Cayden slitting my mother's throat. I just don't know *why*. For revenge? For power? To put Cayden on a stolen throne, so you can pull his strings like a puppeteer?"

He was quiet for a moment, and then he spoke, "Centuries before you were born, Bastile had come to me with his tail between his legs. He was erratic, not of his right mind, going on and on about a prophecy. He said there would come a day when Empyrean wasn't safe for him anymore. He was so spooked to learn of a time when his own people wanted to see him dead that he was desperate enough to beg me for help.

"I had laughed his worries off as nothing more than the ramblings of a madman, but he was serious. He had dreamed up a way to cheat death by creating yet another realm, one that only the dead could preside over for all eternity."

"The Half-Light," I whispered, transfixed on his tale.

He nodded, skimming his hands over the top of the water. "There was a riddle from the prophecy he repeated tirelessly until even I committed it to memory: '*A woman born with violet eyes must be the one to rise. Tethered to darkness, tethered to light, she is the sword, he is the knight.*' Once you were born, he was certain the prophecy was about you. He sought me out and said it was time for him to crossover into the Half-Light to begin his reign in the afterlife.

"But that's not all... In exchange for my assistance in helping him create the Half-Light all those years ago, he betrothed you to me, convinced I was the knight the prophecy spoke of."

I sucked in a sharp breath. "He *what*? No. He... He wouldn't. He *loved* my mother. He would have never wanted to see her daughter wed to a... a monster like you."

Vemdour flinched. It was nearly imperceivable, but I saw it. My words struck him as hard as a slap. He recovered, lips curling into an impassive grin. "Maybe, maybe not. But that was the bargain we had struck, in exchange for his immortality in the Half-Light."

"So you did murder him," I said flatly. "After you secured my hand in marriage."

"I killed him, yes. Because the only way for me to grant him favor over death was if he died himself. Don't frown, pet. He knew it was coming and had set his affairs in order. Now, Bastile is happy in the Half-Light, cherry-picking whatever souls he wants to pluck from Empyrean and the Realm of the Mortals before they enter my groves."

I shook my head, unable to make any sense of this. My gaze drifted to the brand on my wrist, and I felt for the faint hum of the tether between Gideon and me. Why would Bastile betroth me to Vemdour *and* bind me to Gideon? I rubbed my temples. There had to be more to Bastile's plan, to this prophecy Vemdour spoke of.

"But why?" I asked in disbelief. "Why would Bastile believe the prophecy was about you?"

"Because I'm the God of the Forsaken. I am darkness, I am fear, I am your knight. And you're the Princess of Empyrean. You are light, you are hope, and you are my sword. Together, we are unstoppable."

My mouth parted, heart beating rapidly. "Bastile betrothed us, so we could unite our realms."

"Yes, but Ward had other plans."

My brows raised at the mention of my father's name. He must have known about the betrothal. It was why he sent me away to the Realm of the Mortals to keep me hidden from Vemdour, from our marriage, and from any chance of prying the throne from his wretched grip. And that must be why my father wanted to lead a counter-attack against the Realm of the Forsaken, he believed Vemdour wanted the Empyrean throne.

"So that's what you meant when you said my presence in your realm would be an arrangement to piss off the gods and kings who have wronged us," I murmured. "Is that also why my father sent that letter forbidding me from returning to Empyrean? He thinks I came here to wed you, doesn't he? Maybe if you told him that wasn't the case, he'd let me go home..."

Vemdour's expression softened. "As long as Ward is alive, it is unsafe for you to return to Empyrean."

"But—"

"Valeria." He waded through the water that separated us and tilted my head back with a featherlight grip on my chin. "He will kill you if you return to Empyrean. Do you understand me?"

"I have friends there," I said. The words were too loud for the small space. "People I *care* about. If I don't stop my father, they will die. The rebellion—"

"The rebellion will be fine without you for a couple of months until you hone your powers and are strong enough to take the throne by force."

I took a step back, out of his reach, tone turning frosty. "Stop interrupting me. Stop acting like you give a single fuck about Empyrean. You don't. You don't even care about *me*. I'm just something to be used by you, by my father, by everyone, and I am *sick of it.*"

My mind spun as anger simmered under my skin. I needed to get away from Vemdour and the truth of his words, from the fact that if Bastile had it his way, this man, this *monster*, would be my husband. I climbed out of the hot spring before he could respond. Just as my bare feet touched the ground, glittering mist surrounded me, turning the stone to plush carpet.

I glanced over my shoulder, half-expecting to find Vemdour behind me, but he wasn't there.

I had spirited myself away from the god and into my room at the castle.

I collapsed onto the bed, not caring that I was soaking wet. My thoughts were a knotted mess that I tried to work through. Gideon was supposed to come for me tomorrow, but after what I learned today...

What if Vemdour was right? What if I *was* safer in the Realm of the Forsaken? The thought sent a chill across my flushed skin. If I didn't get better with my powers, I was never going to be able to help Empyrean.

There was only one thing I could do now.

I slipped from the bed and over to the writing desk where I grabbed a piece of blank parchment and a fountain pen, and I scrawled a letter to Gideon.

G,

I miss you.

I'm safe. And I pray to Bastile that you're safe, too. I received a letter from my father that he learned of the rebellion, and I'm scared he's going to hurt you and Brini and everyone else I care about. I've come up with a plan to ensure I take the Empyrean throne without anyone getting hurt.

Which means, I don't want you to come for me. I can't tell you why (for your own safety) but know that my reasoning is sound. Just... please, keep your head down until I'm back.

I don't know when that'll be. It might be days or weeks. ~~*I fear that it could be months.*~~

However long it takes, it'll be worth it. I promise.

Trust that I am safe, I am well, and ~~*Vemdour isn't so bad*~~ *I've got the God of the Forsaken wrapped around my finger.*

Until I see you again, here are some papery kisses.

Xx

V

I swiped a layer of red lipstick across my lips and kissed the bottom of the page. While waiting for the ink to dry, I penned Gideon's name across the front of an envelope in cursive. Once the ink dried, I folded the letter in half, tucked it into the envelope, and called for the elevator.

A small part of me feared Gideon would see my decision to remain in the Realm of the Forsaken as a betrayal that he would never forgive me for. But whether Gideon liked it or not, Vemdour was right.

I couldn't help Empyrean if I was dead.

CHAPTER 27

Months have passed since I'd tasked Cayden with sending my letter to Gideon asking him to remain in Empyrean while I stayed in the Realm of the Forsaken to hone my powers.

I didn't think Gideon would listen, but when my seventh day in the Realm of the Forsaken came and went, when my seventh *month* came and went, a part of me felt betrayed that my soulmate didn't even have the decency to write me back.

There was no communication through the bond, no inkling of fear or nervousness or hope. I found it hard to believe he was actually angry with me for my choice, but it was better than the alternatives—that he was dead because of his loyalty to me, or worse, he didn't care that I hadn't come back.

I didn't have much time to worry about Gideon and his feelings, though. From dawn until dusk, I spent the last several months training with Vemdour.

And if I had learned anything about the Realm of the Forsaken, it was that gods were persistent as fuck. With his relentless training, using my power for little things became second nature. Lighting the hearth in my bedroom, changing my outfit, even spiriting from one place to another, had become ingrained habits honed after hours and hours of trying and failing.

The big things like redecorating my room or ripping out hearts... those were another story.

Most of those sessions ended up with me a sweaty, frustrated mess. Not only because I kept failing. But also because I found myself growing increasingly attracted to the god. His careful touches set my skin on fire in a way that made me question my sanity. The way he was proud of me for even the smallest accomplishments sent heat to my cheeks in a blushing school-girl kind of way.

It was annoying in every sense of the word.

But every night I counted down the minutes until I could spend time with Vemdour. An unexpected bonus from the amount of time we've spent together was that the glamour around him rarely showed his monstrous features.

The Realm of the Forsaken's court had definitely taken notice. Especially at formal meals like tonight's where the god no longer feasted on human flesh but instead opted for mortal food. I didn't want to believe he made the switch for my sake, but it was hard not to feel somewhat flattered.

Like every other night since murdering the demon that inhabited Ellody, Vemdour seated me to his left. Pyrtra was discarded like the trash she was, and if the rumors circulating the court were true, she hadn't been to his bedroom since that night in the hot springs.

My breath hitched, wondering if he cast her aside as some kind of allegiance to me. If those all too familiar hands of his stroked himself at night as he thought of *me*. If those teeth that were now tearing through a chicken breast rather than a human limb would ever graze against my skin.

Gods, I think I had a crush on him.

As if he heard my thoughts or felt the bubbly warmth spreading through my veins or saw the slight shift as I crossed and uncrossed my legs, clenching my knees together, he glanced at me. His night-flecked eyes raked over every exposed freckle and pale, thin scar on my skin. He set his fork down, and gently, ever so gently, placed his hand on my bare thigh. His touch burned in the most delicious way.

It had been too long since I'd been touched by anyone other than myself.

I met his gaze and spread my legs in silent permission.

Painstakingly slow, his hand crept closer to the silky wet fabric that—

Vemdour paused, nostrils flaring, as two unfamiliar faces sauntered into the dining hall.

The woman's springy cinnamon curls bounced with her purposeful stride. Her rose-red dress was striking against her dark brown skin, and it flared out at the bottom. It was so unlike anything I'd seen someone wear in this realm that it caught me by surprise, even more than how lovely she was. As if she felt me studying her, she flashed me a grin, exposing paper white teeth with a tiny gap between the front two. And the man trailing behind her was equally as handsome, with bronze skin and eyes like liquid honey. His dark hair had a streak of gold and was tied in a low ponytail at the nape of his neck. Dressed in finery a match to Vemdour's, I could make out the edges of his muscles tensing beneath his suit. Jutting out from behind him were two black wings, as iridescent as a raven's. But he was no Celestian.

The man's gaze met mine for an uncomfortable amount of time, but the bored expression on his gorgeous face did nothing to give away his thoughts.

Vemdour removed his hand from under the table and sighed quite dramatically. He turned toward the strangers, fixing his attention on the man. "Give me one reason not to rip those wings from your back, Søren."

My gaze flickered to Cayden, who pressed his lips into a thin line.

"I'm here on official emissary business," Søren said curtly, his gaze sliding to mine once more. "The Realm of the Divine tasked me to see if the rumors are true."

Vemdour didn't so much as look in my direction as he said, "I don't know what rumors you speak of, but if you're referring to Valeria, then I highly suggest you choose your words wisely."

I smiled at the god's threat.

"My lord," the woman said, bowing. Her eyes slid to Cayden, only briefly, before she brightened. "The Realm of the Divine sent a letter. They are... not happy with the current circumstances."

So, my presence in the Realm of the Forsaken was pissing off the gods. Just what Vemdour wanted. I locked that bit of information away for later.

Vemdour turned to me and tucked a loose curl of hair behind my ear. He leaned in close and whispered, "Play along."

"Say please," I murmured.

"Please." His warm breath sent a shiver through me. "Now, giggle." He nipped my earlobe, teeth tugging it gently. My heart thundered as desire burned under my skin, and the sultry laugh that slipped from my lips wasn't forced. "Good girl." He pulled himself away from me, speaking loud enough for the strangers to hear. "I don't want to trouble you with these matters, my sweet. Retire for the evening, and I'll meet with you after I alleviate the worries of our guests."

Our guests. I didn't miss his word choice, and neither did Søren, judging from the sharp intake of his breath and rustle of his feathers.

"Of course." I stood, grabbing two chalices of wine. The length of my glittering dress was obscene, and I loved watching Søren's eyes bug out of his head as I mock-bowed. "I'll be in the pool waiting rather impatiently for your arrival, *my love.*"

For good measure, I winked at the winged stranger.

The room was silent as I disappeared from the dining hall. Several gazes burned holes into my back, so I added an extra swing to my hips. As the ornate double doors shut behind me, I jutted out my heel to keep one door cracked and lingered to see if whatever show we put on had its desired effect.

"What the *fuck* is going on here?" Søren hissed.

"Do not worry about what is going on in my realm," Vemdour said flatly. "Now, have a drink, Søren, and tell me what I've done to anger the Realm of the Divine this time."

It worked. With a grin splitting my face in two, I headed toward the pool.

EVERYTHING IN THIS fortress was modern with a dash of roughness. I hated it and loved it at the same time. Loved that I could see myself thriving here. And hated that I liked this castle—mostly the amenities—more than the one waiting for me in Empyrean.

Floating in the deliciously heated water, I stared at the night sky peeking through the skylight. The pool was as beautifully brutal as everything else in this realm. Jaggedly carved into the inky-colored stone, overlooking endless ash-covered volcanoes, smoldering red and orange from within as if the land was burning from the inside out.

Much like I was.

Every part of me wished Vemdour would saunter in, his powerful frame as naked as mine. I could've left my swimsuit on, but if Søren had followed Vemdour here, I wanted to sell whatever image the god was trying to portray.

But that was definitely something I would ask him about later because it had been over two hours...

I sighed. Vemdour wasn't coming. And, it seemed, neither was I.

MY HAIR HUNG WET DOWN my back, dripping tiny beads of water onto the floor with every silent step I took down the hall and toward my floor. I'd waited for Vemdour at the pool until I was pruned and not a minute more. He stood me up. Bastard.

The murmur of two hushed voices echoed down the corridor that led to the dining hall. I shivered against the chill of the cold stones as I inched closer. Tugging the wet towel tighter across my shoulders, I peeked around the corner to spy the demon whose arm was taken and given to Mason, standing opposite a woman with long, silky hair and ashen skin. Pyrtra.

"This is good news, Tam," she said.

The demon, Tam, cocked his head to the side. "How?"

She sighed. "The King of Empyrean wiped out the entire rebellion. They're all *dead*. He banished the Witch of the Gray from Seraphicity, and the princess can't step foot in Empyrean without receiving a death sentence. When she learns what's gone on while she's overstayed her welcome here, she'll go ballistic and leave our realm for good."

I sucked in a breath, covering my mouth with one hand. No. This couldn't be happening. The rebels were all... dead? My stomach soured as I pressed my back against the stone wall. The stones lapped at my heat, sending an icy wave of shock through me.

They were lying. They had to be.

A glance at my wrist confirmed the brand was still there; the faint hum from the tether sang in my blood and danced around my soul. If Gideon were dead, wouldn't this and the feeling in the tether disappear? He had to be alive.

This was some kind of sick lie.

"Vemdour will never tell her the truth. She has his favor," Tam hissed.

I craned my neck to hear better, just in time to watch Pyrtra back-hand him across the face. The blow rattled down the hall, sounding like it hurt like hell.

Silence stretched between them as Tam rubbed his cheek.

"She does not have his favor." She lowered her voice. "I do, and I'll rule the four realms beside him. She's nothing but a pawn, the means to an end."

I flinched.

"So, how do you plan on getting this information to the girl?" Tam fidgeted, shifting from foot to foot. "I want to be there when she realizes she's lost everything."

She waved away his words. "Your intel will prove to be useful, my friend."

Pyrtra pushed past him and disappeared down the hallway, leaving him alone. I backed away from the edge of the wall and tried to steady the pounding in my chest. This was bad. I'd spent too much time in this realm trying to master my power, and it ended up costing me everything.

Because of my selfishness, the rebellion crumbled into nothing.

I should've taken my father's warning in his letter seriously. He said he discovered the rebellion, but I didn't believe him. I thought he was trying to bait a reaction from me. I guess that wasn't the case after all.

My mouth went dry as footsteps drew nearer. Tam rounded the corner just as I sprinted into a run. In a blinding quickness, he snatched a fistful of my hair and yanked me toward him.

"Let me go, asshole," I said through clenched teeth.

He obliged, throwing me against the wall. My head cracked against the stone and stars sprung to my vision as I fell to the floor. I reached back to touch my head and hissed. My fingers came away bloody.

He stared down at me with dark, sinister eyes. My mind spun as he knelt beside me. "I've been waiting to find you alone."

I swallowed the lump in my throat. "I'm under Vemdour's protection."

He yanked the towel from me and threw it down the hall. His leer raked over me from head to toe, and I wished I was wearing a parka instead of the skimpy black bikini Vemdour gifted me.

My skin prickled with unease as a blade manifested in his hand. Crap.

I reached for my hidden dagger—

A single sharp burning sensation drew my gaze toward my chest. My mouth parted in shock, registering what had happened. Tam drove his blade between my breasts until the hilt was flush against my skin. A scream poured from my lips and rattled around us, echoing and echoing.

"You'll bleed out before he finds you." He took one long look at where the knife protruded from my chest and laughed as he rose to his feet. Then he turned on his heel and disappeared down the hallway—leaving me for dead.

My breath came in spurts. I glanced down to the hilt of the dagger and hesitated, hand stilling in place. Fuck. I couldn't remember—was I supposed to take the blade out or leave it in?

Vemdour.

With more effort than necessary, I made it to my feet, using the wall as support. I wound through the halls, stumbling toward the elevator, blade still in my chest. My feet were on autopilot, leading me toward the god.

He would help me.

Warm blood trickled down my bare skin. The halls were frighteningly quiet, and for a moment, I feared that maybe Vemdour tasked Tam with killing me and that was why he stood me up. But no, he wouldn't do that. Would he? I thought we'd become close over the last few months. We'd become... friends on the verge of sharing a bed.

Sweat clung to the back of my neck. Every step jiggled the dagger, sending white-hot flashes of pain through my body.

How was I even alive right now?

I made it to the elevator and smashed the button a dozen times. The pain worsened with every passing minute. It hurt to inhale, even worse to exhale. After what felt like a lifetime, the doors dinged open, and I hurled myself inside, pressing the button to the ninth floor before collapsing onto the ground.

What if Vemdour wasn't in his room? What if I died in a fucking elevator?

Oh, gods. There was no honor in that.

My vision came in and out of focus, blurring and whirring as the elevator soared higher and higher. When I reached Vemdour's floor, the doors opened. But I was unable to move. Everything hurt.

"Vemdour." His name was a prayer on my tongue.

He rounded the corner, and shock riddled his beautiful face. Dropping to his knees beside me, he growled, "Who did this to you?"

I cringed. The pain was deep and raw. Another gasp. "Tam..."

A flash of violence flickered in his eyes as he scooped me into his arms and gingerly carried me toward... his unmade bed? The silky black sheets were like spilled ink. He laid me down gently, surveying the wound.

"It's a good thing you left the blade in." His shoulders tensed as he pursed his lips. "Stay still and take a deep breath." I did as he instructed. He yanked the blade from my chest and placed his free hand over the wound. My eyes drifted to the ceiling as a shock of pain radiated through me. Fastened directly above the bed was a mirror, and I watched in silence as something poured from his palm in a dazzling, blinding light. It burned and sizzled as the wound zipped itself shut from the inside out. Even the cut on the back of my head tingled as it closed. He tossed the knife onto the foot of the bed and cupped my cheek with his other hand. "The pain will be over soon."

The burning subsided, shifting into a bleak numbness—pins and needles with a dash of static. One glance at my chest and my jaw dropped. A thin golden scar replaced the bloodied wound, surrounded by tiny black stars.

"You couldn't have just healed me?"

"All healing magic comes with a price, pet. Be thankful the price you paid was pretty."

I rolled my eyes, sitting up on my elbows. "Whatever."

A quiet moment passed between us before he spoke again. "You were wrong, by the way." He ran one finger over my scar, and it sparked under his touch. "That night in the hot spring? You said I didn't care about you, but I do. More than I ever thought I could."

There was an ache in my chest and not from the freshly healed wound.

He smiled softly and snapped his fingers. A fuzzy blanket appeared across my lap, along with a laptop playing a rerun of some reality TV show. "Stay here until I come back."

I snuggled under the blanket. It smelled woodsy, fresh. "Where are you going?"

Vemdour's lips curled into a sinister smile as he grabbed Tam's dagger. "To kill a demon."

CHAPTER 28

Sleep came and went until I jolted fully awake, still alone in Vemdour's room.

I shivered against his sheets, thinking of the death and despair consuming Empyrean as I laid around and did nothing. My heart ached for my... friends? Is that what they were? What Brini was? What Mae and Bex had become? Even Malachi and Sabel... I missed each of them and worried for their safety. And where was Mason? Was he somewhere with Mistress Marjorie?

Were they even still alive?

I hadn't thought much about them since trying to learn more about my powers, and guilt gnawed at me.

I sighed and crawled out of bed. Grabbing a long-sleeve shirt from the floor, I slipped it on to stave away the chill crawling up my spine. It was far too big on me, hanging just above my knees, but it was good enough.

Vemdour's bedroom was a distraction from the relentless worries that prodded at me. The space took up the entire ninth floor of this wing of the castle, and it was so... normal. I half-expected him to sleep on rocks or in a tomb. But no, the room was packed to the brim with furniture dipped in gold. A large, four-poster bed rested against the far wall with a simple wooden chest at the foot of it. I tried to open it, but a spell locked it up tight. Tucked into the corner of the room was a writing desk with a stack of blank sheets of paper.

I wondered if they were the same pages Cayden used to send me his blood letter.

My fingers gently grazed countless artifacts and bones and books as I walked around. Judging by the trinkets taking up every inch of space, Vemdour was a collector. I guess if you've been alive for a millennium, you'd have to have some sort of hobby.

The ornate fireplace was decorated in shades of black and gold, and I stood in front of the flickering flames until my skin was flushed and tender, warmed from the heat. Above the mantle was an elegant painting of a young couple, faces glowing with fondness for each other. Their gestures were beautiful yet straightforward—his hand gently placed on her lap, her hands tenderly holding his. I couldn't help but peer closer as I noticed something familiar. Hanging from the woman's neck was a tiny gold chain with a dagger, similar to the one hanging from my own neck.

In the middle of the embossed frame was the painting's title: "The Boundless and The Bound."

"Ah, you're a fan of art," Vemdour purred from behind me. I jumped, and he chuckled. "You and the mortal boy have that in common."

"His name is Mason," I snapped.

"Yes, yes. Mason. Here, come sit." He patted the loveseat—it was the same shade of black as his hair. I obliged, angling my body away from him. His monstrous features were on full display with that pinprick smile barely reaching his eyes. "Are you sure you're feeling all right? You're never so quick to obey me."

I shrugged. "Tell me more about the painting."

"Worthless. I should burn it, but I can't let it go."

"How come?"

"It's of a former lover and me."

I looked between him and the handsome man in the painting. It was the same man beneath the glamour. A crown of bone dipped in gold and smoldering ember rested on his head, dark shoulder-length locks spilling out beneath it. Brown eyes alight with mischief caught my eye. He was so *human* before, no trace of a gaunt face or leathery skin.

"Don't look so surprised," he continued, circling one finger on his leather pants. I couldn't spot a drop of blood on his finely pressed shirt. Did he change clothes after killing Tam? "I betrayed her, and she cursed me to look as rotten on the outside as she believed I was on the inside. If I ever find her..." His voice trailed off as he stared at the painting. His features darkened as his eyes shuttered.

The woman staring back at him was a fearsome thing with a challenging smirk on her thin lips and a spark in her blue-gray eyes that demanded your attention. She was magnificent. But who *was* she? I almost asked, but thought better of it.

I poked his arm playfully. "I'm surprised Pyrtra allowed you to keep it."

He returned the full weight of his gaze to me. "Pyrtra didn't *allow* me to do anything."

"She was there with Tam before he stabbed me." The words rushed out of me. I licked my lips, recalling their conversation. "They were talking about Empyrean. They said my father killed the rebels, and I lost everything. Is it true?"

He nodded. "That is what Søren and Red came here to discuss."

No, they had to be mistaken. Like earlier, I still felt the muted hum of Gideon through the dyad. He was alive. I would know if he wasn't. But even if Gideon somehow escaped and my father had killed most of the rebels—

"Why didn't you tell me?" I blurted out, unable to hide the hurt in my voice. Somewhere along the line, Vemdour and I became something other than mortal enemies. Or at least, I thought we had.

"I was going to tell you this evening, but other things took priority." He laced each word with a tinge of sorrow, and the anger building in my chest evaporated. This was the side of him that I had grown to like over the last few months, and it frightened me more than the god who thrived on pain. It was a side that craved comfort, and it pulled on my heartstrings in a way that scared me.

Because it was *this* side of him that told me we were the same.

The truth slipped from my lips. "I don't know what I'm supposed to do now."

His hand dropped to my thigh. "You came to my realm under the illusion that you were trading yourself for the boy, but I knew the night I offered to let you go that wasn't the full truth. So tell me what you're *really* here for, pet."

Oh, what the hell. There was no point in lying anymore. "I wanted answers." I sighed. "But then it shifted into a desire for power."

"The darkness in you burns brighter when you're with me." The glamour around him rippled and his eyes danced as he reached to brush a strand of hair out of my face, fingers grazing my skin. "Don't you see? You belong here. You belong with me. Give in to the wrath and join me. Together, all four of the realms will be ours."

The allure of ruling all four realms caught my attention. Pyrtra said something similar a few hours ago. Was that his plan all along? To accept Bastile's betrothal to me and let me rule by his side as he conquered the other two realms? Me? A mortal-raised princess with a foul mouth and a penchant for trouble?

Vemdour stood and hauled me to my feet, using his free hand to tilt my head up. Every fiber of my being told me this was a trap, but my feet locked in place. Something within him needed mending. It called out to me the way he said my darkness called out to him.

"I'll give you everything." His voice deepened as he stared down at me. The air around us went still, almost sacred, as if the realm had been waiting for this moment, for their god to murmur this promise to me, for us to exchange vows. "Everything you've ever wanted—revenge, power, love. I will give you it all."

I wanted all those things. And I wanted them without fear that someone could take them from me or someone could punish me for wanting them. He spoke to my deepest desires like he knew me better than I knew myself, and that scared me. It scared me to have my darkest truths on display. And it scared me even more knowing he wouldn't run from them.

Could he give me the peace that I'd been chasing my entire life? Would one kiss with a monster's lips change me into someone I didn't recognize in the mirror? Could I give myself to him in the hope that I would gain enough power to save Empyrean? That I could protect myself from the malice he nurtured within me?

It was worth a shot.

Gnawing on my lip, I lowered my voice and admitted, "I do want it all." My heart thundered in my chest. "I want it all with you."

He smiled and placed two fingers under my chin. I shuddered, remembering where those two fingers almost were, earlier this evening. "Have you ever been kissed by a god?"

My skin was a live current, sensitive to his touch. He was dark and brooding in that toxic ex kind of way that you knew was so bad for you, but you didn't *care*. Because his touch made you feel alive in a way no one else's had.

"You know I haven't."

His mouth was a breath away from mine. "Do you want to be?"

I searched his eyes for some sign of betrayal, but all I saw was what I imagined he saw in mine. *Wanting.*

Somehow, during the months we spent together, Vemdour slipped into my chest as easily as Tam's blade. The only difference was that no one would be able to heal me from a wound as brutal as the God of the Forsaken.

As he stood before me asking if he could kiss me, I didn't care about the wrongs he committed, the lives he destroyed, or the truths he harbored. All I wanted was to know this version of him—the one beneath the glamour, the god unable to love and be loved.

"Yes," I breathed. "Yes, I want to be kissed by you."

He lips captured mine. My body buzzed from head to toe as if it was electrified like the air before a thunderstorm. His tongue slipped into my mouth, tasting like a tangled web of hope and fear, and I devoured it. It felt wrong, *so* fucking wrong, but my arms snaked around his neck, and my hands wound through his thick, soft hair, slipping through the glamour.

Were we the same? Was that why I could see through his glamour? He said my darkness called to his darkness, and I believed him. How else would he know me so well?

He deepened the kiss, and blue eyes flashed in my mind. Bitter ash replaced the taste of honey. Wrong. This kiss was so, so wrong. And somehow, so right.

Kissing him was like dancing with death—perilous and inevitable.

Vemdour broke away, his breathing ragged. "I've waited a very long time for that." He leaned forward, forehead meeting mine. "I've waited a very long time for *you*. And now that I've tasted you, not a single other soul will ever satiate me again."

His words were mesmerizing as the realization set in. Vemdour *kissed* me. Actually kissed me. And all of the fear I had for wanting slowly dissipated, leaving only his promise of love, power, and revenge.

Yet my thoughts drifted to Gideon. He would never forgive me for what I'd agreed to become, what I'd agreed to do. He'd think I was just like Cayden, maybe worse.

I swallowed, frowning as I glanced at the brand.

Vemdour tensed, his hand cupping my cheek. "There's something you need to know, pet."

I tilted my head back to look up at him as I searched his endless eyes. "And what's that?"

"You should have a seat." He took my hand and led me to the couch. I sat, drawing my knees to my chest. Sitting beside me, he pursed his lips. "There's no easy way to say this."

"Oh, for fuck's sake. Just spit it out, Vemdour."

"We need to sever your dyad." My stomach plummeted. "I've thought about it for a while now, and it's the only thing I can think of that's limiting you from wielding your full power."

I glanced at the brand, at my connection to Gideon, to Empyrean. So long ago, I would've given anything to get rid of this stupid thing. It was a gift from Bastile, but now I didn't need it. Not when I had a god in my back pocket. I could free Gideon from this burden, and we could both go our separate ways. He could have a chance at actual happiness with someone who could love him the way he deserved to be loved—entirely.

We both knew I was never going to be enough for him.

"Tell me what you're thinking." Vemdour leaned toward me, thumb caressing my bottom lip. "Tell me what you want."

"Break it."

"Say please," he said, echoing my command from earlier.

I kissed him, hard and fast, only stopping once I was sure. Once I was ready to fully align myself with the God of the Forsaken.

"Please," I whispered. "Please sever the dyad."

I didn't have to ask him twice. His hand dwarfed my wrist as he murmured a chant in an unfamiliar tongue. The corners of his lips tugged downward, but when he opened his eyes and let me go, he grinned.

Just like that, the brand transformed from shimmering gold to matte black, stark against my creamy skin. Equally dark blooming roses and thorny vines wound around the mark and my wrist, streaking up my forearm in a delicate tattoo. An after-effect of Vemdour's magic, no doubt.

My breath caught in my chest. It was beautiful, but... it felt too easy.

"I thought it would hurt," I said, wrinkling my nose. "Especially since it hurt so much to be bound to Gideon in the first place."

Magic was so weird. So unpredictable.

"First, you should know by now that I would never intentionally cause you harm." He tilted his head to the side, admiring his handiwork. "Second, why would you think that? Severing a dyad like this sacrifices only one of the bodies so that the other can have a full soul."

I inhaled sharply and jumped to my feet, wincing at the pain in my chest—whether it was from his words or the still fresh scar, I didn't know. "*Sacrifices*?"

"What did you think would happen?" He leaned back, arms behind his head. "I'd sever the dyad, and you'd both go on living with half a soul?"

"Yes." I blinked through the pressure of tears welling behind my eyes. A vice wrapped around my heart. "That's precisely what I thought would happen, Vemdour. You should have told me!"

He sat there so casually cruel as if he hadn't dropped this horrid truth into my lap. With a shrug of his broad shoulders, he said, "I thought you knew."

Vemdour had to be mistaken. Searching for the bond, for an inkling of Gideon, I came up empty. There was nothing. No humming. No tether. No Gideon.

"You are a godsdamned *liar*." A wave of emotions rose up within me. "You knew I knew nothing of magic and the dyad. And you tricked me!"

My nails dug into my palms, slicing through the skin. Warm drops of blood dripped to the carpeted floor.

Gideon was gone. He was... gone.

Vemdour laughed, and it sent a shiver down my spine. "No, pet. I *freed* you."

CHAPTER 29

The bathwater in my tub was one degree below boiling, but it didn't thaw the ice in my veins or soothe the soreness in my chest. I submerged myself underwater and screamed until my lungs gave out and then I forced myself to stay under even longer. Heart-stopping waves of pain rattled through me. A part of me didn't want to live knowing what I'd done, who I'd hurt.

A blurry figure stood over the edge of the tub and yanked me up as black dots sprinkled across my vision. I gasped for air. My stomach soured, knowing Gideon would never breathe again.

Cayden swore as he pulled me from the tub and wrapped me in a plush robe.

He shook my shoulders as if he was trying to shake some sense into me. "Valeria, what's wrong?"

"Do you have all fucking night?" My throat was raw and it hurt to speak. "I made a mistake."

A mistake. Was that what Gideon's life boiled down to? One reckless, impulsive decision, and it cost him his life.

Gideon was dead. Because of me.

"He's gotten into your head, hasn't he?" He paced back and forth in front of the bathroom sink. "I thought that necklace blocked your mind from manipulation."

His words hit me like a bus. Manipulation? "What are you talking about?"

"Vemdour. He's promised you things, hasn't he? He's convinced you to join him, to trust him." He raked his hand through his hair. "Judging by the look on your face and the fact that you just tried to drown yourself, I'm assuming he's persuaded you to do something where you didn't fully understand the consequences."

How... how did he know that?

"Thought so." He nodded, continuing, "He did the same thing to me once. A long, long time ago."

"No." My body stiffened, every muscle locking up. "Vemdour isn't manipulating me. I'm not stupid. I know what I'm doing."

He narrowed his eyes into sharp pinpricks. "Do you, little sister? Because this isn't a game."

"I know it isn't a game!" Rage and regret coursed through me as I closed the distance between us, my bracelet quickly becoming a blade. Shoving Cayden against the wall, I pressed the tip of the dagger into his throat. He didn't push me away or fight back. He only watched me with those eyes that reminded me so much of our father's.

"I tried to prevent you from this fate. I did everything I could to protect you."

"Protect me?" I seethed. "You tried to *kill* me when I was a baby."

"You have every right to be angry, but there are things you don't know."

"Angry?" I clenched my jaw, tempted to slice through his skin to see crimson wet the blade. "I'm beyond that. I'm vengeful."

"Vengeful because Empyrean fed you lies against me."

"What lies?" I loosened my grip and my resolve. Cayden had never spoken so openly with me before. What changed? Why was he so talkative all of a sudden? Was it because Vemdour told him I agreed to join him? That had to be it. I reared against him. "Tell me what lies."

He held his hands up in surrender. "I'd rather show you."

"Show me what?" My heart roared in my ears as I took a step back, returning the dagger to my wrist with the one-word command.

"The night our mother was killed."

My mouth hung open. "What the fuck do you mean?"

"This is a Mirror of Memories." A vintage hand mirror manifested in his hand. "It cannot falsify any events that transpired in any given memory. Instead, it will show you exactly what happened to our mother."

He handed it to me, and I ran a finger over the intricate details. It was pretty with flowers, moons, stars, and swirls of filigree etched together on its polished silver frame and handle. It was the kind of antique I would've picked up from the shop on Cornelia Street. I recognized the steady hum of holy magic vibrating through it. Maybe my lessons with Vemdour were paying off after all.

"You should know that you won't be able to interact with anyone or anything. It's only a memory." His voice became softer as his shoulders sagged. "And not something you can change the outcome of no matter how much you want to, so don't even try."

Nodding, I gave him one wary glance before turning it over. Brisk cool air rushed around me, and my vision went white. Moments later, I entered Cayden's mind. His memory played like a podcast through earbuds, and I watched as if I was an audience member watching a play from the front row.

Screaming. There was so much screaming. My blood-stained hands trembled while the whisper of names whipped around my mind urging me to kill, kill, kill.

Following the pulse of a single name—the only one left in this wing of the castle—I strolled down a corridor to the throne room.

When the name registered clearly, my heart stopped—it was Father's name. Father must die.

There was arguing beyond the closed doors, no longer hushed and saved for their quarters. The baby was crying. Mother never let Valeria cry. *Bursting into the room, I found my parents standing in the center of the hall, neglecting the basket where the baby wailed.*

Father screamed as he held a knife to Mother's throat. "You've betrayed me one too many times, Iris!"

"Do it, Ward. End my life so I can meet him in the Half-Light."

He struck her. Blood dripped from the corner of her mouth. Grabbing the basket that held Valeria, he angled the tip of his dagger over her as her little hands reached for the shiny blade.

I tried to call out to stop him. I tried to move from where I stood—desperately wanting to take the baby from his sinful hands. But I couldn't. I was rooted in place by a large, leather-like hand resting on my shoulder. The smell of copper and ash wafted around me. It was a scent that didn't belong in Empyrean. It was a scent of pure, unadulterated evil.

"Don't!" Mother begged. "She's your daughter."

"You and I both know she isn't." He plunged the dagger into the basket, but the monster behind me waved his hand and the blade bounced back, blocked by an invisible barrier.

Mother laughed, smiling to the ceiling as if she was looking beyond it.

Father dropped the basket to the floor, and the baby cried louder. My fingers twitched as I tried to regain control of my body. I couldn't even tap into the magic I wielded as the Deathbringer. Resting my hands on the hilts of my swords, I watched helplessly as Father brought the dagger to Mother's neck once more.

His name was a chant in my mind as his blood sang to me. Ready and willing to be spilled.

Mother looked away from him, eyes locking with mine. My knees wobbled under her gaze. I didn't want her to see me like this—blood-stained and death-fed. She smiled as she said, "Protect Valeria."

Father slit her throat in one swift motion. Blood sprayed across the floor, bathing both him and Valeria in red. He dropped the dagger and spit on her limp body. "Filthy whore."

The weight on my shoulder lifted, and I regained control. I rushed toward Mother, slipping on the blood pooling around her. Her gray eyes were wide open, her final command a whisper on her lips. My hands found the hilts of Life's Song and Death's Promise, and uncontrollable rage pulsed through me. Unsheathing my blades, I turned them on Father, whose name repeated over and over in my mind.

He would die. His blood would satiate me.

Celestians poured into the room, drawing their swords, the Witch of the Gray behind them.

"He killed her," Father cried, pointing to me. "He's working with the Realm of the Forsaken. Seize him!"

"No." I shook my head in disbelief, sheathing my swords. "I didn't do this. I didn't—"

Time slowed to a near stop; only the pounding in my chest was evidence this was happening. Like a savior I never asked for, a voice crooned behind me. "Deathbringer, my name is Vemdour, God of the Forsaken. I'll free you of their unjust punishment if you do my bidding for the rest of your life."

I whirled on the god. "I will never serve the Realm of the Forsaken."

"Such a pity." He turned away from me. "Enjoy death."

"Wait!" My eyes flickered to where Valeria cried—her cheeks as red as the blood splattered across her. Mother asked me to protect her. I couldn't do that if I were dead. "I will accept your bargain. On one condition."

"Humor me."

I glanced at him, choosing my words wisely. "You will never harm my sister, Valeria."

The demon grinned as searing pain shot through my chest, ripping away a sliver of my soul and binding me to the god. "So it shall be."

The memory slipped away, and Cayden stood with his back against the wall, his gaze lingering on the ceiling.

He didn't kill our mother. Our father did.

All I saw was red. Flames danced under my flesh. I'd make our father pay for what he had done. He would feel the full force of my wrath, the full force of my power. Maybe I'd start with Lirabeth and her baby... take from him what he tried to take from my mother. Kill them slowly and make him watch. Then, when he was begging for me to stop, I'd—

No. Gods. What the fuck was wrong with me? Who was this realm making me become? I didn't torture people for revenge. Okay, I did *once*. But that was because it was Ellody, and she was a hateful bitch who was as guilty as any demon. That was *different*. Wasn't it?

Moments passed without me saying a word.

For the first time in my life, I was speechless.

"Why did you make the trade, Valeria?" Cayden's voice was low and disheartened. "I've spent hundreds of years in this realm protecting you, keeping my promise to our mother... all for you to undo it over a mortal boy."

The ringing in my ears drowned out my voice. "*Hundreds of years?*"

"Vemdour didn't tell you?" He sighed exasperatedly. "Time works differently in the Realm of the Forsaken. A year in the Realm of the Mortals and Empyrean is about fifty years here."

"That means..."

"You've been here for about a year in this realm's time, yes. But in Empyrean, it's been almost a week."

"No." I collapsed to the tiled floor, a war drum beating in my chest.

Oh, *fuck*.

By Bastile, what had I done? I drew my knees to my chest, taking several deep breaths.

"All. This. Time." My mind spun as realization set in. The words came in bursts as tears pricked my eyes. "I thought he didn't care."

Cayden knelt in front of me. "Who?"

I couldn't say his name aloud. Every time I tried, it died in my throat.

Gideon. He was dead. *Dead.*

Oh, gods. I should've asked questions. I should've...

No one in Empyrean would want me once they found out I murdered Gideon on a fucking *whim*. Maybe this was all just a horrible dream—a waking nightmare where I'd gasp awake, and the brand would be shimmering gold and not deathly black on my wrist, humming, and I'd know that I didn't destroy the one good thing that had ever happened to me.

I was a monster, worse than my father.

Cayden placed a hand on my shoulder. "Val, who are you talking about?"

The nickname shook me to my core. Only Mason called me that.

Mason. If he was even alive, he wouldn't forgive me either. For fraternizing with the enemy, for willingly staying and being trained by the god who took everything from him. He was going to hate me, too.

How had I screwed things up so badly?

My eyes met my brother's, and I threw my arms around him. I couldn't stop myself. I needed someone, anyone, to tell me that everything was going to be okay. That I had made a mistake or two or three, but I could fix them. He was stiff under my embrace before wrapping his arms around me, hugging me tightly. For years I trained with the intent to kill him, to get my revenge. While he let everyone believe he was the one behind our mother's death and the raid on Empyrean. He let those insidious lies spread throughout Seraphicity like a cancerous tumor no one could cut out. He put a target on his back and let campfire legends morph him into a cruel usurper who was on a constant quest for power.

The realms feared Cayden. Feared the monster that lurked beneath the surface—the weapon that was at Vemdour's disposal.

But that was *me*... that was who I had become. I was the cruel usurper on a quest for power, mindfucked by Vemdour in so many ways. His kindness, his sweet lies, his careful touches, the fury in his eyes when he saw I was hurt... none of it was real. It was all part of the bargain he struck with Cayden. *You will never harm my sister, Valeria.*

Tears streamed down my face. "You traded your soul for my protection."

"It was an easy trade." He let me go and shrugged, adding, "At the time."

"And now?"

He chewed his lip, concerned eyes meeting mine. "It's not so easy with you here because Vemdour has taken an interest in you. Selfishly, a part of me hoped he'd slip up and harm you, so I'd finally be free."

"You sound like you hate him." I picked a piece of fuzz from the bathrobe. "But he saved you."

"Saved me?" He snatched the mirror from the floor, and it vanished in an instant. "He imprisoned me, Val, with the promise of protection and revenge. The same shit he's doing with you."

"No." My forehead creased. "What we have is..."

"A lie. He's using you because of what you can give him."

I sucked in a breath. Vemdour said he wanted me here to anger the gods and kings who had wronged him, but maybe Cayden knew more.

"And what's that?" I asked.

"You haven't pieced it together?" He rubbed his jaw. "Even after the memory?"

"Pieced *what* together?"

"You're the key to all the realms." His face flashed with something fearsome. It sent a shiver down my spine. "Because you're Bastile's daughter."

My eyes went wide. No. No, I wasn't. A scene from Cayden's memory played on a loop in my mind.

She's your daughter.

You and I both know she isn't.

Was that how Vemdour knew I had power? Not because he could feel it? But because he knew who my true father was? Had he been playing me this whole time? My shoulders slumped. No. He spoke as if he knew me—like we were the same, two halves of a prophecy.

A woman born with violet eyes must be the one to rise. Tethered to darkness, tethered to light, she is the sword, he is the knight.

Bastile was certain the prophecy was about me because he was my freaking father.

I was going to faint.

Cayden looked at me for a long minute before rising to his feet. "Sometimes, knowing the truth can be the heaviest burden to bear."

He left, leaving me alone in the bathroom. My lungs still burned from the bath, and my chest ached from the gaping Gideon-shaped hole left in my soul. So much had changed, and so much had come to light. I didn't know where or how to start processing it all. My mind was spinning round and round. Everything was so fucked up because of lies and secrets and layers of manipulation.

My mother's face kept flashing in front of me. She was as beautiful as everyone said, and I took after her with the same blonde hair, round cheeks, button nose, and plump lips. Even our curvy figures were similar. But what I couldn't wrap my mind around was the simple fact that the blood of a god ran through my veins. I laughed incredulously. Gideon told me there were rumors about

Bastile and my mom, and I couldn't help but think about how he would've loved to be proven right.

My breath became ragged thinking of his stupid, cocky grin and the sound of his laugh.

Vemdour said severing the dyad set me free, but I couldn't see the truth in that. Not when I knew my freedom damned someone so... perfect.

Aurick, Gideon's father, would never forgive me. Neither would Malachi or Sabel, or Mae, or Bex, or anyone in the rebellion, if they were still alive. And they *could* be alive. Vemdour manipulated the shit out of me and lied about a lot of things; maybe the rebellion was one of them. Maybe Tam and Pyrtra's conversation was just another one of his tricks.

My mind spun thinking of everyone who would turn on me the moment they found out what I'd done. And for what? The promise of a power I already had. The promise of all four realms. Deep down, I didn't even want that. I just wanted to be loved. Unconditionally loved.

And that was the kind of love a power-hungry god could never give me.

I sniffled, wiping the snot dripping from my nose onto the sleeve of my robe. I should get up. Get dressed. Brush my hair. Do something. But I couldn't. Everything hurt too much to move.

Margie would be disappointed to learn I fell for Vemdour's promises. Disappointed, but not surprised. She knew all along what I'd become. Someone I wouldn't recognize when I looked into the mirror. Thinking back to that day, it was like she spelled it out to me, but I was too caught up in my feelings to listen to her and heed her advice.

You'll need to embrace that you aren't a mortal. You are a princess with power, and that... that could very well be something that takes what's already inside of you, everything dark and vengeful, and draws it closer to the surface.

Gods, she was right. She was always right.

CHAPTER 30

Shadows and screams haunted my sleep. I tossed and turned, sweat clinging to my clammy skin. My hair was in knots at the back of my head. The terrors that plagued me confirmed I made a mistake—aligning myself with the enemy only for it to destroy the only alliance that mattered and the hope of saving Empyrean from Not My Father.

Sometime in the night, I heard Gideon's voice, as crisp and clear as a fall afternoon. He called out to me, told me he was coming. It felt so real that I startled awake with tears in my eyes and an ache in my chest, thinking I felt the faint hum of the dyad once again.

One glance at my thorn-stained wrist proved that guilt was a terrible hallucinogen.

The truth of my situation settled into my blood, icy and angry.

Vemdour played me.

He manipulated me with pretty words that disguised ugly lies.

It wouldn't—

It *couldn't* happen again.

CHAPTER 31

The ninth bell chimed throughout the fortress as I strolled into the dining hall. The glamour hid Vemdour's monstrous form. His brown eyes snapped to mine, and my heart skipped a beat as if it were saying, "Don't ruin this. We have nothing else."

I'd rather have nothing and know it was real than have him and believe a lie.

My steps faltered when my gaze fell on the head of the table. Seated there was Tam's mutilated body—torn to shreds, skin missing, holes gaping sporadically across the demon's chest, like fury alone was the weapon that brought him his death.

I swallowed. Vemdour did that... *as revenge for me.*

My eyes drifted back to the god, and I bowed. I had practiced the movement in my bedroom in front of the mirror a million times until I knew precisely how low I had to tip to ensure my cleavage spilled from the gown he sent for me. It was a simple yet expensive couture piece from the Realm of the Mortals. I recognized the label as soon as I saw it, and I screamed with delight before remembering I couldn't trust him. It was velvety with short black sleeves and a ruched front. The dress cut off mid-thigh, and the slit down the front exposed the glittering scar between my breasts and the stars that adorned it, drawing everyone's gaze to my chest... before their eyes drifted to the roses and thorns that trailed up my forearm. Paired with some strappy heels that wound up my calves with a soft satin ribbon, the outfit and tattoos were a statement—I belonged to him.

Vemdour grinned as I crossed the space and placed a kiss on his cheek. The crimson lipstick I wore left a smudge. He blushed, his olive cheeks turning a faint shade of pink.

How was *that* a lie? He had to feel *something* for me.

Somehow, I'd use that to my advantage to get what I want.

I winked at Pyrtra as I took my seat, and she hissed. Cayden sat quietly drinking wine from a chalice, his expression indifferent.

Half an hour later, the room was buzzing contentedly. The steady chatter of conversation erupted from around the table. That was my cue. I tapped my goblet with a knife. The metallic clanging rung out around us, drawing everyone's attention to me.

"Vemdour." His name was a dandelion in my mouth, thick and fuzzy, a breath away from granting a wish. Cayden tensed, his fists on top of the table. "To solidify our alliance, I want my throne."

The god licked his lips. My cheeks heated, wondering if he was replaying our kiss the way I did over and over again last night until I was numb to the sting of betrayal.

"You'll get a throne when we're wed, pet."

I bristled but quickly corrected myself. Time to play the game. "Easy there, weirdo. I never agreed to marry you."

"How do you think alliances work?" He leaned back in his chair. "Did you believe words alone would ally us?"

"If you want me to marry you, you'll seal the deal with *my* throne," I said flatly. "And not just any throne. I know you'd *love* to wave your little hand and make one. But I want *my* throne—in Empyrean. I want you to murder"—Cayden's eyes flickered to mine, a silent warning to not reveal I knew the truth—"my father."

His shoulders tensed. "No."

"You said you'd give me anything, did you not? Last night in your room?" I cocked my head to the side. "I want my father's head as your next dessert for Worthless Witness."

"Under any other circumstances, provoking a war with Empyrean would delight me," he said after taking a gulp of wine. "But I have bigger plans for us and that begins with burning the Realm of the Divine to the ground."

"If you won't help me, I'll take back my fucking throne myself."

"Absolutely not. Your powers aren't strong enough yet. Give them time to grow, my sweet. Together we will conquer the other realms, but only when I know we will prevail unscathed."

"I *am* strong enough."

"The answer is no, Valeria. End of discussion." His tone indicated his words were final, but as I opened my mouth to object, he added, "You're rash and impulsive, and I won't send my bride into a bloodbath."

"Let me prove that I can do it," I blurted. "I'll fight"—I scanned the room—"Pyrtra. If she wins, I'll stay, marry you, and let you call the shots. If I win, I leave to collect the king's head and serve it to you on a platter. Either way, you get something you want."

The room was eerily silent. Demons *loved* violence. To turn down a spectacle like the one I was offering would make the God of the Forsaken appear weak. The corners of my lips tugged upward. Checkmate.

Pyrtra grinned. "I'll play if it's to the death. I've grown annoyed with her grating presence."

"You've grown annoyed with being cast aside like the trash you are," I hissed.

"I said *no*," Vemdour snapped, picking the skin off a turkey leg. His eyes met mine again, and this time, they were pleading with me to stop while I was ahead.

I didn't, of course.

"What are you scared of?" I took a sip of wine. It was as bitter as the kiss he left on my lips last night. Cayden pinched my arm, and it took everything in me not to react. "Losing the only thing you've ever loved? I'll come back, Vemdour." I crossed my fingers under the table. "Scout's honor."

Pyrtra growled while excited whispers swept around us. They knew there was something deeper going on between us. Everyone knew. Even the Realm of the Divine probably knew, thanks to Søren. The truth was Vemdour and I both understood each other in a way others didn't, and I hated him for it. It was how he was so easily able to manipulate me into trusting him.

"That's where you're mistaken, pet." His lips curled back. "To love, you have to have a heart."

I blinked, taken aback by his statement. Was *that* his curse?

"Let me finish what Tam started," Pyrtra said. "We can defile her corpse together, my lord."

"You will treat my bride with the respect she deserves." Vemdour yanked her from her seat with one wave of his hand and slammed her to the ground. Something cracked. A rib? Her arm? "Say something like that again, and I will sanction the tournament so she can tear you to pieces for simply suggesting such a thing."

She snarled, eyes fuming with rage. "You dare say she'd defeat me? I am the original Succubus. I am poison herself."

The rapid rise and fall of my chest betrayed the calm exterior I was trying to portray. I opened my mouth to speak, but I couldn't find the words. She was the one who poisoned Mason, who destroyed his life with a single scratch.

Cayden cleared his throat, and my shoulders slightly relaxed. "Letting the ladies fight would provide quite the entertainment." He lifted one shoulder. "I think the stakes could be higher, though."

Vemdour crossed one leg over his knee, his black slacks stretching easily, and took a sip from his glass. The contents sloshed, showing a substance thicker than wine. "Tell me more."

Cayden smiled. A smile that had no warmth. A smile that I didn't trust. "It obviously can't be a fight to the death. So, let them have at each other, but incentivize each party to win. Valeria wants to take on Empyrean alone"—he stifled a laugh, and the rest of the table did the same—"so that can be her incentive. And Pyrtra... she can fight for your forgiveness for her betrayal with Tam."

"No," Vemdour said again. His lingering gaze roamed over me once more. "Those stakes aren't high enough. Think bigger." I shot a nervous glance at Cayden, who promptly ignored me. The god continued. "If Valeria wins, she can leave and take on Empyrean. But if Pyrtra wins, Valeria must bind her soul to mine and wed me by midnight on the solstice."

My breath caught in my chest. I would never agree to it. The God of the Forsaken exposed his hand. He wanted me as more than a bride. He wanted to *control* me.

"No," I choked out.

"It's decided." Vemdour winked at me. "Valeria and Pyrtra will enter the arena tomorrow. Cayden, alert the realm and tell them to place their bets."

When Cayden's eyes met mine, he gave me a curt nod and rose from his seat, turning on his heel and striding out of the room, his black cloak billowing behind him.

THE REST OF THE EVENING passed by rather quickly in a realm where time was indefinitely longer than in the others. Word of the challenge spread like wildfire. It was hard, but I kept my mouth shut, stealing nervous glances at Vemdour one or two or twelve times before returning to my room. I didn't understand why he had this pull over me. Was it really because it felt like we knew one another? Or was it something more sinister? Did he manipulate me into this mindset through kindness and pretty words?

I'd spent the last hour pacing, wondering how I lost the upper hand in this game yet again. The challenge was in place, but the stakes were higher than I ever imagined.

The elevator dinged. Cayden stalked into the room clad in fighting leathers with a belt slung around his hips, one short sword sheathed on each side. He pointed to the couch. "Sit. We need to talk strategy."

For once, I didn't object, taking a spot in front of the fire. The embers winked at me, illuminating the room in a flickering orange glow.

"Don't underestimate Pyrtra." He rubbed his hands on his thighs, and I held back a smile. We had the same nervous tick. "She's lethal, but she likes to play with her opponents. She'll try to goad you into a rage, hoping you forget your training."

My mouth parted. My training was the only upper hand I had. "How does she know I'm trained?"

"The entire realm knows about the destruction you left in your wake at your high school. But she doesn't know you didn't do it alone. So don't give her a reason to think otherwise."

I nodded. This *was* valuable insight.

"You will be allowed weapons since Pyrtra has supernatural abilities and you haven't been able to tap into your power completely. I want you to use these." He unsheathed the two swords on his hips. I recognized them from the memory he showed me. "Meet Life's Song and Death's Promise."

I took the weapons from him and inspected them. The silver blades were etched with various runes that cast a demonic glow around them. The pommel on Life's Song housed a deep red ruby adorned by small black glimmering gems. In contrast, the stone in Death's Promise was neon blue with the same jewels surrounding it. Both grips were smooth to the touch and light in my hands. I imagined these swords sang when gliding through the air.

I let out a low whistle. "They're gorgeous. Where did you get them?"

"They're passed down from Deathbringer to Deathbringer."

My eyes flickered to his. "What *is* a Deathbringer?"

"It's exactly what it sounds like. Someone who's sworn to bring death upon those that are deemed guilty by the Scale of Equity. We are dark magic, serving Ryt's justice."

Ryt was the God of War and Bloodshed. He was one of the only gods both Empyrean and the Realm of the Divine allowed free passage between the realms to dole out justice. But...

"I thought Ryt died during the Wrath of Deities war," I said, furrowing my brow. "How in the world are you doling out a dead god's justice?"

Cayden took a deep breath and settled into the couch, his eyes on the fire. "Before the war, there was a prophecy foretelling Ryt's death, and so he had imbued the Scale of Equity, a pendant, with some of his magic and gifted it to a soul he deemed worthy enough to carry out justice on his behalf."

He pulled a pendant from beneath his shirt and showed it to me. I ran my fingers over it the delicate curves of two crescent moons facing opposite each other and across the lines that held them together in the shape of a cross.

"How did you become the Deathbringer?" I asked, curious.

"Several months before you were born, when I had just turned nineteen, my predecessor approached me and offered me the role."

I blinked at him. No one would ever think he was in his late thirties. He looked barely a year older than me, but underneath his youthful face there was evidence that he had lived far longer than me.

"For someone pushing forty, you look terrific," I teased.

"Thanks." He ran his hand through his hair. "So long as I'm the Deathbringer, I will remain forever young."

"And what happens when you stop being the Deathbringer?" I paused and leaned forward. "*Can* you stop?"

"No, I cannot." Cayden's eyes turned sad. "Once the mantle is passed to the next, I will die. But that day is far off." He waved his words away. "Enough about the Deathbringer. There's something you need to know about Vemdour."

"I don't think I can handle any more truths about Vemdour," I said flatly, sitting back and folding my arms across my chest.

Cayden sighed. "I think Vemdour knew what was going to happen the night Ward murdered our mother. For years, I couldn't wrap my head around why the God of the Forsaken was there at precisely the right time."

Probably because Bastile promised me to him. The truth burned on my tongue, and I swallowed it down.

"You think he helped plan our mother's murder?" I asked, skeptical. "That's madness."

"Madness?" He laughed. "That's politics, Val. Vemdour always gets what he wants because he's calculating and willing to wait. He wanted revenge on Bastile for reasons I don't know and he wanted to weaken Empyrean. Ward was just a pawn he used to claim both of those things. It was Vemdour who murdered Bastile. It was Ward who fabricated Bastile's Will and declared himself as the next rightful king. And it was both of them who plotted the attack on Seraphicity, framing me for our mother's murder."

I replayed my conversation with Vemdour. He told me that he killed Bastile in order to grant him power over the Half-Light and that he secured my hand in marriage because of the prophecy to unite our realms... but *why* would he want to weaken Empyrean?

I sucked in a breath. He must have known Ward would do everything in his power to prevent me from claiming the throne... like using the entire Celestian army against me. So Vemdour and his horde of demons slaughtered them to make my path to ruling Empyrean easier.

Everything I had ever known was a lie. I knew Bastile would never appoint a monster to sit on the Empyrean throne. I seethed in place. No wonder Ward had no sympathy for the innocent lives that were lost that day. His ambition and greed were the reason they'd died.

Rage boiled within me. I couldn't worry about all of the lies I was led to believe to keep me powerless and in the dark. I had to focus.

I gestured to Cayden's swords. "Why would you give me these?"

"Enchanted blades." He tapped the polished silver. "They sing for the sweet release of bloodshed."

"Won't Vemdour recognize them?"

He lifted a shoulder. "So what if he does? You're allowed weapons, and he said I could choose them." I chewed my lip as he added, "I'm sorry the stakes have risen as high as they have. I thought I was helping when I stepped in."

"It's fine. I'll win."

My words sounded more certain than I felt.

"I know you will." He flashed me a weak smile, and I itched to wipe away the worry from his downturned brows and glassy eyes. "Promise me that when you get out of here, you won't come back. Not for me. Not for revenge. Not for anything."

Months ago, this would've been an easy promise to make. But now I knew things could have been so different if we weren't born into such chaos. I wouldn't have hated him with every cell in my body. We would have had inside jokes and stupid fights, not bloodshed and torment.

We would have been *friends*.

"I promise," I lied.

Cayden nodded, then stood to leave, and I almost asked him to stay.

I wanted to hear more of what he knew about the politics of this realm and truths about Empyrean. I wanted to know what his childhood was like and if he wished things were different between us, too.

Truthfully, I wanted to get to know... my brother.

But he left without a second glance, leaving me alone with the company of the shadows dancing along the wallpapered walls and enough time to learn the weight of my new swords in my hands.

CHAPTER 32

The arena was alive with a chaotic hum. Demons stood in a line so long it wrapped into a desolate courtyard with charred, lifeless bushes and a fountain made of bones. It was doubtful they'd all have a chance to place their bets before the match began, but they pushed and shoved one another in anticipation. As of last night, the odds were heavily in Pyrtra's favor, ten thousand to one with only a handful of demons betting on me.

Either they were idiots or geniuses. If I had anything to bet with, I would've bet on the latter.

Cayden said stories of my training and skill spread throughout the Realm of the Forsaken. I found it hard to imagine they believed one woman slaughtered over twenty demons single-handedly and then escaped without a scratch.

Maybe my brother spun the tale himself, turning my feats into folklore.

I searched the crowd for him, but he was nowhere to be found.

When I arrived, the tournament keeper, Oisin, a fickle demon with short white hair and deep green skin, gave me the low-down on the rules and the arena—anything goes and Pyrtra and I would remain stranded on the floating stone island until a victor prevailed.

Nope. I didn't like the sound of that one bit.

Soon Pyrtra and I were ferried across the sky on the backs of two plush storm clouds to the disjointed ring—if you could even call it that. My legs were shaking as I slid off the cloud and onto the rocky ground.

I peeked over the edge and sucked in a breath. Hot lava bubbled and gurgled, singing a fiery song. One misstep and that was it. So long, world. I moved closer to the center of the ring. Pyrtra watched my every step with calculating eyes, and I flirted with goading her—a wink here, a bat of my eyelashes there. She tied her long black hair back in a single braid. Her skin-tight clothes clung to her lithe frame like they were painted on, and I briefly wondered how she could breathe. She bared her teeth, tiny and sharp.

Gods, she was the worst.

My hands rested on the hilts of Life's Song and Death's Promise where they were strapped to my thighs.

That morning a thick pair of worn leather pants, a billowing t-shirt, and a matching leather vest sat at the foot of my bed without a note. I knew they were from Cayden when I realized it was my *leather ensemble* from the Realm of the Mortals. Clutching the gift to my chest, I breathed in the faint indescribable scent of Mistress Marjorie's magic and her never-ending lessons—the smell of home and safety. Then I hoped with everything I had that she was all right.

Shrill screams filled the air, announcing the arrival of the God of the Forsaken and his party. They took their seats on the cliffside terrace, the railing made of smoldering bones. My palms were slick with sweat, and I rubbed them on my pants. Vemdour leaned back in an oversized gilded chair, his burning eyes on me.

Pyrtra growled from my left, but I couldn't tear my gaze away from him. I hated how tangled up my feelings were. He lied to me. Played me. Tricked me into trusting him. And yet, a sliver of me wanted to kiss him again.

I was so sick of myself and my warring emotions.

Get it together, girl.

Cayden's lips curved into a tight knowing smile as he zeroed in on Life's Song and Death's Promise. I gave him a slight nod as my eyes passed over to the woman on his right. Red. Vemdour's emissary. She looped her thin arm through Cayden's and rested her head on his shoulder. With her other arm, she waved to me. Why did she seem so... friendly with Cayden? And me? I lifted my hand to—

Something smacked against the back of my legs, and I hit the ground, splitting my palms on the rough stone.

"That's cheating!" I shouted.

Pyrtra wrenched me onto my back and clambered on top of me. She brought her hand to my face and sliced my cheek open with one sharp fingernail. "There's no such thing in a realm made of horrors."

A scream escaped my lips as my face burned, waves of heat pounding my skull. Using all of my strength to push her away, she barely budged. I growled. I weighed at least thirty pounds more than her, but she was heavy as a boulder. My pulse raced, nerves shooting through me.

"I'm going to enjoy this, little princess." Her acidic breath was a weighted blanket on my face, heavy and suffocating. "I'm going to peel your flesh off piece by piece until I can see what makes you so divine."

There was a wildness in her eyes that I'd need to match, or else she was going to destroy me. Fight or flight kicked in, and a primal rage coursed through me as I continued to struggle beneath her grip. Life's Song and Death's Promise were sheathed on my thighs, vibrating in anticipation.

Do something, Val, you useless idiot.

Pyrtra shifted by half an inch. There! An opening around her waist. I lifted my leg and wrapped it around her torso, thrusting myself to the side, knocking her off balance and away from me.

Valeria, I'm coming for you.

Gideon's voice stole the air from my lungs, and I sat up, whipping my head around.

No, that wasn't possible. He was dead. Eyes wide, my brow furrowed. I could've sworn... my gaze fell on Vemdour, whose face danced with worry. Dirt flew up around me, clouding my vision as tiny pebbles pricked my skin. But I could barely feel the pain. Not when Gideon's voice echoed throughout my mind once more. *Answer me, princess. Tell me you're okay.*

This couldn't be happening. Vemdour severed the dyad. The brand... it had changed. My fingers grazed my wrist and a glimmer of gold sparked amongst the black ink. A familiar tug pulled me to my feet. The dyad's outline illuminated, twinkling like pure, unfiltered daylight under the vermillion sky.

Pyrtra stalked toward me, her pitch-black eyes boiling with unleashed rage. I willed time to slow, begged my power to grant me a few precious moments to sort through the truth of what was happening. The cheers from the crowd turned into a distorted murmur, Pyrtra's foot hovered above the ground, as if she had paused mid-step.

Tears wet my lashes as my heart hammered in my chest. I wanted Gideon to be alive more than anything. I... I wanted the dyad. I wanted my thoughts to be an open book. I wanted feelings and strings and stolen kisses in the middle of the night with someone who kept their promises.

With someone I could trust.

And if this was real, I wanted all of those things with Gideon—my soulmate.

Time remained paused granting me those extra seconds to *think*.

Needing to be sure that this wasn't my mind—or Vemdour—playing tricks on me, I let out a deep, shaky breath. *Are you really here?*

A familiar caress stroked my mind through the tether. *I promised you I'd come, fuckwit.*

Oh my gods. He was alive, and he came for me even though I asked him not to. A chaotic giggle bubbled up my throat, and I clamped a hand over my mouth to stifle it. *You do know that's not a term of endearment.*

All he did was laugh. I let it wrap around me as it sparked a feeling deep within my chest that I'd long forgotten. Hope.

Relief coursed through me—Gideon was *alive.*

Maybe I hadn't screwed everything up.

Only a couple of seconds passed as I shook my shoulders out and cracked my neck, and my hands found the hilts of Cayden's blades.

I glanced at Pyrtra. It was time to end this.

Time resumed as if it hadn't slowed, and the crowd gasped the moment I freed Life's Song and Death's Promise from their sheaths. Even Vemdour stood, his worry now masked by confusion. Leaning on the railing, his large hands threatened to crush it. Red clapped from beside Cayden, whose face split in two as the swords illuminated red and blue, ravenous for death.

Moving with the grace of wind through a willow tree, I stormed toward Pyrtra in a series of slashes. The blades sang out in a blood-hungry song, bleeding into a bright purple the moment they connected with her ashen flesh. But she was faster than I anticipated. She ducked under one of my swings and smacked me to the ground with enough force that my ribs crunched on impact. Life's Song and Death's Promise flew from my grip and landed with a clatter. Clutching my side in anguish, I refused to cry. I'd endured worse than a few broken ribs. The coppery taste of blood pooled in my mouth, and I spit onto the stone.

She circled me, light on her feet. Even after taking several slices from the blades, she had a supernatural strength that I couldn't compete with.

Not yet, at least.

I took a shallow breath trying to call on my power as Pyrtra grabbed a fistful of my hair and jerked me to my knees, jostling my focus.

Gideon's concern pulsed in time with the thumping of my heart. *I'm almost there.*

In a panic, I closed my eyes and forced a sentence through the tether. *Stay where you are. I'll come to you.* If it was really him, then I couldn't lose him again. Not when I just got him back.

Pyrtra held one sharp nail to my throat, and the crowd cheered for the Succubus. They chanted her name in various dialects, excited for the currency they were going to win.

Vemdour watched and waited, expression inscrutable. Did he really care about me? Or was every careful touch and delicate half-truth a ploy to lead up to this moment? So he could bind himself to my soul?

Pyrtra's grip tightened in my hair as she preened under the crowd's attention. But she didn't know I had one more trick up my sleeve.

Literally.

I unwound my bracelet, letting it take its crystalline dagger shape. Holding my breath, I lifted the poisonous blade to Pyrtra's wrist and jabbed it through. She screamed as she released me. Her howls fueled me as I scrambled to my feet and paced around the platform. Blood and dirt drenched our clothes and the rocks beneath us. Cayden's swords were on the opposite side of the ring, so all I had was my dagger. It had to be enough.

"You cannot slay me," Pyrtra bellowed. Fire escaped her palms, entrapping us in a cage of flames. She lunged for me once again, narrowly missing as I dodged and rolled away from her with enough time to catch her off guard. I ignored the worsening pain in my ribs and the incessant stinging in my cheek. Flames licked at my flesh. My heart skipped when the fire didn't burn me. Instead, it danced across my skin as if it was *part* of me.

Maybe Vemdour didn't lie about *everything*. Maybe there were still things I didn't know about my powers and what I was fully capable of.

Power—alive and vengeful—coursed through my blood and the fury within me devoured all of my mercy as I reached out to the flames and called them to me. I thought of Mason, of every horror he endured while he was a prisoner here, of Vemdour and every lie he told me and every touch I granted him, of Cayden and the life he missed out on to protect me, of Ward and the terrible things he did to steal what was rightfully mine, of what it felt like to lose Gideon, to lose my birthright, to lose myself.

I channeled all of my pain and anger into the flames, letting them swirl around me.

The God of the Forsaken stared at me in awe—his mouth agape, starry eyes wide, and broad chest heaving in silent panic. No pair of rose-colored glasses would ever hide his true nature from me again. It was seductive and wicked, manipulative and lecherous. His power beckoned me—like calling to like. And I knew after I left this realm, I'd spend the rest of my life wondering why he had to turn out to be a monumental piece of shit.

I stalked toward Pyrtra, letting the flames around me act as a shield, the hilt of my dagger humming in my sweaty palms. She punched and kicked, flinging fire at me to no avail. Reaching out, the blade connected with her putrid skin—a jab here, a slice there. I was patient and careful, taking my time to cut her to bits. Her cries were a sinister song that moved me to keep going, to keep striking. Finally, she collapsed in a heap—no longer beautiful *or* lethal.

This wasn't supposed to be a fight to the death, but it would be.

I'd enjoy taking from Vemdour what he threatened to take from me.

His lover. His hope. *Me.*

In a cloud of swirling black smoke, the god spirited himself to the rocky edge nearest to the island. The electric buzz of his power rolled off him in droves as he focused his attention on me.

Oisin trembled before him. "Shall I call the match, my lord?"

Vemdour met my eyes. Something like deliberation mixed with despair lingered there. "No."

I pressed two fingers to my lips before shifting them into a finger gun, pointing it at him, and pulling the trigger as my other hand plunged the dagger straight into Pyrtra's heart, knowing her body would turn to dust beneath me.

CHAPTER 33

The Realm of the Forsaken trembled as their god fell to his knees, seething in place.

He knew there was something different about me. He had encouraged me to embrace that part of me.

What did he expect?

With the one-word command, the enchanted dagger returned to my wrist.

Gideon's words slipped into my mind. *I'm going to assume the realm is going to shit because of something you did?*

I snickered as I grabbed Cayden's swords and sheathed them.

The storm cloud swooped down from the sky, and I climbed on top, slowing my breath as it carried me toward solid ground.

Cayden swaggered behind Vemdour with Red still clinging to his arm. Sweat collected on his brow as he extended his hand to me and helped me from the cloud. "Let's go."

"She's not going anywhere." Vemdour's head snapped up, and he rose to his feet. He towered over me, his eyes darker than I'd ever seen them before. "You violated the rules of the tournament."

Desperation laced his every word, and I pitied him. Pitied his meager attempt to keep me here, pitied the despair emanating from him.

Oisin cleared his throat, bless his heart, and trembled as he said, "Forgive me, but nowhere in the rules does it explicitly say murder is a disqualification."

A guttural growl escaped Vemdour's throat as he clutched Oisin's head in his hands and crushed his skull. I gasped. The demon's body fell to the ground with a harsh thud.

I tried to tip-toe around Vemdour, but the god grabbed my wrist, tugging me close. I sucked in a sharp breath as my ribs squealed in pain.

"Look what happens when you give in to the darkness." Vemdour's voice was low, taking on that seductive tone that stripped away my reservations and spoke to my very core. "Stay with me. There are still things I can teach you. You'll have everything you want here."

"Everything I want is in Empyrean."

He looked at me for a beat longer. "Deep down, you know they'll never accept you for who you are. Are you going to leave and pretend you haven't changed? That there isn't a part of you that craves what only I can give you?"

His words stung as I wrenched myself out of his grip. I brought my mouth a breath away from his and whispered, "That's exactly what I'm going to do, *pet.*"

At that, he laughed. And he kept laughing until those laughs turned to screams. Rocks fell from the cliffsides, and demons ran haphazardly from their god, who was hell-bent on making someone, anyone, pay for all that he'd lost. With every wave of his hands, demons burst like fireworks, their blood and guts raining over the arena.

Cayden dragged me out of the courtyard and through the halls until we were out of the castle and on the bloody road. The woman followed, humming a song. My head was woozy, my surroundings coming in and out of focus. We drew to a stop across a drawbridge, and I blinked my vision straight.

"Go." He ruffled my hair. "Seek your revenge."

"I don't want to leave you here."

"You must." He hugged me gently, and I winced. "While I'm not bound to remain in the Realm of the Forsaken, it is the only realm where no one innocent is at risk from Vemdour's claim over me. Going with you puts you and everyone you're with in danger. Somehow, underneath the lies, Vemdour's grown attached to you."

With more effort than it should take, I released him and folded my arms across my chest. "Cayden, I'm not leaving you."

It was hard to ignore his comment about Vemdour growing attached. I'd add *that* to the list of things I didn't have the mental capacity to deal with right now.

Cayden softened. "Vemdour isn't the only thing that ties me to this realm. You promised you'd go without me."

"I lied." My gaze flickered to Red. "I don't accept that."

"Val." He ran his hand through his hair. "You met Red the other day, and well... she's my..." She wiggled her eyebrows, and his cheeks flushed. "She's my girlfriend."

My eyes went wide.

He chuckled. It wasn't the menacing sound I was used to, the one he used for show. This was more desperate. The back of his hand brushed her cheek.

I sucked in a breath. "You're dating a *demon*?"

Red laughed. "I'm not *just* a demon. I'm also an emissary to the Realm of the Forsaken. I have clearance to go between all of the realms because I'm not a threat."

Not a threat? All demons were a threat, but maybe she was better at hiding her talents.

"So, you're an assassin," I deadpanned.

"Perceptive." She cocked her head to the side. "I like you."

Valeria, you need to hurry. Gideon tugged on the bond, and it took everything in me not to sprint in his direction with the little bit of strength I had left. I had waited so long for this moment.

A year in this realm, seven days in Empyrean.

I pushed a message down the tether, sweat clinging to my forehead. *Five more minutes.*

Red turned to Cayden. "There may be a way to free you of Vemdour's claim." She took his hand in hers and added, "We could have a life—"

"We?" I cut her off. "You're a demon, Red. Demons aren't allowed in Empyrean."

"There are"—she counted on one hand—"two demons that I know of residing in your realm. One is a spy for Vemdour, and one lives undetected and alongside your kind. We're not all evil soul-sucking wretches, princess. Some of us dealt with an awful hand when we were alive, and we've paid far more than what we bargained for since we've been claimed."

I blanched. "A spy for Vemdour? In Empyrean?"

"Take me with you, and I'll show you who Vemdour's spy is. If I'm lying, you can end my life right where I stand. But when you see I'm telling the truth, I'll swear my allegiance to you. Please." She laced her fingers through Cayden's. "Don't force him to choose between us."

There was a pang in my chest. *Don't force him to choose between us.* Because he wouldn't choose me. I considered her worth as an asset to Empyrean. As an *emissary*, she could be a wealth of knowledge. If it meant Cayden would come with me, we could make it work.

"Fine, you can come." Turning toward Cayden, I added, "Maybe Mistress Marjorie can break the contract."

He looked at me, uncertainty dancing in his eyes. "You really want me to come with you? Even after all I've done?"

"All Vemdour *forced* you to do." Freeing him from this place was my first step to helping him earn forgiveness. And if he could be forgiven for his past, so could I. I didn't have to be the person this dreadful realm forced me to be, or the person Vemdour said he recognized deep down. I could be someone, something, more than myself.

I swallowed the pain blooming under the gash on my face while Cayden weighed his options.

He let out a long breath. "If you truly think the Witch of the Gray can free me, I'll come with you. But if she cannot break the bargain, I'll return to this realm before Vemdour makes me hurt someone. Deal?"

"I've seen enough deals for a lifetime." I tried to smile, but it sent unbearable pain through my skull. "Let's take it day by day. Now follow me."

Valeria, you need to come now.

I didn't object, letting the tether tug me left and right down winding overgrown paths. We moved as fast as we could with my battered body. Each painful step carried me closer to him, but my strength was waning. Feeling light-headed, I crouched, breathing between my knees. Something wasn't right. The realm shook, and my teeth chattered as a chill overcame me.

Red knelt beside me and placed the back of her hand on my forehead. "Cayden, she's feverish."

"We've got to keep moving." Cayden scooped me into his arms. "Direct me."

We followed another path, one that ducked under a hollowed overpass of dead trees, charred and gaunt.

You're close. Turn left.

"Left," I whispered, resting my head on Cayden's shoulder. Each step jolted me, and I winced, small murmurs of pain escaping my lips.

We ventured deeper into the desolate forest, twisting and turning with my directions. Like every time before, I felt Gideon before I saw him. His heart thundered through the bond, fear mixed with concern. An invisible cloak of warmth wrapped around me and staved off the goosebumps snaking their way up and down my limbs.

My heart lurched at the sight of him. Alive. He was alive.

I hadn't let myself fully believe it at first. He was as handsome as ever perched next to a makeshift portal of rocks. It was set up like an arched cairn with runes etched into the surfaces, spelling out an unfamiliar spell. Mistress Marjorie's handiwork, by the smell of it. He drew his sword, and corded muscle flexed and tensed underneath his shirt. My breath caught in my throat. Even with messy, unkempt hair curled at the nape of his neck and dark shadows under his baby blues, I found him beautiful.

He clenched his jaw. "Put her down."

"They're allies," I said, but the words came out as more of a whimper.

Gideon reluctantly lowered his weapon and stalked toward us, tearing me from Cayden's arms. Citrus, spice, and winter fire enveloped me, and tears flooded my cheeks, burning the gash on my face as I drowned in his embrace. I wanted to kiss him and hold him and let him chase away all of the darkness that haunted me.

The sky lit up with strikes of ebony lightning, cracking and thundering as the ground trembled.

"I take it you have something to do with that, too," he murmured.

"She does." Cayden clasped his hand in Red's. "And we need to get out of here before the God of the Forsaken realizes he's losing more than Val."

Gideon arched a golden brow. *Are you sure about this?*

I nuzzled in closer to him—drinking in his warmth, his strength, his everything—letting the words slip easily out of my mind and into his. *The only thing I'm undoubtedly sure about is you.*

Without another word, he dashed toward the shining, swirling silver portal with his arms wrapped around me tight and the steady beat of his heart trickling down the bond.

CHAPTER 34

A rush of cool air whipped around us as we strode through the portal. It felt a lot like skinny-dipping in the deep end of a pool at midnight—chilly but exhilarating. We entered a small clearing in the middle of the woods, where a thick layer of fog settled above the ground.

Footsteps barreled toward us. Malachi pounced on Cayden, grabbing him by the neck and holding a shiny blade to his throat. It reflected the scattering of stars above us. My brother reached toward his hips only to realize Life's Song and Death's Promise weren't there.

I still had them.

"Valeria," Cayden growled like a feral animal caught in a trap. "A little help here."

Red's hand covered her mouth as her eyes darted between the guys and me.

"Malachi, stop." My cracked ribs objected to every breath I took. I cradled my side with my left hand. "He's with me."

Malachi whipped his head in my direction. "What do you mean he's *with* you?"

Gideon put me down and crouched in front of me, pressing the back of his hand to my forehead. "By Bastile, you're burning up."

"Pyrtra scratched me." My throat was itchy and tight. "I think... I think I've been poisoned."

Shock lanced through me. The only person I knew who had been poisoned by Pyrtra had his arm lopped off.

Oh, gods.

"Fuck." Gideon moved toward Malachi, snatching a leather canteen from his hip. In two steps, he was back by my side. Gentle fingers on my chin tilted my head back as warm water poured down my throat, tinged with the bitter taste of dirt. "We need to get her back to camp."

Cayden's throat bobbed against the blade. "The cut on her cheek is a deadly wound from a Succubus. She needs dark magic to slow the poison's spread so that it can be siphoned out of her before it takes her life."

Siphoned. The knot in my chest loosened. Because I wasn't mortal like Mason, I could be healed, saved, when others would already be maimed or dead.

Malachi bared his teeth. "You don't tell us what she needs."

"Cayden didn't lead the raid against Empyrean," I blurted, hoping to ease his anger.

"Lies." He pressed the dagger's edge harder against Cayden's throat. "You fell for his lies."

I swallowed. I didn't fall for *his* lies. I fell for someone else's—someone far worse. But that was beside the point.

"I didn't lead it," Cayden gasped. "Now, let. Me. Help. Her."

"It was Vemdour and Ward." My voice sounded shrill, desperate. "Ward killed my mother, and Vemdour was behind everything else that happened that night."

Malachi ignored me, tightening his grip. "Tell her how I got these scars, Deathbringer."

Cayden's eyes flickered to me. "I—" He cleared his throat. A trickle of crimson pooled along the ridge of the blade. "I'm sorry. I'm so sorry."

"Tell her what you did to me and the others."

"I slaughtered them." His voice broke as his eyes scoured my face. "Every Celestian under the age of six. I strode into the barracks and killed them all. The kids... they knew me. I spent countless afternoons with them, training them, teaching them how to stop people like me. But when the time came... they couldn't do it. They remembered none of their training."

Bile rose in my throat.

"I didn't want to do it," Cayden continued. "But the king had seized the throne, and our mother was dead. I was angry and vulnerable and I had to protect Valeria. I didn't know Vemdour planned to wipe out the Celestian forces, and I sure as hell didn't know I'd be the one forced to do it once I signed over part of my soul."

"You carved us up. You locked us in," Malachi howled, shoving Cayden to the ground. Standing over him, he angled his blade centimeters above his heart. I watched in horror as Red tugged his arm, but he pushed her away, and she stumbled into a tree.

"Malachi," I said, louder this time, scrambling to my feet and closing the space between us. My body fought against the movement as if I was trudging through quicksand. The world around me spun. Gideon grabbed my elbow to steady me. "We need him alive. He's our greatest chance at claiming the throne."

"I wondered what I would do if I ever saw you again." He ran a hand through his soft black hair, his eyes meeting Cayden's. Not even a shadow of his teasing nature lingered in them. "Sometimes, I thought about taking my time, carving a message into your flesh the way you did ours. And other times, I'd imagine the exhilaration I'd feel as I choked the life from your body—watching your eyes roll back in your head, my fucked up face the last thing you saw." He took a steadying breath. "But now I look at you... and I want you to spend the rest of your life with the torment of this memory. The burden of the pain you've left throughout a pain free realm."

"An apology will never undo the wrongs that I have committed," Cayden whispered, his voice too loud for the uneasy quiet. "But I'd like to try and make amends."

Malachi stared at him for a beat longer before sheathing his weapon and stomping from the clearing.

My brother was on me in a flash, tilting my head to the side to look at my cheek. He let out a shaky breath and unclasped the belt from my hips. "We don't have much time."

Gideon's hesitation and wariness flooded into me.

My eyes met his. *I trust him.*

Cayden pulled Life's Song free and sliced his palm open with the tip of the blade. A thick, black ichor bubbled to his skin's surface.

"That's so fucking gross." I cringed. "What *is* that?"

"My essence." He gestured to Life's Song and Death's Promise. "A perk of being made into the Deathbringer. By cutting myself with Life's Song, I'm able to access the dark magic within my bloodstream. The essence should slow down the poison's spread, but we'll need someone born of dark magic to siphon it from you."

"Why can't Red siphon it?" I asked. "She's literally a demon."

Gideon's eyes bulged before his expression shifted back into concern.

"I wasn't born of dark magic, princess," Red said softly. "I was Made, like most demons are."

Satisfied with Red's answer, Cayden dipped two fingers into the goo and smeared it over my cheek. The wound stopped burning almost instantly. I sighed in relief.

"How much time do we have?" Gideon asked.

"An hour, maybe two, before she's comatose." Cayden's voice hitched. "Half a day before she's dead."

That was all my soulmate had to hear. He swept me into his arms and ran.

The others followed.

"Gideon," I murmured into his chest. "Where are we going?"

Don't speak. Save your strength.

Sweat dripped down his face as he carried me through a foggy forest. I traced the prickly blond stubble lining his jaw, wondering where the clean-shaven guy that stole me from the Realm of the Mortals had gone. Had he been unable to sleep without me? Did he toss and turn in a too cold bed, wondering if I'd ever lie beside him again? He looked as tired as I felt, and yet he kept running, carrying me deeper and deeper into an endless sea of fog.

I gasped. *Are we in the Gray?*

Yes.

"Why?" I asked aloud.

He didn't answer me, but I could feel bits of his scattered thoughts drifting through our bond. Some played like clips from a movie—Ward shouting, his father doing his best to keep the peace, and thoughts of me flickered like an old film reel.

The crackling of fire and laughter carried across the mist. It was a joyous sound, one that swelled in the air around us. A single laugh drew my attention. A breathy noise I'd recognize anywhere. A sound I wanted to bottle up and listen to every time I missed home.

"Mason." I tried to crane my neck to look for him. "He's here? In the Gray? Where's Margie?"

Gideon's arms tightened around me. "Relax. We're safe."

We entered a campsite, similar to the one at the portal but with much less fog.

Mason sat on a log in front of a roaring fire, smiling from ear to ear, his shaggy hair kissing his brows. It was easy to imagine this was how he looked all those summers Mrs. Kennedy sent him away to camp. I wasn't ready to face him—to learn about the horrors he suffered in the Realm of the Forsaken while I sat back and did nothing.

"Valeria!" Sabel cried out, clasping her hands in front of her. I peered around her, searching for Brini, but the little girl was nowhere to be found.

At Sabel's outburst, Mason moved toward me, his face alight with so much joy my heart could have burst from feeling so full. Maybe he didn't hate me. But in a split second, his features darkened, shifting from glee to fear, and my heart deflated. He fixed his sight on Cayden. Ugh, he would definitely hate me now. He crouched, touching the ground with Tam's inky hand...

The area around us rumbled.

Gideon groaned. "We don't have time for this."

Roots sprung up from the ground, wrapping and winding their way around Cayden's legs, imprisoning him where he stood.

Red shrieked and clawed at the roots. "Valeria, make the boy stop!"

"Mason," I whispered. His nostrils flared as his eyes snapped to mine. They were jet black, the color a perfect match to his new arm.

My mouth went dry. He was ripped at the edges, torn and broken. But as he wielded whatever newfound power he had, he was also something unexpected—a weapon.

The poison coursing through my system was taking hold as the roots climbed higher, Cayden's gasps for air growing louder.

The pain in my cheek was back ten-fold, simmering with terrible heat.

"Release him," Gideon said. "He's under Princess Valeria's protection."

Mason didn't move.

"You will not disrespect our princess's orders," Malachi said sharply, lifting his chin toward me. His earlier anger had dissipated, and he was all business. He drew his sword and turned to Mason, placing the tip of the blade to the back of his neck. "Release him."

Mason dug his fingers deeper into the earth, his lips curving into a sinister grin as Cayden shouted in agony. Red screamed.

"Mace." His shoulders jerked. "Mason, please, I—" I retched, choking on the sentence I couldn't finish. Heaving in Gideon's arms, I coughed up a chunk of black slime.

Panic flooded me. Not mine. Gideon's grip around me tightened as his heart raced.

"We're running out of time," Cayden croaked with whatever breath he had left.

I knew he meant me. *I* was running out of time.

In a flash, Mason snapped out of his anger. The roots retracted. I tried my damndest to flash him a thankful smile, but my face wouldn't cooperate.

"Summon the Witch of the Gray!" Gideon yelled.

It was the last thing I heard before the world around me went dark.

CHAPTER 35

A single lamp flickered from across the room as I blinked rapidly, my eyes adjusting to the low amber light. Not a room. A large tent, made cozy with fur blankets atop carpets spread haphazardly along the grass. The soft inhale of breath drew my attention to the figure curled up on the ground next to my makeshift bed. I peeked over the edge, and my heart fluttered.

Gideon.

I slipped out from the covers, stepping over him and through a flap that led into what I assumed was the bathroom. A bucket of clean water sat atop a wooden barrel and behind it was a rickety oval mirror. I splashed my face and dried it with one of the towels propped atop another sealed barrel. My gaze drifted to the mirror. The deep cut Pyrtra inflicted was wholly healed, save for a light silver slash. Nothing adorned the scar. I wondered what price Margie had to pay—if any—to heal me.

Now that I was free from Vemdour's temptations, tricks, and manipulation, the roots he nurtured within me should shrivel up. But even I knew the darkness would linger like a rotten perfume, masked by the sweet scent of relief. I kept staring at my reflection, wondering if I was as hideous a creature on the inside as the god. My skin prickled. The dirt and grime of my fight with Pyrtra were washed away, but Vemdour's longing gaze and delicious touch remained. It was still there, invisible to the naked eye. I could still feel it—feel him—calling out to me.

"Come back to bed," a voice murmured from behind me, and I spun around half expecting to see the god's smoldering eyes and towering frame. Half *wanting* it. My elbow bumped into the bucket, and water sloshed over the edge.

"Gideon." His name was delicate in my mouth, and I winced at the slight pain in my cheek. Taking a few steps toward him, I clutched his face between my hands and kissed him once, twice, three times until I was on the verge of drowning in him. The stubble on his jaw tickled my skin. His hands found my hips and tightened, crushing me against him. Without breaking the kiss, he picked me up and carried me to bed, where he placed me down gently as if he was afraid I'd break.

If only he knew he was the breakable one. And that I had almost lost him. Almost.

"Don't frown, princess." He grinned, and my stomach flipped. "You're home."

"This is a tent," I teased, glancing around us. "This isn't home."

"Home to me is wherever you are."

Gideon kissed me again, and happiness flooded through me. I didn't think I'd ever have the chance to be with him again. And now, he was alive, he was real, and we were *alone*. His lips on my body would chase away all memories of Vemdour. Slipping my hand under the frayed hem of his shirt, I ran my sharp nails down his back.

He groaned into my mouth. "By Bastile. You need your rest."

"Will you at least stay with me? And not on the ground?"

A blush crept along his tanned cheeks. "I was being a gentleman."

"Well, stop." I swallowed a yawn. "And get under the covers."

He kissed my newest scar and kicked off his boots before climbing into bed. He stretched, his wool socks finding my bare feet beneath the blankets. Another layer of warmth that I snuggled into. With my head in the crook of his arm, sleep beckoned for me, and I surrendered with a smile.

FOR A FEW HOURS, I laid in bed resting and listening to the unfamiliar noises of camp.

To be honest, I wasn't just resting. I was *avoiding*. There were so many fires to extinguish, I wasn't sure where to start. Probably with Mason. But I was too chicken to face him, too scared he'd confirm my fears—that he hated me.

"She's been asleep for hours," someone complained outside the tent, drawing my attention from the silver narcissus I twirled between my fingers. Gideon left it for me on his pillow along with a note saying he'd be spending the day with Margie. "And worse than that, Prince Charming's been in there like *he's* her boyfriend or some shit."

Okay, so that was Mason. His voice was unrecognizable laced with such animosity. Yep. Definitely avoiding *that* fire for a bit longer.

"Their relationship is—"

"None of your business." A voice interrupted the woman who was trying to comfort him. "Now, go."

Two sets of footsteps scurried away.

A moment passed before the tent flap opened. A short black bob bounced as she shook her head. "Glad to see you awake, Your Grace," Bex said, curtsying. Fine leather pants and a tank top replaced her tweed gown. Fresh purple bruises littered her bare arms, along with several cuts and scrapes.

I gawked at her. "What happened to you?"

"I've been training in my spare time while you were..." Her sentence trailed off, and she averted her gaze, suddenly interested in folding blankets.

"Away," I finished for her. She nodded. "Where's Mae? Is she here, too?"

Sorrow passed over her features before she righted herself. "I'm relieved to see you awake. How are you feeling?"

Weird. "I'm, um, good. Feeling peachy keen."

"Can I get you anything to eat or drink?"

"I can get it myself," I said, climbing out of bed.

I couldn't hide from everyone forever, so I might as well put out the fires now before the tensions burned the camp down. I needed to round up Cayden and Malachi to make sure they weren't at each other's throats, Mason so I could smooth him over, and Sabel because I needed to know where the hell Brini was.

Bex placed her hands on my shoulders. "You need to rest."

Just because I spent a year—er, a week—in the Realm of the Forsaken didn't mean I was something that needed to be *handled*.

I was *fine*. Gods.

"What I need is for you to stop coddling me," I snapped. She raised her eyebrows a fraction, and all I could hear was the memory of Vemdour's laughter as he told me no one would accept who I really was. Pushing the horrid noise from my mind, I added, "I'm sorry. That came out harsher than I meant it to."

"Maybe the fresh air will do you some good."

Bex headed toward a crate overflowing with clothes and pulled out a simple pale blue dress, the color of a cloudless pastel sky. She slipped it over my head and pulled my hair out of the back, the locks a long, matted mess. After running a brush through it and tying it in a braid, she looped her arm through mine and led me outside.

We wound our way through the cream-colored tents in silence, listening to the stream of chatter and grunts. The woodsy scent of low-burning logs permeated the air along with roasting meat.

Mason sulked at a wooden picnic table. He tossed an apple from hand to hand, his mind elsewhere. It was unsettling to see him without a notebook and pen. He wore a loose tunic rolled up to his elbows and leather breeches. A beat later, his eyes snagged on me, and he bolted in my direction, shoving Bex out of the way to grip my face and press his lips against mine.

Out of habit, my mouth parted for him. This was wrong. He would never be kissing me like this if he knew the truth of how I fell hopelessly for Gideon when I never let myself open up to him. And he certainly wouldn't be kissing me if he knew about the time I willingly spent by Vemdour's side, believing his wicked lies. Kissing his wicked lips.

Murdering Ellody.

My eyes snapped open as I stumbled away from him, one hand pressed to the knot forming in my chest.

"Mortal," Malachi called from behind us.

"Val." Mason reached for me, but I took another step back. His brow furrowed. "What's wrong? I've missed you."

"I've missed you too, Mace," I whispered. "But there's a lot we need to talk about."

He dropped his hands to his side, eyes darkening. "Then talk."

"Not here."

"Where would you like to go, Val? You wanna take me back to the bed you let Prince Charming sleep in last night?" His words were acidic, and they cut to the bone. "I would've been better off if you left me in Hell."

Tears stung my eyes. How... how could he say that?

"I can send you back," Cayden drawled from where he was leaning against a table. His hands rested on the hilts of Life's Song and Death's Promise.

"Stay out of it, Deathbringer," Malachi warned. He tied his hair in a loose bun as if he was preparing for a fight.

Cayden grinned, giving a mock bow.

I pointed to the three of them. "Come with me."

Both Cayden and Malachi nodded.

Mason folded his arms across his chest. "I don't take orders from you."

And that's when the final string of my patience snapped.

"Yes, you fucking do!" I shouted. My heart pounded in my ears as my voice grew louder. "You are in this realm under my protection; therefore, you *will* answer to me, and you *will* obey my orders whether you want to or not. *Capeesh?*"

Flames licked beneath my skin, dying to be let loose. A part of me wanted to force Mason to kneel to prove he understood that our dynamic wasn't the same as it was in the Realm of the Mortals, and it never would be again. But that was the part of me Vemdour unleashed.

Four words flittered into my mind. *I'll be there soon.*

I ignored them. I didn't need Gideon's help. Not for this.

My gaze flickered over the three of them and then beyond to Sabel, who stared with her mouth agape.

"Sabel." The darkness threatened to burst to the surface at the sight of her flawless face without Brini in tow. "Come along as well."

She slid into place next to Mason like they'd become fast friends.

With a deep breath, I schooled my expression. "We're all going to have a nice little chat instead of acting like uncivilized demons."

"Not all demons are uncivilized," Red sang from where she perched on a log in front of the camp's fire. The flames danced in my direction, calling out to me with a siren's song, sweet and hypnotizing.

"Right," I said. She flashed a friendly smile. "Would you like to join us, too?"

She looked over the group and shook her head, springy curls bouncing. "Just make sure Cayden comes back to me in one piece."

"No promises," I muttered as I stomped in the direction of my tent.

I PERCHED ON THE EDGE of my bed with my feet tucked under me. The guys took a seat on the ground and gave Sabel the only chair in the room. No one said a word as they waited for me to speak. Bex had run off the moment she heard my stomach growl, and I sighed, thinking of how hungry I was.

"Any volunteers on who wants to go first in clearing the air?" I asked.

Cayden grinned. "I suppose I'm the obvious choice."

"Fine." I clenched my jaw. "You fucked up, Cayden. Big time. But you've been atoning for your sins for years." I glanced at Malachi. "He's been working as an ally—my ally—by protecting me from the Realm of the Forsaken for as long as he could." My eyes met Cayden's once more. "And... he's my brother, and I want him here. You've all seen the lengths I'd go to for the people I care about"—I cast a stern glare at Mason—"so for the love of the gods, just let the Deathbringer work with us, so he can do what he does best—"

"Kill innocents?" Malachi said, interrupting me.

"And torture innocents?" Mason chimed in.

Cayden blew out a breath of air, his brown eyes darkening. "Bind yourself to a god and see how much free will you have afterward."

"Enough. There are other things I need to fill everyone in on, but I want a chance to talk to Mistress Marjorie first," I said. "So... can everyone play nice and chill the fuck out for a bit?"

Somewhat reluctantly, they all nodded.

Sabel picked idly at her gown. It was as blinding as the sun at high noon and as vibrant as her fiery hair. "Can we hurry this along? I don't like leaving Brini unattended."

My spirits perked up. "She's here?"

"Of course she's here."

Relief flooded me knowing Brini was safe. Gideon stalked through the tent's entrance, and the knot in my chest loosened.

He placed a quick kiss on my cheek. "What'd I miss?"

Malachi rolled his eyes. "I'm sure she can catch you up in about a millisecond through the dyad."

Mason blinked. "The what?"

"Let's go," Cayden said to Malachi and Sabel. He stood, brushing dirt from his pants. "We don't need to be here for the lover's quarrel."

The three of them said their goodbyes and left, likely going separate ways.

An awkward silence grew between Mason and me as we sat there. Even Gideon waited for me to say something, anything. But I didn't know where to begin.

"Mason, I'm sorry for... getting you into all of this." I waved a hand around, trying my best to encapsulate everything that happened over the last whatever amount of time. "It was never my intention for you to be hurt. You know that, right?"

He nodded, finally looking at me. My heart threatened to crack open. We never fought during our entire friendship. We'd had disagreements, sure, but we had never spoken to each other the way we did today.

"There's no easy way to tell you, but the dyad between us is more than just a bond." My voice quivered. "We're... soulmates."

Mason snorted. "Soulmates? Really, Val? This is a cop-out, and you know it."

"Perhaps," Gideon said softly, and Mason's dangerous eyes switched to him. "I should let you two talk alone. Besides, princess, you're starving, and it's making me hungry. So, I'll get us something to eat."

I opened my mouth to tell him Bex was already on food duty, but he slipped out of the tent before I had the chance.

Alone with Mason, I feared him in a way I never had before. The way his eyes raked over me with such... indignation. But somewhere underneath his anger was my best friend. And I knew him better than I knew myself.

"Such a gentleman," Mason spat after a moment of silence. "You know, I never pegged you as a damsel in distress who needed Prince Charming to swoop in and save her."

"I never pegged you for one either."

He let out a long breath of air. "I am grateful you saved me from the Realm of the Forsaken."

"You sure about that? You said I should have left you there."

"I was angry." He clenched his jaw. "I *am* angry. Angry that I've lost everything, Val. Everything." His voice cracked. I slid down to the ground and took his hands in mine, ignoring the searing heat that emanated from Tam's. An ache rattled through me as I watched him shatter.

"Mace—"

"Do you even know why you were exiled to Oakwood of all the places in the world?" he asked, interrupting me.

"Margie chose it at random."

"At random?" He laughed, but it was hollow. "They tortured me with more than just weapons and magic in the Realm of the Forsaken, Val. They also tortured me with the truth."

My brow furrowed at his question. "What truth?"

"Your keeper knew of a Seer that had fled from Empyrean and made a life in Oakwood. He had a family. A wife who loved him, a son who adored him." His words were coated in venom as he flung them at me. "Then *you* came along and brought attention to the one place he thought he'd be able to live out his life in peace."

I blinked, stunned at this revelation. "*Aulus*? Aulus Damus was your father?"

"He was." A tear slid down his cheek. "So, I hope you can understand that I am not exaggerating when I say that I have lost *everything* because of you." He took a shaky breath. "I want to go home to my mom and my friends and never see you again."

His words cut deep. Swallowing the lump in my throat, I whispered, "You can never go home, Mace."

He snatched his hands away and shoved them in his pockets.

Pressure from unshed tears built behind my eyes. "There is nothing, and I mean nothing, that I can say to make up for all that you've lost by being my friend. And I know you might hate me forever, but if I had to do it all again and tether you to my realm to keep you alive, I would." The dam broke. Tears streamed down my face, salt coated my lips. "Because I'm selfish and stupid and going one single day without you is something I never want to experience again. I'm so sorry."

"I know you are, Val," Mason said softly. "And I'm sorry, too. I'm... I'm hurting, and I want everyone else around me to hurt, too. Including you."

"We'll find your dad," I promised as I hugged him tight. "When this is all over, I will do everything in my power to bring him home to you."

"I'm going to hold you to that, *Your Highness.*"

I pulled away from him, wiping snot across the sleeve of my dress.

He wrinkled his nose, brushing a few tears from my cheeks with his thumb. "That's gross, Breault."

"Oh, fuck off, Kennedy."

"No, I don't think I will." He laughed and wrapped me in another tight hug, pressing his lips to the top of my head. "You said it yourself, I'm not going anywhere."

My body relaxed, no longer tense and ready for a fight. I sank into his embrace.

Deep down, my heart knew he wouldn't have forgiven me as quickly if he learned how I spent my time in the Realm of the Forsaken. If he knew the god who stole his arm had kissed my lips or if he found out that the hands he held moments ago ripped Ellody's beating heart from her chest for *practice.*

He could never know that I wasn't the same girl he grew up with. Not anymore. My time with Vemdour changed me. But maybe... maybe having him around would keep the cold vice of darkness at bay.

CHAPTER 36

G ideon watched me with a smile on his lips as I scarfed down my bowl of stew—and his—satiating my ravenous hunger. After I'd emptied the bowls and licked the spoons clean, I flopped back onto the bed and groaned at the tightness in my overstuffed belly.

"Okay, I've eaten." I propped myself up on one of my elbows. "Are you going to catch me up on what happened while I was away and why we're in the Gray?"

"Do you want the short or long version?" He laced his hands behind his head, leaning the chair backward on two legs.

I flicked a bread crumb from the comforter. "Something tells me both versions suck."

In agreement, despair and vengeance ravaged their way down the bond.

Climbing out of bed, I closed the space between us and knelt, taking his hands in mine. "Gideon?"

He stood and tugged me to my feet along with him. "You kneel for no one."

"But there are lots of fun things I can do on my knees."

A half-smile ghosted his lips before it waned, and his face turned stony.

My fingers slicked his hair back. "What is it? What happened while I was... away?"

"A lot." There was a weight upon his shoulders that hadn't been there before. "After he discovered you were missing, King Ward put the entire King's Council on trial to test their loyalty to the crown. Those that didn't pass met the end of his sword. Then he imprisoned those he deemed loyal, keeping them in the castle under lock and key."

An image flashed through the bond—a man prone on the marble floor in the Great Hall, blood pooling around him. Life drained from his amber eyes.

"Your father." A frigid ache rattled through my chest. "Oh, gods. I'm so sorry."

Gideon squeezed his eyes shut, forcing the image from my mind.

"Murdered for treason," he said dryly. "My father claimed he was the leader of the rebels. The distraction gave Malachi and me enough time to escape and round up a handful of the others before the wards went up."

His hands shook as I clutched them. The bond was hollow with invisible pain. While I screwed around in the Realm of the Forsaken, Gideon suffered. I would never forgive myself for it. I released his hands and balled mine into fists. The prick from my nails cutting into skin was something to focus on other than the anger swelling within me.

What other deaths stained Ward's monstrous legacy?

My eyes flickered to Gideon. "Who else did we lose?"

He rubbed his jaw. "Everyone who isn't here now."

The words stammered out of me. "What... what about Mae? If Ward did something to hurt her—"

"Mae chose to stay in the castle." He let out a long breath. "She's our eye on the inside, keeping a record of everything that's happening while we're unable to breach the wards."

I felt my eyebrows disappear into my hairline. Mae was the quiet one—the observant one. She was now a mouse wandering the halls of a deadly trap, and she'd need to keep her wits about her if she wanted to stay alive.

"What in Bastile's name are the wards made of that Margie can't breach them?"

The candlelight cast a shadow over his handsome features. "Dark magic, but they're changed hourly." He glanced toward the entrance of the tent as if he saw beyond it. "Once the Witch of the Gray figures out a way through one ward, another replaces it."

"This is so screwed up." I reached for the dagger hanging around my neck and held it tight. It was cool to the touch, even though a fire burned bright within me. "Thousands of innocent hostages are locked up with a power-crazed prick who will stop at nothing to keep the throne. And there's nothing we can do about it."

Vemdour's eyes flashed in my mind, tempting me to surrender to the anger. If I did, I might very well burn the entire realm to the ground.

"We'll figure out a way to get through sooner or later." Gideon watched me as I paced. "But enough about Empyrean. Tell me what happened while you were in the Realm of the Forsaken."

I shook my head, refusing to meet his gaze.

"Valeria. I need to know if it was worth sending you there."

I chewed the inside of my cheek. I was ashamed of my time there. Ashamed of what I'd become. Manipulation or not, a part of me cared for Vemdour. I believed his lies and his promises, and I nearly lost everything because of it.

I nearly lost *Gideon* because of it.

"If it's too hard to tell me"—he pulled me to him until my head rested against his chest—"show me."

I thought that'd be worse than saying it aloud. But I was already hellbent on keeping my truths hidden from Mason. I didn't want to do that with Gideon, too. He was my soulmate. He had to understand. Didn't he?

"Are you sure?" The rise and fall of his chest rustled his shirt against the scar on my cheek. "It wasn't— I didn't— It's probably not what you imagined. I wasn't tortured or anything. But I... I did something bad." I was rambling, and I couldn't stop. "Okay, I did more than one thing that could be considered bad, but gods—"

"Show me everything." He tightened his arms around me. "Even your darkest truths won't scare me away from you. Surely, you know that by now?"

His words were quiet, almost solemn, and it caused me to pull away and stare up into his magnetic eyes.

"I hope that's true." My insides tightened, a ball of tension settling like a brick in my belly. "I'm not sure how to *show* you, but I'll try."

Slowly, my eyelids fluttered shut as my head found his chest once more. I snuggled in close, breathing in his familiar scent. I replayed the memories I promised myself I'd bury once he knew the truth. One by one they trickled down the invisible string that bound us together.

Doing my best to release memory after memory in chronological order, I paused and murmured, "A week in Empyrean is a little less than a year in the Realm of the Forsaken, so if it feels long, that's why."

His body went rigid. "If I knew that, I wouldn't have waited seven days to come for you."

"You didn't get my letter?" I asked.

"What letter?"

"I wrote you—" I paused. *Red.* Cayden must've asked her not to deliver it to Gideon to ensure I still had a way out of the Realm of the Forsaken. "Never mind. Let's get this over with."

The memories played slowly, and he went still the moment they became darker. His heartbeat accelerated and slowed as each day, each moment, each ugly truth, poured through the tether.

When the memories stopped flooding down the bond, he stepped away from me, putting distance between us. A thought raced through me fast enough to make my stomach churn. What if he hated me now that he knew the truth? That I wasn't just a mortal-raised princess, I was Bastile's daughter, and there was a darkness within me that nearly went unchained. That I had fallen for Vemdour and his honeyed lies and almost killed him because of it.

I watched him wearily.

"You weren't joking when you said your time there wasn't what I imagined." He ran both hands over his face and through his hair. "So, let me get this straight. You chose to stay there."

"Yes."

His throat bobbed. "You chose to join *him* and that's why your brand looks different?"

"Yes." I glanced at the delicate black roses and thorny vines that swirled around the golden geometric hourglass. "The brand morphed once I asked Vemdour to break the bond."

It seemed I'd forever be marked by Vemdour, in more ways than one.

"But then you changed your mind?"

"Yes," I said for a third time, running my tongue over my lips. "I thought he killed you, and that... that broke me." Closing the distance between us, I pressed his palm against my chest. "Do you feel this?"

He gave a single jerk of his head.

"My heart beats for *you*," I whispered. "Vemdour tempted me with power and revenge, but the moment I thought I lost you, I didn't give a damn about any of that." My voice hitched. "Because I... I had feelings and strings and dreams all attached to you." I gave a half-hearted laugh. "I'm so far from perfect, Gideon. And I'd understand if you want to be free of me. I wouldn't blame you if you ran and never looked back. I've messed up... a lot. Hooking up with Malachi, hurting you physically and emotionally, abandoning Empyrean for power, allying with Vemdour, *making out* with—"

"Is there a point you're trying to make?" His forehead creased.

"Right, sorry. I'm not one for big speeches." I shook my head, hoping to get my thoughts straight. "I guess what I'm trying to say is... if you're all in, so am I."

There was a long silence as he gazed down at me, his hand still pressed against my heart. The tether between us gave me no inkling of his thoughts or feelings, and I braced myself for what came next, for the realization to settle within him that he didn't want me. It would hurt, but I would heal. It'd be just another scar carved into my heart. No biggie. My palms were slick with sweat, and my throat went dry while I waited. No biggie at all.

His thumb stroked my cheek so tenderly I thought I'd shatter beneath his touch. "You have possessed me since the moment we were bound. I'm yours in every sense of the word."

My jaw dropped, and he chuckled. That wasn't what I was expecting.

He placed a kiss on my forehead. *I'm in love with you, fuckwit.*

Oh.

Warmth spread through my veins as a thousand butterflies tore from their cocoons and fluttered within me, stroking the lonely parts that craved to hear those three tiny words—words that no one had ever spoken to me before.

He loved me.

My heart thumped madly in my chest. It was so loud that I was sure the entire camp could hear it. But I didn't care because *he loved me*.

"Say it again," I breathed. "Out loud."

"I." A kiss on my cheek. "Love." Another on my jaw. "You." A final kiss met my lips, and my knees wobbled. His arm around my waist steadied me as I played those words over and over again.

I love you.

I love you.

I love you.

He knew the gnawing darkness that had burrowed its way into my bones, into every fiber of my being. It was proof that I wasn't perfect, and I never would be so long as those roots remained.

And yet... he loved me anyway.

CHAPTER 37

Beside me, Gideon slept peacefully, worn out from kissing and a passionate—albeit quiet—night tangled up in each other. It was so unlike every other time I'd gone to bed with a man. There was no urgency, no sense of primal desire or distraction needed. Instead, we both took our time as we tenderly touched each other, kissing scars and learning each other's bodies in a way no one else had. And when we finished, tremors raking through us, I fell asleep to the gentle sound of his voice while he told me he loved me again and again.

But Vemdour's bloodthirsty grin plagued my dreams, turning a beautiful evening into something twisted. I'd spent the last few hours lying awake thinking about how a crackling fire sounded a lot like bones crunching. After I couldn't take the noise anymore, I climbed out of bed and slipped into Gideon's cotton shirt. It hung loose and long on my frame, regardless of my curves, stopping mid-thigh. I wrapped an itchy wool blanket around my shoulders and sneaked out of the tent.

My bare feet sank into the cold, soft earth with each silent step as I followed the scent of vanilla and smoke, searching for the one person I needed to talk to. The camp was small, the fire dwindling to a quiet *snap* and *pop* while everyone slept soundly. No sounds of wildlife could be heard. There wasn't even a breeze. The night was still. Almost peaceful.

Before my time in the Realm of the Forsaken, I never would
have noticed it, but now the air was thick with the quiet hum of
dark magic. It was a blanket smothering the camp, and I knew if I
ventured toward the tree line, I'd feel a protection barrier that not
only hid us from view but muted the outside world entirely.

Margie sat at a wooden table in front of a tiny one-story stone
cottage covered in lush green moss. Skeletal trees arched over the
home like they had died reaching for the sun.

My shoulders sagged in relief when she spoke, her voice
sounding like home.

"I wondered when you'd come to pay me a visit, little one."

I raced around the table and threw my arms around her neck,
breathing in the familiar scent of power and secrets, safety and
assurance. She wrapped her arms around me, giving me a gentle
squeeze.

"I'm sorry it took me so long," I breathed.

We held each other for a beat longer before I reluctantly let her
go and took a seat across from her. A single white orb floated next to
the round oval-shaped door as if my keeper used the moon itself to
illuminate her front yard. It cast an eerie glow around us.

Her cloaked gaze burned me, and after all this time, I still longed
to know the face of the woman who raised me. She sat up straighter,
laying her hands flat on the table. "Ask what you came to ask."

"Is it true?" I cleared my throat, masking the break in my voice.
"Is it true that Ward isn't my father?"

"Yes, it's true."

My heart hammered in my chest. "Then that makes me..."

The words trailed off, and she finished for me. "A demigod."

"Right, a demigod," I agreed, nodding as if I had a single fucking
clue what that meant for me. "Is that why Vemdour couldn't sever
the dyad between Gideon and me?"

Her shoulders tensed, her body going rigid. "Did he try?"

"Yep. And he couldn't break it." I showed her my wrist and the inky roses and thorns that adorned the brand, streaking up my forearm. "He was able to transform it into this and mute the tether for a time, but he couldn't sever it." I didn't know if she'd have any answers to my questions, but something in the pit of my stomach told me she would. "Why am I able to see through Vemdour's cursed form to the god underneath? Is it because I also have the blood of a god running through my veins?"

She traced her finger over several runes etched on top of the table. A glimpse of similar black marks peeked from beneath her long sleeves. Her silence—which was once a comfort—was insufferable as it stretched between us.

"As you know, Bastile was a fearsome god in the Realm of the Divine. He helped fight against the Realm of the Forsaken during the Wrath of Deities, a gruesome war that took years to end. During that time, Bastile protected the Realm of the Mortals from the crossfire of both the gods and the demons. And in doing so, he fell in love with a mortal woman he saved from a horde. From that moment on, he spent most of his time in the Realm of the Mortals, watching her from afar.

"That's when he came up with the idea to create his own realm, one that's sole purpose was to protect the Realm of the Mortals from the dangers they couldn't see. But, of course, the other gods found out about his intentions, and they were enraged that a fellow god would dare to revolt against them."

She paused for a moment before continuing. "They banished Bastile from the Realm of the Divine and exiled him to the Realm of the Mortals. He watched the woman he loved wither and die, as all mortals do, and he wandered the earth hearing legends of a sorceress who hailed from the Gray, a place that is neither here nor there, but everywhere, untouched by all the realms. He came to me, and I listened to his desires. After meeting with him and seeing his passion for the mortals, I offered him a pocket of the Gray to build his perfect world—Empyrean."

I cocked my head to the side. "You helped him without expecting anything in return?"

"Of course not." She lowered her voice. "In exchange, he was to help me curse a god."

"Vemdour?"

She nodded. "Yes, but when I knew him, he went by Kieran."

Kieran. It was a pretty name, fit for a handsome god.

"Bastile agreed to my terms, and we used our combined magic to create Empyrean. We spent years sculpting each Empyrean in his image from clay."

My brow furrowed. "You can't make a person from clay."

"A god with a sorceress on his side can do anything," she murmured. "Creating life takes only the breath from immortal lungs and a little dark magic."

"But we age, we bleed, we die," I argued, struggling to wrap my mind around how any of this made sense.

"Let me finish the story, little one." She took a deep breath as her voice turned dark. "Together, we created life. And once that life was born, we sought out Kieran under the guise that Bastile wanted a truce between realms. After a bloody fight, your father tore Kieran's heart from his chest and gave it to me."

Like I did with Ellody. I shivered, remembering the day I challenged Vemdour into admitting he was in love with me. *To love, you have to have a heart.*

Oh, my gods. He told me. He told me that day what his curse was, but why?

Why in the world would *Margie* curse *Vemdour*?

Then it dawned on me. My heart thundered in my ears as I prayed to Bastile.

Please let me be wrong.

"You're the woman from the painting," I whispered. Heat spread across my cheeks. "Vemdour betrayed you, and you cursed him for it."

She was quiet for a long time until she said, "Yes, we were lovers a millennia ago. When I felt like he was growing too possessive of me, I sought comfort in the arms of another. He was angry when he learned of my infidelity and..." She took a deep steadying breath. "And he hunted her down and killed her."

My stomach soured. I kissed the same man that was once *lovers* with my keeper. I may have had *feelings* for the same man that was *once lovers with my keeper.*

"Why are you telling me this?" I asked, wanting to puke.

"Because the curse I cast on his heart had a clause."

I leaned forward, ignoring the dread settling in my belly. "What was it?"

"Whomsoever this heart loves will see the god beneath."

I blinked. Then blinked again. "But you took his heart, so how could it love anyone? Let alone *me*."

She tilted her head back to gaze at the fistful of stars scattered across the inky sky. "Kieran's heart beats steadily in the chest of your soulmate, little one."

I bolted to my feet and took several steps away from the table. "Wait, what?"

My breath hitched painfully. A nightmare. This was a nightmare. I pinched my arm, convinced I was dreaming. But a prick of pain proved I was awake. My mind spun as I tried to grasp what Mistress Marjorie just told me.

Vemdour's heart was *in* Gideon?

"We hid Kieran's heart for years—even going as far as changing my identity—but Bastile grew anxious about some sort of prophecy and the bargain he made with the god in exchange for the

Half-Light. So he gave me an ultimatum—either return the heart or hide it somewhere no one would think to look."

She let the words sink in before continuing. "Two years before your mother fell pregnant with you, Bastile hid it in the only safe place he could think of—an Empyrean, made from clay."

I shook my head. Then shook it again. I kept shaking it as if doing so would erase or help me forget what I just heard. "This is impossible."

Gideon had Vemdour's heart.

"No, little one." She stood and closed the distance between us, clutching my shoulders. "This is the truth. Gideon was the first clay incarnate that we animated since the dawn of Empyrean. Every other Empyrean who came after that was born, except him. He... he was created, sculpted by Bastile's hands with lungs filled with the breath of an immortal and the darkest of magic pulsing through his heart."

My world shattered. It felt like someone kicked me in the gut and then trampled me.

All this time. All this fucking time, I thought Gideon was perfection incarnate.

Too good. Too pure. Too righteous.

And it was because he was created to be that way.

"How can I let myself love Gideon now?" My lips trembled along with my knees, every bit of me threatening to break. "Knowing the heart beating within his chest is that of a monster?"

"Even monsters can love and be loved."

Her words knocked the air from my lungs as Vemdour's face sprung to mind, with the way his endless eyes searched mine for validation, for something more.

"I've seen Gideon bleed," I whispered, disbelief hinging on every single word. "If what you're saying is true, how can that be?"

"Because he is flesh and blood, just like you." The words came out soft, almost comforting. "He just came into this world a little differently."

My chest seized. *He just came into this world a little differently.*

I couldn't blame him for that. He... he had no idea what he was. He mourned the loss of his parents as if they were his blood family. He didn't know the truth.

He could never know the truth.

Because if word spread... Vemdour could find out.

Fear snatched me in its searing grip. "What if Vemdour realizes he couldn't break the dyad because I'm bound to the person with his heart?"

"He can't take his heart back even if he knew."

"Another clause?"

"Whomsoever his heart loves may grant the god peace."

Peace. The only thing I'd ever chased in this world, and I had the power to grant it to one of the deadliest gods that stalked the realms.

It took everything in me to breathe past the deceit, my heart shattering and burning all at once, pain and fury fighting for control. I wanted to hurt her in some way, to rub it in her face that Vemdour chose me, wanted *me* to rule all the realms with him, but I couldn't. I choked on a sob that clawed its way up my throat, not speaking until my anger simmered into hurt.

I turned away from her. "You shouldn't have hidden this from me."

The words came from somewhere deep within me. Somewhere that had been devastated by her betrayal. The one person I thought wouldn't withhold the truth from me had done so more than once.

"I'm sorry," she said softly, placing a hand on my trembling shoulder. "You're right. I should have told you the moment you were bound. But I thought if you knew, you wouldn't give yourself a chance to love him. Gideon isn't Vemdour—even if he bears the burden of his heart."

Tears flooded my cheeks as the pressure in my chest loosened.

Gideon isn't Vemdour—even if he bears the burden of his heart.

She was right. She was always right. Gideon wasn't a manipulative piece of shit like Vemdour. And Vemdour didn't hold a torch to Gideon.

Wiping the tears from my eyes with Gideon's shirtsleeve, I whispered, "But none of this explains why Bastile bound me to Gideon if he truly believed the prophecy was about Vemdour. Did he do it to ensure Vemdour couldn't hurt me in our marriage without hurting himself?"

"We may never know the god's reasoning behind his actions, little one." She squeezed my shoulder. "But you can trust that whatever his actions were, they ensured you were cared for in his absence."

I stepped away from her and rubbed my temples, trying and failing to unravel this tangled web of half-truths and bargains. My life was an absolute mess. I was betrothed to the God of the Forsaken and bound to the man who held his heart in a chest molded by my father's hands. We were on the verge of a war with Ward for the throne that was mine by birthright... and my feelings were so conflicted, so torn between wanting to tell the truth and needing to tell a lie.

"You've hidden so much from me, Margie," I said softly. "I need you to promise me that there will be no more secrets. Not between us."

"For your forgiveness, that is a promise I am happy to make."

"Is there anything else you would like to tell me?" I narrowed my swollen eyes at her. "Like how you knew Aulus Damus was Mason's father and that's why you chose Oakwood?"

"I thought he'd help me keep you safe, but he was a coward."

"He had a family," I whisper-shouted, pointing in the direction of the camp. "He left Oakwood to protect Mason, to protect his wife."

"Aulus Damus should be the least of your concerns."

"Mason is my concern. Not Aulus. *Mason*."

"We cannot change the past," she said sharply. "Aulus made the choice to leave his family, and now you must make yours. Are you going to tell Gideon the truth? Or will you run to Vemdour and free him of his curse?"

What *was* I going to do? I had no intention of freeing Vemdour. He was a manipulative bastard, and there was no way in hell I'd sacrifice Gideon for him. All I knew was that I was going to do everything in my power to keep Gideon safe. He loved me. Maybe those feelings would fade in time, but for now, he loved me with a blackened heart that had never loved before.

And I wasn't going to give that up for anything.

"I'm going to do neither of those things." Wrapping the blanket tighter around me, I lifted my chin. "For once, I'm going to do something I'm not particularly good at."

My eyes roved over her hood, and I finally didn't have to wonder what she looked like beneath it. I already knew. A challenging smirk on thin lips, gray-blue eyes alight with mischief, and snow-white hair that shined silvery under the moonlight. One half of the Boundless and the Bound.

She tilted her head to the side. "And what's that?"

"I'm going to keep my mouth shut."

CHAPTER 38

It took Gideon all of fifteen minutes to wrangle everyone into the large tent, filled with ledgers and maps, a round wooden table, and chairs. He gathered every single name I whispered down the tether as I dressed this morning—Mistress Marjorie, Cayden, Malachi, Red, Mason, Bex, and to Gideon's surprise, Sabel.

They had been patient, making light conversation amongst themselves, as I wracked my brain for the words to a plan I didn't have.

Last night, when I made my way back from meeting with Margie, I had a heavy heart and a spinning mind. I laid awake next to Gideon, watching him sleep. The steady rise and fall of his chest softened me so much that I locked the truth of what was hidden inside him in the recesses of my mind. When I awoke, I nearly forgot.

As he sparred with Malachi, I was awestruck by how beautiful he was in the dewy glow of early morning, sweat glistening against his sun-kissed skin. That was the moment I remembered. Bastile sculpted him, brought him to life, and bound him to me. And that was the moment I decided I didn't care.

Vemdour's heart or not, Gideon was my soulmate.

He loved me.

That alone was enough for me to bury the whole he-has-the-God-of-the-Forsaken's-heart truth so deep that I'd need an excavation crew to bring it back to the surface.

"Can you eye fuck Prince Charming on your own time?" Mason hissed in my ear, leaning so close the familiar smell of his sweat-soaked skin wafted into my nose. "Some of us have demonic arms they need to get under control."

Right. I glanced around the table and took a deep breath.

TWO HOURS LATER, WE all sat around the same table arguing amongst ourselves. A pounding bloomed in my head brought on by the whiplash of the conversation. No one could agree on *anything*.

"Cayden." Malachi slammed his hands on the table, rattling the now empty mugs. "You are not coming with us."

"Yes, the fuck I am," Cayden said, his voice lethal. Red placed a steadying hand on his shoulder. "I'm not trusting the lot of you with Valeria's life."

A tiny spark of gratitude dripped down the tether. Gideon liked Cayden. A little. He wouldn't admit it, though.

"You're a liability," Malachi argued. "Vemdour still controls you. Even now, you could sabotage this plan. We can't risk it."

With a sigh, I glanced at my keeper for some input. We hadn't spoken since last night, and I hoped things weren't going to be weird between us now. "Margie, do you think you can break the bargain between them?"

"I could try, but I offer no promises." The words were clipped. "Contracts with gods tend to be breakable only upon death."

My heart plummeted into my stomach as Cayden's words came floating back to me. *But if she cannot break the bargain, I'll return to this realm before Vemdour makes me hurt someone..*

As if he was replaying the same memory, he frowned.

A heavy silence settled over the tent.

Malachi stared at the map of Seraphicity sprawled across the table, his jaw twitching. Finally, he said, "Valeria, if you're determined to bring the Deathbringer, any innocent blood that he sheds will stain your hands."

"Don't burden her with that," Cayden snapped. "I have control over *that* part of me. It's when Vemdour demands something that I have to obey."

"Like a good little plaything," Mason snickered, drawing Cayden's scrutiny away from Malachi and a glare from Red.

"Enough!" I shouted. I realized they weren't going to take my plan seriously until they knew who I was and what we were fighting for. Cayden, Margie, and Gideon already knew the truth, but the others... "There's something else some of you need to know."

My arms itched from the heat lapping under my skin. The flickering candle flames illuminating the tent burned brighter than a star caught on fire as I willed my anger to rise. The darkness sang to me, purred to me. My fingertips tingled, and I closed my eyes, willing the power to come, if just for a second.

C'mon. Don't fail me now. My heart pounded as I replayed every sting of betrayal from all the lies and half-truths. I relived the crimson swipe splitting my mother's throat wide open and imagined the terror of what Mason had to face, all alone in a realm of ash and shadow.

And then there was Vemdour, the handsome god who nurtured the darkness within me. So quick to challenge me and—

"Valeria!" Bex shouted, and my eyes snapped open to find her face creased with fear. "Your hands are on fire!"

The room broke out into chaos as Mason threw a half-full pitcher of water on me—missing the flames and splashing my face—and Malachi stripped off his shirt to smother the fire, his muscles rippling in the candlelight. Bex's mouth hung open, Sabel looked dazed, and Red's eyes were alight with wonder. Cayden leaned back in his chair, his booted feet crossed at the ankles on top of the table.

"Surprise," I said, doing my best jazz hands. "Bastile's my blood father."

Everyone stilled. I took several deep breaths and willed the flames to settle. After another beat of my heart, they disappeared entirely. Progress.

"Let me get this straight," Mason began, turning to me. "You're a princess *and* the daughter of a god?"

"Yup."

"Cool." A lop-sided grin met his lips, and I dreaded what he was going to say next. "Not many mortals can say they dated a princess *and* a demigod."

"Technically, we didn't date," I corrected him.

He waved his hand. "Semantics."

Sabel's mouth twisted and she stood abruptly. "I've got to go check on Brini," she threw over her shoulder as she darted from the tent.

That was weird, wasn't it? Gideon asked.

Mm-hmm. Very.

I bit my lip, filing that weirdness away for later and steering the conversation back on track. "The plan isn't foolproof. I know that. But I am Bastile's daughter, and that throne is rightfully mine. We will all do what it takes to claim Seraphicity and restore it to my father's—my true father's—vision."

No one spoke as our plan settled into place.

Would I cut down innocent Empyreans if they took up a sword against us? If they were doing what they thought was right by protecting Ward?

I didn't like the part of me that knew I would.

I didn't like her at all.

But I wasn't as powerless as I once believed, and I'd never let myself believe that lie again.

CHAPTER 39

The next morning, Sabel and I marched across an open field smothered in mist, following a tiny glowing orb dictating which direction we should go.

Sometime last night, after Margie failed to destroy Cayden's oath to Vemdour and his screams died out, a second wind kicked in. When silence finally settled upon us, I bolted upright. Gideon pulled me back to bed and tucked me under the covers, securing me in place with his arm thrown over me.

I laid there wide awake until an invisible weight had settled on my shoulders, and I bounded out of bed just to bounce around camp. Malachi couldn't sleep either, and so between the two of us, we spent hours plotting and planning, ensuring there were no loose ends, nothing we hadn't covered.

We could do this.

We *had* to do this.

Sabel craned her neck as if she was trying to catch a glimpse of the rest of our group. But they were nowhere around us, so that was impossible. A small purple bruise on her neck peeked out from behind a curly lock of hair.

I gasped. "Sabel Keogh!"

"What?"

"Is that a hickey?!"

"A what?"

I tapped the delicate space right under my jaw and grinned.

"By Bastile." Her hand reflexively went to her neck as her face reddened. "Please don't tell anyone."

"Let me try to guess who left it."

She groaned. "Please don't."

Ignoring her, I rattled off my theories as we continued walking. "I'm not sure Malachi is your type, though he is a handsome flirt and a deliciously good kisser... A more likely candidate is either Mason or Bex. And while Bex is drop-dead gorgeous, I'm almost certain she's taken, so... that leaves Mason!"

She sucked in a breath. "Are... are you angry?"

"No, of course not." I bumped my hip into hers. "Mason and I are *friends*."

Her shoulders sagged in relief. "I don't know if you know this, but Gideon brought him to me after you rescued him." An easy smile spread across her lips. "He's quite lovely."

I cut her a sidelong glance. Sabel was a great person. She cared for Brini without question, and she cared for Mason when I couldn't.

"Thank you," I murmured, grabbing her hand and squeezing it. She didn't ask what I was thankful for, she only squeezed my hand in return.

The towering statue of Bastile loomed on the horizon. Gideon's nervousness seeped through the tether the closer we drew to the invisible line that separated the Gray and Empyrean.

Soon, the perpetual misting of fog dissipated, and the field was no longer a dead graveyard of crops. Instead, we trekked through calf-high cotton the color of polished quarters. The air was fresh, and the sun warmed my cheeks.

It was a beautiful day to die.

A few more hours passed, and we reached the elusive northern entrance.

"So it does exist," I mused.

The gate was iridescent, almost like a portal built between two arched columns that twisted together at the top to form a knot. A single metal bar cut horizontally through the middle barring any passage.

"Are you sure you can do this?" I asked Sabel as we waited for Gideon to give the go-ahead that he and the others were at the Bygone.

She batted her lashes. "Unlike you, I was born to play the part of a damsel in distress."

We're ready. Gideon spoke the two words into the tether, and my heart lurched.

"It's go-time." A grin spread across my lips as I handed her Malachi's dagger. "Make it believable."

Sabel snatched a fistful of my hair and positioned the blade against my throat. Then she pushed me out of the brush and toward the gate where only two guards were on duty—one thin and gangly, like a rodent with scruffy hair and buckteeth, and one short and stocky, like a dwarf from a fantasy movie, who could probably deadlift me without breaking a sweat.

"Halt!" Stocky called out. "Name yourself."

"Sabel Keogh. And this"—she tightened the fist wound in my hair, and I yelped—"is the leader of the rebel filth, Princess Valeria Breault."

The guards exchanged nervous glances while I bit back a laugh. They weren't even Celestians. This was going to be a piece of cake.

"Don't move," Rodent said from behind the gate. "We're sending word to His Royal Highness."

"Please hurry," Sabel begged. "I don't know how much longer I can hold her."

That was my cue. I thrashed in her arms, acutely aware that I was stronger than her. She gritted her teeth, trying to hold me still. The guards weighed their options before unlocking the gate.

There was no sound, no evidence that the wards had dropped, but Stocky yelled, "Come quick!"

Sabel shoved me forward, her breath hot on my neck. Each step brought us closer to claiming Empyrean.

Now, I urged Gideon as Sabel thrust me into the guard. Stocky grabbed my arms with both hands, and I wiggled away from him, stomping on his foot. She pushed me again. But this time he wrapped his arm around my decolletage and held me against him. His fingers bit into my flesh as I struggled to free myself. My eyes met Sabel's in panic as he reached for the knife sheathed to his thigh and pressed it to my throat.

Oh no. I—

Sabel fainted. Her body collapsed into the guard, knocking us both over. Malachi's knife clattered to the ground and both Stocky and I looked at it and each other before we scrambled toward it. My fingers had just barely scraped the hilt before he yanked me away from it.

I kicked at him aimlessly, landing a blow to his groin. He howled in pain, and I leapt to my feet bracing myself for a fistfight with the other guard.

We're through, Gideon finally said through the tether.

Rodent struck me across the face with the hilt of his sword, and I hit the ground. Hard. Blood pooled in my mouth. He pinned one knee to the center of my back, holding me in place.

Took you long enough.

Sorry. His words were clipped. *We ran into some trouble.*

What kind of trouble? Dread coursed through me. A small part of me knew the answer before I even asked the question.

Specters.

Sabel moaned and held the back of her hand to her forehead.

I blinked twice in rapid succession at her, so she knew phase one of our plan was complete. The corners of her lips twitched up before she bit her bottom lip to stop herself from smiling.

Stocky regained his composure and kicked Malachi's dagger through the wards, out of reach. Malachi wasn't going to be happy about that. Then he switched places with Rodent, who moved to console Sabel as he guided her to a pair of thick steeds tied to a tree just to the right of the gate. Within moments, the guard was curled around her finger, handing her a black handkerchief to blot her eyes. She wasn't lying when she said she was born to play a damsel in distress.

"You'll regret this," I screamed, trying to channel the vibe of a scorned rebel leader. I shifted beneath Stocky's weight and whimpered when he wrenched my hands behind my back. He tried his best to pry the bracelet off me, but I warned him against it. "I wouldn't do that if I were you."

He grunted and hit me once more—this time with his fist—before locking a pair of heavy manacles around my wrists. He dragged me toward a finicky horse. It neighed as the guard drew near. In one fell swoop, he tossed me over its back, climbed onto the saddle, and took off down a winding overgrown path.

This way into Seraphicity was entirely different from the Bygone, and I wished I weren't upside down to experience it. We twisted and turned down various paths as branches clawed their way up to the sunny blue sky. Trees and dirt were nothing but a blur around me, and Sabel's curls were a torch blowing in the wind.

Minutes later, we stopped. I was dizzy and unable to stand, stumbling the moment my feet hit the ground.

Stocky drew his sword, his face riddled with disgust. "I should kill you right now."

"You don't have the balls." I spat at him, half-expecting another blow.

"Barrett," Rodent said, leaving Sabel atop a set of marble stairs in front of a swirling silver portal. When his back was to her, she winked. "King Ward will have your head if you don't hand her over."

Barrett grumbled and sheathed his sword. "I'll escort the girl. You escort the traitor."

CHAPTER 40

The market was in its normal state of chaos as the guards escorted Sabel and me through it, the point of a sword digging into my back. Murmurs spread among the sea of people, my presence causing mixed reactions. Some spit at my feet while others fell to their knees, praying to Bastile.

Somewhere in the crowd, my friends were ready to strike the match needed to ignite what was coming next.

I faced forward, staring at Sabel's back as the weight of Gideon's eyes raked over me.

His anger swelled and drifted through the bond. *Did they hurt you?*

Nah. Just a couple of bruises. They'll heal.

If I lived long enough to let them.

We made it through the market without incident and to the castle as the sun cast a heavenly glow over the grounds. Unlike the day I arrived, Ward waited in front of the castle surrounded by guards and bastards from the Pry. Lirabeth stood by his side, cradling a baby swaddled in yellow.

Bile rose in my throat, not from the joy and rage that spread across Ward's face. But from a gruesome display of power—several severed heads protruded from pikes lining the entryway. A strangled cry clawed its way out of me as the faces registered, gray-skinned and flesh torn by hungry ravens. All of their wide-eyed gazes stared at me in horror.

Squeezing my eyes shut, I refused to look.

I refused to remember them this way.

Aurick and Royston.

And countless others.

Dead.

Their heads were a brutal reminder not to plot against the crown. My breath was fast and heavy as the world spun around me. I pictured Gideon's face up there next to Mason's and Malachi's. The guard didn't catch me when I fell to my knees, leaving me to retch in place. Sabel's cries were louder now, and I wondered if they were real. Because mine were.

What's going on?

Nothing, I sobbed into the tether. *Stay away from the front of the castle.* Gideon couldn't see Aurick like this. It'd awaken something dark within him. *Promise me you'll stay away.*

I promise.

Anger made me climb to my feet and lock eyes with Ward through the gate. My wrath was palpable, a drum of darkness that thrived on the promise of revenge.

My nails dug into my palms as my fingertips tingled. Not now. Not yet.

Ward barked an order, and the gates swung open. The guards flanked me and dragged me through, their rough hands digging into each of my arms.

I willed myself to settle, to stick to the plan.

Deep breaths. In for five counts, out for seven.

Sabel rushed into her father's arms, who graciously comforted her, taking off his cloak and draping it around her shaking shoulders. Her mother placed kisses all over her face. Then Sabel dove into an intricately fabricated story about how Gideon kidnapped her and held her hostage. Her voice broke when she cried that she'd never be able to marry now because the rebels *ruined* her. A line I was sure Red fed her.

Even though every nerve in my body wanted to weep for the dead, I schooled my features into annoyance at the story she was telling. I'd have time to mourn after this was over, after we put them to rest and sent them off into the Half-Light.

To make Sabel's story even more convincing, I interrupted her with curses and promises of death. Of course, I was no actress, but I'd say it added a certain layer of authenticity to the exchange.

She continued telling them she overpowered me in a fight when I returned from the Realm of the Forsaken, poisoned from letting demons feed on me. At that, Vemdour flickered into my mind, and the two times he ate from my hand. I shivered. The people standing in the courtyard lapped up everything she said even though she was lying through her perfect teeth.

She glanced at me with puffy eyes as she finished her story.

It was my time to shine. I knew what I was supposed to say now, what image I needed to paint of myself. Mason would tell me to color the lines a darker shade first before filling in the middle. It'd add depth to any picture. It'd make any lie believable. But with the heads of the dead on display behind me, I couldn't disgrace my name in front of them.

They died for me.

I wouldn't lie before them.

So I made a promise. "When I'm through with you, Ward, your head will be dessert for the God of the Forsaken."

Shocked whispers broke out, and Ward seethed, turning to Sabel first. "Thank you for your strength and courage in coming forth with the truth. You served the crown well. Fear not for your reputation"—he ogled her from head to toe, his gaze lingering on her chest—"I will see to it that you receive an advantageous betrothal."

She bowed to him, and the witnesses murmured their approval.

I scoffed. Ward didn't give a fuck about Sabel or her reputation. He wanted to get to the best part—what he was going to do with *me*.

"As for you, Valeria..." His eyes sparkled. "We will do what we were unable to do to Cayden. We will set you ablaze at dawn and pray you find mercy in the Half-Light."

Another piece of our plan clicked into place.

The cackle that bubbled up out of me was something dark and twisted, and I couldn't stop the sound from pouring out of me no matter how hard I tried. I followed the guards through a heavy wooden door to the left of the courtyard that led deep underneath the castle—to the Condemned, an abhorrent prison meant to break its prisoner's minds with endless darkness. The walls were sharp and jagged and cold, so very cold. Their boots on rock echoed as they dragged me down and down and down until I was sure we'd hit the bottom of the floating island.

They shoved me through a door into a cell smaller than a half-bath. I shook violently with laughter. As if the Condemned would contain the magnitude of what we'd planned.

The guards cursed me, drawing my racket to a deafening silence.

"I'll remember each of your voices when I'm free," I whispered into the pitch-black blanket of darkness. Their breathing stilled as they listened intently, waiting for me to continue with a threat they could mock.

I didn't say anything else, though.

Their imagination would do the rest for me.

CHAPTER 41

The guards changed shifts at least twice after they locked me up, proving it'd be more challenging to free me than we thought it would.

I'd spent the last couple of hours going over our plan and wondering if leaving me here was the best course of action. If I escaped, Ward would know others were helping me. And by the end of the day, we'd all be rounded up and executed. But if I were still in my cell by the time dawn broke...

We're altering the plan.

No, Gideon argued. *We're getting you out of there, just waiting on the next shift change.*

Ward's waiting for someone to try and free me, Gideon tried to object, but I kept forcing my thoughts down the tether. *We should wait. Bide our time. Let him tie me to the pyre, and then Mistress Marjorie can strike. Empyrean will never let me burn knowing the truth.*

Time passed without a reply. I tried again. *Gideon?*

Sorry. I was getting everyone's thoughts.

I smiled into the nothingness before me. *And?*

Your insane ideas have gotten us this far. It's a dangerous risk, but you're right... striking publicly is the smartest move. Gideon sent a gentle caress through the tether. *Please try to get some rest. There are only a couple of hours until dawn.*

THE DOOR TO MY CELL swung open and collided with the stone wall. The high-pitched clang of metal rattled through to the marrow in my bones. A guard yanked me from the dry-rotted cot with one thick gloved hand, and I yelped. They chuckled at my fright, unable to see my scowl in the dark, as they dragged me out and up the winding stairs back to the courtyard. I blinked, shielding my eyes from the change in light. The sun had barely risen. A sliver of its orangey hue peeked from beyond the skyline.

I craned my neck to take in the faces of my guards, only to find them hidden behind shiny silver helmets.

Not guards, then. Celestians.

The tether hummed. Gideon felt close, but I couldn't spot him.

Empyreans of all ages shouted obscenities as we walked toward the market. Stones pegged my skin, bound to leave bruises. Others watched without pity like I *deserved* to be paraded through Seraphicity and led to my death. Children clung to their parents as they pointed at me, tears running down their too-thin cheeks. In every face, I saw Brini, and I prayed to Bastile that she was safe and somewhere far away from here.

The spectacle came to an end as we ventured to a part of Empyrean I'd never visited before—the Pit. It was a vast circular arena with little to no shade and a dirt floor. Slabs of stone encased it with two heavy gates on either side. Rows of silver-veined marble benches surrounded the inside of the arena as all of Empyrean poured out to watch my execution.

I scanned the crowd for the faces of my friends and came up empty. Sweat dripped down my spine. Where were they?

The Celestians pushed me forward, and we circled the edge of the arena to a separate door that led underneath. Below, one of them rummaged through a bag and handed me a simple cloth nightgown that reeked of what smelled like gasoline.

Oh, gods. My heart thundered in my chest. The tiniest of sparks would set me ablaze.

"I can't change with these." I gestured to the manacles. "Take them off."

The one with a metal ring of keys obliged, removing them from my raw and chafed wrists. I slipped out of my tattered lilac gown, appreciating that they turned around to give me the tiniest sliver of decency. I took a deep breath, swallowing the pungent air. A pang of sorrow mixed with worry seeped into the bond. Gideon had to be close, but *where*?

Once the gown was on, they led me through a gate and into the Pit. The sand was cool on my bare feet, not entirely warmed by the rising sun. My gaze fell on the center of the arena where a dais, carved from obsidian and silver, waited across from a thick wooden stake. It was driven into the ground and surrounded by kindling.

A pyre for my death sentence.

My heart thundered in my chest. I needed to run. I needed—

"Princess Valeria Edelyn Breault." The realm quieted as Ward spoke. He sat on the dais with Lirabeth by his side. The latter held their newborn cradled in the crook of her arm. "You are sentenced to death by fire for treason against the crown. How do you plead?"

I straightened my spine and glared at him. "You're sitting on *my* throne."

"Guilty!" He waved one fat-fingered hand to the Celestians, and they dragged me onto the pyre, tying my arms behind my back with thick rope. Sharp pinpricks bore into my feet from the splintered planks beneath me. I swallowed my cry as I scanned the crowd once more for the familiar faces of my friends. Everyone blurred together until one set of ruby lips smiled at me. Red sat behind Ekon, a knife to his throat. She gave me a reassuring nod.

Glancing back to Ward, who was waiting all too patiently for the torch-bearer, I worried my lip.

Where are—

Mistress Marjorie popped up behind Ward, just as a familiar raven swooped down and snatched Ward's crown from his head, granting Margie access to dig her fingers into his skull. Lirabeth's screams for help were cut off as the Celestians surrounding the dais shucked their helmets to the side.

Oh, my gods.

Cayden, Mason, Bex, and Gideon stood there, a wall between me and the other Celestians rushing into the Pit from both doors.

"Found it," Mistress Marjorie chirped, pulling an illuminated iridescent orb from Ward's head. She cupped it in her hand along with a vial of silver liquid. Then, carefully, she poured the concoction onto the memory and widened her hands, creating an enormous bubble shaped like a drive-in movie screen.

My knees buckled.

All of Empyrean watched as Ward screamed and berated my mother. They gasped when he brought the knife over the basket where I cried. They cursed when he slit my mother's throat, and they raged when he spit on her body. And when Ward framed Cayden, they went ballistic.

The realm delved into chaos, with everyone fighting someone else.

I couldn't tear my gaze away from the sight of my mother dying. The memory played over and over as Mistress Marjorie stood holding the spell intact.

A guttural scream drew closer to me as Ward rushed toward the pyre, fumbling with a pack of matches. He halted in place, chest heaving, as a sword met his throat.

"I promised my queen she could have your head," Gideon growled. "Kneel before her."

Ward jutted his chin and glared at me with his soulless eyes. How did I ever compare Cayden's warm brown eyes to his muddied ones?

On my left, Red screamed for Cayden. Blood drenched her ivory dress. My eyes scanned the dais and found my brother standing there with Death's Promise held against Mason's throat.

No, no, no, no, no. This wasn't happening.

We were so close to ending this. So fucking close.

Gideon glanced between Ward and Cayden.

"Help him," I screamed.

But there was no time now.

Vemdour emerged through an inky portal, whispering something in Cayden's ear. His endless eyes flickered to mine, and I gawked at him, still struck by the handsome god beneath the curse. He took a step away from my brother, his mouth coiling into that sinister grin that haunted me ever since I left him.

Hundreds of Vemdour's minions wreaked havoc around us. Mistress Marjorie broke her spell to fight alongside Bex. Bursts of power exploded from her hands. Malachi, still in raven form, clawed and bit at the demons, relentlessly tearing away bits of flesh with every strike. Screams of terror lashed me as demons plucked Empyreans from their seats and dropped them to their deaths.

They outnumbered us.

My heart pounded in time with the bodies hitting the ground as my wrists chafed against the ropes binding me. I needed to be out there fighting.

The coppery scent of blood and sweat tinged the air, and I cried out, "Vemdour, stop!"

But he didn't. He wouldn't. I told him everything I wanted was in Empyrean, and now he threatened to take it all from me until all that was left was *him*.

As if the sound of my voice jolted him into action, Gideon struck the back of Ward's head with the hilt of his sword. The false king collapsed with a thud, unconscious but breathing.

"Hurry," I begged.

Gideon rushed behind me, struggling with untying the rope that bound me.

I tried to call my power to me, tried to singe the ropes from my wrists, but it wouldn't surface.

My eyes drifted back to Cayden, silently pleading with him to fight whatever command he was given. His face was tight, lips thin, eyes full of sorrow. The hand holding Death's Promise trembled.

"Please," I said softly. "Please, Vemdour, don't."

Mason murmured to Cayden, who gave a curt nod. When Mason met my gaze, he smiled, even as the blade dug in, parting the skin with a silent scream. A loud ringing exploded in my ears as Mason's life drained from him, blood staining the sand crimson. He crumpled to the ground—one hand clutching his bloodied throat, the other extended toward me.

Gideon yelled something, but I was too far gone.

Too broken. Too angry.

Everything I'd done was to keep the people I cared about safe.

And I failed. Again.

Rage, anger, and vengeance clouded my clarity. Howls clawed up my throat as I released the pain. Flames burst from beneath my skin, igniting the pyre. But, like the fire that Pyrtra unleashed during our duel, it didn't burn me.

No one did this to Mason but me. I murdered Pyrtra. I begged Cayden to come with us because I thought he was worth the risk.

Guilt devoured my chest, rattling the pieces of me that shattered.

Mason was dead. And it was no one's fault but mine.

My body levitated from the ground, higher and higher, with every painstaking pound of my heart.

Gideon's cries were painful through the tether, but I couldn't help him. No matter how much I willed the flames to disappear, they wouldn't release me. I trapped myself in a fiery cage of wrath.

The darkness won.

Vemdour won.

The god grinned as I hovered above the Pit, vibrant purple flames licked my flesh and spread out behind me in the shape of two magnificent wings.

A perfect match to Bastile's.

Time nearly stilled as his voice carried across the screams. "I promised you power, pet. And I always keep my promises."

He spared me one more knowing look before he clapped his hands and vanished, taking Cayden and his minions along with him.

His revenge was swift, the consequences everlasting.

Fire danced along my skin, bathing me in its warmth.

I should be the one lying there with blood pooling around me.

Not Mason.

Margie shouted to Gideon and Malachi, pointing in various directions while I watched from above. My heart broke again as Sabel stumbled over numerous bodies and collapsed onto the ground beside Mason, half slung over him. She trembled as she cried, and it was like thunder shuddering in the sky. On the dais, Lirabeth sat cradling her baby, eyes wide with shock, focused solely on Ward's limp body, a prayer on her lips.

A prayer to my blood father that would go unanswered.

My mind drifted to the peace I chased and the desire to restore Empyrean to its former glory. But how could I do anything for Empyrean when all I wanted was revenge?

Screams turned to sobs as I slowly descended to the ground, recalling the flames and charring the dirt around me. The fire-fueled dress I once wore was ash somewhere in the breeze, and I stood broken and naked in front of Empyrean.

Gideon stripped off his armor, slipping his shirt over my head. I trembled. If anyone looked close enough, they might see everything broken within me. He sucked in a breath when his hands cradled my face, but he didn't pull away from the burning. He drew me closer. Clutching me against his bare chest, the familiar scent of blood, sweat, and citrus grounded me in the present.

My pain was his pain.

I burrowed my face deeper into him, not wanting anyone to see what emotions ravaged my features.

The shock. The sorrow. The outrage.

My mouth parted, letting in shallow breaths.

Ward stirred from unconsciousness at my feet. Pulling away from Gideon, I stared down at the man who murdered my mother and betrayed his firstborn son. At the monster who destroyed a monster-less land.

When he blinked his vision clear, the fear in his eyes was a living thing.

And I wanted to snuff it out.

I untwined myself from Gideon's arms and picked up the sword he used to knock Ward out earlier. It was light in my hand when I stalked toward him, accusations dripping from my tongue. "You murdered my mother, you framed my brother, and you've destroyed my realm." My voice was steadier than I thought it would be. "How do you plead?"

Ward's eyes raked over me, begging for mercy.

When he opened his mouth to speak, I cut him off. "Guilty."

With all that I'd lost in mind, I swung the sword against his neck. Blood splattered against my bruised cheeks.

Ward's body fell to the ground as blood gurgled from his wound, soaking into the charred sand.

It only took three blows to behead him completely.

My stomach soured knowing that was a quicker death than he deserved.

CHAPTER 42

ONE MONTH LATER

I never thought I'd return to the Realm of the Mortals, let alone to my hidden house. My shoulders sagged as I glanced up at the tower where I spent so many days dreaming about perfect worlds and limitless happiness. Now, I no longer dreamed at all. Instead, I tossed and turned, waking from nightmares drenched in sweat, to a life without Mason in it.

A life too colorless to bear on most days.

After Mason died, the mortal-raised part of me died, too.

And to heal, I needed to visit home.

I needed to say goodbye.

I chanted the spell to lower the wards, and the words fumbled through my lips as I butchered the old tongue. A moment later, the soft hiss of dark magic dissipated, and I stepped through the wrought iron gate unscathed.

The wind carried the scrawl of Mason's hand drifting across paper into my ears as I crossed the front yard, overgrown grass tickling the skin between the cuffs of my jeans and my sneakers. Three steps up the stairs and the familiar creaks were the weight of Mason's body as he settled in place on the porch, waiting for me to come hang out.

A knot burgeoned, sending an icy chill through my hollow chest.

I bounded inside and upstairs, acutely aware I had only a tiny bit of time to grab the things I wanted before I said goodbye to this part of my life forever.

Nothing tied me to the Realm of the Mortals anymore.

The air was stale in my room as the door swung open, and I cracked the windows to let in the fresh scent of summer. It was early morning, the sun barely over the horizon. If I closed my eyes, I could pretend Mason was waiting for me on the outskirts of town, ready to run through the woods.

I thought killing Ward would satisfy my ache, but it didn't. His bloodshed did nothing to soothe the rawness in my chest or slow the darkness burrowing its inky tendrils into my bones. Lirabeth wept when his head rolled from his shoulders, a stark contrast to the cheers vibrating the stands. Maybe she loved the monster within the man. My mother made that same mistake once. And so did Margie. A part of me did, too.

But when Lirabeth begged me for her life, I listened. She swore to raise her son with the knowledge that he had no claim to my throne, that I was the sole blood heir. I thought letting her and the baby live would thaw the ice spreading throughout my veins, but it didn't.

It made me colder, regardless of the divine fire I carried.

I shivered and wrapped my arms around my chest to hold myself together.

I didn't let myself think of that day too often. It hurt too much.

And the clock on the nightstand told me I didn't have time to hurt.

Unfolding the enchanted bag Mistress Marjorie gave me, I crammed my belongings into it—books, clothes, shoes, makeup, perfume, and jewelry I found at the antique store on Cornelia Street. All of the little treasures I'd accumulated over the years. Margie had promised it'd fit everything I wanted to take back to Empyrean, and then some.

My eyes snagged on the portrait Mason gave me for my birthday.

I didn't look like that anymore. Now, streaks of ebony bled throughout my blonde hair, and the flames in my eyes shifted, rimming my pupils with silver.

I was finally favoring my father—finally favoring Bastile.

Gideon told me the changes suited me, though I couldn't stand to look at them. They were further proof that danger lurked beneath my pretty face. They were evidence of what I was at my core—something wicked and holy.

Unbreakable now that I had already shattered.

And what did it take to unlock the divine power within me?

One life. Mason's life.

Vemdour knew what he was doing when he destroyed the powerless girl I once was and replaced her with the woman he saw beneath—a woman who was his equal, a woman who rivaled him in every way.

A woman who sent him Ward's head on a platter along with a promise. *Soon you will be where you were meant to be all along, my dearest Vemdour.*

Six feet under. Ashes in the wind. Blood on my hands.

A shiver slithered down my spine despite the room's warmth.

My eyes flickered to the door where Vemdour leaned against the frame, arms folded across his broad chest, his gaze roving over me. His glamour was wholly gone now; not even a ripple exposed the monster's exterior.

We stared at each other for a long minute.

The desire to set him ablaze with a single wave of my hand took over, and I squeezed my hands into fists—nails cutting into the skin. I couldn't make good on my promise now. Not until I knew the full extent of the consequences. Not unless I knew Gideon would survive. And Cayden would go free.

I wrapped the picture in an old-band t-shirt—one of Mason's—and gently placed it in the bag. "How'd you know I was here?"

"I have spies all over, pet."

"Stalking isn't a form of flattery."

"Red delivered your gift." He stepped through the threshold, and sirens sounded in my heart. "Along with her resignation as emissary to the Realm of the Forsaken."

Red was a blessing. She was the only one I could ask to remove the pikes from in front of the castle, and I wept when she offered to say an Empyrean prayer to help guide those spirits into the Half-Light. A demon saying prayers for those made to destroy them? It was kind of poetic.

After that, I asked her to remain in Empyrean as my emissary. She agreed under the condition that we didn't stop trying to free Cayden from his contract with the God of the Forsaken. It was an easy enough promise to make, considering I didn't blame my brother for Mason's death.

That blame fell on the god who stood before me today. And me.

Vemdour ran his large hands over the quilt I stitched so many summers ago, and I snatched it away from him, cramming it into the bag, too.

He sat on the bed, crossing one knee over the other. The springs whined under his weight. "Is this how it's going to be between us now?"

"There is no us," I snapped.

I pinched the bridge of my nose to steady myself. I couldn't lose control. Not now.

Another glance at the clock. Five minutes, and I had to go.

He was quiet again, almost contemplative. "Valeria, the boy's death was necessary to free you. You were never going to embrace yourself as something more, so long as you believed you were something less."

"His name was Mason." I let the flames licking under my skin flicker to the surface as I locked eyes with him. "If you're going to talk about him, use his fucking name."

"You think I don't know his name?" He jolted to his feet. "You think I don't bear the tally of his death?" A step toward me. "You think I *wanted* to make you hate me?" Another step. "That power coursing through you? The one you're trying so desperately to control?" He was so close now that if I reached out, I could trace the curve of his lips and the shape of his jaw. I tilted my head back to glare at him. "Mason's death unlocked it."

I jabbed a finger into his rock-solid chest. "Get out."

He didn't move. "Are we enemies now?"

"We've always been enemies."

He let out a long breath, lifting his hand toward my cheek only to drop it to his side. "Because of our... time together, the Realm of the Divine doesn't think so."

"I don't care."

"You should," he said softly. "I received word this morning from Sørin that Ward had a letter drafted to be sent to the Realm of the Divine should he meet an untimely death."

"And?"

"It said that you had aligned yourself with the Realm of the Forsaken and that securing the Empyrean throne was only the beginning of our conquering." He licked his lips, eyes scanning my face. "He warned them that we're coming for the Realm of the Divine's throne next."

"There is no *we*, Vemdour."

If I didn't know any better, I would have thought he flinched. "You aren't safe in Empyrean, Valeria."

Another lie. Another manipulation.

Stepping away from him, I pulled the vial from my pocket and shook it while simultaneously giving the bag a testing lift. It was as if it weighed nothing at all. Gods, I loved magic. Without having to bear the bag's weight on my shoulders, I slung it on like a backpack and tossed the vial to the floor. An incandescent portal opened, and I stalked toward it—spine straight, eyes dry.

"They're coming for you," he whispered. "Because of me, they're coming for you."

I stilled a breath away from my one-way ticket back to Empyrean.

With more bravado than I felt, I turned to face the god and said, "Let them come, Kieran. And I'll be sure to tell them all about how you mean *nothing* to me."

THE MARKET WAS ALIVE with music and dancing when I returned to Empyrean.

I was only a *little* late to the festival after dropping my mortal goods off in my new chambers, the Queen's Quarters. After Sabel's parents kicked her out for the part she played in the insurrection, I gave Brini the girlish bedroom Lirabeth designed and let Sabel take the chambers directly under Brini's.

Gideon unofficially moved in, too. We hadn't had *the talk* or anything, but his clothes hung in our shared closet, and he had his own dresser. It made things... easier to have him around. He kept me together during the aftermath of the Battle of Forthrightness—what Empyreans had taken to calling the day I claimed the throne—and he did everything he could to ease my suffering.

Margie said time would heal my pain, but we both knew that wasn't true.

Fractures of the heart scar over and become rougher, sensitive to the changing seasons.

Gideon sent a gentle caress through the tether. My head whipped around, searching the crowd of smiling faces for his, and I found him with ease—blond hair, magnetic blue eyes, and sun-kissed skin.

Perfection incarnate, made just for me.

Malachi and Red trailed behind him.

"Did you get everything you needed?" Gideon murmured, wrapping his arm around my waist and nuzzling into the crook of my neck.

I grinned. "And then some."

Malachi surveyed me from head to toe. "No threats on your life while you were there?"

It was hard to hear him over the music, so I shook my head, forgetting I was wearing Bastile's crown. *My* crown. It was heavier than I had imagined it would be.

That morning, I instructed the guys to remain in Empyrean because I knew Vemdour would make an appearance once he heard I was in the Realm of the Mortals. Part of me wanted him to come, wanted him to apologize or offer to bring Mason back, but that part of me was delusional, still hung up on his honeyed lies.

They're coming for you. The echo of Vemdour's warning sent a shiver down my spine, but on the off chance he was telling the truth... that was something I would deal with later.

Today was about celebrating.

A pair of thin arms looped around my thigh and squeezed, screaming, "Queen Valeria!"

Sabel stalked toward us, her cheeks flushed and eyes red-rimmed. Her gown was the color of a raven's feather, so stark against her fair skin and the sea of jewel tones that it was haunting.

"Godsdammit, Brini," she panted. "You can't just run off like that, you little shit."

Brini giggled and smacked Malachi's leg. "Tag, you're it!"

And then she was off, quicker than a rabbit, Malachi bounding after her with a wink in my direction.

A slight breeze whipped the sweet and rosy scent of flower blossoms around us. It was fragrant and refreshing, considering the market used to reek of piss and shit and decaying bodies.

But, a little bit of magic and voilà. All cleaned up!

Together, Mistress Marjorie and I would use our combined magic to erase and undo every trace of Ward's rule. Of course, we still had a lot to do, but this festival was the beginning of something new—something fun and wholesome. Something to bring everyone together again.

In front of the band, Mae and Bex danced, alight with life. Red dragged Sabel over to join them, and I could have sworn there was the ghost of a smile on her lips.

Gideon placed a kiss on my temple, and I leaned into his warmth as hope sprung in my chest, clawing its way through the despair.

CHAPTER 43

Later that night, the moon was high and the stars glittered in the sky, casting a silvery sheen through the windows. Gideon laid on our bed, one hand propped behind his head while the other held one of my romance books as he read it aloud to me.

I couldn't wait to curl up next to him.

Too tired to put away my things from the Realm of the Mortals, I shoved the bag from the bed. It clattered to the floor with a heavy thud and the sound of something shattering.

"Oh, no." I groaned, picking it back up and dumping the contents onto the duvet.

I rifled through my belongings, palms slick as I grabbed Mason's drawing.

Please don't be broken, I prayed to Bastile.

I unwrapped it to find the glass still intact; only the back of the frame had popped off.

Easy fix. I squeezed the prongs into place, but it popped open again.

My brow furrowed as I took the back off entirely, and an envelope fell to my feet. What the hell? I bent to pick it up as my heart thundered in my ears.

It bore my name written in Cayden's familiar handwriting. Worrying my lip, I cracked the wax seal and withdrew a silver emblem. I recognized it immediately.

The Deathbringer's sigil—two crescent moons connected by lines in the shape of a cross.

Fastened to the back was a note with a single sentence:

Use this to bring Mason back, but you won't like who he becomes.

CPSIA information can be obtained
at www.ICGtesting.com
Printed in the USA
BVHW051923220323
660958BV00009B/103